# The Unicorn Girl

Cover Illustration by May Jones


ISBN: 1-4196-8696-8
ISBN-13: 9781419686962

Visit www.booksurge.com to order additional copies.

# The Unicorn Girl

M. L. LeGette

*For Casie, Ben, Mom and Dad*

*For May who painted Leah so beautifully.*
*For Grandma with her generous contribution.*

*And last but by no means least,*
*to my friends and teachers—*
*your wonderful interest*
*and support throughout this process*
*has been more appreciated*
*than you will ever know.*

# Table of Contents

Table of Contents

# The Witch

In a stone cottage, deep in a dark and entangled forest, sat a tall, thin woman in a high-backed chair. She drummed her bony fingers slowly on the chair's thick arms, her black eyes roaming the room. She had inky black hair with a few streaks of gray and her high cheek bones were heavily pronounced under her sickly pale skin. Her name was Mora... and she was waiting.

She was a witch—a witch who had lost one battle that had cost her her powers, her life, and her freedom. Her skin grew paler as she thought about that horrible night, and she glowered at the room. She had been forced to live here. *They* had forced her. They were fools for ever challenging her! But she could wait. She had waited for nine years. She could wait a little longer. She *knew* she would get out of this tomb; she could feel it in her bones. All she had to do was wait.

She had been anticipating its arrival for years . . . ever since they had stripped her powers from her. There was only one potion that could return Mora to full strength. Her piercing eyes focused on the wooden cabinet where her potion ingredients were hidden and a smile flickered across her face. She allowed herself a chuckle—a hollow, bottomless sound—as she pictured the shocked and frightened faces of those who had trapped her.

The fools thought they were safe from her. No one was safe from her! Her hands gripped the chair's arms in a strangling grasp...then, she relaxed. Mora breathed deeply through her nose. They thought they had saved themselves by the spell that had bound her powers. They thought she would never be able to find the main ingredient to the potion. After all, no one had seen the creatures in many years. They were hidden, guarded by some powerful entity. Surely, she would never be able to get her hands on *that* ingredient.

Mora smirked as she continued to drum her fingers. Oh, how they would regret the day they had underestimated her. She'd hunt them down, one by one, and torture them slowly—she would let *them* feel the torment she had felt for these past nine years!

All she had to do was wait. She had slowly collected all of the ingredients but one, but she had had to be careful—oh, so careful, for she was being watched.

She had seen the pesky owls in the trees—but they had never dared hop onto *her* window ledge.

A sudden sharp caw interrupted her thoughts. A raven swooped down from the top of a tall bookshelf, swallowed in shadows, to land on the chair.

"Patience, my dear," Mora whispered to the raven. One long finger stroked its inky black feathers. "She will appear. When the sleeping sickness takes its hold, she will appear... and then... then we shall see how things unfold. When she comes, we will be ready."

The raven ruffled its wings as the witch continued to stroke its feathers. The thin smile on her lips broadened, showing yellowing teeth as her eyes landed yet again on the closed doors of the cabinet. Her name was Mora... and she was waiting.

# Chapter 1
# The Riding Lesson

I didn't know Mother for very long. She died when I was two. I hardly remember anything about her, actually. Sometimes, if I strained my memory, I could see an indistinct smiling face, but that was all. I think it greatly disturbed Father that I had no memory of her, so I hardly ever asked him questions about her. It was a few years after her death, when I was six, that he was first able to tell me about her without his eyes darkening or voice cracking, but even then he never spoke in much detail.

Even though I was an only child, I never felt very lonely: instead, I was very much the center of attention. Ann, my favorite servant, told me when I was five that it was lucky that I had even learned to talk. It had taken me forever to learn to form words thanks to a little trick I had picked up when I was a baby. I realized very early that if I simply pointed to something that I wanted, then at least three people would rush to get it for me. No matter what Ann says, I still think it was a lovely way to get spoiled.

Now that I look back on it, just about everyone treated me as their own—the exception being my wonderfully dreadful governess, Miss Perish. Miss Perish bore a striking resemblance to a tall bird of prey, one who'd had a run-in with a jar of face powder. I was introduced to my first governess the day that I discovered my 'duty in life': becoming a lady. A young girl in a wealthy family was supposed to start learning how to be a lady when she was twelve—I started when I was eleven. Miss Perish would always say, "Stay ahead of them, that's what we must do, stay ahead." Or, "Just think Leah, you'll be the finest lady in Torona with me instructing you." The problem was, I had no intention of being a grand lady.

For starters, I didn't *look* the part. Father had taken me to a ball when I was nine where I had seen grand ladies up close. They laughed imperiously; they had rosy cheeks and slender necks. They moved with grace and elegance. I, on the other hand, was not rosy or graceful. I was pale and small with straight, black hair and large, green eyes. Not to mention I often tripped over my trailing hems.

But somehow Miss Perish could overlook my less-than-striking appearance, in the hope, I'm sure, that one day I would blossom under her care. Yes, my life certainly took a painfully embarrassing swing once Miss Perish entered the doors of Willow Manor. It started with sewing. At the end of the lesson I was supposed to present to her an embroidered copy of my name. When she called for it I furnished a magnificent example of jagged scribbles. I didn't understand why she was so furious with me. After all, why on earth would you do something that pricked your fingers?

Proper etiquette was no better than sewing, with its curtsying and tea-pouring. And at dancing I was as clumsy as a rag doll. My embarrassment only grew as I swayed awkwardly before the orchestra, holding onto my partner for dear life. Then after dance there was voice. Miss Perish would glare at me as I tried not to sound like a mouse caught in a trap. Every day she made me sing scales until I was hoarse. At least when I danced I had someone accompanying me. When I sang I was all alone on the battlefield.

I was shocked that Father would have hired such a horrible person to teach me. When I was loudly complaining to Ann about this after my first encounter with Miss Perish, she informed me that my Aunt Roseanne had badgered Father constantly about not having made a step toward any proper schooling, and that she finally took the matter into her own hands. Figures.

I may sound like I loathed my life at Willow Manor but the truth is, I loved it. Father was always wonderful to me and so were the servants. The only time that I wished to be anywhere else was during lessons—though some good things came out of them. Once, for example, I had a very rough dancing lesson where I tripped on my skirt and banged my nose on the hard floor. Frank Boon, the manor's chef who had generously agreed to be my partner, helped me up while Miss Perish screeched around us, waving her arms like a bird that was trying to take flight. Frank gave me a damp cloth for my stinging nose and led me to the sitting room.

I sat on a window seat looking out over the grounds to the distant hills of the Langdale Mountains. Occasionally I rubbed my nose and sniffed back tears. I felt a shadow creep over me and heard Father's voice; I didn't move my eyes from the window for shame of my cherry-colored nose.

"What are you looking at Leah?"

"Nothing much," I mumbled.

"Is there something on your mind?"

"There's no need to act like you don't know." A lump began to form threateningly in my throat.

"I can understand that you do not enjoy dancing, but—"

"Oh, please, I saw you dance at Aunt Roseanne's ball—you're wonderful at it," I said, completely frustrated.

"That doesn't mean that it came naturally, if that's what you mean. I had to practice."

I looked at him with tears blooming in my eyes and my lower lip began to tremble.

"What you need is something fun to do," Father said with a smile.

"And what's that?" I asked thickly.

"How would you like it if I taught you how to ride a horse?" asked Father as he leaned over, placing his hands on his knees.

This was not what I'd expected. Father was grand at riding horses—he was a hunter, after all. I can't count the times that I'd wished he would teach me.

"You mean it?" I said, putting my weight on the palms of my hands as I leaned toward him. "Can we start now?"

"Of course!" he said straightening up. "Hurry upstairs and put your traveling clothes on—I'll wait for you at the entrance."

"Oh—thank you! Thank you!" I wrapped my arms around his neck in a tight embrace.

"You're welcome," he laughed.

I was gasping for breath when I finally reached my bedroom (it was one stairway and five corridors from where I'd left Father). I tripped over my dress in my frantic state and had to grab hold of the dresser to stop my nose from continuing its sudden attraction to the floor. I flung the doors of my closet open and snatched out the plain traveling dress I had received for my birthday the year before. Quickly, I yanked off my gown and replaced it with the brown dress. Then I kicked off my delicate shoes and pulled on my boots.

Father stood waiting for me at the bottom of the last stairway in front of Willow Manor's large double doors. I was still trying to put my hair up when I reached the last step.

"I'm ready," I said enthusiastically, as I rubbed my side where a stitch had begun.

"Follow me, then."

As we drew closer to the stables, my stomach twisted nervously. The closest I had ever come to a horse was petting it timidly before Father went off on one of his hunts. Miss Perish loathed animals and did all she could to keep me far from them. I smiled weakly up at Father, hoping that my face looked somewhat calm.

"I'm going to put you on Iris," he said as he opened the stable door and stepped aside for me to pass. "She's had plenty of people ride her before, so you needn't worry about her being jitterish around you."

"I'm not worried," I said, with my head high in the air, though I gulped. Father smiled down at me.

Iris was in the twentieth stall. She was entirely white. She lifted her graceful head toward Father and me as we opened the door of her stall.

"Leah, bring her out here while I get her saddle."

I grabbed her halter and led her out of the stall to Father who was holding the saddle in his arms. He explained to me where each strap connected and which buckle went where. Then he showed me how to put on the bridle. I listened intently as Father went on and on. Iris held herself carefully as if she was being judged on her behavior.

"Now, let's see how you do on her," he said, stepping back and dusting off his hands.

We led Iris to one of the fenced-off meadows. The one that Father led us to was empty, which I thought was for the best. The only ones that would see me make a fool of myself on my first riding lesson were Father, Iris, the bugs, and the birds.

"Come over here and I'll show you how to mount," Father said, beckoning me with a wave of his hand.

"Now, what you do is very simple. You put your foot in this stirrup," he indicated the stirrup with his hand. "And grasp one hand on the saddle here and the other in her mane, like this. When you have a good, steady grip and your foot in the stirrup, pull yourself up and throw your other leg over the side and hook that foot into the other stirrup. I promise Miss Perish won't be watching," he added with a wry smile.

"What makes you think that Miss Perish makes me nervous?" I asked, as I grabbed the saddle and placed my foot into the stirrup.

Father held onto Iris's bridle.

"I see you tense up every day before lessons at breakfast."

I cleared my throat loudly as I ignored him. With a firm grip, I pushed from the ground only to fall back down heavily. I hadn't noticed how tall Iris was until I tried to get on her back. Without waiting to give Father time to respond to my failed first attempt, I rewrapped my hand in Iris's mane and pushed hard from the ground. As I lifted I hurriedly swung my leg over Iris's side and sat down in the saddle.

"Very good, well done," Father said, smiling proudly at me. Iris nodded her head as if she were congratulating me as well. I couldn't help myself; I smiled broadly, shining down at Father.

It turned out that Father was right about riding being easier than dancing; at least it was for me. It seemed to come so utterly naturally, like a bird knowing how to fly—I *knew* how to ride.

Every day, Iris and I grew more attached to one another. I never once fell off Iris and Iris never did anything that would startle me; it was as if we could read each other's minds. Soon Father stopped attending since I simply didn't need him there anymore.

However, what with my new obsession with riding, I began to hate my other lessons even more—if that were possible. Each day I sat inside with needle and thread; tripped over my feet while I danced; and saw Miss Perish's face twist in agony at the sound of my voice cracking as I sang.

"Sewing, dancing, and learning how to present yourself will get you where you need to be if you would only *pay attention*," she once said to me crisply. "While you're *not* riding a horse."

One day I stood outside of Father's sitting room door with my ear pressed against it, listening in on Miss Perish and Father discussing this very problem.

"She is a *lady*, Sir James. Not a boy!" She said passionately.

"Are you telling me, Miss Perish, that women cannot ride horses and still be considered ladies?" Father asked calmly. "Why it was just yesterday that I saw the Duchess of Calamar riding her prized stallion."

"Sir James, you misunderstand me. I am not saying that Leah is not allowed to ride a horse. I am simply asking if that is more important than the lessons that will help Leah with her future. Being able to ride a horse will not get her a husband."

"Miss Perish, I will hear your ideas for Leah's future and the reasons behind them and consider them. However," Father's ring tapped against a wine glass. "I will make the decisions. I want as much as you do Miss Perish; I want my daughter to have everything that will prepare her for her future—to live happily and safely—and that is why Leah will continue with her riding."

"But sir—"

"Thank you Miss Perish," said Father firmly.

I jumped back from the door just before it flew open and a disgruntled Miss Perish walked through it, nearly running into me.

"Excuse me Miss Perish," I said with a quaint smile.

Miss Perish glowered down at me like a vulture, flared her nostrils, and marched off down the hall, her flowing gown billowing out behind her.

I looked after her as I stepped into the sitting room. Father stood next to a huge table sipping his wine; the many animal heads fixed on the walls stared down at us.

"I needn't tell you what our conversation consisted of, then," he said when I entered the room.

"No, I suppose you don't," I said with a small smile. "Thank you."

"Now don't you start thinking that you're not going to continue with your daily routines." Father shook a finger warningly. "You're still going to do all the things you always did before you had Iris; I'm just giving you something to look forward to when you've had a rough day." His tone lightened and a crooked smile wrinkled his face.

"I know," I grabbed him round the middle and hugged him tightly. "I won't let you down, I promise. I'll work harder, I really will … you'll see."

"I know you will, Leah."

## Chapter 2
# Dinner Guests

Four years later, I was still shackled to Miss Perish and her never-ending attempts to turn a duckling into a swan. It was easy for me to tell (even after four long years) that Miss Perish had suffered a significant blow the day she hadn't gotten her way with Iris. She never spoke directly about my horse, but it seemed to me that she was even more determined to point out my shortcomings: "Why can't you keep in tune?" or "How many times do I have to tell you to step with your right foot, Leah, your *right* foot?" and my all time favorite, "*Why* can't you be more like Miss Lydia? She is growing into a *true* lady."

Miss Perish enjoyed nothing more than comparing me with my cousin Lydia, Aunt Roseanne's only daughter. Aunt Roseanne was Father's sister, but she looked nothing like him. She was a very plump woman with wavy blonde hair and rosy red lips. I could usually hear her coming before catching sight of her (and hopefully make a quick getaway) because of the many dangling bracelets she wore. Her daughter Lydia was everything I wasn't, and it didn't help that we were the same age. She had perfectly curled blond hair that fell softly onto her shoulders, her cheeks were rosy, and her lips beautifully formed. Whenever we were forced together I felt like a rock next to a gleaming jewel.

Maybe it was because I was always small for my age or because my hair was as straight as a plank and refused point blank to curl; I just never seemed to shine the way Lydia did so easily. Where her lips were plump, mine were small and thin. Her complexion was perfect and her cheeks were always rosy. The way Miss Perish went on about Lydia, I knew that, if given the chance, she would drop me in a second to be Lydia's governess.

But a promise was a promise. I did try harder to please Miss Perish and by some miracle I did. When I was fifteen, the angels smiled down at me during one of my dance lessons.

Miss Perish was teaching me a waltz.

"One two three, one two three ... that's it Leah ... one two three." Miss Perish waved her hands slowly through the air and swayed side to side on the spot. "Listen to the music. Let it lift you ... You are a cloud drifting on a breeze ... one two three ... one two three ... "

I concentrated hard on the music, searching for the beat and letting the galloping motion move me ... Galloping. It was just like Iris galloping. I tried to remember everything about riding Iris when she galloped. The soothing motion of rocking backward and forward surged through my body and planted itself in my feet. I moved my feet to the same rhythmic music. Slowly, very slowly, the music seemed to guide me across the floor. When the music stopped, I had the strangest feeling in the pit of my stomach—as if I had lost a piece of myself.

"Bravo Leah, bravo!" said Miss Perish as she walked gracefully to me and pushed Frank aside. "That was perfect! I knew it was just a matter of time! You've proven yourself to me at last! Well done!"

I smiled a smile that I hoped was pleasant. My face felt slightly numb.

"Goodness, look at the time," said Miss Perish pulling out her watch. "It's almost time for dinner. Hurry off and get ready for your father. He will be so pleased to hear what I have to tell him."

I silently nodded my head, not trusting my mouth for a response. I was moving to the door when Frank touched my forearm with his hand.

"That was a nice dance, Leah. I knew you would get it eventually," Frank said with a wrinkled smile.

"Thank you Frank," I said, when I had found my tongue.

I usually went straight to my room to change for dinner, but today the only place I wanted to be was with Iris.

The late afternoon sun was blinding. Shielding my eyes, I ran quickly to the stables, not caring that I was splashing specks of mud on my dress.

When I reached Iris's stall, I threw the door open wide, making Iris raise her head curiously. I rushed forward and flung my arms around her neck, sobbing. I didn't understand why I was crying. And I didn't care that I was collecting heaps of straw on my dress as I kneeled next to her.

Iris did all that a good friend could do in times like these. She nodded her head, tried to wipe my tears away, and neighed soothingly. When I was at last comforted I brushed the straw off, gave her a final hug and left.

The sun had begun to set as I made my way up to the manor's stone steps. The grounds were stained a deep red and my shadow stretched long before me.

*I hope I don't run into Miss Perish,* I thought as I cautiously moved down the corridors. Somehow I didn't think she would be too happy about my muddy dress and puffy eyes. I crept through the manor like a mouse watching for a cat. When I finally reached the sanctuary of my room, I closed the door and leaned up against it, breathing in deeply with my eyes closed. After a moment had passed, I opened my eyes and saw that a bath had been made for me—as usual. I touched the warm water with my hand and watched it slowly ripple.

I quickly shed my clothes but just as I was getting comfortable in the bath, Ann threw open the door so forcefully that it banged off the wall. She hurled a towel at me while she shrieked, "*Get up!*"

"What's going on?" I asked, stepping out of the tub and wrapping the towel around myself. Ann's brown hair was falling out of its bun, giving her a slightly unhinged appearance. She rushed to my closet and pulled out a white dress with lavender trim.

"Quickly, girl!" said Ann frantically. "Madam Roseanne and Miss Lydia are here! Oh, dear Lord, *why* do they always drop by without telling us?"

"Lydia's here? With Aunt—" I trailed off in horror.

"Yes, with her mother," said Ann feverishly, her eyes darting around the room. As her eyes lighted on me still dripping water she shrieked, "What are you doing just standing there? Get moving!"

I jumped, finished drying myself off, and dived into the dress Ann had given me.

"Oh, there's no time to dry your hair," said Ann, running a brush through my tangled ends. "We'll just have to put it up."

I grimaced and squinted as Ann pulled and twisted my hair tightly into a bun. "There," she said breathlessly as she grabbed my elbow and pulled me out into the hall. "If you hurry you may not be too late!"

She pushed me down the stairs and I stumbled on the hem.

"*Hurry!*" she hissed frantically.

With a deep breath, I rested one hand on the banister and made my way to dinner.

Father, Aunt Roseanne, and Lydia were already at the table when I walked into the dining room. They stopped their conversation and looked at me as I walked through the door, my stomach twisting queasily. Aunt Roseanne stared down her prominent nose imperiously while Lydia smirked eloquently. Guinevere, a tall, quiet maid, walked through the kitchen door, holding our salads, as I hastily unfurled my napkin.

"You've grown a bit taller since the last time I saw you," Aunt Roseanne observed, her eyes running up and down my figure. "But you look a bit too brown for my liking. James, I would do something about that, if I were you."

I glanced down at my hands, feeling heat creep up my neck. I had become much tanner ever since I started riding Iris.

Aunt Roseanne's wrists jingled as she reached for her glass. She took a sip of elderberry wine, hiccupped softly and continued, "What have you been having her do? Manual labor? I understand that a healthy dose of sunshine can heal the soul in more ways than we can possibly imagine, but too much of a good thing can turn sour indeed. Why, look at Lydia"—my eyes shot upward and glowered at Lydia who smirked haughtily back—"her complexion is perfect."

"You needn't worry, Roseanne," Father replied with a smile. "I doubt Leah will be turning sour any time soon."

Father's eyes caught mine and twinkled brightly before returning to Aunt Roseanne, but a salad had just been placed before her, attracting all of her attention.

"I heard you did very well in your dancing lesson today, Leah" Father said as Guinevere laid a salad before him.

"Oh—you heard," I said, twisting my napkin.

"Miss Perish told me right after the lesson. She was extremely proud."

I smiled, momentarily lost for words. I couldn't possibly tell him how I had felt afterward at a time when he looked so proud, and especially not when Lydia and Aunt Roseanne were in the room. Out of the corner of my eye, I saw Lydia snort silently and roll her eyes.

"James," said Aunt Roseanne, her eyes piercing. "How has everything been at Willow Manor?"

"Very well," said Father.

"Good, because I must tell you, I've been worried about you."

"Worried about me?" Father asked humorously. "Why would I make the short list of your fears?"

"Why, for over a year now I've heard not a peep from you. That sort of disconnection makes a woman worried."

Father laughed heartily.

"You need not worry about anything here, my dear sister."

"I see," said Aunt Roseanne, her eyes lingering on my dripping hair. "Yes, everything must be running quite smoothly." The sarcasm dripped like oil.

I smiled and leaned back slightly in my chair. I could tell this would be a long evening. As we were eating the main course, the conversation drifted away from Willow Manor, thank goodness, to the kingdom of Torona.

"I've heard that King Rowan's son is doing well, learning how to rule a kingdom," said Father, leaning his elbow on the table.

"Oh, yes. The last time I heard talk of him was when he went to Christon and shook hands with the poor, the darling." Aunt Roseanne sighed deeply. She always had a fevered respect for those with more power than herself. "Of course, he could have had someone else do that for him, but . . . " To listen to Aunt Roseanne, you'd think she was on speaking terms with the Royal Family. "I keep reminding Lydia, here, that he is only one year older than she is." Her eyes twinkled dramatically over her wine goblet.

Lydia smiled rapturously.

"Really Mother, that doesn't mean anything."

"Nonsense," thundered Aunt Roseanne, spilling wine down her front. "Who says that Prince Philip shouldn't be interested in you? You deserve to have some royalty attached to your name. Everyone knows you're the prettiest girl in Torona."

Lydia stared at me over her wine glass, her eyes cold and smirking, as if daring me to ask why I didn't deserve to have royalty attached to *my* name. I raised my head slightly and glared right back at her. Royalty suited Lydia perfectly—I could see her now, sitting on a thrown and bellowing out orders.

Our scorching glares were interrupted, however, as our butler, Owen, entered the dining room.

"Pardon me, Sir James."

"Yes, Owen?" Father raised his chin from his hand.

"Sir William Shanklin is here to see you, sir."

"Sir William?" gasped Aunt Roseanne. She twisted around in her chair to see Owen.

"Show him in, Owen," Father said, rising from his chair.

Owen bowed from the room and soon returned with a tall, handsome man in his mid thirties. He flashed a dazzling smile at us that made Aunt Roseanne positively flutter with excitement and shook hands jovially with Father.

"I am terribly sorry," Sir William said, gazing at our plates. "Are you in the middle of dinner? I can wait."

"Have you eaten?" asked Father.

"Some hours ago."

"Then you must dine with us."

"No, I couldn't be a bother!"

"*A bother!*" ejaculated Aunt Roseanne. "Really, Sir William."

"Come, come," said Father, indicating a seat. "Guinevere, set another place, please."

"Well, if you insist." And without further ado, Sir William took the seat in between Father and Lydia. Lydia looked extremely pleased with herself.

"I take it that you already know Madam Roseanne and her daughter Lydia?" asked Father.

"No, I'm afraid I haven't had the pleasure," Sir William replied.

"Who does not know Sir William Shanklin?" laughed Aunt Roseanne in a flowery, girlish way as Sir William inclined his head.

*I don't know him,* I thought. His name seemed slightly familiar, but that was all. From his elaborate dress, I guessed he must be a knight, and one of high rank at that.

"Yes, we know Sir William from his daring deeds in the Braxton Bog," said Lydia.

"That one adventure seems to have given me more honor than I could have ever dreamed." I suddenly noticed how bright Sir William's eyes were. With his large smile and wide eyes, he seemed a little too intense to me.

"I can't say that I've heard of it, sir," I said. Even as I heard the words form, I regretted speaking.

Aunt Roseanne stopped laughing as if her voice had been snatched from her throat and stared at me accusingly, as if shocked that I dared speak before such important company. Lydia wore a crooked smile and mouthed 'You don't know?' behind Sir William's back.

"I'm sorry, but I—" Sir William began, looking at Father inquiringly.

"This is my daughter, Leah, William."

"*Leah?*" Sir William gasped with an over exaggerated jump. "The tiny little child you wrote to me about? No!"

"Sir William was an old hunting partner of mine," Father explained, in response to my raised eyebrow. "I haven't heard from you though in ... it must be twelve years now."

"My apologies," Sir William bowed his head mournfully. "But being a knight is a demanding profession."

"Well, I'm sure the pair of you will spend plenty of time getting reacquainted, James," interrupted Aunt Roseanne sharply. "But I'm sure Sir William would like to tell us of his daring achievements."

"Well, I might as well tell you what happened in the Braxton Bog," said Sir William excitedly, turning to me. "If, that is to say, it won't bother the ones who have already heard the story?"

"Oh, no, of course not," breathed Aunt Roseanne, on the edge of her seat.

I felt like I was about to be sick so I pushed my plate away slightly.

"Well," began Sir William dramatically, "the Braxton Bog is located, as I'm sure you already know, in the Ash Moors. The Moors are unpleasant enough with the heavy fog that is always settled over the muddy ground, but the Braxton Bog … " Sir William closed his eyes and shook his head. "The Braxton Bog is by far the most terrible place in Torona. There is nowhere else like it. The dense fog, the large pools of mud … it is like a trap … a maze that you fear you will be wandering through forever." His eyes opened and they seemed to bore into mine. "The Braxton Bog is home to some of the most *fearful* creatures you could imagine. The ones my party was dealing with were … *the vors.*" Sir William stopped to savor the looks of terror on Aunt Roseanne and Lydia's faces. "Now, I'm sure you don't know what a vor is … " Sir William trailed off staring pointedly at me.

"Well—"

"Of course you don't," said Sir William smugly, smiling largely again. "Vors are *foul* animals that look like large black dogs." His voice dropped significantly as if he was telling a ghost tale to frighten children. "Some call them *demons.* Their fur hangs in thick matted knots off their skeletal frames and smells profusely of something decayed in water." Sir William stopped here to relish the tense atmosphere and the horrifying picture he had just created. Lydia stared at Sir William as if transfixed, her mouth slightly open, and Aunt Roseanne kept fanning herself and moaning. "You might be wondering why my party was out in the Bog dealing with these dreadful monstrosities?" Sir William whispered. "A large group of vors had attacked the small innocent village of Bell Sound so ferociously that many of its inhabitants didn't dare leave their homes!" I actually felt as if the candles had dimmed. "King Rowan felt that the vors' population was growing too large, and the low amount of food had made them venture into the surrounding villages for sustenance. He decided to send a group of his most trusted knights, myself included, to deal with the problem." Sir William's chest expanded at the mere memory. "When we reached the area around Bell Sound, we stopped and set up camp." Sir William's voice now dropped to such a low whisper that I had to lean forward to hear. "We sat there in the muck and mud, barely able to see through the fog that covers the Braxton Bog. The night seemed to press down on us, muffling all sound. And then ... "

"And then what?" asked Aunt Roseanne. Her eyes were as round as coins. Father chuckled faintly but Aunt Roseanne and Lydia seemed too transfixed with Sir William's story to hear.

Sir William drew a rattling breath and closed his eyes as if in pain.

"I will never forget what happened next. I fear these memories will haunt me to my grave."

I couldn't keep myself from rolling my eyes.

"I was on watch and even though my eyes were itching with exhaustion I stayed awake, for I knew I must give the alarm if the vors sprang an attack. And right when I was tapping my cheek to stay awake, *I saw a figure in the gloom.* I could not mistake its hulking mass! Its foul stench! The vors were upon us!" Sir William slammed down his fist on the table, making everyone jump. "There must have been forty of them, the hellish beasts! They blended in and out of the darkness so effortlessly that at times I thought there were eighty. I bravely sounded the alarm but the vors were too quick! In moments we were surrounded and horribly outnumbered. My fellow knights were trying to fight them one on one but there is only one way to stop a vor." A triumphant grin spread across Sir William's face. "Even in that horrific battle, where men were screaming and running, my head alone was clear. I remembered from long ago when I was a squire, training to become a knight, that the only thing a vor fears is fire. The few trees you'd find in the Ash Moors are usually too damp to set flame to, but I had luckily found a small handful of branches on our way to the camp site and lit a small insignificant fire to stay warm. I ran furiously to this pitiful fire and grabbed one of the branches just as a vor bounded toward me. I drew the flaming branch behind me and gave a good swat at the bloody beast!" He narrowly missed knocking over his goblet as he swung his arm across the table. "He gave a tremendous howl and bolted as I made my way to another vor and another. Quickly the other knights realized what I was doing and grabbed the remaining branches from the fire. Needless to say," he gazed nonchalantly at his fingernails, "Bell Sound is safe thanks to me." Sir William leaned back in his chair, an annoying grin playing on his lips as Aunt Roseanne and Lydia applauded loudly.

"The King must have been very proud of you," Father said, barely concealing a smile.

"Oh he was. He promoted me to the top ranks."

"Well done!"

Dessert was brought out just then by Guinevere, a delicious rose petal pudding. As I ate it, I reminded myself to compliment Frank.

"How long will you and Lydia be staying?" Father asked.

My head jerked up from my pudding. *Please don't stay very long. Please leave in the morning.*

"I was thinking 'till at least the end of the week," said Aunt Roseanne.

*Damn.*

"Sir James," said Sir William, snapping his fingers at Guinevere to refill his goblet, "there are some things I need to discuss with you."

"Yes, we can do that now," Father said, rising from his chair. "Leah, you may go to bed if you wish."

I rose with poise, and smiled happily. As I walked past Father, I saw him smile back at me slightly. He knew how much I disliked Aunt Roseanne and Lydia's visits. Sir William didn't seem so terrible—annoying and pompous, yes—but he would most likely be gone in the morning after his business with Father. He was after all, a top ranked knight, and who knew how many more awe-struck females he still had to impress.

## Chapter 3
# The Warning

I woke the next day with a small, hopeful prayer. More than anything, Lydia enjoyed flirting with the men that worked at Willow Manor. Hopefully, what with my lessons, I wouldn't have time to run into her. I pulled myself out of bed with a groan and dressed. Luckily, I didn't see Lydia or her mother at breakfast. I ate quickly and went to my first lesson of the day, embroidery.

I entered to find Miss Perish seated in a large chair, fabric and needles on her lap with more draped over a table before her.

"Take a seat," she said without looking up from her needles.

I closed the door and walked across the room, where I sat down opposite her.

"Today, you will embroider a design on a gown." Miss Perish stood up, placed her fabric on the table, and walked to a closet where she pulled out a simple turquoise dress that I had outgrown. She placed it on the table in front of me and gave me a sample drawing of a wavy, intricate design. "I want you to embroider this design on the neckline." And with that, she turned on her heel, sat down in her chair, picked up her needles, and continued to knit.

I stared at the neckline, my needle poised. I glanced back at the design and with my lips pursed began to work. In the beginning I thought I was doing rather well, but all too soon I found a mistake. Holding back a grumble, I pulled out the thread and started again. This time I only had a few mistakes that were near the end. An hour later I placed the needle down to consult the design once more and saw that mine was much narrower and the curves were slightly jagged. I sighed and let my shoulders droop. I looked up tentatively at Miss Perish who was staring at me.

"Done are you?" She stood and held the dress up. I saw a grimace pass over her sharp, pointed face. "Leah," she said, staring down at me, "I would have thought that by now you would have mastered a design as simple as this?"

I glared down at my hands.

"Really," she continued, starting to fire up, "sometimes it seems to me that whatever I say goes in one ear and out the other. I thought that since you seemed to have improved in dance that you just might have done the same in your other classes! But how *obviously* wrong I was!" She waved the dress around in her fury. "I keep telling myself that it must be my fault. That if

I had gotten hold of you right after your mother died then you wouldn't be such a mess!"

I looked up shocked. Miss Perish's face was suddenly stony. It wasn't her insults that had my stomach twisting oddly. It was the fact that this was the first time my mother had been mentioned in years. Miss Perish breathed deeply through her nose.

"That is all for today, Leah," she said, her voice rather constricted. "I want you to spend the rest of the day practicing what *you* think you need improvement in. Obviously, what I am doing is a waste of time." Miss Perish opened the door and stood beside it, waiting for me to leave.

I rose from my chair, still too shocked at what was happening to reply, and left. The door slammed behind me.

When Miss Perish had first entered my life, she had been able to make me feel ashamed of my failure to please her, but after four years I had decided that her lessons were simply pointless. I had come to terms with the fact that I would probably never be as good as she wanted me to be. But her insults still stung.

I sat on a large, thick rug in front of an empty fireplace, rubbing the head of one of the many hunting dogs Father owned. He pressed his head closer against me, his eyes closed in pleasure. *Why did she have to blow up like that? The embroidery wasn't that bad anyway.*

"I see you're not practicing."

My eyes lifted from the rug to rest on Lydia, who stood in the doorway.

"Your observation skills are impeccable as always," I said sarcastically, turning back to the fireplace.

Lydia laughed dismissively.

I stood up (the dog at my feet snorted and looked up at me reproachfully) and left the room with Lydia fast on my heels.

"I met Miss Perish. Don't you want to know what she told me?" she asked.

"Not really."

"She said that you're completely useless. That—"

"Lydia," I said, turning around to face her, "we've known each other for a long time, so I hope you won't mind me asking you to keep your large nose out of my lessons."

Lydia gasped and clapped her hand over her nose. I turned on my heel and walked down a corridor and into another room, slamming the door and turning the key that protruded from the lock with a satisfying *click*. I walked across the room to stand before a large portrait of Mother that had been moved here the day she died. It used to reside in the great hall, but I don't think Father could bear to see it every day, so he ordered it to be hung in this small, unused room. For some reason, I had never spent much time in this room. The twisting in my stomach seemed to intensify. It was my fault more than anyone's that I didn't know much about Mother. Why didn't I ever bother?

I turned from her portrait and leaned against the wall. It suddenly seemed painful to realize how little

I knew about her. She had died when I was much too young to remember her; the only things I knew were what Father and the servants had told me, but they were few and far between. In fact they had stopped mentioning her when I had stopped asking. Why didn't anyone talk about her? Miss Perish's sudden mention of her had jarred the empty space inside me that she should have occupied for thirteen years. Why hadn't anyone talked to me about her? I glared up at her portrait, a sudden rage ringing in my ears. Was her death so painful that she was automatically shunned from my life? Did they think I didn't *deserve* to know anything about her? That I couldn't handle it? My fists clenched tightly, I crossed the room and sat in a chair opposite her portrait. I pulled my knees up close to my chest and wrapped my arms around them.

I don't know how long I spent in that room, curled up, looking at Mother's portrait. My stomach growled in protest but I ignored it. I knew it must be late in the day as I watched the sun's rays stream into the room. Knowing I couldn't hide there all day, I rose from the chair and left Mother's staring eyes.

I breathed in deeply as I walked onto the brightly-lit grounds. I stood still, staring at the sky, letting the wind brush across my skin. I couldn't let Miss Perish ruin a perfectly nice day. After all, hadn't she canceled the rest of my lessons? That was definitely something to smile about. Just as the idea of visiting Iris slipped into my mind, a voice reached my ears.

"Leah!"

I turned and saw Sir William making his way down Willow Manor's stone steps toward me.

"Hello, Sir William," I said in a falsely cheery voice.

"How are you spending your day off?" Sir William asked, raising one eyebrow.

*Does everyone know?* I thought disgustedly.

"You could call it that," I said.

"You needn't feel sorry for your performance," Sir William boomed, tapping me on the shoulder. "You must learn from your mistakes and inaccuracies. Becoming a lady is what all women strive for." He pumped his fist in the air and sounded like a general pepping up his army before battle. "One must not get disheartened by a few flimsy attempts, but carry on and become what you were meant to be."

I looked up at him, too annoyed to comment. Was dancing and sewing all that was expected of me? To grow into a beautiful, obedient, perfect wife? *Become Lydia?!*

"I must say," he continued with a humorous laugh, "that I had forgotten Sir James had a daughter."

I breathed deeply, searching the grounds desperately for an escape.

"But Sir James told me you *finally* learned a waltz!" Sir William exclaimed, like I was a four-year-old who'd learned to buckle her shoe. "You should be proud."

"I—"

*It's coming!*

“What?” I said, startled. The voice I had just heard echoed in my ears. I stared around wildly, looking for who had just said those words.

“Yes, I believe that your talent for dancing will give you confidence for—”

“No, didn’t you hear that voice?”

“What voice?” Sir William said, looking down at me with a frown, obviously annoyed I had interrupted him.

“The one that—the speaker must have been standing right here!” I said, beginning to get frustrated at the sight of Sir William’s deepening frown. “It was so loud; you must have heard it!”

“Maybe the stress of the day has tired you,” Sir William said soothingly, but his eyes didn’t reflect concern. “Shall I go and tell Miss Perish to cancel tomorrow’s lessons as well? Yes, I think I will,” Sir William decided as I opened and closed my mouth like a fish. He didn’t hear it? How could he not have heard it?

“Yes,” Sir William continued, “yes, I think it would be wise for you to come inside, Leah.” And placing his hand firmly around my upper arm, he pulled me back into Willow Manor.

He led me into Father’s sitting room and said, “Stay here, and I’ll call the doctor.”

“I don’t need a—” but Sir William was already through the door.

I sat on the edge of the chair, my fingernails burying into the arms of the chair as I replayed the message in my mind. The voice had been so panicky—chill bumps prickled my arms and legs. Why hadn't Sir William heard it? Had he been lying? No, that didn't make sense. Why should he lie about some panic-stricken warning? He was a knight. He had been taught not to take things like this lightly. But he had looked at me as if I was sick, insane even.

"I make such wonderful first impressions," I mumbled to my knees.

As I sat, my mind miraculously became blank. My eyes moved in and out of focus and for five minutes I felt calm. Until...

"I must see her! Let me through, *let me through!*"

Miss Perish's frantic, sharp voice reached my ears. I lifted my gaze to the door where seconds later, Miss Perish marched through followed closely by Sir William, Aunt Roseanne, and Lydia.

"What's this?" she yelled looking at me. "Voices? You heard *voices?*"

Her hysterical tone made me lean back in my chair to get away from her. I shot a glare at Sir William over Miss Perish's shoulder. Why did he have to go blabbing about this?

"The doctor should be here shortly," Sir William said excitedly, now that he had an audience. "I sent one of the servants to go and get him."

"It shouldn't take that long," agreed Aunt Roseanne glancing at me (but turning quickly away when our eyes met). "Doctor Baldwin lives only ten minutes from Willow Manor." (In addition to being a well-known hunter, Father also owned a large portion of land that he rented to others).

Miss Perish bent over me, touching my forehead and fussing about how pale I looked.

"Just horrible," she was saying. "Hearing voices! I tell you, what's next? Seeing vors in your bedroom?"

"Miss Perish, stop, please!" I said, trying to push her hand from my forehead. "I'm fine, I—"

"Where is that doctor? Where is he?"

"He should be—"

"I'm right here."

We all turned to see Doctor Baldwin, a short, round man, walk steadily through the sitting room door.

"What seems to be the problem?" he asked, while feeling my forehead.

"She seems to have heard something, but I was standing right beside her and I did not hear a thing," Sir William stated immediately.

I was beginning to regret telling Sir William about the voice. For a fraction of a second, I saw fear in Doctor Baldwin's eyes. I looked over at Lydia who was standing in a corner staring at me, her face icy, and I immediately knew why. She hated being pushed aside while someone else got all the attention. She probably thought I was acting to impress Sir William.

"What activities have you been doing today?" asked Doctor Baldwin, now staring into my eyes. "Anything intense today?"

"No," I answered, directing my attention back to the doctor.

"Eaten anything?"

"Breakfast."

"Sleeping well?"

"Yes."

"Have you fainted any today?"

"No," I said angrily.

Everyone was looking at me with either a fearful expression or a frown. Why were they acting like I was crazy?

"I think it's best if you stay in bed for the rest of the day, and maybe tomorrow," said Doctor Baldwin. "Where is Sir James?"

"He had a business arrangement," Sir William said promptly. "You can be assured that I will inform him of everything when he returns."

Doctor Baldwin nodded and left the room, leaving me quite speechless.

"Well, you heard what he said," Miss Perish announced sharply, pulling me out of the chair. "Upstairs! Now! You need rest!"

"But—" I started meekly.

"No buts."

Miss Perish piloted me past the others and up to my room, muttering savagely all the way. It had seemed strange to me how caring Miss Perish had been back in the sitting room, but now that we were alone, she vented her rage upon me.

"Really, hearing voices? *Hearing voices?* Never in all my days have I even contemplated such a ridiculous excuse to get attention!"

"What?" I said blankly.

She opened the door and pushed me into my room roughly.

"You heard me!" Miss Perish spat. "I know exactly what was going through your brain. You were jealous of Lydia and pretending to need a doctor was the perfect way to be the center of attention!"

"I don't want to be to the center of attention!" Frustration welled up inside my chest. Did any of them believe me? "I did hear that voice!"

"ENOUGH!" Miss Perish bellowed and slammed the door in my face, leaving me standing very still, a gnawing twisting emotion eating at my stomach.

# Chapter 4
# A New Teacher

I sat on my bed, my mind working furiously. No matter what any of them said, I had *not* imagined that voice. Its words still rang clearly in my head. It had been so fearful. Why? And why hadn't the speaker revealed itself? Why hadn't it tried to communicate with me again?

Three knocks sounded on my door, abruptly halting my reverie.

"Come in," I said, and my heart lightened as Father entered the room. He looked pale and rather shaky.

"How are you feeling?" he asked sitting next to me.

"Fine," I lied.

Father stared at me and said, "Miss Perish told me what happened."

"Did she also tell you I did it for attention?" I asked viciously.

"No, she left that part out," Father said with a weak smile.

"You don't think I imagined that voice do you?" I asked desperately.

"No," Father said, "but I do think it is possible that you could have overreacted. What did it say?"

"That something was coming."

"And it didn't say what it was?"

I shook my head and when Father didn't respond I said, "And Sir William said he didn't hear it."

To my surprise Father laughed.

"Tell me, when this happened was Sir William giving some grand advice or talking about one of his accomplishments?"

"Yes, actually," I said.

"Then the only way you could have gotten him to listen to anything else would have been to ring a gong some inches from his ears. It's one of his drawbacks," he added with a small smile.

"But, Doctor Baldwin and the others thought there was something wrong with me," I said, wanting to get out all the feelings I had been containing for the last few hours.

"Leah, I know *you* and I know that there is nothing wrong with you." He squeezed my hand. "If you hear the voice again, come to me and we'll decide what to do, but if not, then I wouldn't worry about it. What harm is it doing you?" he said with a shrug.

I looked into Father's eyes and smiled. What was that voices to me? It wasn't hurting me or Father, so what was the point in worrying about it?

"Now then," Father said, slapping his hands together, suddenly businesslike. "Have you eaten dinner yet?"

"No."

"Would you care to have it brought in here or would you rather eat with us?"

I smiled widely at his complete understanding.

"Here," I said, blushing slightly.

"I will give your excuse," Father said turning to the door.

"Father?"

"Hmmm?" he asked stopping at the door and looking back at me.

"Where were you today?"

For a moment, his eyes darted away from mine.

"It was nothing. Just someone I've known for awhile . . . a problem had arisen. It's a long story. Ann will bring up your dinner soon." And he closed the door.

I woke early the next morning. Quietly, I dressed and left Willow Manor to see Iris before anyone could stop me. When I reached the spot where Sir William and I had stood the day before, I stopped and listened intently to the early morning sounds. Birds sang cheerfully and, oddly enough, an owl swooped into the forest, but there was no foreboding voice. With a sigh I continued to the stables. Father was right; I shouldn't worry about it anymore unless it happened again. I ploughed through the dew-covered grass feeling better every minute.

Iris let out a low neigh in greeting as I opened the door of her stall.

"Hello," I said as I grabbed her reigns and saddle. "Ready for a run?"

She nodded her head up and down vigorously as I led her into one of the fields.

It felt wonderful as we galloped across the grass. This was where I belonged. I enjoyed some blissful hours, getting farther away from my world with each stride, when I was roughly brought back down to it with a jolt.

"Miss Leah!"

I pulled on the reigns and turned in the saddle to see who had called for me. Adam, the stable boy, was waving at me by the fence.

"You're needed up at the Manor," Adam said when I had reached him.

"Why?" I asked dismounting.

"Miss Lydia called for you."

My insides turned glacial. What did Lydia want with me? Wishing that I could refuse, but knowing I'd never hear the end of it if I did, I gave Iris over to Adam and trudged up to Willow Manor. I had just walked through the front oak doors, wondering where Lydia was, when her head poked out of a door to my left. She waved me over to her.

"What?" I asked as I walked through the door.

Lydia closed the door behind her and said, "I am here to tell you that I will be tutoring you today, as Miss Perish still feels reluctant to do so."

"Tutor me?" I asked, momentarily stunned.

"Yes," Lydia replied briskly. "She felt that it would be for the best—to learn from me, that is." She smiled wryly. "We shall start now."

She walked to a sturdy table and sat down, looking up at me expectantly, back straight and nose up.

"You're not going to tutor me," I said.

Lydia raised her eyebrows into her blond bangs.

"I'm not, am I? That's not what Miss Perish thinks."

"Why doesn't Miss Perish teach me today?" I asked, balling my fists, trying desperately to keep my voice steady.

"Like I said," Lydia replied with a curved smile, "Miss Perish is unwilling to do so."

I glared at Lydia, refusing to sit.

"If you truly have a problem," Lydia continued after glancing at my expression, "then I suggest you go to Miss Perish immediately. I'm sure she would *love* to hear from you."

Trying with all my might to keep my hands from shaking, I sat down in front of Lydia. There was no way I was going to deliberately go near Miss Perish, not after what had happened the day before.

"Good," Lydia said as she lifted a teapot that I hadn't noticed and set it down in front of me. "Miss Perish has informed me that you aren't very smooth when pouring tea. We'll start there."

I picked up the teapot with one hand and a cup in the other. As I poured I shot icy daggers at Lydia.

"Your hand is shaking," Lydia observed happily.

I breathed deeply through my nose and focused on steadying my wrist.

"Did you really hear that voice?" Lydia whispered.

"What?"

She was leaning forward, her hands pressed flat against the wood.

"Did you really hear that voice?" she repeated.

"Why should you care?"

She blinked and glanced up at the door, her eyes wider than usual. I turned and looked at the door, but it was still closed. Puzzled, I turned back to her.

"Lydia, what—"

"What would be coming?" Lydia interrupted, her eyes wide.

"I don't know," I replied, trying to ignore the urge to slide my chair away from her. "Why should you care? I thought you thought I'd made it all up."

Lydia suddenly looked embarrassed. Taking her hands off the table, she straightened in her chair. Her upturned nose and imperial air had returned.

"Are you going to hold that pot all day or finish fixing the cup?" she asked sharply.

It was by far one of the strangest and most painful lessons I had ever had to endure. Lydia quickly regained her usual manner and seemed to have completely forgotten about her strange behavior towards me moments before. She didn't waste any time in criticizing my techniques and correcting my movements. When I went to bed, I spent a good while staring up at the ceiling trying to decide who was worse, Lydia or Miss Perish.

When the day—the blessed day—of Lydia's, Aunt Roseanne's, and Sir William's departure (he had decided to leave on the same day as Aunt Roseanne and Lydia, much to their delight) arrived I woke with a light, happy feeling of freedom.

"You must come back again," Father said to Aunt Roseanne, kissing her hand.

"Of course we'll be back!" Aunt Roseanne replied imperiously. "We should do this much more often." Her eyes strayed once again to my small frame. I could only imagine how much she wanted to fix me.

"I fully enjoyed the stay," said Lydia curtsying.

"You must leave then, William?" asked Father, turning to shake hands with Sir William.

"Afraid so, duty calls—" Lydia sighed and Aunt Roseanne batted her eyes, "—and I must be getting back. Upon my departure from Torona, King Rowan made it quite clear that I should return as quickly as possible."

Sir William nodded to Father, bowed to me, and walked out into the gray day followed by Aunt Roseanne and Lydia. I held my breath as he mounted his steed and they climbed into their carriage and did not let it escape until they had exited Willow Manor's main gates.

## Chapter 5

# A Cup of Tea with a Witch

❧

It had been several months since Aunt Roseanne, Lydia, and Sir William had left, and life at Willow Manor had returned to its usual state. The disembodied voice had remained silent. I didn't hear a murmur, not even the slightest trace of a whisper. At first, I was relieved, and over time I began to doubt if I had even heard it. Like Father said, why worry if the speaker remained mute?

Miss Perish continued to teach me, though her patience with me was even shorter than before. But as much as I hate to admit it, Miss Perish's lessons were starting to work. I couldn't believe it at first, but I could curtsy without my knees trembling. I could pour hot tea without a drop spilling. (This, however, always gave me bad memories of Lydia). Dancing came as naturally to me now as riding and I could carry on a good conversation with a duke or duchess if ever I should meet one. As much as it soured me to admit it, the many years with hawk-like Miss Perish had proved fruitful. Of course I still wasn't the best lady by any means, as Miss Perish was quick to point out. No matter what she said, though, I felt that I was doing just fine, thank you very much.

Then, one day a letter arrived for Miss Perish, announcing the marriage of her sister. When Miss Perish told me that she would be gone for at least a week ("or Heaven forbid more!") I almost shouted for joy. However, I decided that was a tad too exuberant, so I had to channel my excitement into a smile of good fortune for the bride to be. As I watched her leave, my only prayer was that Miss Perish had more sisters waiting to be married.

It was a fine summer's day with the sun aglow and the trees in full bloom. I didn't have much to do because Miss Perish was gone and Father had taken Iris with him on one of his large hunts. So there I was all alone on the grounds, kicking at the grass nonchalantly as I walked. As the breeze picked up and whipped my hair straight back like a horizontal black waterfall, I heard the creaking of trees. The forest that surrounded half of Willow Manor waved around at me. It was called Raven Wood. I cautiously looked around to see if anyone was watching before I slowly moved into the trees.

I had never been in the forest by myself before. When I was nine I took a walk through it with Father, but he always told me to never venture into it alone. *And what am I doing?* I asked myself, as the green foliage blocked Willow Manor from sight.

Rays of light broke through openings in the trees to give the woods a magical, peaceful air of solitude. I walked on, deeper into the forest. It didn't take long before I understood why the forest was called Raven Wood. The cawing of a raven echoed shrilly through the trees every few minutes, sending shivers up my spine. I stopped and leaned up against a tree. I had to be sure I could find my way back home. My eyes followed a small sparrow fluttering to the ground. I blinked. Surely not. A few feet away from me, where the sparrow stood, lay what was unmistakably a path. Small pebbles lined the edges of a narrow grassy trail with uncanny precision. I knelt down to examine it closer. Each pebble was the exact same size and color. Although I knew perfectly well that exploring an unknown pathway was not only stupid, but dangerous, I moved onto the path and proceeded.

I couldn't have been walking for very long—ten or fifteen minutes at most—before I walked around a substantial oak tree and stopped dead in my tracks. A very small wood cottage was right off the path—in fact, the path led straight to its front door. I had never known there was a cottage in Raven Wood. I stared at a crooked stone chimney from which lavender smoke rose into the air in large hoops, growing larger the higher they floated into the air. As I gazed transfixed at this strange house, an owl flew into an open window and my heart stopped. I hadn't yet considered who might live in that peculiar house. The strange smoke, the crooked roof, the owls, they all led to only one conclusion: witches.

Father had told me about witches—how they were evil and dangerous. As I backed away, a loud voice came from within the cottage.

"There's *who* outside?"

I stood frozen; how could the witch know I was here? I heard the screech of an owl and the woman's voice again.

"Really, it's Leah Vindral? How wonderful!" The cottage door suddenly burst open, revealing a short old woman with wide owl-like eyes and gray fly-away hair.

"Oh it *is* you! Come in my dear, come in," the old woman said, clapping her hands together. I stood stunned. How did she know my name? The woman, with amazing speed, walked up to me, grasped my wrist in a remarkable grip for someone her age, and pulled me inside. Before I knew what had happened, the door had swung closed and the woman stood looking up at me, her eyes twinkling, a smile spreading across her face.

"Please, sit down," she said, indicating a chair behind me with an outstretched hand. I didn't want to upset the witch for fear that she would attack sooner, so I sat and was startled by a rush of wings and the indignant screech of an owl as it took off by my ear.

"Hush you!"

I looked up startled—I certainly hadn't said anything. Then I realized the woman was addressing the owl that had now landed on a large pot.

"Leah, I'm so glad you're here," she said, turning from the ruffled owl. "Would you like anything to eat? I was just making lunch."

"No ... thank you," I said nervously, starting to rise. "I really should be going ... didn't mean to intrude—"

"Nonsense!" She waved a wooden spoon energetically through the air.

I hastily sat back down. Maybe if I kept her talking, I could distract her long enough to figure a way out of this mess.

"I never knew there was a house in Raven Wood. Who are you?"

With a clatter the woman dropped the spoon in her hand. "You don't know who I am?"

"No, why should I?" I asked puzzled, my guard dropping slightly.

"Because your mother told me about you the moment she could get her hands on quill and paper."

"You knew my mother?" I asked, shocked. *Who was this woman?*

"'Course I knew her," the witch said, sitting down opposite me, sounding slightly impatient. "You mean he hasn't told you?"

"He?"

The woman shook her wild head dismissively.

"Your father, Sir James. I've been *trying* to get him to let me meet you."

I stared at her blankly.

"Well—then I'll just have to introduce myself." She stared across the table rather roughly, her frown even deeper. "My name is Lavena. I am your godmother."

My mouth dropped open.

"*You're m—my godmother?!* But—but, aren't you a witch?!"

"I am." Lavena raised her eyebrow questioningly, "Does that bother you?"

"Yes it does!" I yelled in panic.

"In heaven's name why?"

"Because ... because witches are ... I mean, aren't you ... ?" I trailed off weakly.

"Evil, you mean?" Lavena said with an amused smile. "Well, you needn't worry about me. I'm, what you might call, a good witch."

"You mean you won't hurt me?" I asked dubiously.

"Of course not! Why would I harm Castilla's only daughter?" Lavena said, waving her hands as if to dismiss an irksome fly.

"But my father?" I began.

"Oh, Sir James and I go back many years. We have had some rather rough times that I'm sorry to say have scarred our friendship. And good Lord, that man's stubborn. Been sending him letters ever since poor Castilla's death, but he's absolutely refused to let me near you." Lavena glowered down at her hands, and I suddenly realized who Father must have been meeting on the day I had heard the voice. But then Lavena looked up and blinked her eyes hurriedly, a smile spreading across her face once more. "What must I do to convince you?"

She suddenly gasped and raised her right hand.

"I know!" She leapt to her feet and ran to an old trunk pushed up against the wall. She opened it and started throwing papers and odd-looking contraptions over her back. "Aha! Here it is!" She rose, brandishing a tattered yet well-preserved piece of parchment. "Read this."

I took the parchment that she had thrust under my nose and unfolded it. On it was a short, scribbled letter, as if someone had written it in a hurry, or perhaps couldn't keep her hand steady.

*Dearest Lavena,*

*She is more beautiful than any of my dearest dreams! You must come and see her immediately! James and I have decided to name her Leah. I hope you will agree to be her godmother. Leah deserves the best!*

*Castilla*

I stared up at Lavena wide-eyed after I read it through twice.

"She wrote this?" I whispered.

"Yes."

"Could I keep this?" I asked, still staring at the letter.

"Certainly," Lavena said kindly. "I've been hoarding it long enough."

We sat in silence. Lavena stared at me while I stared at the letter.

"Well, now that we've gotten over introductions," Lavena said, bringing me back to the present, "are you sure that you don't want anything to eat?"

For a moment I hesitated. She could have stolen the letter from the real Lavena; she could have forged it, but there was something about the old woman ... something I trusted. "I'd love something. I'm starving," I said as my stomach gave a growl.

Lavena bustled over to the stove and started frying something that smelled delicious.

"Are you mad that my father never said anything about you to me?" I asked.

"No dear," Lavena said with a dry chuckle. "I completely understand why he didn't."

"Why then?"

"Your father, I give him all the respect that I can—dear Lord—but that man hates all magic ... and he's as stubborn as an ox," she added sourly.

I snorted quietly. That wasn't a good enough excuse for keeping the knowledge of a godmother from me all these years, even if she was a witch.

"Then why did he agree for you to be my godmother?"

"Because he hasn't always disliked magic," Lavena replied shortly.

"Father told me that witches kill people. They fly on their brooms and snatch up their prey."

"That," Lavena said, turning to look at me over her shoulder, "is a misconception." She turned back to the oven. "Never have I heard of a witch that was a cannibal. We eat the same things the average non-magical person does." She picked up a plate. "I frankly don't enjoy flying as my means of transportation. The only brooms you'll see here are strictly for sweeping."

Lavena carried over two plates with the largest poached eggs I had ever seen, two pieces of black bread, a nice serving of goat cheese, and a large heap of steaming hot ham. "Would you like some tea?"

I nodded, dumbfounded by all the food that she had made so quickly. Lavena sat down at the wooden table and gave me a cup of tea that smelt of chamomile. As I took a sip I caught sight of Lavena. She was staring at me serenely over her lunch.

"What?" I asked.

"You look so like Castilla."

"I know," I said, smiling down at my fork, remembering my hours of studying Mother's portrait. "Except my hair. Hers was brown."

Lavena continued to gaze happily at me.

"Why did Mother want you to be my godmother—if you don't mind my asking?" I said to try to stop her from staring at me. I found it a little unnerving.

"Of course not dear," she said taking a sip of tea. "I told you that Castilla and I go back many years. You see, Castilla used to live in a town called Fairanex. She was the only daughter of a—but you know all this."

"No, actually, I don't."

"Oh." Lavena looked startled. There was an uncomfortable silence before Lavena said in a more cheerful voice, "She was the only daughter of a candlestick maker in Fairanex. I met her when she was a little older than you are now. I was passing through the town, visiting an old friend of mine, when I overheard a doctor informing Castilla that there wasn't much he could do for her ailing mother. She was in such a state, the poor girl; I just had to help her," Lavena added with a shrug.

"What happened?" I asked.

"I healed her mother and Castilla insisted I visit whenever I was in town. Your mother and I certainly bonded—we were great friends. I can't tell you the shock I received when she told me she was to marry a man called James Vindral who lived essentially right down the road from me." Lavena laughed merrily. "I don't think he ever knew that I lived in Raven Wood until he married her and we were introduced. She told me that it took her some time before Sir James agreed about me being your godmother—but then Castilla was always a convincing person. She's why I laid the path out to my home, so she could visit me and not get lost."

It felt odd to be discussing Mother with someone I hardly knew over a cup of tea, but it also felt strangely satisfying. I began to ask questions I had never thought to ask: What was her favorite food? Did she laugh easily? Was she quiet? Lavena chuckled at the constant flow, but there was something in her gaze that I pretended I didn't see ... something sympathetic.

When Lavena and I had finished our huge lunch and I had talked for so long that my throat was scratchy, I said a pleasant farewell and left her cottage. As I walked down the pebble-lined path to Willow Manor, I replayed the pleasant hours of conversation with Lavena. It was funny now to think that I had thought she was dangerous.

When I exited the forest I began my search for Father. I wanted to talk to him about Lavena. There were so many questions I wanted answers to. I rushed into Willow Manor's main hall and spotted Ann at the top of a stairway dusting a clock.

"Ann," I called.

She looked over the banister, still wiping the clock's face.

"Yes?"

"Ann, has Father returned from his hunt?"

"No, he said he wouldn't be back till three."

"Thank you," I said with a swift glance at the clock's hands before turning away.

"Anything I can do?"

"No, Ann. Thank you, though."

"Anytime," said Ann, returning to her dusting as I made my way through a side door that opened to the outdoors. A rose garden lay just behind Willow Manor. Separated from the rest of the grounds by beautiful lush hedges, it gave an immediate sense of peace and solitude. That was where I wanted to be. A large trellis covered with wisteria led to the rose garden. The wisteria walkway was deserted and soft sunlight filtered through the many leaves. Halfway through the wisteria tunnel a gap the size of a door appeared on the left, opening to the garden.

The perfume of roses exploded onto my senses as I stepped into the garden. I walked over to a weeping willow located at the far corner of the garden near a small pond and sat down with my back leaning against the trunk.

It seemed strange—amazing even. Mother had hardly been mentioned for so long, and suddenly I ran into someone who had been the best of friends with her. It seemed that Father and Lavena had gotten along fairly well before, so what had happened to sever their friendship so badly? It didn't make sense for Father to still be silent on the topic of Mother, either. Hadn't he loved her? Hadn't he ...

I opened my eyes and stared at the petals floating lazily in the breeze. Questions and feelings that had never entered into my mind were now sprouting roots.

There was only one thing I could do to understand why my godmother's identity had been kept a secret: I had to talk to Father. The clock on the wall next to Ann had said two forty. I was sure I would be able to hear the pounding of horses' hooves from my location in the rose garden. It wouldn't be long. Father was usually very precise with time.

I sat there, musing over how I could broach the subject. No matter what, I was not going to allow him to make some sort of half-hearted excuse and—

I jerked my head to the left and hastily stood up. The distant pounding of hooves had reached my ears, and it was steadily growing louder. I left the garden and ran to the stables to find Father. The hunters were dismounting when I arrived. There must have been ten others, all of them Father's close friends. I recognized the majority of them, each one having been to dinner a couple of times.

I walked up to one of the hunters.

"Sir Fredrick."

"Hello, Miss Leah, pleasure to see you today," said Sir Fredrick, turning from his steed and bowing.

"Likewise," I said, curtsying slightly, "do you know where my father is?"

"I saw him over there a minute ago," he said, pointing to the far edge of the group.

"Thank you," I said, inclining my head. I made my way carefully through the crowd of men and horses and spotted Father talking to a burly man with a grizzly black beard that I did not know. The bearded man had finished his conversation with Father and was leading his horse away when I walked up to him.

"Leah! Good to see you," said Father, turning around and spotting me. "Have you had lunch yet?" he asked, as Adam took his horse down to the stables and we made our way up to Willow Manor.

"Yes," I said as Father waved farewell to the other men.

"Would you mind watching me eat then?"

"No ... there are some things I want to talk to you about, actually."

"Wonderful!" Father strode through the oak front doors.

We settled down at the dinning table and Guinevere brought out lunch for Father.

"So, Leah, what is it that you wanted to talk to me about?" Father asked, spreading cheese on a slice of poppy-seed bread.

I took a deep breath. It was now or never.

"I met Lavena."

Father's knife clattered down on his plate. "How did you meet Lavena?" His voice was hushed, his eyes wide.

"I went for a walk in the woods and found her house." I didn't look at him. "We talked and—she told me she was my godmother."

"Really?" He leaned back in his chair and surveyed me with darkened eyes. He then leaned forward and lifted his fallen knife. "I don't want you to see her again."

"Why?" I asked, shocked.

"I have my reasons," Father said brusquely.

"And what are they, may I ask?"

"You're too young—"

"I'm fifteen!"

Father, his fork in midair, looked at me. He was frowning but not from anger. I had the feeling he was thinking carefully.

"I will not deny that Lavena is you godmother," he said quietly. "It is my wish, however, that you stay away from her."

"But—"

"That's final, Leah," said Father sharply, and he directed his attention to his lunch once more.

# Chapter 6
# Something Practical

Father forbidding me to see Lavena certainly caught me off guard. Lavena hadn't been joking about she and Father having deep scars. But if he thought that I was going to pass up the opportunity of getting to know a witch, he had another thing coming! It was hard for me to take Father's warnings about witches seriously now. I had been alone with her for a few hours and nothing had happened. I wanted to learn more about this strange woman who seemed perfectly comfortable talking about my mother.

The next morning, I was making my way, slowly and silently, down a staircase. I had done a lot of thinking as I lay in bed last night. If Father was testy about me seeing Lavena then I would just have to make sure he never found out about it. I had told Ann before dinner that I was old enough to wake myself now and not to bother. She had seemed a little surprised by the abrupt decision, but didn't question it. It was very early in the morning, right before dawn. I would have a few hours with Lavena and still have plenty of time to make my first lesson. No one need ever know.

I peered left and right at the bottom of the stairs. Not even the servants could know of my plan to enter Raven Wood. The coast was clear so I crossed the shiny wood floor on tip toe and snuck through the door. With furtive looks up at Willow Manor's windows I sped to the edge of Raven Wood and disappeared behind its leafy foliage.

It didn't take me long to find the pebble-lined path. I marched down it, invigorated by my own rebelliousness. I hadn't disobeyed Father many times before. But what harm could it do? Really, it wasn't like Lavena was going to blow me up. Mother had trusted her, so why shouldn't I?

I had reached Lavena's cottage. I walked slowly up to the door and hesitated. I didn't know how early Lavena got up. Swallowing, I rapped on the door. No one answered. I knocked again, louder. Nothing. I frowned and let my arm fall. Dejected, I was turning to head back to Willow Manor when I heard the soft pattering of feet inside the cottage and the door opened a crack. I whirled around.

"Lavena?"

"Oh, it's you." The door opened wider, revealing Lavena in a gray dressing gown. "Come in, come in."

I stepped inside and sat down at the kitchen table. Owls eyed me blearily, perched on pots, pans, and rafters, fluffed up to get ready for a nice long nap.

"What brings you here so early?" Lavena asked, putting a kettle on the stove.

"I want to get to know you," I said truthfully, shrugging my shoulders.

Lavena smiled contentedly as she sat down.

"You told James, didn't you?"

"Yes," I said, looking at my hands. When Lavena didn't reply I continued. "He's forbidden me to see you."

"I'm glad that didn't stop you!"

"I was wondering if it would be all right if I came to see you in the mornings," I said tentatively. "That way Father need never know."

"Certainly, my dear. But I must say, I think I might miss my sleeping in."

"I don't have to come every day," I said quickly, "maybe twice a week or something."

"That would be wonderful." The kettle gave a loud whistle and Lavena rose to tend to it. "I don't mind telling you Leah, that us old people need our beauty sleep."

"You're not old, Lavena," I said chuckling.

"Hah! You might think so, but if I told you my age you'd probably fall out of that chair."

"Do witches live longer than non-magical people?"

"Yes, quite a bit longer." Lavena placed a cup of tea and a plate of biscuits before me.

After we had finished our tea, Lavena took me on a tour of her house.

"Now this, my dear, is the library."

Lavena opened a door with a large brass handle and my mouth fell open. Inside were countless shelves that towered ten feet tall, at least, and each one was crammed full with books.

"Lavena," I gasped, following her inside, "how is this room so large? It can't possibly fit!"

"Well, I am a witch," said Lavena with a wink. "If you just use an expanding charm, you'd be amazed at how much you can store."

"But what are all these books about?" I asked, astounded at the thousands of volumes.

"Oh, a wide variety of things, from *The History of the Universe* to *How to Remove a Stain.* People kept giving me books until I had them coming out of my ears. So I decided to do some renovating."

"Can you teach me magic?" I asked excitedly.

"'Fraid not, dear," Lavena said kindly. "Magic's usually in the blood. A witch or wizard needs to be in the family, and the closer to your generation the better."

I gazed up resentfully at the shelves.

"Not fair," I mumbled.

"Magic isn't everything, dear," Lavena said, leading me out of the library, "just useful when you need it. But I can teach you some things," she said, closing the library door.

"Like what?" I asked enthusiastically.

"Herbs and other useful things," she said. "I could teach you how to make potions."

"Would you?" I asked, hardly containing my glee.

"If you want to."

"I would!" I yelled, hopping up and down like a three-year-old. I couldn't believe my luck. Potions sounded much more fun than proper etiquette!

"Let's get started then," Lavena said, in between chuckles.

❦

On the second morning with Lavena, I blurted out something that I had been sitting on since I'd met her.

"Father doesn't talk about Mother that much. Nobody does."

"It's a shame," whispered Lavena gravely. "Castilla was the most charming woman for miles. Her memory shouldn't be … "

"Shouldn't be what?" I asked. Lavena turned her back to me in a hurry. She took a deep breath.

"It isn't my place," she said, her back stiff. "Your father has the first say at how to raise you … isn't my place."

I could feel the tension in the air.

"Should you use expanding charms only on rooms?" I asked, trying to change the subject.

Lavena turned back to me and breathed through her nose.

"Expanding charms can be used on a variety of objects. For instance … "

She moved to a part of the kitchen where a large cabinet resided. Hanging limply off a hook on the side of the cabinet was a tattered old sack covered in patches. "This," she said, putting the sack on the table, "is a Replenisher. It may not look very fancy, but you would be amazed at what it does."

"Which is?" I asked, poking the frayed bag. It was rough to the touch. I knew right away that Miss Perish would have burned it immediately.

"Exactly what the name says—replenishes. Here," Lavena opened the sack. "Look inside."

I gazed inside the sack, looked back up at Lavena, and did a double take. Inside was food. Neatly wrapped sandwiches, a variety of fresh fruit stored in a basket, two flasks of juice, cheese, napkins, and utensils filled the sack. Somehow there was an incredible amount of room in the Replenisher so none of the food overlapped each other.

"How?" was all I could say.

"This satchel is a fine example of mixing two charms."

"You can do that?" I asked, impressed.

"'Course I can. Now, this satchel has an expanding charm *and* a replenishing charm. They're wonderfully useful for a journey. The bag isn't very heavy, so it'll never slow you down."

"Is there always food in it?"

"Only when you need it. That's where the replenishing charm takes effect. Whenever you want food, envision what you want and open it. It's very simple."

"And when you close it… "

"It disappears," Lavena finished as she fastened the top.

"How did you get it?" I asked.

"Been in my family for generations, as you can see by its appearance."

I smiled down at the shabby Replenisher.

*Bong!…*

"What time is it?" I asked, a knot of panic forming uncomfortably in my throat.

"Nine," Lavena said turning in her chair to look at an old tattered, brass clock hanging on the wall.

"Good Lord! I'm LATE!" I said a rushed good-bye to Lavena and ran as fast as I could to Willow Manor.

Up the stone steps, down a corridor, up a flight of stairs, down another corridor, left, right, right, left, and, completely out of breath, I entered the ballroom. Miss Perish turned to face me as I came through the door. She stared at me with pure contempt, her arms crossed over her chest dangerously.

"You're late! I have been waiting for you to arrive for ten minutes! Where have you been all this time?" She said, bearing down on me, tapping a finger on her watch. "No, you don't even have to tell me—I know. You were out with that *horse* of yours. We'll see if Sir James will change his mind about that when I tell him you were late for one of my lessons!"

"I wasn't near Iris!" I yelled furiously. She *still* wanted me to get rid of Iris, even after all this time. I was so angry at her I could have slapped her across her face.

"*How* dare *you speak to me like that!*" She hissed dangerously. Then she closed her eyes and said in a deadly calm voice, "Then tell me, where were you?"

"I was taking a walk and forgot the time," I said, not looking at her. I had a feeling she knew I was lying.

"Really? You had no idea that this lesson started at nine o'clock sharp and always has?" Miss Perish's words were so full of sarcasm that they made me even more irate.

"No," I said, balling my fists. "I knew when it started, I just lost track of the time. It was a mistake, that's all."

"We'll see about that," Miss Perish said with an obnoxious air of victory. The bottom of my stomach dropped as she led me out of the room. She knew something. Had she seen me walk into the woods and figured out where I had gone? Then again, did she even know Lavena? Miss Perish walked out of the ballroom and back down to the first floor. She moved purposefully to Father's sitting room and knocked on the door. I stood quite still, unable to think of anything to say. Father, however, was not to be found in his sitting room.

"No problem," said Miss Perish pleasantly. "We'll find him."

We went in other rooms where Father could usually be found, but not today. But we did find him. He stood staring down at a patch of wildflowers as—*it couldn't be.* I stopped walking so abruptly I might have run into an invisible brick wall. Sir William stood beside Father talking animatedly. Sir William. *Sir William?!* I couldn't believe it. Of all times to have Miss Perish argue about me with Father it just had to be in front of Sir William. I didn't even know he was expected to arrive. If I'd had the nerve I would have turned around and walked straight back to the manor.

"Leah!"

Miss Perish's voice snapped at me like a whip. She had continued walking and had only just noticed that I had halted in my tracks. Swallowing with difficulty, I started to walk again.

"Excuse me, Sir James," Miss Perish said cutting in on what Sir William was saying. "I need to discuss a problem with Leah. It's very urgent."

Father straightened himself and his eyes shifted from me to Miss Perish.

"What is it?" he asked curiously, placing his hands behind his back.

"Leah was late for her dance lesson," Miss Perish said.

"What was the reason?" A line formed slightly between his eyebrows.

I opened my mouth to say something, but Miss Perish jumped in before I could make a sound.

"She said she was out walking and lost track of the time. Obviously, she is lying."

"Why do you think she is lying, Miss Perish?"

"It is clear to me that she must have been spending this time with that horse of hers," Miss Perish said, nose high.

"Do you have proof of this?" Father asked, gazing up at a slowly passing cloud.

"Yes, of course. Leah arrived ten minutes—"

"You misunderstand, was she in fact with Iris?"

"I hardly think that matters." Miss Perish bristled in defense. "The point is that that horse has been distracting Leah from her lessons."

"And what do you wish for me to do, Miss Perish?" Father asked calmly.

"Why, take away the horse of course," Miss Perish said as if this was obvious. "As I told you before, sir, I knew that that horse would prove a problem—"

"Yes, I remember."

"Then you agree."

"No, I don't. I have only your word that Leah was late because of Iris, but you have no proof. Therefore, unless you do find proof Leah will continue to have a horse."

"As you wish." Her jaw tightened and a vein rose on her temple. "Come Leah, we've wasted enough time."

As we walked back to the Manor I heard Sir William say pompously, "Late for lessons, honestly James, what else has that girl got to do?"

The dancing lesson that day was very uncomfortable. I could feel Miss Perish glaring at me the whole time. Plus, I was hungry from missing breakfast and I couldn't concentrate so I made more mistakes than usual—which didn't help the atmosphere at all.

After the lesson I rushed down to see Iris. After I had brushed Iris and fed her an apple I left the stables. I was still reminiscing about Father shattering Miss Perish's dreams of depriving me of Iris while I dressed for dinner.

I was so happy that Miss Perish hadn't gotten her way that it didn't even bother me to have Sir William's company for dinner. Apparently, he had arrived just a little before Miss Perish's confrontation with Father.

"Great things are happening James!" Sir William said happily over his leg of lamb. "Great things indeed!"

"Like what?" Father asked, taking a sip of wine.

Sir William leaned forward and said in an audible whisper, "King Rowan is making *very* large plans."

"I have the strangest feeling that what you are telling me is against the rules," said Father smoothly.

"Absolutely right, you are. Only the highest ranked knights were told," Sir William's chest protruded smugly, "and we must uphold the highest level of secrecy."

"Which you are fulfilling in every way possible," said Father with a smile.

"Of course!"

Father laughed loudly.

"Tell me, why all the secrecy?"

"Ah," Sir William said, in between a mouthful of potatoes, "That I cannot say, but I will tell you that King Rowan is looking for the best hunters in Torona." Sir William looked at Father with narrowed eyes and his mouth curved up at the edges.

"Really?"

"Ah yes…"

I could feel my attention ebbing away as I ate the last of my dinner. Sleep itched at my eyes, and as Father and Sir William left to have an after-dinner drink in the sitting room, I made my way up to my bedroom. I pulled the covers up under my chin and gazed happily out of the large window. The twinkling stars were slowly disappearing behind dark, thick clouds.

# Chapter 7
# The Death Caravan

As Lavena and I walked through the woods on a perfectly clear morning, I told her about Miss Perish's explosion.

"That woman sounds like she gets more dreadful everyday," said Lavena sourly, "I'm glad I've never met her."

Lavena was taking me for a walk in Raven Wood, a pastime I had quickly grown accustomed to. I was carrying a basket that was already almost full.

"Now look here Leah!" Lavena said, almost jumping with glee.

I looked at a short, dark green plant with blue leaves that had uneven shapes, as if something had violently tried to rip them from the stem.

"Is it supposed to look like that?" I asked.

"Yes. This plant is called Farlex. When a few of its leaves are placed on a wound, it stops the flow of blood.

Put three leaves on the cut and wrap it in a cloth. In five hours the wound will be healed and there will be no scar. Pick a few of these—my supply of them is running low."

I picked a handful of the strange leaves and placed them in the basket.

"Feverfew, that sticky plant with the pink flowers—yes, that's the one—protects you from dragon fire—when used in the correct potion, mind. The potion is unfortunately very difficult to prepare—takes about three months to mature. And testing it is dreadful." Lavena pinched her eyes closed and shuddered as if remembering the experience.

"Now, if you ever get a toothache," Lavena said, as we came upon a patch of wild roses, "Put a petal from a rose in your mouth. The yellows are always the best, but reds do just as well."

After a few more minutes of walking Lavena stopped again and knelt down low to the ground, indicating for me to do the same.

"This," she said, pointing a finger to a small purple flower that I would have walked past without the slightest glance, "Is Lavender Marsh. It may look small but when ground or chopped up, it makes an extremely powerful sleeping draught that will knock out the victim for three days." Lavena held up three fingers for emphasis. "Never look at size alone, Leah, for some small things are more powerful than larger ones. Never be deceived by outward appearances."

"It's amazing that one simple flower can do that. Put a person to sleep for three days! It's hard to believe," I said, astonished.

"Another thing you will learn is that Nature lives in a completely different way than what you would expect. Always the impossible is mastered here—remember that."

We left the Lavender Marsh and walked back to Lavena's cottage. I laid all the plants on a wooden table outside her cottage to dry. The sun had slowly risen higher into the sky while we had walked through the woods, and breakfast would soon be served at the manor. I waved good-bye to Lavena, and made my way back home.

When my lessons with Miss Perish finished for lunch I decided to see Iris. I had just brought her back in from a wonderful ride and was cleaning her up when Adam came to see me.

"Miss Leah," he said, "Sir James would like to see you in his sitting room."

"Why?" I asked, feeling a little disappointed at being taken away from Iris.

"I don't know," Adam said shrugging his shoulders. "He just told me to go and get you."

"Tell him I'm coming. Just let me finish up here."

I quickly finished brushing Iris, filled her trough with some more water, and left for Father's sitting room. I opened the sitting room door and poked my head through.

"You wanted to see me Father?" I said.

"Yes, Leah. Come in," he said turning from a window.

He was not alone. Three other men that I recognized from his hunts were standing near him. They smiled at me as I nodded to them.

"You're in for a real treat, Leah," Father said, as I moved to stand in front of him. When I didn't say anything he continued. "How would you like it if you went on my next hunt?"

I didn't know what to say. Father had never asked me to go on one of his hunts before. I didn't want to be rude, and I would miss my proper etiquette and singing lessons.

"I would love to go," I said smiling.

"Wonderful! We're leaving tomorrow bright and early," Father said and then turned to converse with his guests.

I left the room wondering what a hunt would be like.

The next day as I ate breakfast and put on my riding clothes, I tried to ignore the nerves bubbling in my stomach. They grew steadily worse as I walked to the stables a little stiffer than usual, wondering what on earth I had gotten myself into. The stables were crowded with the hounds of Willow Manor and the men who would be accompanying Father on the hunt. The men bustled around, talking jovially as stable boys readied their horses. Tension and nerves flew into my heart and, quickening my pace to leave the men, I went to find Iris. Her ears were pricked up and she nervously danced in place as she sensed the excitement blowing through the air. I calmed her down as much as I could—which wasn't much as I felt my stomach do another flip—and put the saddle and bridle on her. I led her out to the crowd that had now formed outside of the stables and tried to find Father. After much searching, I saw him on his most prized stallion,

Crescent. Father's eye caught mine and he waved me to him.

"How are you feeling?" he asked once I'd reached him.

"Fine," I lied in a hollow voice.

"Let's move then," Father said loudly, and sitting straighter in his saddle he turned Crescent's head toward Raven Wood's edge, followed steadily by the other hunters.

Crescent's black coat glistened in the early morning sun as he cantered off with the dogs running madly up ahead. I noticed that Father was leading the group in the opposite direction from Lavena's cottage. I glanced up to see what his expression was—to see if this was deliberate—but he was talking with Sir William who had just ridden up beside him.

It took awhile, but the dogs found a scent and ran exuberantly as we followed closely behind. I loved the wind whipping through my hair as we hurried on in a rush of excitement. The sound of the horse's hooves pounded the ground like falling rocks. It was odd, though, after riding full out with the dogs rushing beyond us, to suddenly slow down and stop.

I was near Father at the front of the group. The dogs had abruptly stopped barking and stood like statues staring at a huge stag in between the trees. The first sight of him startled me. His antlers were enormous with threatening sharp points. He was simply gazing at us curiously with large amber eyes, not understanding what we were or why we were there. My heart pounded in my chest as if it wanted desperately to get out. The trees bent and swayed in the wind and it seemed so clear that I couldn't deny it: the stag turned its head ever so slightly and stared at me, his eyes boring into mine.

A burst of air whizzed by my left ear so close that I jumped. Everything seemed to happen so quickly. An arrow sank deeply into the stag's chest. He dropped to the ground in a limp heap, blood staining the mossy carpet of Raven Wood. Blood pounded in my ears. I blinked and found my hands cramped in a strangling grip on Iris's reins. My shirt was plastered to me in a cold sweat. I couldn't make my eyes leave the dead stag.

But then, I heard laughter. My head turned so fast I heard it crick. Sir William was holding his bow in his hand laughing jovially as he gazed at the dead stag. Victorious glee radiated from his eyes. Men were huddled around him, thumping him on the shoulder and giving praise for such a wonderful shot.

Anger thrashed inside me like a powerful storm getting ready to unleash something dreadful upon the world. I glared furiously as five men gathered the stag on a horse and headed back to Willow Manor. They all seemed very pleased with themselves. I listened to them congratulate Sir William over and over again on the beast he had just killed.

"I think this one will bring a high price, don't you?"

"Yes, look at the size of its antlers—he's quite the prize."

"My God Leah, why do you look so serious?" Father asked, looking down into my face.

"It's nothing ... I'm—I'm fine, Father," I said, looking at Iris's ears.

"Don't worry James. She's just excited about the hunt... I'm sure she's thinking of how to congratulate me on my shot." I recognized the gloating voice that was sneering in my ear. Sir William was the one who had killed that stag. Before I had even realized what I was doing I heard my voice shouting.

"*How dare you say that!* I am not excited about this hunt, this murdering crusade, this—this *death caravan!* I will *never* congratulate you on what you have done! *NEVER!*"

"Leah!" I felt Father grab me by the waist to keep me from falling out of Iris's saddle and jumping on Sir William. "Stop it, Leah. STOP!"

I turned back to face the back of Iris's head—and focused all my energy on her ears. Heat was rising in my face as I sensed all the eyes of the group upon me.

As we set off again, the unease of the argument slowly lifted and conversation came back to the group. I, however, didn't move my eyes from Iris's ears and Father would only speak if someone asked him a question and even then it was a sharp reply. I knew I had not only embarrassed myself but had severely humiliated Father in front of a large group of hunters, all of them his close friends.

The ride back to Willow Manor seemed to take twice as long. When Willow Manor's sloping grounds appeared I sighed inwardly. All I wanted was to get as far away as possible from the dead body of the stag.

When Iris stopped I quickly dismounted and called for Adam to take her. Father didn't try to stop me nor did anyone else as I made my way to the front steps.

I seemed much more aware of my body now that I was alone, and there was no one talking in the background or the sound of heavy hooves hitting the ground. My heart was beating furiously, and its beat seemed to be in my ears rather than in my chest. As I walked my legs were weak and seemed to hit the ground too hard, and I was breathing like I had just run a mile. I was angry with myself. I had never let my temper get away from me before. *Well, not entirely*, said a voice in my head. *It was just three summers ago that I yelled at Miss Perish because she said that I would never amount to anything… That I would never make Father proud because I wasn't proper. I threw the books that I had placed on my head at a night stand. Father did tell me that what I did was awful and I should be ashamed, but after time it all became a joke.* I doubted that my first hunting experience would ever be made a joke. But why—*why* had I felt so infuriated by the death of that stag? Hunting had never bothered me before. Why should it affect me so greatly now?

I was so occupied with my thoughts I hadn't even noticed that I had crossed the grounds, gone through the oak doors, and was now walking down a corridor. I didn't know where to go, so I decided to let my feet lead me.

I needed to be alone and think this out and the rose garden would suffice. I was sure Father would start looking for me when he had finished seeing his companions off.

I stepped into the garden, walked over to the weeping willow and leaned my head against the rough trunk. I hadn't even changed my position before I heard heavy footsteps thudding their way into the garden. I turned to face the opening in the walkway, my hand resting on the trunk, breathing steadily. Just as I had expected, Father burst through the opening and, seeing me, marched to the tree.

"Leah," Father said, coming to a halt before me. "Explain."

I had never seen him so angry before. His hands were clenched and his forehead was set in the deepest of frowns.

"I'm sorry," I said truthfully.

"Sorry?" he said with mock sarcasm. "You have humiliated me in front of some of the most important men in Torona. I have not raised you to behave like a crazed wild animal!"

"I didn't mean to!" I said. The weeping willow's branches swished lightly between us.

"You didn't—" Father repeated breathlessly. "If I hadn't pulled you back you would have strangled William!"

I didn't reply. How was I supposed to explain if he kept interrupting me?

"I hate to say this," Father continued, his voice full of bitterness, "but I'm beginning to wonder if Miss Perish has been right all along? Really, why can't you be more like Lydia?"

My mouth went dry in a matter of seconds. I had the feeling, as I pushed by him and ran to my room, slamming the door behind me and collapsing on my bed, that I had seen a flash of remorse in his eyes. I had hated to embarrass Father but there was no reason for him to yell at me! *He should know that it was a mistake,* I thought darkly. *And to wish I was more like Lydia! That was the worst thing he could ever say! If he wanted Lydia to be his daughter so much then why didn't he throw me out and adopt her!*

A knock sounded at my door and Ann entered it.

"Sir James wants me to tell you," she said, "that you are to apologize to Sir William tomorrow."

"Why doesn't Father tell me himself?" I asked acidly, rolling over on my elbow to face her.

"Because he has to go and apologize for your behavior to the others that are still here," Ann replied roughly.

I gripped my pillow tightly as Ann shut the door. What did I care if they all thought I had acted like a nine-year-old child? Could Father no longer bear to share my company? *Well that's just fine,* I thought miserably. *I'll stay in here for the rest of the day and spare him from any discomfort I may cause him.*

## Chapter 8

# Midnight Messages

I had trouble sleeping. My dreams were filled with creatures, beautiful with life, and the death cries of arrows slicing through the air everywhere, killing everything in sight. After waking sweaty with my heart racing for the third time, I slammed my fists on the feather blankets around me in frustration. The branches blowing in the wind outside my window scratched their long fingers across the wall. I winced at the screeching noises as they passed the window.

*How dare you…*

Chills ran down my spine as I sat up straight as a candlestick. The voice had been so quiet that I wasn't sure if I had really heard it. My ears felt like they were widening as I tried to hear the voice again.

Silence.

Taking in deep breaths, I tried to calm my racing heart, but just when I placed my sweaty head on the pillow, I heard it again.

*How* dare *you!*

"How dare I what?" I asked the room, sitting up again. When no one answered I crept cautiously out of bed to the window, the unease in my stomach increasing.

I looked out over the grounds and saw the huge intertwined trees of the forest stirring in the breeze. They looked like soulless skeletons reaching their grasping fingers toward me. As I watched, more voices joined the first, growing louder and wilder.

*You are a fool! Blood drips from your hands!*

I slammed my cold hands tightly over my ears and mumbled, "Stop. Stop it."

But the voices wouldn't stop; they cried louder in retaliation. I was on the floor—my hands clamped tightly over my ears—now screaming at the top of my lungs.

"STOP! STOP IT! LEAVE ME ALONE!"

A door banged open and someone put their arms in a tight embrace around me, rocking me like a baby, but I couldn't understand what the person was saying. As I was rocked, the grasping voices subsided and I realized Ann was holding me.

"Shhh child, *shhh*! Everything's all right... no one's going to hurt you," Ann whispered soothingly, rubbing her hands on my arms and rocking me back and forth. "You're safe here. There's nothing to worry about, child."

I wanted to tell Ann what had happened but my throat was too dry. Resting my head against her shoulder, somehow I fell asleep.

When I woke I was in my bed and the sun was up in all its glory. The birds sang happily as they whizzed outside my window. I stretched lazily, thinking that it was promising to be a wonderful day, when I suddenly remembered what had happened in the middle of the night. I walked over to the window cautiously. I tried to see into the edges of the forest to see if someone was standing there but it was useless. I never would have heard anyone from the forest. The invisible speakers seemed to have yelled in my ears. But that was impossible. A shiver ran through me.

I turned from the window and observed my room critically. Everything was in place. The small table stood beside my bed, a lamp and some books rested upon it untouched. I frowned at the walls. Could the voices have come through them? Could I have imagined everything? I brushed my hair out of my eyes and glared at the floor, thinking hard.

"Ah, I see you're awake, good."

I jumped and saw Ann walk through the door.

"That was quite a night you had, wasn't it?" Ann said softly, as she looked through my closet, searching through the dresses for one that she wanted to have me wear. "Tell me, did you have a bad dream?"

"You remember what happened?" I asked.

"How could I forget?" Ann said with a dry laugh. She pulled out a misty rose-colored dress from my closet. "You were thrashing around like a mad thing when I came in."

"I was?" I asked, heat filling my cheeks.

"And screaming at the top of your lungs like some wild animal!" Ann said, nodding her head. "What had you dreamed?"

"Umm, oh … I don't remember," I said, waving my hand and getting out of bed. "Thank you." I held out my hand for the dress she was holding. There was a slight silence between us before Ann said, "I'll just be going."

I watched her go to the door and said, "There isn't much point in telling anyone about this, especially Father. He's had enough on his mind."

"How right you are," Ann said with a wink. "You're growing up. Thinking maturely about other people's feelings is a wonderful sign of coming of age."

I smiled slightly. "Sure … "

I didn't think Ann would believe me if I said that I thought I'd heard those voices again. I didn't want to have to go through all that fuss with Miss Perish and Doctor Baldwin again any time soon.

*Nothing happened,* I thought to myself as I descended the stairs. *I was just overreacting from my dream. I probably imagined hearing those voices—yes, I'm sure of it.* With a determined nod I entered the dinning room where Father was just finishing his breakfast.

"Good morning, Father," I said politely, sitting down at the table.

"Hello, Leah. I trust you slept well?" Father replied stiffly, dabbing his mouth with his napkin.

"Wonderfully," I lied.

"Marvelous," Father said.

Breakfast was unusually tense, with hardly any talk. At least he never brought up the hunt and, following his lead, neither did I. But then, as I was climbing the stairs to join Miss Perish in the library:

"Leah, Sir William will be in the stables at noon. I want you to talk to him there."

"Of course," I said turning around to look at him. "I'll see him at noon."

"Leah."

I looked over my shoulder at him.

"I never should have said what I did about Lydia."

"I know," I said curtly. I made my way up the stairs feeling grimly satisfied. I didn't care that I had just been rude to Father. For the first time in some years, I didn't care what Father said to me, even though I knew that by the end of the day my conscience would probably win out and I would end up apologizing to him as well.

I didn't pay much attention during my lessons—a fatal mistake to make, I can tell you. Miss Perish had to resort to slamming a book on a table to get me to pour the tea, after I had ignored her order for the third time in a row. Even though I had tried to convince myself that I had made the voices up, I couldn't stop my mind from revisiting the scene. Finally, lunch came and I left Miss Perish to work up my nerve to apologize to Sir William.

I disliked—no, that wasn't the right word, *despised* is more along the right lines—I *despised* the idea that I would have to apologize to Sir William, but I knew it was the right thing to do. Finishing the remains of my lunch I left the dinning room. With a deep intake of breath, as if preparing for a storm, I walked down Willow Manor's front steps. The thought of apologizing to him made my stomach squirm like I had a handful of snakes slithering inside it. I could just picture his face when he heard me. I would probably never hear the end of it. I grimaced at the thought of Lydia ever finding out.

I didn't have to look long to find Sir William. I had just passed the fourth stall when I found him brushing down his horse, a powerful-looking stallion the color of dark molasses. If he saw me he didn't show it. He kept his eyes down, concentrating on making every hair shine in its place. When he finally moved his eyes to me I was standing on the other side of the stallion.

"Is there something you need?" Sir William asked in a calm cold tone, "or are you liable to try to choke me again?"

Deciding that there was no point in beating around the bush, I rushed an apology with my face as expressionless as possible.

"I am sorry about what I said to you yesterday on the hunt," and I turned on my heel, not wanting to see how he would react.

"I tried to tell James that something like this was sure to happen," Sir William said pompously. "A woman should never go on a hunt. You can't handle it. A woman should be meek, docile, obedient ... "

I whipped around and shot him a glare that would have melted ice.

"Looks like Father didn't listen to you, though," I spat.

"No," Sir William said coolly. "I've always felt that his downfall was marrying a—well, let's just say he and I have a difference of opinion, shall we?"

Before I could even ball up a fist to pound him with, he'd passed by me and strutted away.

A cloud of straw and leaves billowed about me as I pounded out of the stalls. I stopped abruptly before the Manor's steps. I was really tempted to skip the rest of my lessons and go visit Lavena but my better judgment came into play. It would be foolish to visit her in the middle of the day and I would never hear the end of it if I missed any more lessons. I breathed deeply through my nose and entered the Manor.

❧

The wind howled like mad during dinner. Positive I would never get to sleep with the trees scratching against my bedroom wall, I slowly closed my bedroom door, sat down on my bed, and stared down at the floor. I sat like that until I heard the clock in the hall toll midnight. Everyone must have been getting ready for bed by now. Knowing I was completely out of my mind, I slid on my cloak, crept out of my room, and made my way out of Willow Manor as silently as a mouse. I had to talk to *someone* about the voices.

With my heart beating much faster than usual, I nearly ran to Raven Wood's edge. I had never been to the forest at night. As I walked under the canopy of whirling trees, I realized I could only see an inch in front of me. What a waste of time! How would I possibly find the path? But just then, I saw it. The pebbles were illuminated by a light glow, as if a small flame were trapped inside each one. I sprinted down the path and a short time later, was knocking frantically at Lavena's door. After a few moments, it opened a crack, revealing only a sliver of a face.

"Lavena, can I come in?"

Lavena opened the door wide for me.

"Yes, yes," she said, looking tired and highly confused. "Come in."

"I need to talk to you," I said, taking a seat.

She looked at me expectantly, but I couldn't help noticing that she seemed anxious and distracted.

"I heard these voices last night... at least I think I did."

Before Lavena could open her mouth a windblown owl flew through the window. It landed on a pink teapot, its feathers sticking out in every direction. Lavena rushed to it.

"What news?" Lavena asked the owl.

The owl clicked its beak three times.

"She—she *what*...?" Lavena gripped the stove tightly.

"Lavena, what is it?" I asked, but the owl was clicking its beak again.

"She gave it... why would she give it to him?" Lavena asked the owl.

The owl snapped its beak.

"Do they know?" Her voice was so low, I had to lean forward slightly.

The owl hooted.

Lavena nodded her head and, as if she had just noticed me, gave a start and sat down, apologizing.

"Sorry, you were saying?"

"I heard these voices last night," I repeated, slightly offended by her lack of attention.

"Voices?" Lavena's own voice cracked slightly, but she recovered quickly. "What kind of voices?"

"Hollow." I said after some thought. "Raspy, hollow voices."

Lavena stared at me across the table, her face expressionless.

"What did they say?" she asked carefully.

This wasn't hard to answer. Their words had been playing over and over again in my brain.

"They kept blaming me for something and saying there was ... blood on my hands."

"Well, Leah I wouldn't worry about it," Lavena said calmly, closing her eyes and leaning back. "Not if you've only heard them once."

"But I haven't."

Lavena's eyes shot open.

"You've heard ... "

"Twice."

I was taken aback by her sudden change in attitude. She had turned deadly pale and her hand gripped the table until her knuckles turned white.

"Do you remember what they said ... the first time?" she asked quietly. For some reason I felt that she had already guessed before I answered.

"The first time it was only one voice, but it sounded the same as the others. It said that something was coming."

Lavena jumped as one of the owls let out a screech.

"Have you told anyone else about this?"

"The first time I told Sir William, Aunt Roseanne, Lydia, Miss Perish, and Father. Is there something wrong with me?"

"Wrong?" Lavena said, her eyes wide. "No, Leah. Nothing is wrong."

"Then you can hear them too?" I asked hopefully.

Her shoulders tensed, "No … I can't."

My heart dropped in disappointment. Was I the only one that could hear them? That didn't make sense at all.

Her bright eyes startled me when I looked up again.

"Leah, I think it would be wise to forget about these voices … for now."

"Why?" I asked. Of all people I hadn't thought Lavena would want me to forget about them, Father yes … but Lavena?

"They aren't doing you any harm," Lavena said, rising and opening the door. She poked her head out to make sure no one was there. Her face was still frighteningly pale. "If they threatened you, then we would do something but as they haven't … "

I walked through the door, "But?"

"Leah, trust me," said Lavena with a bit of an edge to her voice, "and I'll walk you back to the edge of Raven Wood. I don't want you visiting me at night anymore, understand?"

Before I could reply she shut the door behind us and marched up the path, leaving me jogging to catch up. I tried to pry more information from her but all I got were grunts. I was actually relieved to leave her company when we reached the edge of the forest.

# Chapter 9
# Unwelcome News

Sir William had only stayed in our company for two nights before leaving during a spectacularly blustery storm. As I watched him leave I evilly hoped that the wind would blow him straight off his horse. Fall passed by briskly and winter harshly took its place. Lavena and I had bottled my first potion and had moved on to harder ones. She said that making potions was a good pastime during the long winter months. ("There isn't much growing when six feet of snow plops down on it"). I don't think Lavena ever enjoyed the winter.

Lavena seemed to be back to her normal self, but there were times when I would enter her home to find her talking feverishly to her owls. I would also catch her staring at me. It became a usual occurrence to be asked if I felt sick or dizzy. But despite the strangeness, she never mentioned my late night visit and I never dared to bring it up. No icy voices fell upon my ears during the change of seasons and I found myself relaxing once more, though this time I did not forget them. And I also couldn't deny that I was very curious about the person Lavena had spoken to her owl about. No matter how normal Lavena tried to behave, I knew she was deeply troubled about the news her owls were sending.

One day, I was sitting in my proper etiquette class, staring into space, trying to guess who the illusive 'she' was. I was alone in the room. Miss Perish had blustered off when Owen had entered, informing Miss Perish that Father wished to see her. She had ordered me to continue practicing my posture, which, of course, I had ignored. Suddenly, the door banged open and Miss Perish bustled in in a wave of excitement.

"Leah! Leah, I have wonderful news!"

I quickly changed my slouching position to a straightened back, but she seemed too excited to notice the transition.

"We are going to have a ball!"

"What?" I asked blankly. Her face hardened at my lack of excitement.

"A ball, Leah, a *ball.* The Royal Family is attending along with a grand number of dukes and duchesses! They will arrive in a month so we must start preparing now! This will be a wonderful test to see how much you have improved!"

"But why are we having a ball, Miss Perish?"

Miss Perish rolled her eyes, sighed with exasperation (as usual) and said, "Honestly, girl."

I raised an eyebrow and she said with irritation, "Sir James wants to show you off! You're nearly a lady and time is precious. There should be plenty of possible young suitors—"

"*S-suitors?*" I spluttered. "I'm not ready for marriage!"

"That's obvious," Miss Perish replied acidly. "But girls should have a list of potential husbands in mind by the time they reach fifteen and then decide at sixteen. We are a little late. Usually young ladies have the ball on their fifteenth birthday." She gripped her hands together and breathed through her nose. "But Sir James makes the decisions."

It was clear that Miss Perish had been annoyed about this for some time.

The lesson that followed was the worst one I had ever had to endure. It's not that I did everything wrong—it was just that Miss Perish was asking for complete perfection. I wanted to scream! The closer I got to the day of the ball the more nervous I became. The only thing *I* was looking forward to was the day the ball would be over.

It seemed at first that it would never come, but the nearer the ball approached the faster time went. It seemed to me that the clocks had sped up. Before I knew it, the day of the ball had arrived, on a bone-chilling day in December.

I didn't mean to be, but I seemed to be underfoot everywhere I went. Ann and Guinevere were inhuman with their cleaning. I couldn't stand to stay watching them—my nerves were already close to the breaking point—so I went into the kitchens. The second I walked in I realized what a mistake that was. Frank was screaming out orders, his eyes bulging out of his head, veins popping out on his neck, and his chubby face turning a disturbing purple color. One look around the frenzied room made me turn on my heel and rush out the door, only to run directly into Guinevere, who was carrying a huge glass vase overflowing with white roses. With an ear splitting *crash* the vase smashed on the wooden floor, the roses carpeting it like snow.

"*Leah!*"

"I'm sorry!" I said weakly as I bent down to clean up the mess. "I didn't see you. I—"

"Miss Leah," said an exasperated Guinevere, rubbing her eyes, obviously trying to stay calm. "Why don't you go outside until we're done here?"

"Please, let me do something," I pleaded. "I'll find some more white roses."

She looked at me, "There aren't any more white roses. These were the only ones remaining in the greenhouse."

"Please," I begged. "I'm sure I can find something."

As if against her better judgment, Guinevere nodded and fetched a basket. "Take this and fill it up to the top. But I don't know where you'll ever find any, not in this weather."

I nodded and quickly left the messy scene to her. I was glad to get away from all the hustle and bustle of the manor.

I entered the greenhouse and felt my face fall. Guinevere hadn't exaggerated. One look told me that there was no hope of picking any white roses. The ones that remained were turning brown at the tips from old age and drooping their once beautiful heads to gaze at the ground mournfully. I cursed silently and gazed at the pink and yellow roses that filled the stuffy room instead. I knew that Queen Mariah's favorite rose was white (a little fact I hadn't yet dispensed with from one of Miss Perish's lectures). I looked through the nearest snow-filled window and moaned. Maybe Lavena knew of a way of conjuring white roses. Tightening my grip on the handle of my basket, I left the greenhouse and fought my way through the snow to the woods. The wind blew through me like knives; I pulled my cloak closer about me and ducked under the trees. The sky was steadily darkening with threatening clouds. Quickening my stride, I headed to Lavena's.

The more I walked the darker the woods became. Quickening my pace to a jog I found the path, trying to ignore my gnawing awareness of the storm growing above me. I had passed the halfway mark, a tree with three owl holes in its side, when I saw something twinkling out of the corner of my eye. It shocked me at first, because the woods had now grown so dark it seemed as if someone had draped a black fabric over the canopy. I moved toward it, wondering what light could have been playing through the clump of bushes.

I drew back a bush that was hiding it from view and my heart skipped a beat. There they were, white roses, the most beautiful I had ever seen. They were growing in the middle of a small clearing almost covered in snow. I moved cautiously to stand before them, strangely afraid that they would disappear if I moved too loudly or quickly. Roses didn't bloom in the winter; the cold was too much for them and yet, here was a small but healthy-looking bush just bursting with flowers. The scent that danced from their petals was delicate and sweeter than any other scent I had ever smelled. I would have to ask Lavena how they were able to bloom. I pulled out a clipper from the basket and snapped the stem of one rose... and another... and another... until my basket was full.

I rose and was fumbling with the basket on my arm when the hairs on the back of my neck prickled with the feeling of being watched. I whipped around, looking frantically for the thing that had been observing me.

"Who's there?"

The wind whipped the trees around me, sending chills up my spine. I might have imagined it, but I thought I saw the same glimmer of light the roses had shed playing in-between some trees to my right. This one seemed brighter, though, and I could have sworn that it moved. If I just moved a little to my left I would be able to see it clearly—

A sudden burst of wind nearly swept me off my feet. By the time I had steadied myself and brushed my hair out of my eyes the strange light had gone. Large buckets of snow poured down from the branches above, covering me instantly. I gave a final look to the place where the light had been and ran as fast as I could back to the manor.

I was soaked to my knees and shivering violently when I ran into Willow Manor. The guests hadn't arrived yet. I still had time.

"Leah!"

I spun around and saw Ann rushing toward me looking positively frantic.

"Good Lord child! I've never seen someone in such a state. Hurry, people will be arriving any minute!" she said as she ushered me off to my room.

I don't think many people paid much attention to me, even in my snowy state. They were moving even more quickly around the halls and rooms, making last-minute adjustments. My stomach twisted uncomfortably. I was glad when I entered my room and it was just Ann and me.

"I can't believe it's almost time!" she said filling up a bath for me. "We haven't had a ball in so long—I think the last one we had was for your first birthday."

"Why did we stop having them?" I chattered through my teeth.

"I'm not that sure."

I bathed quickly and with the help of Ann put on a beautiful sky-blue dress. The material was light and flowing. When I moved it swung softly around my ankles. She pinned a delicate silver brooch at my breast. A small sapphire twinkled happily in the middle of its thin web. There was one thing I didn't like about the dress, though. I rubbed my bare shoulders and felt goose bumps rise under my fingers.

Ann looked at the clock on the wall and jumped.

"We have no time! Leah, will you stand still!"

"Now what can we do about your hair?" Ann asked, looking at the mop of hair on my head with disgust. "Ahh, I know!" She grabbed a comb and ruthlessly ran it though the tangled mess. As she worked she opened one of the jewelry boxes and pulled out a valuable hair piece made of silver and blue diamonds. She folded my hair in an elegant bun and placed the clip at an angle to hold the hair in place. With a sigh of joy Ann moved me in front of a mirror, where I saw someone completely different from me. The girl had my face but the dress and done-up hair made her look too old—too mature.

"You look like a princess, my dear," Ann whispered in my ear.

"You're just saying that," I said with a smile.

We were standing before the mirror, watching our reflections when…

"THE TIME! Hurry Leah, they'll be arriving any minute now!"

"Wait!" I said turning away from the doorway. "I have to put those flowers in a vase."

"Don't worry, I'll take care of it," Ann said, pushing me out of the room. "You get down to the entrance. Sir James is waiting for you there."

"But—"

"HURRY!"

I walked quickly down the staircases, my hands clammy with sweat. Just before I walked through the pair of doors that led to the entrance hall, I wiped my hands on my dress and lifted my head. With as much poise and grace as I could muster, I walked into the bright, gleaming entrance hall. My heart pounded in my chest when I spotted Father in his best attire. For some reason, all I could think about was all the different chances I would have to mess up.

"Leah, I thought you'd never get here," Father said, holding out his hand to me.

"Well, you know how Ann can be," I said, faking a laugh and taking Father's hand.

"She certainly did a fabulous job. You look amazing, Leah," Father said taking a step back to look at me.

"Thank you," I said, my cheeks coloring with pleasure.

I took my place beside Father and took a deep breath as the large oak doors opened.

## Chapter 10
# King Rowan's Request

As I gazed out the front doors, I was amazed by the change that had taken place. Carriages led by the most elegant horses moved smoothly down the snow-covered gravel path, where they lined up one behind the other, waiting for their loads of passengers to disembark. Footmen jumped off their carriages, holding umbrellas to keep the snowflakes from landing on the guests' perfect heads. The footmen led them to the hall where I stood, struggling to make my parched mouth somewhat damp.

I recognized a good number of the people from the times they had 'dropped in' to see Father. I welcomed them and curtsied after Father greeted them.

On and on it went until my feet roared in protest and I noticed uncomfortably that I was shifting my weight frequently.

"Ah, James! How *are* you doing?" came an imperial voice that made my skin crawl most unpleasantly.

Feeling my heart plummet, I turned to see Aunt Roseanne speaking to Father. Lydia stood a little behind her, exchanging glances with the Duke of Aronian's son.

"Hello Madam, Lydia," Father said with a bow. "I am doing quite well, as I hope you are."

"Lovely. Tell me, has King Rowan arrived?" she asked, narrowing her beady eyes and looking from left to right as if hoping to see him jump out from behind one of the towering vases.

"No, I must say that he has not."

"Oh, that is dreadful. I so wished to speak with him about some business of mine."

Aunt Roseanne looked at Father through the corner of her eye. I had the feeling that she was just hoping Father would ask for more details.

"Really?"

"Yes—I won't say much ... but it revolves around Prince Philip and Lydia."

Lydia smirked at me over her mother's shoulder.

"You must inform me of it," said Father with a polite smile. "But I am afraid that now is a terrible time ... greeting my guests."

"Oh yes, of course. Come Lydia." And with that Aunt Roseanne and Lydia ruffled past Father. "Leah," Aunt Roseanne nodded her head crisply and marched on. The many diamonds and jewels clattered happily against each other on wrist and neck as she walked down the hall.

ශ

I continued to greet more guests; I thought the line would never end. It was so tiring saying the same things over and over again ("How are you?" or "It's lovely to see you" or "I hope you enjoy the evening") that I just decided to settle on simply nodding my head and smiling.

Finally, when I thought I wouldn't be able to stand for another minute, the King's carriage arrived. It was easy to recognize because it was the largest and most stunning I had seen that evening. A dozen white horses, glimmering with freshly groomed coats, trotted down the road with rubies and diamonds winking from the crowns on their heads. Two footmen dropped down from behind the carriage and opened the door, and I got my first good look at royalty.

King Rowan was the first to exit the immensely large carriage. I had been told what the king was like, but I had never seen him before. He had a strong face with a prominent jaw and sharp nose. Even though his hair and beard were gray with age, I could tell that he still had plenty of fire left. He wore a white and red suit with three gold chains around his neck, and medals decorated his prominent chest. As he walked past the footmen, they bowed so deeply I feared they'd topple over. Beside King Rowan walked Queen Mariah who had just stepped delicately from the carriage. She was dressed in an impressive red gown. Her dark hair was set in an elegant bun that (I thought) must have taken hours to complete. After the King and Queen came Prince Philip. Prince Philip was extremely handsome with his smooth, brown hair and blue eyes. My stomach did a small jump that I was sure had nothing to do with nerves.

King Rowan walked up to the oak doors and Father bowed low with respect. The king took Father's hand in a firm grip and shook it heartily.

"We'll deal with business later," he said in a deep voice, with a secretive smile.

"I wish you would tell me what this very important business is, dear," Queen Mariah said as Father kissed her hand.

"Patience Mariah, you will find out soon enough," King Rowan said with a deep laugh. He moved on to me, leaving his wife and son to greet Father. He looked down his prominent nose and smiled.

"This must be your daughter Leah," he said.

I lowered my head and curtsied, "I hope you enjoy the evening, Your Majesty." Even with my eyes directed downward, I could feel his eyes studying me. I didn't like the feeling.

"I'm sure I will."

King Rowan moved on and Queen Mariah put her hand under my chin and tilted my head back to look at my face.

"Charming," she said simply.

My stomach turned again when I saw Prince Philip stop before me. I curtsied so quickly I almost fell over.

I heard him say as if in a dream, "It's a pleasure."

I thought I was going to melt right there on the floor. His voice was so perfect. He thought it was a pleasure to meet me! Me, of all people!

After the royal family had arrived there were only a few remaining guests to greet. The time seemed to go by very fast, maybe because my mind was still replaying my introduction with Prince Philip. When everyone was in the ballroom Father and I followed the stragglers into the most beautifully decorated room I had ever been in. Five fires crackled from the walls and a large array of ales and wines covered one long table. As I walked by one of the tables filled with the most succulent foods I had ever laid eyes upon, I thought, *Frank has outdone himself.*

I weaved my way through the crowd to one side of the room and took a solitary place in a corner to watch the people dance to the sweeping music of the orchestra.

"Did you see what the Countess of Bline is wearing?" said an elaborately dressed woman who I recognized as Catherine Zoran, a rich lady who loved to drop by Willow Manor to discuss the latest gossip with Father. She got a bit tiring, but she was entertaining.

"Absolutely horrible, I must say," said her sister, Raleen, excitedly. "Orange does not suit her in the least."

I couldn't keep from grinning as I watched the women pass. I hardly ever saw Father as I stood there people-watching, but my ears picked up his loud laugh that reverberated around the room. The snow storm was still billowing outside, but inside it was warm and comfortable. I was just about to grab a goblet of cider and a slice of honey crumble when I heard someone call my name.

"Leah, there you are."

I turned and found Lydia standing inches from me.

"Hello Lydia. How are you?" I asked as pleasantly as I could, taking a step back.

"I'm having the most wonderful time. I know everyone here."

"Really? The King has visited your home?" I said, raising an eyebrow.

"Well no—but Mother and he have written letters—mostly about me. Oh, don't you love my hair? And my gown? It's brand new. Mother personally sent for it the day before we left to come here. Oh, yours is all right, I suppose," she said, glancing at mine and flicking her hand. "But really, light blue clashes with the season, doesn't it? Take mine for example, dark green is much richer in color than light blue. Light colors have been out of fashion for months now."

I had the urge to slap her across her long-nosed face. Instead I moved away from the table, but to my horror she followed.

"Mother has business with the King and you won't ever guess what it's about," she said, walking beside me.

"I know Prince Philip is involved," I said looking at the people around me, wishing I was one of them.

"Have you seen him yet?"

"I have."

"Well, he's getting close to the age when he should be thinking about a bride and, well—Mother hasn't told me *everything*, but—"

"Shouldn't you already have a suitor chosen?" Lydia had been sixteen for a month now. Miss Perish had said that sixteen was when a girl made her decision from her list and I knew for a fact that Lydia's was a *long* list.

"Well, yes, but these are delicate matters," Lydia replied huffily. "You wouldn't know anything about that, though, would you?"

I opened my mouth angrily to put her in her place and—

"Pardon me, may I interrupt?"

My stomach did another flip as I whipped around to see the very person Lydia had been talking about standing next to me. Sound abruptly ceased between us as we both stared wide-eyed at the prince. Lydia recovered much quicker than me and batted her eyes like a pro. But he wasn't looking at Lydia—he had his eyes fixed on me. Knowing that I must be dreaming, I watched him extend his hand toward me.

"Would you care to dance?"

It was as if the entire world jerked to a stop. My training forgotten, I stared open-mouthed, thinking that he *must* be talking to someone else, but he kept looking at me, waiting for an answer.

"Yes—yes I would love to," I said breathlessly, placing my shaking hand in his.

As we walked onto the floor, leaving a furious Lydia, I sensed that everyone stopped what they were doing to watch. As he raised the hand that held mine, I picked up some of my suddenly enormously heavy dress in my other hand and inwardly thanked my lucky stars that I could dance.

Prince Philip led and I twirled, my dress swirling about my legs. My eyes never left his face and when he returned my look, my face glowed brightly. We soared across the floor all by ourselves. I didn't pay much attention to the whispering that seemed to follow us—I was too mesmerized with the event that was taking place to care.

When I heard the orchestra play the last note, my heart dropped like a stone in a pond. As we separated, a flock of young, rich daughters rushed forward between us, blocking my sight of Prince Philip. While I watched him give his attention to the jittering crowd surrounding him, a sickening knot burned in my gut. How could I be such a fool? To think that the prince had been interested in me? I wanted to laugh bitterly at the thought. Trying to act as if nothing had happened, I walked slowly back to my corner. However, the moment I reached it I saw Lydia trying to maneuver herself into the prince's line of sight, jumping up and down on the balls of her feet to get a better look. The sight was so disgusting that I turned away, only to see Miss Perish trying to get at me. I knew she would want to force me back onto the dance floor to compete with the other girls. Without a moment's hesitation I made my exit.

I had so many thoughts rushing through my mind that I didn't pay attention to where I was going. Suddenly I looked up and found myself standing at the door of Father's sitting room. I looked around but everyone was in the ballroom, so I turned the knob and walked in.

I always felt like I was being watched in this room. The animal heads on the walls stared at me from every angle, following me with their eyes, hearing my footsteps—my breathing. The only thing I liked about the room was the tapestries. They hung from the ceiling in the most extraordinary colors. Sometimes if I looked hard enough I could swear that the animals woven into the tapestries were moving.

"Your Highness, why don't we talk in here. It's my most precious room and no one will interrupt us. I'm sure you'll enjoy it."

I jumped at the sound of Father's voice. My brain was still strangely cloudy from dancing with Prince Philip—I almost felt drunk. If I was in a better condition, I would have just excused myself politely and left, but because my common sense was somewhere else, I panicked and dived behind a large chair in the corner. Just as I pulled my dress around myself I heard the door open. Holding my breath, I prayed for them not to come where I was hiding. Then I'd really look like a fool.

"Please, have a seat Your Highness," Father said.

"Thank you. You have a very impressive sitting room, Vindral. This just shows how well you hunt," replied King Rowan.

"Thank you, Sire."

Pride swelled in Father's voice.

"Now to get to business." King Rowan clapped his hands together. "I am in the process of planning a most extraordinary hunt."

"What animal is your target, Your Majesty?" Father asked with interest.

There was a pause.

"Unicorns."

"Unicorns?" Father started to laugh, but quickly stopped. "Please excuse me Your Highness, but they don't exist."

"Come now Vindral, I hoped that you of all people wouldn't be so narrow-minded. *They do exist.* I tell you they do. I have found proof!"

I dared to peek my head from the confines of the chair to see. Father sat with his hands on his knees looking politely incredulous.

"You are to arrive at my castle a week before the hunt. Be sure to arrive promptly. I will discuss the plans for the hunt in full at that time. For now—is there something wrong?"

Father's expression was peculiar. His brow was slightly furrowed and his checks had lost their color.

"I am terribly sorry Your Highness, but I cannot accept."

"Excuse me?"

"I cannot accep—"

"Yes, I heard you," interrupted King Rowan impatiently. "I meant why?"

"Do you have any other hunters, other than your knights, I mean?"

"Yes, of course," King Rowan said with a distinctive bite in his voice.

"Good. Then I won't feel so guilty refusing."

"I don't understand! With your experience, this hunt won't last longer than a month, at most!"

"Thank you for your belief in me," Father said kindly. "But I cannot leave my home for a month or longer. I am needed here, Your Majesty."

"Your daughter is old enough to take care of herself," King Rowan said dismissively. "And you have servants."

Father shook his head.

"I'm terribly sorry, Your Highness. Please forgive me."

"I don't understand!" the king repeated, as he thumped his armrest with a clenched fist.

"My deepest apologies, Your Majesty."

Silence expanded thickly in the room and I was sure that they would hear my unsteady breathing.

"I see," said King Rowan harshly, breathing heavily through his nose. "I will honor your decision."

"Thank you, Your Majesty."

I ducked behind my chair again as Father rose out of his chair and the squeaking of another told me King Rowan had done the same.

Father's back was to King Rowan, but I could see the king's face. It may not have been obvious to Father, but I got the impression that King Rowan wasn't ready to give up. There was a glint in his eyes that I didn't like at all. I ducked back out of sight and looked up to see a boar's head staring down at me. The candles in the room flickered as the snow pelted heavily against the windows.

"I assure you Vindral, you are making a mistake," King Rowan said casually. "But tell me more about your charming daughter—she is close to being of age, is she not?"

"Yes, she is."

The door opened and closed and I was left alone with the mounted heads.

# Chapter 11
# Schemes of the Governess

I rose jerkily from behind the chair. It didn't make any sense why such a conversation would make me this unsteady. I didn't even know what a unicorn was. My legs shook as King Rowan's expression flitted before my eyes once more. I left the room and stood in the hallway, afraid I was going to be sick to my stomach. The floor spun and cold sweat prickled on my forehead. I had a faint awareness of someone running toward me and catching me before I hit the ground. But just as quickly as it had come, I opened my eyes and the room abruptly stopped turning.

"Are you all right?"

My cheeks flamed crimson as I looked at the person holding me in his arms—Prince Philip.

"I'm fine," I said in a rush.

"Here, have a seat," Prince Philip said as he awkwardly led me to a chair in the hall.

A moment of uneasy silence pressed between us as distant sounds of the ball echoed down the hall.

"I'm fine, really," I said. I couldn't bear the silence any longer. "I just need some air."

"It stopped snowing—but, do you think you're strong enough?"

If I hadn't been feeling so queasy, I would have laughed at Prince Philip's worried frown.

"Of course I am."

I stood and my legs wobbled dangerously. Prince Philip quickly placed a hand under my elbow to steady me.

At the oak doors, we retrieved our cloaks. Pulling them tightly around us, we made our way into the chilly night. It was beautiful. The snow storm had calmed to a gentle flurry. Snow carpeted the ground and the moon shined brightly in between slowly drifting clouds.

"There are some benches over there," I said, as my legs shook under my weight again.

The benches were free of snow as they were under a trellis. The wisteria vines were so thick that the snow flakes couldn't even drift through to settle on the walkway.

Prince Philip led me to a bench and I gratefully sat down. He, however, stood before me with his hands placed patiently behind his back, as if he was waiting for me to get back up again so he could help.

I looked up at him embarrassed. I didn't know what to say… I bent my head and watched my fingers twist my dress nervously.

"Are you sure you are all right?" Prince Philip asked.

"If you keep asking me that, I might begin to believe that there is something wrong," I replied, happy he had made the first step to conversation.

"I have enjoyed the evening, Miss Vindral—as I hope you have."

His smile sent sparks down my spine.

"Everyone worked very hard to get it prepared, Highness," I said.

"They did a wonderful job. And please, call me Philip."

"And you can call me Leah," I replied, blushing even more. Thank God it was so dark.

When I had the strength, we walked around the garden, talking about anything that came into our heads. Philip told me of life at Torona Castle. I told him about Willow Manor. He seemed very interested in Iris. And I had to tell him about Miss Perish. He found her most amusing and in turn told me about his teachers. The more I talked with Philip the more relaxed I became.

"You must come to Torona Castle," he said.

"Thank you, but I—"

"No, I insist that you come," he said intensely.

I stared at him, taken aback.

"My apologies," he said quickly, smiling once more. He took hold of my hand and bowed slightly. "I only meant that I do not want this meeting to be our only one." He continued to smile handsomely and my stomach lurched yet again.

The gentle snow began to fall faster and soon it became too thick to see through. Laughing, we rushed back to the warm comfort of the manor. I didn't want to revisit the ball, but Philip immediately led the way to the ballroom. I hadn't realized how much time had passed while we had been taking our stroll. The hands on an old clock rested just past ten.

The guests had fanned out a bit. They stood in the corridors near the ballroom, talking and sipping on glasses of wine and mead. Just before we passed through them, the guests stepped back and bowed low to show respect for Philip. It was odd being on the receiving end of the lowered heads. I glanced at Philip and frowned slightly. There was an odd smile playing on his lips. Cocky, smug even. *Well, he has a right to enjoy himself,* I thought. *He's respected.*

"Is there something wrong, Leah?"

I jerked in surprise. Philip had been watching me.

"No," I replied quickly.

"Surely you're used to all of this." He waved his hand lazily at the guests.

"No, actually. Why should I be?"

"You are the daughter of one of the greatest hunters of Torona," said Philip, amazed that I had such a question. "Servants should care for you on bended knee." He chuckled at my bewildered expression.

"But why would I . . . "

We had just entered the ballroom and the moment Philip's face shined through the door, all the princesses and young duchesses flew to him like moths to a flame. Once again I found myself standing uncomfortably outside of the circle of jittering girls. My stomach twitched uneasily as I watched Philip smile broadly at all the attention. Sighing, I turned my back on them and left the ballroom. My feet led me to the library where, closing the door gently, I settled myself in a large comfortable chair and watched the snow fall smoothly past the window.

*BONG ...*

I jerked awake as the clock on the wall tolled the hour. As I peeked my head through the door, I heard guests giving their farewells and the sound of many feet climbing up the stairs. The Royal Family and a handful of the guests were to continue their stay at Willow Manor while the others left for home. Grateful that the ball was finally finished, I made my own trek to my room. The moment my head touched the pillow I was swept away into blissful, quiet, darkness.

But the darkness didn't last as long as I wished it would. I was sure that I had only been asleep for five minutes, but the sun was shining rudely through my window and settling on my closed eyelids. I was just about to roll over when Ann bustled in in a flurry; the door slammed against the wall as she rushed to the bed and threw the covers off me.

"Get up Leah!" Ann scolded. "Miss Perish will be furious if you're late!"

"Wha?" I said as I squinted around the room, flooded with bright sunlight.

"You've slept in late enough!" Ann said, her hair already falling out of its bun. "We can't give a bad impression to the Royal Family!"

"Why not?" I said crossly, as I slid out of bed. "It's not like we haven't already met them."

"Leah!" Ann gasped, clutching a ruffled, pale green dress to her breast.

"Sorry, but it's true. I mean, why do we need to prove to them how well we live?"

"It is an honor to have the Royal Family sleep under your roof!" Ann scowled. "Frankly, I don't think Miss Perish has done a good job teaching you."

She pushed the dress into my hands rather roughly and left the room, slamming the door behind her.

Dressing quickly, I arrived just in time to see Father and Sir William walking through the oak doors with King Rowan and Prince Philip. Hesitating, I stood in the great hall, not knowing if I should say good morning. In the end, I hesitated too long and they were out of sight, marching through the crisp air. After breakfast, I solemnly and dutifully began my search for Miss Perish. I didn't know if she even wanted to have a lesson today. With Lydia and Queen Mariah to content herself with, Miss Perish must have been ecstatic. Why would she want to waste this moment of a lifetime with me? However, I had just turned a corner when a loud screech echoed down the hall.

"Leah! *There you are!*"

I looked up just in time to see Miss Perish running up to me, her dress flapping like a flag in a high wind about her legs. "We *must* talk!"

Without any further ado, Miss Perish grabbed my elbow and—half pulling, half yanking—led me into one of the sitting areas. I had enough time to notice that a large, comfortable fire was burning happily in the corner before Miss Perish pushed me into a chair.

"I've been looking forward to discussing your first ball, Leah," Miss Perish said, clasping her hands together. "What were your strengths?"

"Umm . . . "

"Come, come. What were your triumphs?"

I thought Miss Perish's eyes were about to jump out of their sockets, she was staring at me so hard. For some reason the memory of the ball was hard to find in my brain.

"The ball is a little fuzzy for me," I replied.

Miss Perish's smile twisted. "I should think so. You spent a good portion of the night with the prince."

My neck was distinctly hotter.

"The way he danced with you made me wonder," Miss Perish continued silkily. "I can't tell you how glad I was to know I had finally knocked dancing into your hard head."

It suddenly came back to me in a rush. The night of the ball was in my brain in bright colors, as vivid as if it had happened three minutes ago. I squirmed uncomfortably in my chair. Miss Perish smiled wider.

"I also saw you walking outside with Prince Philip from a window. The two of you were talking for quite some time."

I wanted to disappear. If it weren't for my lady-like training, I would have sunk as low as possible in my chair.

"Though I still don't understand why he chose you," Miss Perish said as if she were discussing clothes. "Why would he have picked you over Lydia? I must say she is far prettier than you."

This scenario honestly seemed to puzzle her. I was too angry to question it myself. Philip *had* chosen me. *Me.* Not beautiful, perfect Lydia. She had been standing right beside me; he surely saw her. Why did he choose me? If he thought she was a better catch, wouldn't he have asked her to dance? Of course he would. But the fact is, he didn't. A smile crossed my lips.

"Now, it's time to make your next move." Miss Perish scooted her chair closer forward so that our knees were almost touching.

"My next move?" I asked nervously.

"Prince Philip took a liking to you, why I'll never know, but by God, I'm going to do whatever I can to finish the job."

Miss Perish spoke as if my tiny encounter with Prince Philip was the beginning of a life-long business arrangement.

"Miss Perish, I hardly think that a meeting as insignificant as Prince Philip's and mine could amount to anything," I said timidly.

"Nonsense! The look in his eyes when he led you across the dance floor!"

I bet an egg could have fried on my face at that point.

"We must do it slowly," Miss Perish continued. "We can't be obvious. I'm sure Lydia could teach you a few pointers."

"Lydia's not teaching me anything!" I spat. Lydia was probably in her room, formulating a plan to win Philip over.

"Whenever we eat with them," Miss Perish said without missing a beat, "I want you to sit on the opposite side of Prince Philip. That way you won't be pushing the envelope. Sit just a few seats down from him and keep a steady flow of conversation with whomever is sitting around you. That way you can sneak glances at him. Let him run after you, that's the way to do it."

Miss Perish continued to organize and devise the most extravagant plan for me to snare Philip. She twisted my simple girlish fantasy into the beginning of a long, prosperous love with five children. When she finally let me go, lunch had come and gone. I asked Guinevere if Father had returned with King Rowan or Philip. It turned out, though, that they weren't expected to return from their tour of the grounds for a few more hours. With that information, I walked out into the white world outside of Willow Manor and trudged my way through the snow to Lavena's cottage.

Lavena was standing outside her door, sprinkling a powder on the heaping snow, muttering darkly under her breath. She looked up when the crunching of my footsteps reached her ears.

"My dear!" she exclaimed. "What a pleasant surprise!"

"I hope I'm not interrupting," I said, coming to a halt beside her.

"Oh, no, you can help me if you like."

In her hand was a small pile of what looked like tiny black seeds.

"Just sprinkle them on the snow," Lavena said as I took a pinch.

I did and the moment the seeds landed, the snow began to steam, leaving large patches of cold ground.

"Vaporin seeds," Lavena said as she sprinkled some more, "an easy and fast way to get rid of snow on your doorstep. Well," Lavena dusted off her hands, "have you had lunch yet?"

"No."

"Come in, then. Let's get out of this freezing weather."

Over lunch I told Lavena about the ball. For some reason, I didn't lie about my slight attraction toward Philip. I finished my story by reciting Miss Perish's plan of how I could marry Philip. The moment Lavena heard of the extravagant plan, she leaned back in her chair and laughed so hard that some of the owls took startled flight and hooted indigently.

"That woman is completely insane, isn't she?" Lavena said, once she had gained her composure. "Are you going to go through with *the plan*?"

"I don't think I have much choice," I shrugged.

"I just hope your governess doesn't know about love potions," Lavena said with a giggle.

My stomach jerked.

"You don't think so, do you?" I whispered, horrified.

Lavena nearly fell off her chair laughing.

"Well I wouldn't put it past her," I said angrily, my face hot.

Lavena continued to chuckle annoyingly.

Thinking of a change of topic, I suddenly remembered something.

"Lavena," I said, "what lives in Raven Wood? It's just that the night of the ball, I was in the Forest and—"

"You were here?" Her attitude changed abruptly. "At night? Didn't I tell you never to come here at night?"

"Yes, but—"

"No buts. Never, ever come here at night!"

"But why? Nothing happened."

"I don't care. And you look pale," Lavena eyed me critically.

"I feel fine," I said defensively, but Lavena had already risen and was rummaging in her herb cabinet. She thrust a small bag of dried flowers into my hand and said, "Brew yourself some tea before you go to bed with this."

"But I don't need—"

"You may want to head back up to the manor now; James could have arrived."

⁂

That evening during dinner, I thought about Lavena's strange behavior. Why did she insist so firmly that I couldn't go to Raven Wood at night? Lavena didn't used to be so paranoid. In fact it all started when I told her about those strange voices. I had forgotten about those voices. Philip's arrival had completely brushed them aside. I glared at my plate, trying to bring back to mind what they had said.

"Leah, are you feeling all right?" asked Father.

I nodded and caught Miss Perish's eye. She had decided to join us for dinner, something that she never did. I glanced up the table where Philip was sitting and when our eyes met, I quickly looked away.

That night I had a hard time sleeping. I lay in bed, tossing and turning, the sheets tangling tightly around my legs. I couldn't make sense of it, but I was nervous, scared even. I just knew that it had to do with the thing Lavena was hiding from me. I looked at my bedside table where the tea leaves Lavena had given me still sat unattended. Glaring at them, I decided that I would go to Lavena tomorrow and refuse to leave until she told me what was wrong.

# Chapter 12
# Silence

I woke after a few hours, a plan fresh in my mind. Jumping out of bed, I quickly dressed and was about to leave when Ann came in and closed the door, blocking my exit.

"What is it Ann?" I asked.

Her mouth was bunched up, as if she was convincing herself to do something.

"Ann, if you want to say something, say it," I said, with a little exasperation. I wanted to see Lavena.

"I don't know if I should, but you have the right to know."

"Well, go on."

"I just came from King Rowan's room. I was gathering up the sheets when that knight, Sir William, came in. They started talking about Sir James and Lady Castilla."

My interest was up.

"What did they say, Ann?"

Ann leaned forward slightly, "When Sir William came in King Rowan clapped him on the back, and Sir William asked if Sir James had joined. *What* he was asked to join, I have no idea—"

"A hunt," I supplied without thinking.

"A hunt? Why would you say that? I never heard them mention the word."

"Oh! I just assumed that if King Rowan had business with Father it would involve a hunt... him being one of Torona's best," I said quickly.

"I guess you could be right. But King Rowan said that Sir James refused to join—whatever it was. You should have seen Sir William's face! He looked as if he'd been slapped. Then all of a sudden he spat, 'It's all his dead wife's fault! That damn woman kept him from greatness!'"

I covered my mouth, shocked, while Ann nodded fiercely.

"Why would he blame Mother for Father not wanting to go on a hunt?" I asked, stunned.

"I'm not sure. Lady Castilla didn't have any problems with your Father hunting."

"What did King Rowan say then?"

"He told Sir William to quiet down. Ha! I must say, I enjoy watching that knight be put in his place. But what puzzled me was that King Rowan didn't seem as worked up as Sir William. In fact, he told Sir William that there were other ways of enlisting Sir James's assistance."

"Like what?" I asked, puzzled.

"I don't know, but Sir William seemed to have an idea. He said, I believe it was, 'Do you mean his royal highness Prince Philip?' King Rowan nodded his head. I got out of there after that. Whatever was in King Rowan's mind, I'll tell you, it's not good," she said severely.

"How is Philip going to make Father join … whatever it is King Rowan wants him to join?" I added quickly.

Ann frowned.

"I don't know, but I tell you, something is not right about whatever they were talking about. I know what Perish thinks, but it's my advice to you to steer clear of Prince Philip." Ann shook a finger sternly at me as she walked out the door.

There was nothing wrong with Philip. I was out on the blustery grounds, struggling through the heavy snow. Why would Ann think he would hurt me when it was Father King Rowan wanted? It was just a hunt. A hunt like any other.

As Lavena's cottage, white with snow, came into view, I couldn't deny that what Ann had told me had unnerved me. There was something about King Rowan that I didn't like at all. The sooner he left the better.

I pounded my fist against the door, but Lavena didn't answer. I knocked louder.

"Lavena, are you in there?" I called.

I continued to knock for five more minutes before admitting defeat and trudging back up to the manor. I was just to the stone steps when something odd happened. I stumbled forward, catching myself on the oak door. My vision blurred, my head throbbed and I was close to retching. Then, moments later, my vision improved. I breathed heavily, leaning against the oak doors, feeling physically drained. Was I ill? There was still a numb pounding above my right eye and my stomach twisted nauseously. With a steadying breath, I walked slowly to my room. Just as I closed my bedroom door, I though I heard a faint whispering:

*Soon…*

The day finally arrived for the last of the guests to leave. Even though they stayed a week, I didn't get to see much of Philip, but Miss Perish seemed to think this was a good thing. He was usually with Father and King Rowan.

"They must be discussing marriage plans!" Miss Perish would always say when she'd spot them talking.

I couldn't deny that whenever I would pass them, they would grow silent and watch me go by. I didn't tell Father or Ann about my weak spell. I was worried they would overreact and call Doctor Baldwin. I didn't feel bad all the time. There were some days that I felt perfectly normal and others where I was more tired than usual. Waves of dizziness and queasiness continued, but they would only last a few minutes before I would feel normal again, except for an annoying throbbing above my eye. I thought that maybe it was the pressure I had been feeling lately. I was worried about Lavena and I was tired of Miss Perish quizzing me on ways of snatching Philip. Between Lavena and Miss Perish, it didn't seem odd to feel more exhausted than usual. I had thought that I had been hiding my symptoms from everyone, but I was proven wrong when Ann asked me, after I had to sit down quickly during one of my spells, what was wrong.

"Nothing. I think I'm just stressed," I had said.

"I'm not surprised," Ann had replied, nodding roughly. "With what Perish has been putting you through."

Miss Perish had been much more intense as the days Philip would be in reach dwindled away. She felt this was our last chance to make a lasting impression. On the day the Royal Family was to leave, Miss Perish got her wish; Philip saw me in the library.

"I feel we haven't had enough time together," Philip said.

I put down the book I had been reading.

"I hope that means we'll see each other again?"

"I was actually wondering if you would permit me to write to you."

My heart stopped.

"I would love that," I said quietly.

Philip smiled handsomely and kissed my hand.

"Leah! Leah, where are you? Leah—ah, there you are!" Miss Perish came bustling toward us. "Your Highness," Miss Perish said curtseying when she caught sight of Philip. "The Royal Family is about to leave, Leah. You need to see them off."

I stood in the same place as I had on the day of the ball. The most satisfying moment was seeing Lydia and her mother's faces when they saw Philip standing next to me.

"I had a wonderful time," I said to him.

"So did I." Philip replied, nearly making my knees buckle.

I stood and watched their carriage until it rolled out of sight.

By mid-day, all of the guests had left, including Sir William, Aunt Roseanne, and Lydia. Willow Manor seemed like an empty shell after all the festivities. Once more, it was just Father, Miss Perish, me, and the servants. My lessons hadn't been true lessons during Philip's stay. Most of every hour was spent practicing different ways to ensnare him. Now that he was gone, Miss Perish felt it was time to revisit the old lessons. It was during my dance lesson that it happened.

From the moment I started dancing I knew something was wrong. The more I danced the more I began to remember what had happened when I was in Father's sitting room. The room began to swim around me in circles... I hid behind a chair in the room when I heard Father's voice... the music sounded like it was playing from underwater... King Rowan wanted to hunt something... everything was turning dark... what did he want to hunt?... I was falling... what *was* it?... falling... *unicorns*... silence...

# Chapter 13
# Broken Reflection

Heaping, suffocating darkness pressed against me. I was scared… lost. I had no idea where I was. I tried to move but the darkness was wrapped tightly around my arms and legs. I opened my mouth to scream for help but no sound issued from my parched throat.

"Let me see her!"

A voice! Someone was near by! I tried to yell again but it was useless.

"*You're not going to touch her!*"

I knew that voice. He was panicky, frightened, powerless.

"This isn't about us, James! She'll die if I don't see her!"

Father. A small light flickered in my heart and the darkness constricted as the meek happy thought touched it. Lavena was there, too. They were going to help me, *they had to help me!* I screamed again but to no avail. The voices were leaving me now, drifting on and off until I was left alone with the darkness once more…

Something cool brushed my forehead. I moved my hand and felt the darkness lift away from it. I opened my eyes and heard someone near me gasp and yell out.

The darkness had lifted and in its place was soft filtered light from a covered window. I was in my room, in my bed, completely drenched with sweat.

"Leah! You're awake! You're finally awake!" Ann cried as she flung her arms around me.

My throat was too dry to ask what was wrong.

"Sir James! Sir James! Leah's awake—she's awake at last!" Ann yelled hysterically. There was a commotion down the hall and a wide-eyed, shaggy-bearded Father rushed into the room.

He knelt next to Ann with tears in his red eyes. He looked like he hadn't slept in a week. I was worried he might collapse as he pressed a shaking hand to my cheek.

Worry and annoyance gripped me. Why were they acting so strange? All this drama over a little fever?

"What's wrong?" I croaked. My throat felt scratchy, as if it hadn't been used in a long time.

"Leah, you were sick. But you're fine now—you're fine!" Father said, his voice shaking. If he burst into tears I would never get any answers.

I couldn't bear to see his strained face any longer, so I looked down and saw four heavy blankets over me.

"No wonder I'm so hot!"

To my surprise Father laughed through his tears.

"I suppose we can take some of these blankets off," said Father.

"Sir James, I don't know. Do you think she's well now?" Ann's hand stopped him from rising.

"I think so. Lavena said that once she woke up, she'd be fine."

The blankets were lifted and Ann opened a window. A breeze blew in and played on my face, blowing my hair. I bolted up, making the others back away in shock. A damp cloth on my forehead fell in my lap with a soft thump. I grabbed a handful of my hair and held it in front of my face. My hair had always been jet black. But this hair in my hand was unknown to me. Delicate strands of white hair waved at me from my clenched fist.

*White* hair?! *White hair*? How could I have *white hair?*

"What happened to my hair?!" I yelled.

"Leah, dear, don't worry. It's alright." Ann said soothingly. She placed an arm around my shoulder.

"No, it's not! How did this happen?"

"The cure that saved you had side effects, Leah," Father said gently.

"You'll get used to it, dear. You'll get used to everything," Ann said with a sweet smile.

"*Everything?*" I yelled in panic. What else had changed? Did I now have something growing out of the top of my head?

"Ann, bring her a mirror," said Father.

Ann hesitated for a split second before rising and retrieving a mirror from my dresser. As she placed it before my face, I saw a stranger.

The girl in the mirror was paler than I was. Her white hair flowed down her head gracefully to land fully on her shoulders. But her eyes, her eyes struck me the most. There was not a trace of green in those eyes, only blue. They were two beautiful deep blue pools; each one glinted and glimmered brightly. There was something about those eyes that I didn't like at all. Something that made my skin prickle.

I grasped the mirror to look closer at the strange girl in the reflection. Yes, I could see some similarities. The shape of the face was the same, but with all the changes it looked unearthly. The reflection was beautiful... extremely beautiful—more beautiful than I could ever have been—small, pink lips... pale and glowing skin... fine white hair. But I couldn't stop focusing on the eyes. The bottomless blue was shocking in the midst of white. She could have competed against Lydia. No, she would have blown Lydia out of the water.

"I know it's different, Leah—but Ann *is* right. You will get used to it," Father said, caressing my cheek.

"How long have I been sick?" My stomach twisted as I saw the reflection's lips move.

"Two weeks."

I stared at him, disbelieving.

"What's today?"

"January sixth," Father said.

I couldn't believe it. I had been sixteen years old for nearly four days. I looked from Father's unshaved face to Ann's strained eyes. I didn't know what to do, so I did what I knew they would like to see—I forced that strange girl to smile.

Father stayed with me, making sure I finished my bowl of chicken broth. Then Ann closed my window, and urged him to leave me, so I could rest.

As they left, Ann gave me letters Philip had sent to me while I was ill. As I began to tear one open, it happened: a violent chill ran down my spine. Suddenly, I felt like I was being watched. My eyes jerked to the window just in time to see something large and dark fly by the glass. *It was only a bird,* I told myself, but my heart didn't calm. I focused on the distant outline of the Langdale Mountains, trying to steady my breathing. I gave myself a little shake and tried to return to the letter.

"And how is my little patient doing?"

I jumped and nearly dropped the letter.

"Lavena!" I said happily, hoping she hadn't noticed me flinch.

"Well, how are you?" she asked, sitting in the chair Father had occupied. She folded her hands in her lap and gazed at me happily.

"I'm fine," I replied looking at my knees.

Lavena continued to smile at me.

"Lavena, I think I heard you and Father arguing while I was sick."

"Which time?" Lavena asked with a smirk.

"The time when you were trying to get Father to let you treat me."

"I can tell you, I was ready to jinx James unconscious if he wouldn't let me near you. But luckily, we didn't come to that," she said pleasantly.

"Why wouldn't he let you?" I asked with a frown.

"Ah, my girl, for the same reason we've been so cold to one another over the years. But I convinced him in the end and that's all that matters."

"Does he know you're here now?"

"No, I don't believe he does. But I wasn't going to be kept from seeing how you were doing." Lavena fiddled with the bed sheet and asked gently, "How are you doing with the change?"

"I have to get used to it, don't I," I replied quietly to my knees.

"That's right," Lavena said kindly. "You—"

A sharp tapping on my window interrupted Lavena. A small screech owl hovered outside, tapping its beak against the glass.

"Leah, dear, I'm very sorry but I need to go." Lavena rose and kissed my forehead. "You should be up and about by tomorrow."

She left and when I looked back at the window, the owl was gone.

I spent the rest of the day reading Philip's letters. Each one after the first asked why I hadn't written back and then left tantalizing clues of something wonderful King Rowan was planning. I would quickly jump to the next letter to see if he revealed it, but he never did.

I put the letters beside me and looked at the mirror lying on my bedside table. I had been so shocked at my new appearance—they should have warned me before I looked at myself without knowing about the drastic changes. I felt like a stranger in my own skin. I looked away from the mirror, then looked back. Frowning, I picked up the mirror and looked at the girl that I had to get used to. I hated her. I loathed the girl staring at me with those strange eyes. She was an intruder.

Glaring at the girl, I threw the mirror face-down on the table, shattering it to pieces.

The next day I felt completely refreshed. Even though I knew I was healed, Father wouldn't hear of me visiting Lavena until he was sure I had regained all my strength. It seemed he had finally put aside whatever it was that had made him hate her. Lavena curing me must have healed a fragile cord. I was allowed, however, to leave my room and resume my activities. I started my lessons again, but Miss Perish had a strange gleam in her eyes the day I first re-entered the library.

"So, my Leah is finally able to walk through the halls."

Her cold, slippery tone put me on edge. She was up to something.

"Father feels that I'm well enough to start lessons, Miss Perish."

"Ahh, yes," Miss Perish said, pouring a cup of tea as I sat down. "We can start by discussing your new life."

"Sorry?" I said as I took a cup of tea.

"Your *looks*, girl!" Miss Perish hissed with the eyes of a playful cat. "With your new looks, you could easily snare Prince Philip. You could have hundreds of the richest men in Torona begging for your hand! We'll have to do something about your hair, though. I wonder if we dyed it . . . " Miss Perish left her sentence hanging, studying my face.

Before I could open my mouth, she was off again, waving her hands wildly through the air.

"We must have another ball. You will be the centerpiece. We can dedicate it to your successful and *prosperous* return to health."

The idea of being a tasty morsel to a bunch of drooling men might have appealed to Miss Perish, but it certainly didn't excite me.

"Miss Perish, I'm feeling a little lightheaded. I would like very much not to continue," I said firmly.

"What?" she asked, confused I had interrupted her. "Not feeling well? Are you sure?" She stared at me critically.

"Positive," I said, rising from my chair.

"Well, if you must. We will continue this later. I shall speak to Sir James about the arrangements."

I might have been imagining it—a silly exaggerated observation—but by a week after my recovery, my shadowy suspicions seemed more concrete. The first time I noticed it was during my first lunch in the dining room. Everything seemed normal, sitting at the table talking to Father, when Guinevere entered with our food, gave an obvious start, and dropped the dishes. Her eyes darted to me as she quickly cleaned up the mess, and I knew I was the reason she dropped our lunch.

I understood that my drastic change of appearance would take getting used to, but life at Willow Manor just seemed different. Frank was kind to me as usual, but there was sympathy in his gaze. It was now common for Guinevere to drop what she was holding or run into something whenever I passed her. Adam, the stable hand, didn't seem to be around anymore. I finally snapped at Ann to talk to me normally instead of whispering quietly like I was on my death bed. She didn't take that very well and was huffy around me for the rest of the day. Life was tenser than ever before... and quieter... so much quieter.

Even Father was acting strange. Not a single visitor had entered the manor since the day I had awoken. We usually had dinner guests twice a week, but now there was no one. I often spotted Father talking on the grounds to a duke or duchess who regularly visited us, but their conversations were short and Father would send them on their way, all the while never getting close to the manor's stone walls.

One blustery day, I was passing the time, walking around the manor. I tugged my cloak tighter about me, but my white hair whipped wildly in the wind. I was standing in the courtyard, when a duke I recognized as Sir Alfred Berrybond walked around the corner and nearly ran into me.

"Oh, terribly sorry, I—" he stood frozen, as if rooted to the spot. His wide eyes roamed over my face and frame, and he seemed to have forgotten that his mouth was hanging open.

"It's alright, Sir Alfred," I said, trying to ignore his stunned expression. "Are you here to see my father?"

"Your father?" he repeated with difficulty. He blinked rather quickly as if trying to make his eyes see correctly.

"Yes, Sir James?" I asked, holding some of my hair out of my face as it blew violently in the wind.

"No, no, n-no. Quite a bit to do," he said, speaking quickly and stepping away from me. "Just remembered… urgent business… "

And before I could say anything he had spun around and walked quickly back through the archway he had just come through, leaving me feeling much colder than before.

Then, one cold gray morning, I was walking under a covered walkway when I saw Guinevere receiving a large amount of produce from a farmer who delivered his vegetables to Willow Manor. He was having a lengthy conversation with Guinevere, but when he caught sight of me, he stopped speaking abruptly, as if someone had snatched his voice away. He jerkily snatched his payment away from Guinevere and ran as quickly as he could to his wagon, stumbling and tripping in his haste. Guinevere curiously looked over her shoulder to see what had frightened the farmer, but I had ducked out of sight behind a stone pillar.

Dinner that night was tenser than ever before. I couldn't get that farmer's terrified expression out of my mind. I would only grunt replies to Father's comments and didn't look him in the face.

"Is there something wrong, Leah?" Father asked halfway through his toffee pudding.

I hesitated, then blurted, "Why aren't we having dinner guests anymore?"

Father put down his spoon and cleared his throat. "You haven't been well. I didn't want you bothered with people."

Guinevere refilled my glass of cider with a shaking hand that sent drops of the amber liquid splattering on the white tablecloth.

"I'm not ill anymore. I feel fine." My voice shook.

"I would rather not continue this conversation, Leah," Father said firmly as he picked his spoon back up.

The next day, without asking permission, I marched down to Lavena's cottage. I needed someone to tell me I was being foolish. Someone *had* to tell me that everything would be okay. Lavena opened the door before I had even knocked.

"I saw you coming through the window," she said as she closed the door. "Have a seat."

But I didn't sit. I stood by the fire, my back stiff.

"What's the matter, love?" Lavena asked quietly. "Would you like some tea? Yes, that's what you need."

She hurried to the stove and I heard her put on a kettle as I continued to stare at the fire as if in a trance.

"Is this permanent, Lavena?" I asked in a voice terribly unlike my own.

She hesitated before saying, "Yes."

I couldn't swallow. I couldn't look her in the eye. It was much easier to focus on the fire.

"Leah, it's difficult, I know," Lavena said, putting her arm around me and hugging me. "But you'll get used to it."

"Don't you think I'm trying?" I snapped.

Lavena pulled away from me.

"Then what's the fuss about?" Lavena said with a slight laugh.

Now that it was time for the problem to show its face, I found myself inching away from it. Voicing it meant it was true.

I swallowed and said in a hollow tone, "Nothing's the same anymore. Frank pities me, Ann treats me like I'm glass. Father—" my throat constricted painfully.

Lavena nodded solemnly. "I thought something like this might happen. The non-magical are very superstitious."

"But these people have known me since the day I was born," I said, sickened. "Why should they suddenly be scared of me?"

"They're not scared of you," Lavena said patiently. "They're scared of what *touched* you."

"I don't underst—"

"It's been said that when anything with evil magic harms a non-magical person, they receive a lifelong mark to warn others of their foolishness," Lavena interrupted. "Your stunning appearance is like a witch's mark to them. They've never seen anyone like you. They don't want to be near you for fear they will catch whatever you have. But they won't. There is nothing they will catch from you," Lavena added with a wry smile.

"Is that why Father has been saying I'm still ill? He's been thinking I'm not over it?"

"You are completely healed," Lavena said firmly. "You don't need to worry about that."

I groped for questions, anything to help me understand.

"Father refuses to let anyone see me. He's ashamed of me," I added bitterly.

"He doesn't want you hurt, love," Lavena replied with a small smile, pity lining her weathered face. "He's afraid of what might happen if people see you."

My stomach jerked as if I had missed a step as I remembered Sir Alfred Berrybond and the farmer.

"Miss Perish wants to use my looks to sell me to the highest bidder," I said, my voice expressionless. "She wants to dye my hair." Lavena chuckled dryly.

"She'd be better off not bothering—it won't work, love," she said, her eyes soft.

"Isn't there anything you can do?" I exploded. "A spell—a potion? Anything?"

Lavena slowly shook her head, her eyes unnaturally bright.

"I'm sorry, Leah. There is nothing that magic, or any herb, or any dye, can do to change you back. Nothing."

## Chapter 14
# The Choice

No matter what Lavena said, life at Willow Manor was never going to be the same. It was as if the freezing cold had seeped under the doors to infect the people as they walked through the rooms. I had never been so lonely.

When Miss Perish had asked for permission to host a ball to show off my looks, Father had decided lessons would be best halted for some time. Without half of my day devoted to Miss Perish, I ended up ambling around Willow Manor, or spending time with Iris, waiting for the hours to crawl by.

I even found myself drifting away from Lavena, and that's what scared me most. She was my only ally, my only supporter in a steadily darkening world. Almost every time I sloshed through the snow to Lavena's cottage, she was gone, and the few times she was there, she was jumpy and kept speaking to her owls about some woman. I'd ask what all the fuss was about, but she would quickly change the subject. She'd also remind me at the end of our meetings to stay away from Raven Wood at night. She even went so far as to say that it might be best if I didn't visit her for some time.

"Stay in Willow Manor," she had said two days before. "It's safer there. I can't explain now, but you will understand."

"Why is it safer there?" I asked as she shooed me out of her house. "What's going on?!" But she had closed the door.

I couldn't deny that Lavena's behavior scared me. Who was this strange woman that her owls were watching? I could tell when she was thinking about her—Lavena's eyes would darken as if a thick cloud had passed behind them. Even though I had no idea who this mysterious person was, a nervousness was with me night and day because I knew Lavena was frightened.

It was a cold, dreary day. Rain had started sometime in the night and continued steadily on. It was clear that I wouldn't wander the grounds today, and I wasn't up to sprinting through the rain just to find Lavena's house empty or to be scolded for leaving Willow Manor. So I walked moodily through the halls, glaring at the blurred windows as I passed.

Without thinking about where I was going, I let my feet lead the way. I walked up a darkened stairway that led to a deserted landing and stopped, staring at a closed door that led to the attic. I hadn't been in the attic for years. I remembered it being horribly dusty and dark, but I was so bored that I decided to investigate. I grabbed a lit candle from a tall candelabra in the corner by the stairs and opened the door. It creaked loudly as I turned the knob.

I stepped into a very dark room with only one small circular window. A stale smell hung heavily in the still air. A thick layer of dust carpeted the floor and covered the objects littered here and there. Rusted candle holders with short, cracked candles stood close to the door. I used my candle to light them, and soon weak, flickering light illuminated the attic. I crossed my arms and shivered, stepping farther into the room.

Faded chairs and tarnished mirrors took up most of the space, but a few of my old toys littered the floor, and a wardrobe full of dresses that I had stained or outgrown stood in a corner. I lifted my candle higher above my head so the flame's light illuminated more of the room. In a corner, next to the dirty window, was a small chest beside several large objects covered by white sheets.

Nothing else in the attic was covered. Curious, I pulled one of the sheets away and sneezed loudly as a dust cloud flew into the air. It was a painting. I held the candle closer to its surface and my hand jerked. My mother—my mother was staring at me.

I ripped the rest of the sheets away and flung the candle light forward. Five—*five* beautiful portraits of my mother. The only painting I had ever seen of her was the one in the unused room on the unused corridor. Here were five detailed portraits. One of her and Father—it must have been their wedding day—one with her standing in a poppy field with a red horse, another—my heart quivered. I drew the candle dangerously close to the painting—one with me.

I don't know how long I sat there, gazing hungrily at the portraits. But then I realized that the attic was suddenly darker. The candles I had lit were nearly burnt out. I dried my cheeks on my sleeve and was making an attempt to stand when the candlelight fell upon the chest. Could it have been Mother's?

I set the candle down and with shaking hands—numb from the cold—I opened the lid. Inside were a small number of things; things, I suppose, she had taken from her home when she married Father: some blankets, an intricate tablecloth, a small box of jewelry, and a journal. I carefully lifted the journal and closed the chest.

I had never been more captivated in all my life. I spent the rest of the day curled up in the library, getting to know Mother. She had a wonderful dry sense of humor and a constant curiosity. One passage in particular grabbed my attention—I'm not sure why. In the passage, Mother wrote that when she was twelve, a strange woman appeared at their door. She was old, stooped and nearly blind. It was raining heavily and the woman's heavy, tattered cloak dripped large puddles on their kitchen floor. She asked for food which my mother's family provided. As the woman dined, my grandfather offered her room and board for the night, but the woman shook her head.

"I won't let you fine people be bothered with my presence," she replied with a toothless grin. "I'll eat and be gone." When the soup bowl was empty and bread reduced to a few crumbs, she smiled again and beckoned my mother to her. From within her tattered cloak she withdrew a small money bag. The woman indicated for Mother to hold out her hand and the old woman turned the money bag upside down. Something that looked like a small, white stone dropped onto Mother's palm. Mother had never seen any stone like it. It was smooth with hardly a scratch and it seemed to shine with an inner glow. The old woman winked at my mother and said, "My most prized possession, m'dear. Tis from a unicorn." And with that strange pronouncement and another wink, she scooped the stone from my mother's palm and dropped it back in the bag. She rose, nodded her thanks and left. Mother never saw or heard of her again.

Unicorns. Where had I heard that word before? Then I remembered; King Rowan wanted to hunt the unicorns. I closed the journal and rose from the small table where I had been sitting.

I walked to the closest bookshelf and ran a finger along the spines, scanning the titles. Why were these mythological creatures so important to that old woman and King Rowan? What didn't I understand? The hours ticked by as I searched through volumes, but unicorns were hardly mentioned. There was plenty of information on sphinxes, dragons and vors—real, breathing animals—nothing on unicorns. Finally, when all the candles circling my table were nearly dead, I found something: a drawing of a unicorn standing in a grassy area with a mountain in the background. There was a very small description under the drawing:

Unicorn. *Unicornus.*

*A mythical creature believed to have the body of a horse, the tail of a lion, and a single horn protruding from its forehead. It has been conjectured that the unicorn's horn contains healing powers. There have been a few rumored sightings of unicorns but these speculations have never been confirmed.*

I bent closer to the drawing. The candles I had grouped around me weren't shedding much light. It looked like a horse, but smaller. Its white mane flew around its head wildly. Its tail was long and thin, with a tuft of white at the end, and a sharp horn protruded from its forehead. Its eyes rolled fiercely … its nostrils flared.

I cocked my head to one side and frowned at it curiously.

"Leah! *Leah!*"

I looked up from the book.

"There you are!" Ann had appeared from behind a bookshelf looking thoroughly harassed. "Where have you been? Dinner started fifteen minutes ago!"

"Sorry, I didn't realize," I began.

"What do you mean you didn't realize?" Ann suddenly looked worried. "Dinner always starts at eight. Are you feeling all right? You shouldn't be in this drafty library, you—"

"Ann, please," I said, exasperated. "I'm fine."

I rose from the table and went to dinner. I shouldn't have been rude to her. She was just worried about me. *But that doesn't stop it from being annoying,* I thought bitterly.

Dinner was quiet. I shot glances at Father before steeling myself and lowering my fork abruptly. It clattered loudly in the silent room.

"Father, we need to talk."

He nodded to show he had heard, but didn't look up from his plate. My anger boiled in my chest. I glanced at the kitchen door to make sure Guinevere wasn't about to come out before continuing.

"I feel like things have changed here," I said to his bent head. "Everyone acts differently around me."

"Do you want me to talk to them?" Father asked. "Have they done something to hurt you?"

"No." My frustration rose. Why was this so difficult? "It's not just them. You've been ignoring me."

He looked at me then.

"I've been *ignoring* you?" he asked incredulously.

"Yes," I answered.

"Just because I'm trying to help you recover by not letting visitors in the manor doesn't mean I'm *ignoring* you. I'm trying to protect you. Why can't you see that?" He spoke as if I was a child.

"You're keeping me locked up," I exploded, "just like you've locked Mother away!"

He went paler than I had ever seen him.

"I'm with you right now!" he said loudly. "What more do you want?"

I stared at Father, trying my best to control my stinging eyes. I rose from the table without a word and ran as fast as I could.

I slammed the door of my bedroom (one bottle of perfume on my dresser wobbled dangerously). I picked up a pillow and threw it with all my might across the room. I wanted to kick, punch, scream! I wanted to shatter everything around me!

Quickly, I walked to the window seat and curled up on it. Pressing my knees against my chest, I stared out over the wet, gray grounds. My world had now become that lonely, cold stretch of land outside of Willow Manor. I felt suffocated… trapped. I had to do something.

A fire erupted in my brain. I ran to my cabinet and pulled out a traveling bag. Hastily, I shoved a simple dress into it, pocketed a small bag of money, and grabbed my cloak. What I was doing was beyond foolishness. It was beyond reason. I pulled a piece of parchment toward me and scribbled a brief farewell.

I sat perched on my bed, my runaway note folded on my pillow, anticipation prickling across my skin. No one would hear my escape—for that's what it was. I was escaping from this cage. When the clock tolled eleven, I slid off the bed and with the stealth of a mouse, left my room.

As I slipped down a corridor, something flickered in the corner of my eye. Turning to look, I gasped and fell against a tall candelabra. I barely kept it from smashing against the wall. My heart racing, I stood frozen, holding the impressive metal. If anyone had heard…

The halls of Willow Manor remained silent and deserted. With an angry face, I returned the candelabra to its proper place. I had been telling myself ever since my conversation with Lavena that I had gotten over my drastic change. But the honest truth was I hadn't.

I glared at my reflection in the wide mirror on the opposite wall—my white hair gleamed; my pale skin glowed like a ghost's. I had almost given myself away! Cursing, I turned away from the mirror and made it to the front doors without any other surprises. Holding my breath, as if expecting some alarm to sound, I gripped the cold iron door handle and gently pulled it open.

I needed the Replenisher. Most likely, Lavena would question me, but I thought I knew a way around that. There was nothing that anyone could say to stop me. I was sick of being told to just get used to people's reactions. Why did *I* have to change? Hadn't I already changed enough?

I sprinted through the rain and barreled down the lighted path. I knocked on Lavena's door and waited, shivering slightly. When she didn't answer, I made to test a window. But then, the door opened, flooding the spot where I was standing in light. But Lavena wasn't the one greeting me. A tall, slender woman stood in the doorway. She narrowed her eyes and stared down her sharp nose at me.

"I need to speak to Lavena," I said nervously, stepping farther into the circle of light, "is she in?"

"Out," the woman replied shortly. Her eyes traveled from my wet white hair to my blue eyes, down to my muddy boots, and back to my face, "Who are you?"

"Leah Vindral. I live up at the manor. Are you sure Lavena's not in?" I asked, standing on my toes to try to see into the cottage.

"So you're the little secret she's been keeping from all of us," she said quietly, her eyes roaming over me again.

"Excuse me?"

"Leah, what are you doing here?"

I spun around and saw Lavena standing behind me with a large group of people, none of whom I had ever seen before. Some of the ones in the back stood on tiptoe to try to see me more clearly, while others turned to their neighbors to whisper in an undertone.

"Is there something you want, Leah?"

Lavena's crisp tone and icy glance at the woman behind me made it clear that this wasn't the best time to have a longwinded conversation.

"I wanted to know if I could borrow the Replenisher. You see, I told Frank about it and he didn't believe me. I couldn't sleep, so I decided to get it tonight."

Lavena stared at me, her eyes searching my face. For a minute I thought she wasn't going to believe my lie, but then she walked past me and the woman into her cottage and returned shortly with the old weather-beaten satchel.

"Is that all?" she asked.

"Yes, thank you."

"Good, hurry up to the manor. I've told you not to come here at night."

"But shouldn't she be here?" the woman in the doorway asked silkily. "I think Leah Vindral would be very interested in this particular meeting."

There were murmurs behind me.

"Myra," Lavena said calmly, "I don't want—"

"She's the one, isn't she," Myra said intensely, pointing a bony finger at me. "She's the one who—"

"Leah is not to be involved!" Lavena snapped.

I had never seen Lavena like this. Her fury radiated off her old features like a towering inferno.

Myra didn't reply, though she stared daggers at Lavena. Lavena turned away from her and said with a commanding edge, "Go back to the manor, Leah."

I didn't need any more convincing. I nodded and made to leave as the others trooped past me into Lavena's cottage. Her door shut with a snap, leaving the woods once more in darkness. I hesitated. Who were those people? Lavena had never mentioned them. Myra seemed to know about me. What didn't Lavena want Myra to say in front of me? Praying Lavena wouldn't find out, I inched close to the door and pressed my ear against it.

"You can't keep her safe forever!" Myra said furiously. "Mora will find her and when she does—"

"Mora doesn't know about Leah," Lavena interrupted.

"Not yet, she doesn't," Myra argued, "but when she does, Leah would be better off *prepared* than the sitting duck she is now! She *will* find out."

"I don't want her killed, Myra!" Lavena yelled.

There was a horrible silence. All I could hear was the steady splattering of heavy rain drops.

"Then tell her," Myra replied coldly, "tell her the danger she is in."

My heart hammered in my chest. I was in danger? How? Why? Who was Mora? I'd never heard of her—but, wait, there was something familiar about that name … like I had heard it somewhere …

A piercing *hoot* came from above my head. A soggy owl was perched on the edge of the roof and was staring reproachfully down at me.

I gripped the strap of the Replenisher and ran to the stables, slipping and sliding on the wet leaves.

It had only taken Iris a few hours to adjust to my new appearance, but she was certainly startled to receive such a late visit.

"Shh ... shh, it's all right, Iris." I stroked her nose as she pawed the ground nervously. "I need your help." It was a plea more than anything else. "I need to get away from here."

Iris stopped prancing and bent her head closer to mine. Sniffing back fresh tears, I saddled her up as quickly and quietly as possible, shooting nervous glances up at Willow Manor's dark windows.

When Iris was ready, I led her out of the stables and stood looking at Willow Manor. Who knew when I would see it again? Fearing that if I didn't go now, then I never would, I mounted Iris and cantered to the forest.

As we galloped away into the woods I tried to keep my mind calm and emotionless, but a battle was raging in my soul. The steady thud of Iris's hooves increased the distance between me and the place I had once called home. I gripped the reigns in a strangling grasp and tried to pretend that the tears on my cheeks were just raindrops.

# Chapter 15
# The Elves

That night was the longest I had ever experienced. Never before had I ventured so deep into Raven Wood. The farther we went, the slower Iris walked, carefully placing one hoof in front of the other as the rain fell harder.

I didn't know where we were going. We weaved between the trees all night. My eyes were as large as an owl's as I continuously surveyed the pitch black forest. It was only my bitterness toward Willow Manor that kept me going. Only when I could no longer keep my eyes open and my muscles screamed in exhaustion, did I stop and fall asleep.

A cold wind brushed harshly across my face. I moaned, wondering why Ann had left my window open. Something beside me shifted and when I opened my eyes, I was nearly blinded by the brilliant white light around me. I bolted up, my mind and senses completely awake, as if someone had yelled in my ear. I wasn't in my room. I was in Raven Wood, cold and stiff. The rain had turned to snow as I slept. Small flakes drifted lazily from the sky to add to the already thick mounds covering the ground. I looked around the forest and nearly jumped out of my skin. Two ravens stood a few inches from my feet. One tilted its head and eyed me with one dark eye while the other ruffled its wings. They didn't seem to be glaring at me, furious for intruding upon their forest; it was more like they were sizing me up. Without warning, their wings shot out and they rocketed into the branches of the tree I sat under. As I looked up, my stomach turned unpleasantly. No less than thirty ravens, each staring at me with that same calculating expression, were perched on the gnarled braches of the old weathered oak.

Iris was awake now. As she looked up at the raven-filled oak, her ears twisted and snorted. I slowly rose and placed the saddle on Iris, never taking my eyes off the ravens. They didn't stir from their perches. They didn't caw. Only their heads moved the slightest inch as I led Iris away from them. For a moment, I thought they would follow me or attack, but when I looked back over my shoulder the trees had hidden them from view. It was only when I had mounted Iris and had trotted for some minutes that their loud cawing echoed through the trees. *It wasn't odd,* I told myself. *The forest* is *called Raven Wood for a reason. There have always been tons of them here.*

There were many paths that weaved through Raven Wood, but I wasn't sure where they were in relationship to my location. I didn't even know if I should risk taking a path. Ann would have found my empty bed by now, along with the letter. If Father searched anywhere, it would be the roads leading out of Willow Manor. If I ran into Father or one of the servants, would I run from them? I pushed Iris to a faster trot.

I tried not to think about Willow Manor. There was a part of me that wanted to go back—that thought, perhaps, I had overreacted. But there was a large part of me—the angry part of me—that refused point blank to return home. And I couldn't help thinking about what I had overheard at Lavena's cottage. I was in danger? It made absolutely no sense! *But Lavena had sounded so worried,* said a small voice in my head.

I glared moodily at a passing robin. This Mora person seemed to be the biggest threat. Even though I tried to deny it, I felt a tightness in my chest whenever I thought about her; I kept picturing a faceless figure cackling evilly.

Iris and I moved steadily through Raven Wood. The isolation was frightening yet invigorating. There were no staring eyes—fearful or pitying. No monotonous walks through Willow Manor's stone corridors. And no mirrors. Even though I was freezing and my damp cloak felt weighed down, the forest was beautiful. The snow sparkled and glittered in the sun. But everything changed when night arrived.

No longer were the trees welcoming, beautiful, nurturing. In the dark, their limbs were gnarled, long fingers, each one grasping and tearing at my hair and clothes. No longer was the snow a fluffy play world for little children. It was ice that I had to scrape from the hard ground when I slept. Every night I slept less and less because I was steadily moving farther into the wilder depths of Raven Wood. The simple sound of a breaking twig or the ruffle of wind through the trees left my heart throbbing uncontrollably. The morning was what I lived for.

I was walking beside Iris through a particularly thick section of trees when I felt it—the creepy feeling of being watched. I scanned the area, turning slowly on the spot. But… *nothing*. Nothing but trees. I turned to Iris, but then whirled back around.

The hairs on the back of my neck stood straight up, and it wasn't from the cold air. I *knew* there was someone standing just out of my sight. Why? Why hide from me? But then again, I was in a forest full of animals. Maybe it was just a fox, crouched behind a bush. With one more quick glance at the trees, I mounted Iris and pushed her to a gallop, forcing myself not to look over my shoulder as we went.

❧

The days passed and I began to lose count. Who knew how far I was from Willow Manor? I had not yet come across any travelers, nor had I heard the barking of dogs. I was deep in the wildest part of Raven Wood.

So far, it seemed completely uninhabited by people. I never once spotted a path.

After so many days of snow and rain, I was beginning to wonder why I hadn't yet caught cold. I had been out in the winter day and night and not even a cough. My body was numb to the bone (I sincerely doubted I would ever be completely warm again) and dead tired, but not ill. The winter claimed more lives than I cared to dwell on. Maybe the Replenisher magically fortified one's immune system? Somehow, I didn't think that was it.

A small peripheral doubt that had been nagging at the corners of my mind had now grown substantially to become a loud, piercing cry. I was beginning to have second thoughts about my hasty decision to leave Willow Manor. I couldn't force myself to turn around and face the humiliation, but my anger had ebbed. Maybe it hadn't been so bad? They *were* my family. Maybe I had been gone long enough and I could return and we would all laugh over it and live merrily?

I closed my eyes in frustration and breathed deeply through my nose. This was a fine mess I had gotten myself into: wondering around Raven Wood with absolutely no idea where I was going. I was cold, lonely, and tired. But there was something else, something that I couldn't identify... as if someone or something was gently tugging at an invisible cord, leading me farther away from Willow Manor.

My eyes tingled with the threat of tears, but I rubbed them roughly. I was tired of this forest. I was tired of thinking I was being watched, tired of fighting with myself. Willow Manor couldn't be as bad as this, could it?

I walked slowly beside Iris, rubbing my throat in irritation. I grabbed the Replenisher to help relieve my dry throat, but Iris rubbed her head against my side.

"Hold on, Iris," I said crossly, a hand in the Replenisher.

She snorted and nipped my arm.

"Ouch!" I yelped. "What?"

Iris arched her head back and directed her gaze a little to my left. I followed her gaze and almost hollered in joy. Before us lay a large, crystal-clear lake. I ran full out to the water with Iris at my heels.

It had been so long since I had had a proper bath; even though it would be freezing I didn't care. But I was momentarily shocked that it wasn't frozen. The Replenisher slipped from my hand as I knelt at the water's edge and gazed at my reflection. For some reason my reflection blurred around the edges, as if it wasn't in focus. But what caught me by surprise was that my appearance seemed much too bright. It was almost as if someone was on the other side of the watery surface, holding a tiny lamp to make my figure shine with an ethereal light. I lowered my hand down to the water and touched its smooth surface. How odd; it was slightly warm and my finger tingled.

"Remove your hand," said a commanding voice behind me.

I jumped and whirled around on my knees. An extremely tall, thinly-built man stood only a few feet from me. He held a cocked bow and arrow pointed directly at me. With a gulp I slowly rose. There were twenty other archers behind him, each one aiming at me. Iris nervously snorted behind me. The man and I stood face to face, or, I should say, face to arrow point. He was enormously tall! He had long dark brown hair, so dark it could have been black. His ears were much larger than any humans and the tops were pointed.

"You're an elf!" I said, shocked.

He cocked an eyebrow and said, "You sound surprised."

"I didn't know there were elves in Torona." I had heard from dinner guests at Willow Manor that elves existed but were rarely seen. His eyes suddenly hardened and narrowed.

"We are not in Torona," he replied. Miraculously, he lowered his bow. The twenty other elves lowered their weapons as well, but didn't relax their strings.

"Are you of magical birth?" he suddenly asked quizzically.

"What?"

For a second, I thought my ears were playing tricks on me. Magical birth? Of all questions, I never would have expected that one.

"If you will kindly follow us," he said firmly, his eyes even harder than before, "we will be on our way."

Before I could say anything, one elf picked up the fallen Replenisher with a slightly curious eye as the others swarmed around us. I grabbed Iris's reigns as an elf nudged me in the back to get moving.

Iris and I walked in the middle as the elves formed a slight oval around us. I couldn't help but notice how antsy they seemed. Their heads never stopped turning on their shoulders. It was as if the elves were wary of something in the forest.

We continued to walk beside the lake until we came upon a group of large, intricately-decorated boats, each swaying gently by the bank. Four elves, including the one who had spoken to me, who I imagined to be the leader, filed into a boat. I stood on the muddy bank, still holding onto Iris. Should I run for it? The elves behind me must have suspected my thoughts because they menacingly gripped their bow and arrows. With a glare I led Iris closer to the boat, but another elf thrust out his hand and grabbed Iris's reigns.

"She goes in the other boat," he said gruffly.

I allowed Iris's reigns to slip from my hand as I was pushed into the boat the leader had taken. The boats cut quickly through the calm, crystal-blue water.

Even though I was terrified at my situation, I couldn't help but be amazed at how vast the lake was. The glassy blue water stretched for as far as I could see. Huge, white trees, protruded from the water to towering heights. They were so smooth they didn't seem to have bark at all. The overcast sky and the hazy, yet lantern-like, light that seeped up from the water bathed the trees in a misty grey.

Onward the elven boats pushed through the water, silently weaving between the giant trees. The elves in my boat shot strange glances at me, but when I caught their eye, they would quickly look away. Only the leader continued to gaze fixedly ahead.

My legs ached from the relentless standing. None of the elves spoke and I didn't dare ask where we were headed. The long poles that propelled the boats continued to be thrust into the glowing water.

Other boats now dotted the vast lake. The elves in these were pulling up thinly strung nets filled with wiggling fish. As we passed, their heads followed our convoy. Their eyes moved from elf to elf to settle on me, and grow rather wide. Annoyance and embarrassment mixed in with my fear and I covered my head. I turned my eyes away from the working elves and gasped.

Perched atop a large hill was a gleaming city with a gigantic castle towering impressively in the center. The castle seemed to be made of a strange and unique material, like something between marble and ivory, which glowed with a bright brilliance. Some of the elves couldn't contain smirks at my reaction to their home.

A soft thud and the boats hit the edge of a smooth curving dock made of cobblestone.

"You are to follow me," the leader commanded as the elves from the other boats disembarked.

"What about my horse? Where will you take her?"

"To the stalls."

A darker-skinned elf moved toward Iris, but I stepped in between them.

"Why can't I take her to the stalls?"

"Because *we're* not going to the stalls," the leader answered calmly. "Rendor, take her horse."

## Chapter 16
# Shadowy Silver

There wasn't anything I could do. Rendor held Iris's reins tightly in his hand and led her out of sight.

"Follow me," the leader said again.

When I didn't move, I received another sharp poke in the back by one of the elves and, grudgingly, started up the cobblestone hill. The other elves formed a tight oval around me much like the one in the forest. We passed through a pair of large, iron-locked doors, and I saw winding, narrow roads and alleys with houses and shops.

On the other side of the doors stood two heavily-armed elves. Each eyed me suspiciously, their eyes lingering on my face. I nervously looked down and tugged my hood lower over my eyes. They grasped their swords a little tighter, but then the elf in front of me said calmly, "Angora will wish to see her."

The two guards nodded silently and stepped aside to let us pass. I looked over my shoulder and saw the guards with bent heads, whispering intensely.

"Where are we going?" I asked the leader.

"To Angora," he replied shortly.

"Who's—"

"Your questions will be answered when Angora sees fit."

I glared at the back of his head.

We continued to walk through the crowded streets. The elves going about their daily routines stopped and stared at me, some fearfully, some with wonder, and others with dark brows and serious eyes.

We must have walked for thirty minutes, steadily climbing higher and higher. With each step, my stomach twisted sickly. Who or what was Angora? Was it some monster they were going to feed me to? Was it someone who would decide what would happen to me next? Why did they even want me? It seemed a little harsh to be punished for touching a lake. I wondered if the elves had dungeons.

We turned a corner. This street was much more crowded and the elves traveling with me pressed against me to get through the street without breaking rank. A left . . . a right . . . a sharp hill . . . right again and I stopped so suddenly an elf ran into my back.

A large pair of towering white doors stood imposingly before us. We stepped through these doors and entered a large courtyard. We didn't stop, but continued up a set of stone steps and through an even larger set of doors.

The inside of the castle was simple yet splendid. The walls were impressively tall, connected to the ceiling in smooth, graceful arches. Staircases curved along the walls and disappeared through tall archways.

The leader turned to the other elves around me. "You may go, thank you."

They nodded and walked away from us, murmuring excitedly as they went and continuously glancing back at me.

My eyes moved from their retreating backs to the leader staring down at me.

"Follow me," he said yet again.

"Are you taking me to Angora now" I asked, walking quickly to match his lengthy stride.

"Not yet," he said starting, up a staircase. "You need to be more presentable before you meet her."

Heat flared in my cheeks. Did they think I was supposed to keep neat and clean after spending weeks tromping through a frozen forest? My annoyance grew the farther into the castle we went. Elves we passed would jerk to a stop and stare agape. The elf leading me, though, never seemed to notice this odd behavior. He continued his quick pace, and then stopped and opened a door.

"You will stay in here until Angora calls for you." He held the door open for me, his face once more set in a deep frown.

I had time enough to notice a fine-looking bed, a huge gold-framed mirror, and a happy crackling fire before the elf shut the door with a loud snap. Turning to look at it, I distinctly heard the sound of a key scraping in the door's lock.

It was to be expected. I was a stranger and the way the elves acted around me left no doubt in my mind that they harbored suspicions, just like the servants at Willow Manor. Would there ever be a time when people wouldn't stop and stare or flinch? I tried to leave these unhappy musings behind by exploring my prison cell.

I ranked higher than the common thief, it seemed. The room was quite inviting, especially when I had been expecting cold stone walls and a straw-covered floor. The bed looked freshly made with soft goose-down pillows and blankets. The room was small and had only one window which stretched from ceiling to floor for nearly the length of one wall. Delicate, white draperies hung loosely over its clear glass face. I crossed the room to it and drew the drapes back an inch. I must have been in one of the towers. The white trees stretched far into the distance, while the water below them sparkled like diamonds. Odd, especially on such an overcast day.

*I must be far from home.* An empty gnawing sensation crept into my stomach as I watched the boats move gently over the glassy water. I removed my hood and glanced to my left where a ragged-looking girl was reflected in a gold-framed mirror. I stepped closer, hardly believing what I was seeing.

My dress was torn, with sections ripped in long jagged strips, and the material was damp up to my knees. My hair was wild and tangled and dirt streaked my cheek.

With a wry smile, I said to my reflection, "You see, it's not that they're scared of you, they've just never seen someone so dirty before."

*Click!*

I jumped and saw the door open slowly. A young female elf leaned her head through the crack.

"Kindlen sent me," she said politely. She entered the room and closed the door behind her, staring at me with a wide smile on her face.

"Who's Kindlen?" I asked with an edge of rudeness. All elves must be very tall, for she stood a head above me.

"The one who brought you here," she said simply, still smiling. "I'm sure you would like to get out of those clothes," she said.

Without so much as a nod from me, she put down the burden in her arms on a chair and filled the tub in the far corner of the room with water. Even as she did this, I could feel her eyes boring a hole in the back of my head. Trying to act as though I didn't notice, or care, I focused instead on what she had put on the chair.

A folded towel lay on top of what I guessed was a snowy, white dress.

"There you are," she said pleasantly, "if you need anything, pull the bell." I turned to see her indicate a long, silk rope hanging near the bed.

"Thank you."

She inclined her head slightly, opened the door, and closed it. Once again, the harsh scraping of the key in the lock echoed loudly through the room. With a slight shiver, I undressed and sank into the warm water.

It was bliss—complete, indescribable bliss. My mind was completely devoid of thought, as if someone had gently swept all memories and emotions from it.

But all too soon, my eyes began to wonder once more around the room. Where was I? How long *had* I been traveling before I came upon the elves? Had Father sent anyone to look for me? Did Lavena know that I had left? And what about Iris? What had the elves done to her? In a rush, I lifted myself from the tub and wrapped myself up in the towel on the chair. For a moment I stood in the center of the room, shivering slightly, dripping water pooling at my feet. I blinked, shook wet hair out of my eyes, and grabbed the dress the elf had brought.

It was quite warm and fitted me beautifully. I stood before the mirror wondering if Lydia owned anything made of this material. That's when I noticed it. My right hand had just swept a few stray strands of hair out of my eyes. I frowned, staring at my hand.

On the tip of a finger was what appeared to be a dull, silvery rash. I looked at it closer and noticed that it seemed to have a faint glow. I rushed to the tub and plunged it in the water, scrubbing it furiously. But it didn't wash away. It actually seemed to shine a little brighter, as if proud I hadn't succeeded in ridding it from my skin. I stared around the empty room, hoping to see something that would remove it, but there was nothing. I sank down in a chair and continued to rub it.

Where had it come from? Surely it hadn't been there when I was still at Willow Manor? No, I would have noticed. It must have appeared recently. Maybe just now? I thought back, trying to remember what would have caused such a strange reaction.

A sudden knocking came from the door. Trying to sound braver than I felt I said, "Yes?"

The door opened and the elf called Kindlen entered, followed closely by the female elf from earlier. I curled my fingers into the palm of my hand, my stomach dropping as he stood imposingly before me.

"Angora will see you."

## Chapter 17
# Angora's Plea

"Let me dry her hair first," said the female elf. "Hurry."

She rushed to a dresser and picked up a metal comb.

"It won't take long," she said, as Kindlen folded his arms, a look of annoyance on his sharp face.

She gave the comb a sort of wave and it started to vibrate. She slowly dragged the comb through my wet hair and steam filled the room. What seemed like two minutes later, she pulled the comb out of my hair and said, "There, done."

"Come then, Angora's waiting," Kindlen said, an edge of impatience in his voice. I rose, shaking slightly, and followed him from the room, hoping that I would finally understand who this Angora was. As we went down the corridors, I unconsciously ran my hand through my hair and was surprised to find it completely dry.

Angora must have been located on the other side of the castle. If I hadn't been so terrified of what was going to happen to me, I would have felt sorry for someone who might get lost, wondering aimlessly for days through the many corridors and rooms of the castle.

My knees wobbled dangerously as we neared a large set of elaborately-carved doors. I wiped my sweaty hands over my dress as Kindlen stopped before the doors and turned to me.

"Angora is through there."

"I go alone?" I asked, my voice unnaturally high.

Kindlen nodded.

"Angora only wishes to see you."

Wishing desperately that I hadn't left Willow Manor, I pushed the door open and stepped inside.

It wasn't a very large room. I had expected some grand, elaborate chamber with luxurious rugs and priceless jewels encased in glittering gold cabinets. Instead it was very simple, with only a large table completely covered by maps and documents.

A thin elf sat at the far end of the table, bent over the many papers and documents. She put down a long scroll and stood.

"Come," she said, her hand outstretched. Her voice was clear and authoritative, but there was a softness in her gaze as I walked slowly toward her. I jumped as the door shut behind me. Her eyes lingered on me before she sat back down. "Please, have a seat." She intertwined her fingers together and stared at me with piercing eyes as I settled a few chairs down from her.

"I am Angora, the queen of Aris."

"What *is* Aris... Your Majesty?" I asked, trying to calm my frantic heart. This didn't seem too bad. She didn't look dangerous, at least.

"The elven country and please, call me Angora. It is the area that we control. May I ask who you are?" She sounded inquisitive and I shifted slightly in my chair under her scrutinizing gaze. She didn't seem to have to blink as much as human beings do.

"Leah Vindral," I replied.

"Do you have magical blood?" Angora asked frowning.

"No."

Angora's frown deepened.

"It is you then." She nodded grimly. "You are the one I've been hoping for."

*Hoping?* Then why the foreboding demeanor?

"Sorry, but I don't understand."

"Have you had any magical contact?" Angora asked, ignoring my question.

"Yes," I said as Lavena sprang into my mind. "But—"

"Good, that's good. That will help." Angora clasped her hands together and looked at me over the top of a large pile of papers. She seemed to be making up her mind about something. Finally, she said, "King Rowan has made his move. I need to know if you will help us." She gazed at me expectantly.

I sat in dumb silence. What in the world was she talking about? I swallowed and said as politely as possible, "I'm terribly sorry, but I don't know what you're talking about."

Angora's eyes widened and her eyebrows disappeared behind silvering hair. "What do you know?" It was more like she breathed the words than really voiced them.

"About what?" I asked impatiently.

"*About?* Why, about the sleeping sickness of course!" Angora said slightly exasperated. Then she added at my bewildered expression, "You don't know?"

"Know *what*?" I nearly yelled. I was tired of going around in circles.

Angora's frown was the deepest yet. She leaned back in her chair, her eyes searching my face.

"Someone has taken a great risk in not telling you." Her voice was different now. It was quiet and deadly serious. "Especially if you are wandering through the country without protection."

"And why *exactly* do I *need* to be protected?" I asked harshly, losing the last of my patience.

Angora raised her eyebrows slightly at my snappy question.

"Because you are in danger, more danger it seems than you realize."

I swallowed.

"Could—c-could this have anything to do with Mora?" I asked slowly.

Angora's eyebrows rose even higher.

"Oh, so you know of Mora? Good. That's good."

"Well, no, you see I don't really know anything about her," I said carefully as Angora's eyes narrowed. "Someone tried to warn me about her not too long ago."

Angora's thin mouth tightened. She stared unblinkingly at me while I waited with bated breath. If all went well, I might finally find out about this elusive person that seemed to frighten Lavena so much and actually discover why she was endangering me.

"Mora is a witch. The most dangerous one in Torona. There was a time when she killed hundreds on her journey to power," she suddenly said, her tone harsh and blunt. "After many years of bloodshed, a group of magical beings cornered Mora and stripped her of her powers."

Mora sounded dangerous all right, but why hadn't I heard of her before now? Somehow Angora guessed what I was thinking because she said, "It was a horrible time when no magical or non-magical being was safe. They were days of deception and distrust. But that was many years ago and though some still speak about it, many don't. They have forgotten—living in their pleasant time of peace—or perhaps they simply wish not to remember."

That made sense. Miss Perish never mentioned any wars or battles in my lessons. But something was still bothering me.

"What does Mora have to do with me?"

"It is my hope she has nothing to do with you," Angora said solemnly and she suddenly looked tired. "I am praying that she doesn't have a clue you exist."

"Why would she care if she did know about me? I mean, I'm not special or anything," I said uneasily.

"She would be interested in you because you're connected with the unicorns."

I stared at Angora stupidly.

"*What?*" I couldn't have heard her correctly.

"The sleeping sickness," Angora replied simply. "I can't give you every detail—it might hinder you more than help. The important thing is, do you know that King Rowan has planned a large hunt for the unicorns?"

As if from another life, I remembered hearing King Rowan talking to Father the night of the ball about his desire to find the unicorns.

"Yes," I said slowly. "Are you telling me that unicorns are *real?*"

"They most certainly are," Angora replied seriously. "They just haven't been seen as often as an ogre or a fairy. But they are most definitely living, breathing creatures."

I stared at her shrewdly, "How can I believe you?"

Angora's eyes seemed to bore into me.

"You tell me? Why are you wondering the forest?"

"I-I wanted to get away from my home," I said, taken aback.

"You have been sleeping in the snow simply because you wanted to leave your family?" Angora asked curiously. "From your appearance, Kindlen believed you had been traveling for weeks. It seems to me that disliking your—"

"I don't dislike them!" I said angrily. "I just . . . "

Angora smiled.

"Like I said," she said calmly. "There was something else driving you from your home."

I frowned at her as she continued to smile. Why had I left? At the time it seemed like an act of frustration and rage . . . could my decision have been fueled by something else, something that I hadn't even recognized? Why had I spent so many hours searching the library for a passage on unicorns? Why had I read and reread the small paragraph about them in Mother's journal? With an uneasy twisting in my stomach, I felt again—more distinctly than ever before—the sensation of being gently pulled by some invisible force.

"You are connected to the unicorns," Angora repeated. "You don't need me to give you proof they exist, for in your very soul, you know they do."

"Why are you telling me this?" I asked. There was a horrible pleading in my voice.

"Because I need your help, Leah Vindral," Angora answered carefully, as if she was walking past a sleeping dragon. "If King Rowan finds the unicorns or if Mora gets wind of what he is doing, then she has the potential to return to power. She needs the unicorns in order to regain the powers once taken from her."

"But what can I do?" I asked frantically, my heart pounding under my ribs.

"You are the only one who can communicate with the unicorns." She flung up her hand to stop me from interrupting. "Explaining *how* is not important, what *is* important is that you are the *only one* who can warn the unicorns of the danger they are in. Will you help us?"

"Wait," I started to laugh. This had to be a joke. A sick, ridiculous, terrible joke. "You want me to go wondering around Torona and talk to some unicorns while a crazy murdering witch and a horde of knights are searching the forest for them as well? I've had enough sleeping in snow for my liking, thank you very much. I'm going home," I said forcefully. "In fact that was exactly where I was going to go before your elves brought me here. I don't care if I'm connected to them or not. I'm sorry, but even if I decided to help you, I would be rubbish. Believe me, a simple manor girl is not who you're looking for."

"So your comfort is more important than an impending war?" Angora snapped harshly, her smile gone.

"This is not my problem," I replied coldly. "Who's to say that King Rowan will even find the unicorns? If he doesn't then Mora doesn't return and everyone lives happily ever after. Isn't it possible that by tromping around the countryside, we'd create *more* attention?"

"That is a risk we will have to take," Angora answered, breathing heavily through her nose.

"Well, I wish you luck." I started to rise, but Angora grabbed my wrist.

"Mora will not take 'no' for an answer if she discovers you."

Myra's warning ran through my brain as I glared into Angora's eyes.

"What are you talking about?" I said trying and failing to sound indifferent.

"Don't you see?" I was startled to hear a painful begging note in her voice."You are a key that can be used by either side. If the king learns of a girl that can call the unicorns to him—it is a prize he would kill for."

I tried to twist my wrist away, but Angora tightened her hold. "And if Mora finds out—she will make you do whatever she wants. Even without her powers she is a deadly force. Don't you see," she whispered, an urgency in every word, "this will not go away if you return home. You are not safe anywhere until the threat of Mora has passed and the only hope is for the unicorns to be put on their guard."

I felt like someone was crushing my chest. I couldn't think.

"I will not rush you," said Angora gently, releasing her hold on my wrist. "This is a great task that I ask of you and one that should not be taken lightly. You shall have a nice warm meal and a comfortable bed." She rose and called in a ringing voice, "Kindlen."

The door opened and Kindlen stepped inside. He inclined his head. "Yes?"

"Take Leah back to her room and send for dinner."

I numbly walked from the table and followed Kindlen back to my room in silence. Our footsteps echoed loudly as we retraced our steps. The trek back to my room didn't seem to take long at all and I hardly noticed any elves that we passed. My mind was blank as it tried to absorb everything I had just heard. Without comment, Kindlen shut the door and I stood in the darkening room and waited for the familiar sound of the turning key in the lock, but it never came.

## Chapter 18

# The Wall of Names

It took me a moment to realize where I was when I woke. I turned my head on the pillow and saw falling snow through the drapes. I frowned at the flurries. So I was a key, was I? A tool that could be used by anyone—including Angora. How could I know whether to believe her or not? But everything she had said fit with what Myra had said to Lavena about my being in danger.

I rolled on my side and pushed myself up. Even if I stayed in the room, Angora would call for me when she wanted to. I slid off the bed and crossed to a cabinet. Inside were a dozen dresses that I had a feeling had been placed there during my time with Angora. I dressed slowly and cautiously turned the knob on the door. It opened and I looked down both sides of the corridor. It was deserted. Kindlen had taken me to the left to see Angora, so I faced right and marched down the corridor.

Since my door hadn't been locked I got the impression that Angora wanted me to explore. It was a sign of welcome and trust. Certainly none of the elves I met along the way tried to force me back into my room. They only stared at me. It struck me then, more so than ever before, just how easy I was to spot. My hair was so striking and so unnatural, it made sense that people would stare. I couldn't hide. Even with a hood over my head, people close by would be able to see some of my hair. And my eyes were such a strange piercing blue. I felt like I had a large sign hung around my neck, weighing me down. I closed my eyes as my chest tightened. I was trapped... trapped inside myself. I had thought that running away from home would free me, but I wasn't free—I never would be free. Wasn't that what Angora had meant? That no matter where I went, the stares would continue, the danger would continue. I averted my eyes from the elves and kept walking.

I wanted more than anything to see Iris, to see an old, friendly face, but I didn't have a clue where the stables were. When I passed the same portrait for the third time in a row I decided to put away my pride and ask for help.

"Excuse me," I asked a passing elf who seemed much younger than Kindlen. "Could you tell me where the stables are?"

"Stables?" he repeated.

I tried to ignore the way his eyes widened and strayed over my hair, but my insides twisted angrily.

"Down this hall, take a right and walk down two staircases," he said. "Take a left when you get to a large statue and keep walking until you come to the double doors. If you keep right you'll come across it."

As I followed his instructions I couldn't help but feel that the castle's confusing corridors must be intentional. Who would *want* to have six-step directions for every destination?

Ten minutes later I was crunching my way toward the stables. *I wish I'd brought a cloak,* I thought darkly as I plowed through the whirling snow. I stepped into the stables and spotted Iris almost immediately. Her head was stretched to its limit, her nose sniffing the frosted air. When she saw me she neighed loudly.

"Did you miss me?" I asked her quietly, scratching her nose. She rubbed her head hard against my arm in reply. I led her from the stables up to a long stone wall. I sat on it and looked up into Iris's large eyes. I rubbed her muzzle absentmindedly as I thought about last night.

There were still questions I wanted answered. Why was I the only one that could help? Was it because of the illness or the cure? How could they be sure I could speak to unicorns? Had this happened to someone else and if so, who? Did the elves know where the unicorns were, or was I expected to track them down as well? And who's to say that if I called them then they *would* appear? I looked at the white field before me and whispered, "Unicorns, come to me."

A cold wind blew harshly, but no single-horned creatures appeared; no sense of enlightenment came to me. I grunted and grumbled, crossing my arms moodily as the wind continued to swirl. Why was this happening? What was I supposed to do? Should I trust the elves, people who I hardly knew? Mora's powers were gone. What *serious* danger could we possibly be in from a woman who couldn't cast the simplest of spells?

Iris nuzzled me kindly. Iris wouldn't mind going on an adventure. She was happy just being with me. As I sat there with Iris, I constantly looked over my shoulder and watched any elves near me in apprehension. But they never spoke to me. The lack of contact was surprising and, though I didn't expect it, depressing. When I finally couldn't handle the cold anymore, I returned Iris to her stall and walked back into the castle.

It didn't take long before I was completely lost. The instructions the elf had given me to the stables had become muddled and I soon found myself passing a statue I had no recollection of ever seeing. I hadn't run into any elves for some time. I turned a corner and walked down a long corridor that was completely empty. My footsteps echoed loudly on the marbled floor. Even the air here seemed colder than elsewhere. There were no windows, no tables, no chairs, no portraits, no statues. Only tall candle stands, each holding a single candle. They were placed a few feet apart, in a straight line against one side of the corridor wall. Then, halfway down the long corridor, I came across something that was different. The candle stands had stopped and on a large stretch of wall was a huge roll of parchment. On the other side of this parchment, the line of candles continued. The corridor was so long, I couldn't see either end from where I stood before the parchment. There was no sound. It was as if this corridor wasn't connected at all to the rest of the castle.

The parchment glowed softly so I could easily read what was on it: names. Rows upon rows, column after column. Thousands of names. I touched the parchment, and I was surprised to find my hand trembling slightly. It felt like linen. There was not a tear or smudge. The ink glistened brightly as if the names had been freshly written.

"What are you doing here?"

I jumped and spun around. Kindlen stood beside me, staring at me with a puzzled yet stern expression.

"I-I got lost," I said, trying to catch my breath. Why hadn't I heard him approach? "I'm sorry if I'm not supposed to be here."

But Kindlen wasn't looking at me anymore. His eyes were on the parchment. I looked at it too. We stood in silence a moment.

"What is this?" I asked.

"This?" he repeated, a strange note in his voice. "This is the Wall of Names. Names of those who died in the war against Mora."

I stared at the names, horrified.

"All of these people?" I asked, my voice hushed.

"Semira," Kindlen said, pointing to the name, "a witch who betrayed Mora by joining us. Yaser, a noble fighter. Mora sent her minions to burn his home. He and his family were locked inside."

I stared up at Kindlen, wishing that he would stop, but I couldn't find my voice. On it continued,

Zara, Conlan, Laqueta, Nolan… all killed, some tortured for information by Mora, some merely used as bait to get members Mora thought more dangerous.

"Elmen," Kindlen's voice was soft. There was a bitter edge so faint, I could have imagined it. "Elmen, my brother."

"Your brother?" I asked, stunned.

"He needn't have died," Kindlen continued, his voice empty. "I told him to stay away… he was much too young."

Fifteen minutes later, I sat in my room, staring into the burning flames of the fire. Kindlen had told me how to get there. He had stayed, standing before the parchment as I had walked away. I was cold… cold in my chest, a cold that I didn't think the fire could ward off. I couldn't rid those names from my mind. No matter how hard I tried to concentrate on the red and yellow flames, I could only see Kindlen, standing before the parchment.

When I had re-entered my room, a cold lunch had welcomed me sitting on a tall silver tray. I had devoured it quickly, and then took up my post before the fire. There I stayed as the end of the day quickly approached. I didn't want to leave my room and wander around the castle anymore. My room darkened as night neared and the female elf who had dried my hair earlier entered and lit the candles. She left with the empty serving tray and I continued to stare silently into the fire. A short time later, my door opened again and Kindlen stood in the doorway.

"Angora wishes for you to dine with her," he said.

I felt like I was leaving my stomach in the room as I followed him into the hall.

"Why does Angora always send you?" I asked, trying to break the heavy silence.

"I'm the highest-ranked elf after to her," Kindlen replied. "When she passes on, I will become king."

"Really?" I said hurrying my steps so that I walked beside him. I barely came up to his shoulder. "Are you related to her?"

"No, there is no such thing as 'royalty'. We are chosen to lead because of our abilities and accomplishments."

"Sounds like a better way to pick a leader than some silly blood line," I said, thinking of King Rowan.

I looked at him sideways and actually saw his thin stern lips form a small smile.

"Does Angora eat in the room she was in last night?" I asked, happy that I had made Kindlen loosen slightly.

"Yes."

"Will I just be dining with her?"

"No, the court will be joining as well."

"Who's the court?" I hadn't expected more people to be there. My nerves, stretched so tightly already, were nearing snapping length.

"A group of the elves closest to Angora. And yes, I am on the court," he added at my inclined head.

We had arrived at the room where I had first met Angora. Kindlen opened the door, I entered, and my nerves quivered violently. The court numbered a dozen. The moment I entered they stopped talking abruptly and stared at me intensely.

Angora rose from her chair at the far end of the table, which had been cleared of the piles of parchment from yesterday, and as she did, the others followed suit. The scraping of their chairs reverberated loudly around the room.

"Leah, please have a seat." Angora indicated a chair beside her.

I took my seat as Angora sat down, followed by the others. Kindlen took the chair on the other side of Angora.

"Let me introduce you, Leah, to the court. You are already acquainted with Kindlen. Beside him sits Blen, Orena, Rendor"—I nodded to each in turn—"Qual, Etren, Rina, Yora"—Yora waved at me and Etren smiled widely—"Intra, Ollen, and Lemor." Angora then turned toward me and asked, as three elves entered the room with plates of extravagant food, "Has your stay been well?"

"Yes," I said, ill at ease with all their eyes on me.

Angora lifted a fork and began to eat her steamed fish. The others followed suit. Angora didn't look at me or address me for the rest of the evening after that. By the end of the meal, sleep itched at my eyes and the vision of my warm bed filled my mind.

"But now we move to more pressing matters," Angora said. "Have you made a decision yet, Leah?"

My eyes snapped to her face. She stared at me expectantly. The other elves seemed to be holding their breath, their eyes wide.

I leaned forward, sitting on the edge of my seat, and cleared my throat. The Wall of Names drifted yet again before my eyes. It was now or never.

"I have."

I looked at the faces around me, wondering what was going to happen to me … wondering when I would see Father again.

"I will help you."

A relieved smile spread across Angora's face and a sigh traveled around the table.

"Then we must make plans," Angora said quickly. "We will need thirty from the army. They shall be your guard, Leah. You will leave early in the morning. We can't afford to waste any more time. I am sure King Rowan has been on his hunt for some weeks and I'm sure Mora has her ears and eyes open. Kindlen, Rendor, please bring the elves that were with you when you found Leah. I would like to speak to them about joining the guard. Leah," Angora turned to me once more, her voice softer. "I want you to go up and try to get some sleep. You have a long journey ahead of you."

I nodded and rose. The others stood as well.

"Thank you again, for joining," Angora said quietly. Many of the elves nodded seriously.

My mouth had gone dry. I still wasn't sure if I was doing the right thing. I nodded foolishly again and left the room, still not fully believing that I would be of any help at all.

Five minutes later, I closed the door of my room and leaned against it, breathing deeply. For strange reasons, I had suddenly jumped into a dangerous but exciting predicament. I wasn't sure if I was happy or scared. The prospect of no more lonely frightening nights in Raven Wood, however, greatly elated me. With a slight smile, I crept into bed and drifted to sleep.

I dreamed I was home. I was trying to convince Father that I had found the unicorns—that they really existed. He laughed at me.

"There's no such thing as a unicorn," he said, hands on hips.

"There is too! I've seen them!" I protested. I wanted to shake him to make him stop laughing. "I tell you I have!"

He stopped laughing. He looked at me as if he were consoling a temperamental child.

"Leah, you shouldn't work yourself up the way you do. You're ill after all."

Lavena appeared beside him.

"Lavena," I said, rounding on her for support, "tell him I've seen the unicorns!"

"The child needs rest doesn't she?" Lavena muttered loudly to Father.

I was about to protest longer, but my surroundings suddenly changed. Father and Lavena drifted away into blackness and in the place of Willow Manor's wooden floor was a forest floor. The trees swayed dangerously in a high wind while loud screeches pounded in my head, as if from a group of people being tortured somewhere near by.

I threw my hands over my ears as the wailing grew more intense. The screams were incomprehensible. I didn't know where I was anymore—I was going mad!

As I jerked awake, drenched in sweat and feeling nauseous, I could have sworn that I continued to hear a faint scream and as I listened I heard it whisper, *"Go forward."*

# Chapter 19
# Ambush

I slid off the bed, crept to the window, and drew the thin, white drapes from the cold glass. The sun's pale golden rays bathed the city in their weak light. I was too unnerved to even contemplate going back to sleep, so I sat perched on the edge of the bed, watching the sun rise, wondering if I had really heard that voice say, "Go forward," or if it was simply part of the dream.

My stomach gnawed uncomfortably and it had nothing to do with hunger. I was leaving today. I was headed to who knew where. The excitement that had flooded me right before I had fallen asleep had evaporated. Instead, nervousness and dread filled its place. I didn't doubt any longer that I was in danger or that Angora was telling the truth. But it still all seemed so strange to me. How could one group of creatures be so important?

I rose from the bed, dressed and heard a knock on my door.

"Come in," I said.

The same female elf entered that I had seen the first day I arrived.

"It's time," she said quietly.

I picked up the Replenisher and my traveling bag, but as I began to pass her at the door, I stopped and turned to her.

"What's your name?" I asked.

Her eyebrows raised and she said, "Naya."

"Thank you, Naya." And I walked past her into the corridor. She hurried past me, a smile on her face.

Naya led me to Angora's room where the court, as well as a much larger crowd who I guessed were making up the guard, were already gathered. They rose from their chairs when I entered. Angora nodded solemnly and said, "Eat. You'll need your strength."

I sat down and the others did as well. Angora clapped her hands and a few minutes later an elf entered carrying a tray of fruit, meat and cheese. It seemed that the others had already eaten because the elf placed the food in front of me and left without a word to the others. Angora turned to me and repeated rather forcefully, "Eat."

The elves discussed directions, but they seemed vague—or maybe it was just that I was so unfamiliar with the area. Trying to ignore the tension that hung heavily in the air, I focused all of my attention on trying to swallow my food. Thinking gloomily that the food would taste much better if I wasn't facing a long, dangerous journey, I continued to chew the bread until it seemed like a lump of cement.

After ten minutes, Angora put down a set of papers and said, "Then it is time. The boats are waiting for you—you know what to do."

With that, the elves' faces became their darkest yet and they filed out of the room silently, holding their bows rather tightly. I was making to follow them when Angora held me back.

"Leah Vindral, a word please," she said quietly. She looked at the elves' retreating backs and said in a hurried whisper, "Be wary. If anything happens, do not give your name to strangers. Do not stay anywhere too long. I do not think Mora or King Rowan know of you yet, but they may and you will be in severe danger if they find out." She paused, glancing over my shoulder again.

"Some argue that Mora has no powers remaining," Angora continued quickly. "But I disagree. Mora was too strong a witch. It is hard for me to believe that she hadn't anticipated the possibility of losing her powers and fortified herself as best she could against it."

I stared at her.

"Certain information has been lost, Leah Vindral," Angora continued, her eyes wide and fearful, her voice hushed. "Information that I possessed somehow made its way to Mora. Be wary. Go now and may you go in stealth!"

I suddenly realized that her hand was gripping my wrist painfully. She released her hold and I quickly left the empty chamber and followed the elves to the dock.

There were twenty boats bumping the bank gently. Iris and the other elves' horses were being led into some of the boats while I was shuttled into a boat with four other elves. As the boats pushed away from the bank I watched the city on the miniature mountain slowly fade into the distance, until we turned a bend and lost sight of it completely. Yet even with my eyes focused on the mist and towering trees before me, Angora's eyes still burned into my mind and her words echoed like the screaming from my dream.

Gnawing worry ate at my insides as the boats cut smoothly through the still water. I looked around me at all the other elves. I spotted Kindlen two boats away. He stood much like Angora did—still and steady like the trees surrounding us. *'Be wary.'* Information had been leaked to Mora. Did Angora suspect one of the elves? I shivered at the thought and focused on my feet.

The journey to the other side of the lake seemed to take much longer than the one before. I shifted my weight from one foot to the other uncomfortably. When the sun was high above us, the boats softly hit the bank and we stepped onto the damp soil.

"Leah," I turned and saw Kindlen mount his steed. "Come."

I nodded and mounted Iris as the others moved away from the lake.

We traveled for the rest of the day, only stopping to eat and sleep. I began to lose count of the days that crept by. The elves hardly ever spoke to me; their heads moved restlessly from side to side, their eyes constantly scanning the forest. It was this behavior that startled me most. They acted as if there could be an ambush at any moment. The farther and farther we traveled the more the uneasiness grew. The forest was strangely silent and void of life. I overheard a group of elves talking quietly many days after we had left Aris.

"I don't like this. We should have seen something by now."

"I'd rather keep it this way," said a hard-faced elf that I recognized as Rendor.

"I agree with Dorn," said a female. "It's been too easy."

"Do you want to get attacked?" spat Rendor.

"No, of course not," the female replied. "It just seems to me that, given who we're traveling with, we should have gotten a lot more attention."

"That's a good sign, then, that Mora doesn't know," said Dorn.

I moved Iris past them and pretended not to have heard. I could feel their eyes staring at me and my cheeks grew uncomfortably hot. I once tried to talk to Kindlen but he didn't seem interested in conversation. He actually sounded as if I was distracting him. It seemed that the elves enjoyed traveling in silence.

I was only too grateful when we made camp that night. The monotonous trudging through the forest made me want to scream and my muscles ached and burned with every movement. With a sigh, I lowered my throbbing head down to sleep in my tent as the soft voices of the elves slowly drifted farther and farther away…

A loud crash jerked me awake. Yelling, screaming, and a loud, ear-splitting screeching left me momentarily stunned. I threw open the tent flap and saw a wild, roaring battle. The elves were furiously fighting creatures I had never laid eyes on before. They were much taller than the elves and their thick hide was a sickly gray. Their arms and legs were unnaturally long and they moved slightly hunched over. Their teeth were broken and yellow and their huge, perfectly round eyes a glowing, burning red.

As I watched, one creature drew back its hand and threw a large rock at an elf. Another one of the monsters grabbed one of the burning branches from a fire the elves had made. It ran at the tents setting them ablaze. Horses galloped through the chaos, retreating into the forest. The elves yelled loudly, trying to get organized as the monsters steadily demolished their ranks. Blood splattered the ground. I watched in horror as one of the creatures ran at an elf and threw him ten feet; he hit a tree, slid down its side, and didn't move again. That same creature turned its head slowly and rested its pupil-less red eyes on me. Its mouth gaped open and it let out a screech that made my ears ring. I snatched the Replenisher and my traveling bag, but seconds later a hand as large as my face swiped at the tent, which flew ten feet and lay crumpled on the ground. I fell over on my back, staring up at the creature's horrendous face. I wanted to scream, to yell for help, but there wasn't air in my lungs! The creature reached a hand toward me and then it jerked wildly, screeching madly. It turned sideways and I saw an arrow deeply embedded in its back. With the monster's attention elsewhere, I rose shakily and ran, stumbling. In a blur, I saw Iris galloping through the crowd toward me. As she passed I grabbed her mane and lifted myself onto her back. She fled into the darkened forest. The shouts and screams from the elves and monsters slowly faded and disappeared, but Iris didn't slow down and I didn't try to stop her.

# Chapter 20
# Ian Grinshaw

I was slightly aware of a slow rocking motion. My hand swung numbly, brushing something smooth and hairy. Long strands of thread tickled my face, but my eyes stayed rebelliously, stubbornly closed. The rocking motion stopped and I fell to the ground with a hard thump. Even then, my eyes stayed shut. Time didn't have any meaning. I could have stayed there for a moment or a day—I didn't know... I didn't care...

Something wet and soft brushed across my cheek and when I didn't react it pushed me roughly. Slowly, painfully, I opened my eyes. Iris was lying next to me, her long face directly over mine. She brushed her nose against my cheek again and I lifted a hand covered in old bloody scratches to her muzzle. Hunger gnawed at my stomach, but I didn't have the strength to move.

Staying still was so much easier... Iris pushed me with more intensity.

"Alright, alright!" I croaked.

Sluggishly I pushed myself up and pulled the Replenisher open. I gave Iris a sack of oats and a few carrots while I downed a jug of water in one gulp. I lowered the empty jug and looked at my surroundings for the first time. I didn't recognize where we were. We were still in a forest, but whether it was Raven Wood or not, I didn't know. Iris had stopped in a very small clearing next to a narrow stream. I pulled out a sandwich and devoured it feverishly.

I don't know how long we stayed by that stream. I was in no hurry to leave it. I didn't want to go back into the depth of the forest once more. I hadn't forgotten those creatures. I shivered at the thought of them and drew my cloak tighter around me. What was I supposed to do? Continue the mission? Were the elves alive? Did they think me dead? Were the survivors looking for me? What I really wanted was to go home, but I didn't have a clue where I was.

One morning, after several meaningless days by the stream, I lay on my back scowling up at an equally scowling gray sky. I was stuck, trapped once again. I had to move; I had to at least leave this stream! I rose from the ground and Iris jumped up and pranced excitedly. I threw the Replenisher over my shoulder and mounted her for the first time in some days.

I didn't have a clue where I was going. The elves had never entrusted me with the unicorns' location. Then again, maybe most of the *elves* didn't know their location either. Maybe Angora, fearing one of them had turned traitor, only confided that information to one or two elves. Maybe Kindlen was the only one who knew. Praying that Kindlen was alive and well, I pushed Iris to a faster trot.

It seemed as if I was starting over. Day by day I kept going, only sleeping for a few fretful hours before continuing onward. I had no direction … no destination … all I knew was that if I stopped moving, I would lose my mind. I was so terrified of looking over my shoulder and seeing those red, glowing orbs in the dark that I jumped at every sound. I had also had the increasing sensation that I wasn't alone in the forest. Multiple times I was sure someone was watching me, hidden behind trees and bushes, just out of sight. Was I crazy? Had I been pushed to paranoia by the monsters with red eyes that wouldn't leave my dreams?

On one particularly dark day, that had been overcast since dawn, my mind was completely void of all thought. It was better that way. Staying in a numb state of mind seemed to keep my fears from taking over my senses. The light was so obscured in the forest that I could only see a few feet around me. And then I felt it: a creeping, icy sensation that started at my neck and spread down my spine and arms. I stopped Iris and sat up straighter in the saddle. I had a strong sense that I was being watched, so strong in fact that I turned my head and stared intensely around me … but there was nothing. I scanned the forest, my ears straining for a breaking twig … the rustling of leaves …

Without even thinking, I dismounted Iris and turned in a small circle. For a moment I stood as quietly as the trees around me and then my chest constricted:

"LEAVE ME ALONE! GO AWAY! GET AWAY FROM ME!"

Iris reared in surprise. My voice echoed through the silent forest as I breathed raggedly. I jerked my head upward as a sudden clatter erupted in the high branches. Directly overhead there was a frantic flapping of many wings. Flocks of ravens were soaring into the air, cawing loudly. Maybe I was still in Raven Wood, after all.

I swallowed and grabbed hold of Iris. I mounted and she galloped away from that spot as quickly as possible, with my heart hammering madly.

The farther I rode the more I began to notice clumps of snow falling from branches as it began to melt. Soon after I made this observation, it began to rain. It rained continuously for a week—this time I counted the days. On the third soggy day Iris and I came upon a muddy, slushy road. As if from a different life, I remembered the night I had left Willow Manor and how I had stayed away from paths, fearing I would run into Father. I pushed Iris onto the road.

Finally, at the end of the week, the sun peaked her way out from behind the clouds and the rain stopped. The sun's rays washed over my frozen, damp body, warming it. A few days later the road widened, the trees thinned, and a village emerged in the distance. I could tell that Iris was near exhaustion but her head perked up at the sight of the smoke unfurling from the chimneys and her hooves moved faster.

The village was a small one; I'm sure Iris and I could have gone to the other side and back in thirty minutes at a good trot. But nonetheless, its light-filled windows and smoking chimneys filled my heart with glee. I stopped at the first inn I saw and, leaving Iris to stand outside, stepped into the warm, brightly-lit room.

A bearded man stood behind the bar. He looked up at the sound of the door opening and shutting. He gave a slight start and I saw him blink rapidly as I walked up to the bar.

"How much is room and board for a few nights?" I asked without preamble, as I dug into my pocket and pulled out a small bag of money that I had taken on the night I left Willow Manor.

"Fifteen lurets a night," he said gruffly, still staring at me as if he couldn't believe his eyes.

I dropped thirty gold coins on the counter.

The man stared at the coins and back at me, his mouth hanging slightly open. It was obvious he hadn't expected such a shabby person to have the money for his establishment. I knew I must look dreadful.

"Hem hem," I coughed quietly. He shook his head slightly, grabbed the money and threw a small, bronze key at me.

"It's room seventeen," he said roughly.

"I need a place for my horse. Do you know of any—"

"Pan! Get out here!" the man bellowed, making me jump in turn.

The frantic movement of feet came steadily nearer and a few seconds later a young boy came scuffling through a door behind the bar.

"Yes?" he panted.

"Take the miss's horse to the stables," the man grunted, jabbing a thumb at me.

Pan's eyes flew to me, grew wide, and immediately looked back at the man.

"Her horse?" he whispered.

"Yes boy! Who else is here?"

Pan jumped and ran quickly to the front door, tripping in his haste to follow orders.

I watched him go and when I turned back to the counter, the man's back was to me and he was busying himself with drying a glass. I hitched my bag more securely on my shoulder and walked up the stairs to the right. I found the door with an iron seventeen nailed to the face, inserted the key, stepped inside, closed the door, fell onto the bed, and in seconds was completely asleep.

The sounds of boisterous voices woke me from my slumber. I turned on my side and quickly fell back asleep. The next time I awoke it was still dark outside, and there were still voices singing and laughing energetically below. I rose from the bed and felt around for a candle and matches, which I found sitting on the bedside table. Guided by the light, I took off the dress that Naya had given me, opened my traveling bag and pulled out a simple green dress I had taken from Willow Manor. I quickly dressed, washed my face in a basin in the corner, and walked down the stairs to the loud, raucous noises below.

As I reached the bottom few stairs, I looked around the bar and was slightly surprised that the room wasn't full. From all the noise, I had expected it to be filled to the brim with people. However, the room was only half occupied, mostly by drunk men. A small vacant table by a window at the other side of the room attracted my attention. Trying to ignore the fact that the inn had just gone completely silent, I crossed the room and sat down. I looked around and saw eyes flicker away, and eventually talk slowly began again. There was a group of men, however, at the bar that were still avidly staring at me. This group seemed to be the drunkest of the lot. They kept downing endless glasses of beer and ale and talking excitedly amongst themselves, stealing glances at me all the while.

"What would you like, dearie?"

I looked up and saw a plump woman with wavy auburn hair.

"What do you have?" I asked, glad for an excuse to ignore the men at the bar.

"Rabbit stew or roasted pheasant," she said. "Barley bread comes with both."

"I'll have the rabbit stew."

"What to drink?" she asked as she scribbled on a piece of paper.

I looked at the bar, my eyes suddenly burning. What was wrong with me? The woman leaned down and said gently, "I'll get you something warm, how 'bout that dearie?"

I nodded as a lump formed in my throat. I didn't understand why ordering a meal would make my insides curl.

"It'll be out soon, dearie," the woman said as she turned away.

"What's the date?" I asked to her back suddenly.

"Why, 'tis sixteenth of March." She turned away and disappeared in the crowd.

*March.* It was March? How could I have been gone that long? I sat without really seeing or listening as if in a numb daze. My food and drink was brought to me and while I ate I saw the little boy named Pan who had taken Iris. He caught my eye and hesitated but then walked up to my table.

"Your horse is well," he said squeakily. "I've been feeding her and I washed her yesterday when you didn't come down."

"Yesterday?"

"Yes. You've been in your room for nearly two days now."

I stared at him, hardly daring to believe how exhausted I must have been to sleep for so long.

"Thank you very much for taking care of her," I said smiling. "Here," I pulled out a coin and held it out for him.

He held out a quivering hand and quickly pocketed the gold before running from my table, a shy grin over his round face.

"Hello, mind if I sit here?"

A tall boy who looked about my age—with flaming red hair and freckles running across his nose—was staring down at me happily, a mug with froth dripping down its side clamped in his hand.

I hesitated and my eyes snapped to the group of drunk men at the bar. One had risen and looked like he was headed my way, but he had stopped, his gaze wavering on the boy standing before me. "Go ahead," I said quickly. Out of the corner of my eye, I saw the drunkard slowly return to his barstool, grumbling darkly to his companions.

The boy sat down opposite me and immediately thrust out a hand.

"M'name's Ian Grinshaw. What's yours?"

I stared uncertainly at his hand. Angora's warning echoed through my brain. His hand fell limply to one side and for a moment he looked crestfallen, then he hitched a smile on his face and said, "No matter, I've met loads of people who like to keep secrets. It's actually quite fun—like figurin' out a riddle. Now let's see," he rubbed his chin and hummed, "are you from here?"

I didn't answer.

"Ahh," he said with grim satisfaction, "you've been runnin'. But from whom?"

"What makes you think I've been running from anything?" I asked uncomfortably.

"Obvious, miss. You aren't from here and you look like you're well off with the looks of that dress, even as tattered as it is. Why else would you be here on your own if not runnin'?"

I picked up my mug and drank as an excuse not to reply.

"Anyway, I'm on my own too," he said. "I'm in search of m'future or fortune or whatever the hell it is... I hav'n' made up m'mind yet."

I smiled slightly into my mug and Ian let out a jovial holler.

"There you go! That's better! You look good smiling! You know, you really shouldn't be gloomy all the time. I've met a good amount of gloomy people and they were just that—gloomy. Mopin' around like the end of the world had happened. Thinkin' that if they crack a grin they'll be carried away by goblins and such … "

Even though I didn't admit it to Ian, that evening was one of the happiest I'd had in weeks. I sat and listened to him ramble on until the inn was nearly empty, until even the drunks had left.

I rose with a yawn.

"Are you stayin' here?" he asked, rising as well.

"Yes."

He sighed and shook his head.

"Smart you are. I'm stayin' at the inn down the street." He lowered his voice. "Crappiest food you'll ever have."

I smiled and turned toward the stairs.

"Sleep well, miss!" Ian yelled back at me.

This continued for two more days. Each night, I sat at that table (it was never occupied), ordered my dinner, and waited for Ian to show up. He always did. First, he'd go to the bar, order some kind of steaming drink and make his way to my table where he would once again start rambling.

"Yes, it was my mother who cornered me and forced me out of the house. She thought I was mak'n a bad example for my younger brother and sisters, you know, about me bein' sixteen and not havin' made anythin' of myself. I had thought of bein' a dragon tamer but then I realized that it could bite m'head off and then I thought about bein' a knight," I choked on my drink and looked over my glass fearfully, "but they only take you when you're eleven and as I was fourteen at the time ... " Ian sighed and buttered a piece of bread.

He never asked me again who I was or what I was doing on my own. He never flinched or gaped when he looked at me. Never asked why I had white hair. It just didn't seem to bother him like it did all the others.

"Honestly, a person shouldn' have to worry about *work* when there are chickens to chase," he said, as if this was the most obvious thing in the world. "Don't you agree miss—"

"Leah."

Ian stared over his plate of roasted pheasant, his fork halfway to his mouth.

"My name's Leah," I repeated.

"Why, it's a pleasure!" Ian said enthusiastically, grabbing my hand and shaking it energetically. "M'name's Ian Grinshaw. I believe we've met before, why, I think I've seen yeh at this very table!"

I burst out laughing. My voice echoed through the room and many people turned and stared at me. My sides ached as I laughed and tears bloomed in my eyes. When I opened them I saw a blurred Ian grinning widely, looking very pleased with himself.

## Chapter 21

# Mora, the Witch

I rose from the table, said good night to Ian, and walked up the stairs to my room. I had to pass the group of drunken men at the bar, as they hadn't left yet. Each night they had stayed a little later. As I passed, they turned on their stools and watched me go by with bloodshot eyes.

Three minutes later I closed the door to my room and leaned against it. I was still amazed that it had been one month since my departure from Willow Manor. I wondered, as I stared at the mirror opposite, what Father had been doing all this time. Did he think me dead? Was he still searching the countryside? Then my thoughts strayed to Kindlen and the elves. What were those creatures? Had the elves managed to escape from them? Were the elves now trying to find me to continue the mission? The mission … I sighed and slumped against the door. I had purposefully not thought about the unicorns. I didn't like the idea of going off on my own to find them. I didn't know where to start. But turning a blind eye to the situation made my stomach twist guiltily. They needed me. What if the knights or Mora had gotten word of me and were waiting at Willow Manor for my return? One thing was clear: I couldn't go back home, not yet. It would be the most obvious place to look for me. As I gazed into the mirror against the wall, my reflection scared and pale, I couldn't deny a strange feeling in my chest. Angora had said that I was connected to the unicorns. How *was* I connected? Was that why I had this strange desire for something that I couldn't find words to describe? Would they be able to tell me *why* this had happened to me? *Why* I now looked the way I did? Lavena had said there wasn't anyway to change me back, but she couldn't speak to unicorns ... maybe they knew something ...

I stood in the darkened room lost in thought until I distinctly heard footsteps and the scraping of a chair being dragged along the floor. I pressed my ear close to the door and heard the scraping sound stop abruptly. The hall was silent once more.

Five minutes later, another pair of heavy, uneven footsteps thudded down the hall toward my door. It sounded like there were two people. Then, like the first footsteps with the chair, these stopped as well, right outside my door.

"What ya doin' 'ere boy?'" slurred a man.

"Just keep'n a watch on the young lady," I heard Ian reply pleasantly.

"No need," said another man. He sounded a little less intoxicated, but I still got chills from his oily voice, "You and I both know that a girl like that doesn't need a *boy* keeping her guard. That's a man's job, that is."

"I beg to differ, sir," Ian replied conversationally. "You see, I've taken a right likin' to her, and I would hate to see her bothered by a pair of drunken fools like yourselves."

"Drunken fools!" roared the first man. "If you don't move from that door, then by hell *I'll* move ya!"

There was a frantic scuffle and a yelp.

"Orrin! ORRIN!" yelled the second man. "You're not fit for a fight! Come on man, come—PUT THAT KNIFE AWAY, BOY!"

"You better take your friend to his room so he can lay down his drunken head before he does somethin' he'll regret."

There was silence except for heavy breathing.

"Come on, Orrin. We'll have another chance to see the girl later."

"Righ'," panted the first man. "I'll get ya, boy! I'll get ya *and* that girl!"

I continued to lean on the door, not daring to breathe, until their footsteps had died away. I was just about to open the door when Ian said loudly and forcefully, "Good night, Miss Leah." With that, I turned the lock and went to bed.

I woke the next morning with a plan set in my head as if my mind had been working on it all night. I wasn't safe here anymore, no matter how many nights Ian stayed up by my door. I had to face facts. I knew what the king was doing and I knew that I was needed to help the unicorns... and maybe, just maybe, they could help me, too. I couldn't just stay hiding in this inn forever, clinging to Ian as protector.

I quietly dressed and looked around for a piece of parchment and quill. I found them crammed in the drawer of the bedside table, and scribbled a thank you and goodbye to Ian. I folded the note in half and inched the door open. Ian was sitting in a chair opposite my door, snoring spectacularly. As I closed the door behind me he gave a small grunt but didn't wake. Carefully, I placed the note on his opened hand and tiptoed past him and down the stairs. I mounted Iris and peered around. I still didn't have a clue where to go. With a weary shake of my head I turned Iris onto the road.

We continued to follow the road, the town far behind us. To the left and right was nothing but fields of sheep and cows. Once and a while a farmer would pass us, staring at me as he went by. It was when I saw the first sign of a forest that I turned off the road and, taking a deep breath as if about to dive into the fathomless depths of the ocean, plunged once again into the woods.

This forest seemed much wilder than Raven Wood. It was darker and denser. Large spider webs hung from tree to tree. The trees themselves were thicker and their branches intertwined into gnarled knots. I knew I had reached the heart of the forest when I could no longer ride Iris but had to squeeze in between trees to get through. Spending a night in that wood was no picnic. The frogs croaked almost as if they were in a contest. I hardly got any sleep at all simply because of the noise.

I was not looking forward to spending another night in that forest. When morning finally came, Iris and I ate our breakfast quickly and had set off even before the sun had completely risen in the sky.

We had been walking for only a few hours when Iris suddenly stopped, her ears pricked forward, her eyes wide. I looked around, praying that the red-eyed creatures weren't in this forest, and heard faint voices coming from the right. I softly crept closer with Iris behind me, her neck stretched out, her eyes wide. I pulled a bush's branches slightly aside and saw ten men with an equal number of horses standing before a very small stone cottage.

I could tell that the men were dressed in armor because their shoes were sparkling metal. Green robes draped over their broad shoulders and flowed to their ankles. On every man's chest was an emblem that caught my eye right away. It was in the shape of a shield and colored gold. On it were two swords crossing each other in the formation of an X in the center. There, in the center where the swords met, was a large letter T. It was Torona's emblem, worn by the knights. Fighting back a moan, I crouched down. Just my luck, bumping into a group of King Rowan's knights.

Through the middle branches of the bush, I watched one of them step out of the group. His back was to me, but there was something about his stance that seemed strikingly familiar.

"Go ahead and knock on the door," said one of the knights, who was staring nervously at the door. For some strange reason, I felt a wave of apprehension as I looked at the heavy, wooden door.

The man I had just been studying turned to look at the knight who had spoken, and I got a good look at his face. I covered my mouth as a very audible gasp escaped my lips.

"Would you care to repeat that?" Sir William Shanklin replied with a deadly calm voice.

I cursed silently behind my bush. I just *had* to run into the one person I never wanted to see again, well—other than Miss Perish. But, of course, Sir William was one of King Rowan's knights. It would only make sense that he would be out looking for the unicorns.

After a long piercing glare at the knight, Sir William stepped up to the door and knocked. The knights inched back a little, as if wanting to get as far away from the cottage as possible without looking cowardly. Two knights' slightly panicky murmurs reached my ears.

"I don't like this forest—give me an ogre any day."

"The sooner our business is over the sooner we can get away from here."

"*Yes*," came a cold voice from inside the cottage.

"By order of His Royal Majesty King Rowan, ruler of Torona, I command you to open your door and answer His Majesty's inquires," Sir William said in a pompous billowing tone, with his chin jutted out.

No answer.

Sir William knocked louder. His pounding thuds echoed through the unnaturally silent clearing. The knights seemed to be holding their breath as Sir William's knocks faded.

"By order of His Royal Majesty, King—"

"I heard what you said, boy," said the voice. It was cold and crisp. "Come in if the king wishes you to. Don't stand there pretending to be important."

I smiled at the sharp remark and watched Sir William puff out his chest, frowning deeply. As his cheeks deepened in color, he glared over his shoulder at the snickering, yet huddled, knights behind him, all of whom quickly stopped at the sight of his gaze. With his nose in the air he opened the door, and without hesitation, disappeared into the house.

I couldn't contain my curiosity. I touched Iris's face and mouthed, "Stay here—I want to see what's going on."

Iris looked as if she would rather not but didn't move from her position.

I sneaked my way to the back of the house. The knights were too busy dealing with their horses and shooting edgy glances at the cottage and surrounding trees to notice me.

There was a door and an open window at the back of the house. I crouched down, peaked through the window, and saw a small room, with a fire crackling in a corner. The floor was wooden and there were shelves filled with jars of sickly-colored objects floating in thick liquids. There was a wooden, splintered table covered with herbs and plants drying. I thought I recognized a pile of the small purple flowers called Lavender Marsh that Lavena had told me were used in sleeping draughts. Sir William stood with his back to the flames in the fireplace, staring at a tall, thin woman sitting in a large green chair.

She had black hair with streaks of gray set in a tight bun. The paleness of her skin was shocking and seemed to glow in the dark room. She pressed her thin lips together as she surveyed Sir William with deep disdain. The woman sat like a queen, dressed in a long dark blue robe that touched the floor.

"Witch Mora, by the great King Rowan's orders you are to tell me important information that His Majesty wishes to know," Sir William barked, looking down his nose at the woman in the great chair as if she were some lowly creature.

My stomach plummeted and my heart stopped. Mora, *Mora?* Not only had I blundered into the knights, but Mora, too? I shrunk lower behind the window, trying to steady my thumping heart. If she saw me ... I'd rather be taken by the knights.

"If the king is so *great,* then why has he sent a messenger boy to find him this *important* information?" she sneered, her lips curling. "Shouldn't the *great—King—Rowan* want to see me in person like a *brave* king? Shouldn't he show his people that he is not afraid to walk outside his safe haven and face me like a *great, brave* king would? Why would such a *powerful* king send little messenger boys to deal with his most *pressing* matters?"

"How *dare* you speak of His Majesty in such terms! You have no idea what he can do to you," Sir William said angrily, and small patches of red appeared on his cheeks at the insult to his knightly status. He flinched as a raven cawed loudly. I hadn't spotted it for it had been perched atop a tall bookshelf in a dark corner. It descended from the bookshelf to the top of Mora's chair, shifted its weight slightly, and scowled at Sir William menacingly.

"Your king has no power here," said Mora in a frigidly calm tone, as if she were merely stating a fact.

Sir William seemed to decide to get on with business.

"Well, I—the king is undergoing a hunt and needs information on the whereabouts of the creature he has set his eye upon. That is where you come in, Mora. As a witch that knows much of her surroundings, you have interested His Majesty. He believes you have the information we seek—"

"Do hurry, I don't want to spend my entire day listening to you jabber on," Mora said, resting her hand lazily on her cheek.

"His Majesty wishes to know where to find the unicorns," Sir William said in a rush, though still trying to retain some dignity.

Her eyes shot to Sir William and a wide smile spread across her thin lips.

"It's finally happened. It took the old goat long enough. Listen carefully, boy"—Sir William sniffed haughtily at being called 'boy' again but didn't say anything—"because you'll only hear this once from me. No one knows *exactly* where the unicorns are. Their home has been kept secret, guarded for centuries. Not even I know the exact location."

Sir William made a choking noise in his throat as if to interrupt, but Mora kept talking as if she hadn't heard.

"But there is a way of finding them," she said quietly, her eyes glittering. The raven perched on her chair shifted slightly. "Find the one who can speak to the unicorns and your king will have what he desires."

She knew? Sweat prickled on my forehead.

"Where can I find this person?" Sir William asked, a hungry expression on his face. Against my better judgment, I leaned closer to the window.

Mora stared at him coolly, "She is young—between twelve and twenty. She has an unnatural beauty... and white hair."

I dropped down and stared at my knees with my heart pounding against my ribs. She did! She knew about me!

"*White* hair?" Sir William said incredulously. I risked raising my head to look through the window again. Sir William stared at Mora with one eye cocked. "Between twelve and twenty with *white hair?* Surely you jest."

The raven perched on Mora's chair cawed sharply. Mora lifted her left hand and stroked the raven's chin with a long finger.

"Ask people if they have seen a strange girl. You'll be surprised how many have." Mora's eyes burned. For a split second I thought her gaze swept to my hiding place, but when I looked again her eyes were fixed upon Sir William. "One other thing before you go; just to add some more fun to the game, I'll tell you that the person you seek is *very* close by," and she smiled wickedly. I ducked down quickly.

"WHAT?" Sir William bellowed.

"I'd search the forest," Mora said lazily.

I heard rushed footsteps, the opening of a door, and Sir William shouting at the knights to search for the key to their success—me.

I didn't know if I could get up; my legs felt like jelly.

"I would move if I were you."

I swung my head up to the window and saw Mora standing on the other side of it, inches from me with her eyes bearing down on me like burning fire. I sprung up like I was sitting on hot coals and raced to the place Iris was hiding.

By the act of some miracle, I was able to find Iris without being spotted. I grabbed her reins and pulled her into a run. Men were shouting and their horses neighed loudly.

I ran with no sense of direction. We had to hide, but where? Through the trees, I spotted a rundown barn—half its roof had collapsed. It was still in sight of Mora's cottage. Perhaps it was hers'? Without hesitation I flung the door open and pushed Iris inside one of the stalls. I tore off her saddle and bridle, placing them on a bench beside the wall. I could hear horses' hooves pounding the ground as I looked frantically for a place to hide.

I spotted a ladder and climbed it as quickly as I could. In the loft there was a pile of hay bales. Frantically, all the while listening for approaching horses, I dragged them to one side and crouched against the wall. Just as the doors of the barn swung open I pulled the bales around and on top of me—hiding me from view.

As footsteps clunked their way around the floor below me, I hoped the knights wouldn't notice that Iris's coat was still a little wet with sweat.

"You stay down here and I'll search the loft," said one of the knights.

I pressed myself farther against the wall as the ladder groaned from the weight of the knight. His feet hit the floor heavily. Then, he must have started scanning the room because I didn't hear any movement. My heart pounded against my ribs as I heard the knight start to move slowly around the loft. Louder and louder his footsteps thudded on the weak floor. My heart was beating in my chest so furiously I thought it would explode and give away my hiding place. My hand that rested on the floor jerked up in surprise as I felt the prickling sensation of a spider's legs touch it.

The footsteps stopped and I could see the knight standing inches away from me through a small space in the hay. I saw his hand reach out to the hay bale on top of me—he was seconds from pulling it off and discovering me! I closed my eyes tightly, bit my lip—but a spider was on my neck! Without thinking, I gasped and flung the spider off just as a knight downstairs yelled up the ladder.

"Adrian, there's nobody down here. Some of the others are standing outside waiting to go."

I didn't dare breathe. Had he heard me? There was a slight moment of hesitation before the knight next to my hiding place said, "All right, I'm coming." I flung my hand over my mouth to stifle my gasp, the speaker was so close.

The knight's footsteps thudded on the floorboards and the ladder creaked once more. I didn't move until I heard the closing of the barn door and the sound of the horses' hooves grow distant.

I threw off the suffocating hay bales and gulped in fresh air. Shaking, I brushed myself off and rushed down the ladder. I looked cautiously out of a small window. They had gone.

# Chapter 22
# Torona City

Luckily there was no sign of King Rowan's men as we made our way through the trees. I had to get out of this forest as quickly as possible. With Mora's information, Sir William would have the knights search every inch of the forest for me. I tugged my hood farther over my head.

I didn't stop for the rest of the day, not even to sleep. It didn't matter, because I knew I couldn't have fallen asleep, even if I'd wanted to. Mora was still so clearly etched in my mind that I kept looking over my shoulder uneasily just to make sure she wasn't there. Iris didn't complain. She was still going strong when the sun rose the next morning and I finally stopped to eat.

I gave her a basket of grain and I had my bread with cheese and fruit. When we were finished, we started again. I spent two more nights in the forest. I had the terrifying feeling that I was merely going in circles, everything looked so much alike. On the third day, when I was in complete despair and panic, we finally exited the forest.

Brown pastures, and a few trees laid themselves out before me. Feeling happier than I had in days, I directed Iris onto a narrow, sunny, dirt road. If there was a road here, then there must be a village. I didn't know what I would do in a village. Unicorns certainly wouldn't be there, but I didn't care at the moment. Being out of Mora's forest was wonderful, and who knew, maybe I would hear of the elves or find something else that would help me find the unicorns.

I wasn't on the road very long, compared to my long trek through the forest. We went at a much faster pace now that we didn't have to dodge trees and branches. After a few hours, I came across a sign with gold letters: *Torona City*. I frowned at the sign, feeling my heart sink. It seemed stupid to purposefully wonder into King Rowan's city. It would be crawling with knights. I looked around, biting my lip. Sir William would search every inch of the forest before heading back to the City. The trees from the forest waved at me threateningly. I didn't want to go back. I gave Iris a small nudge and she galloped down the road to Torona City.

I reached the city just before the sun began to set. I had never been to Torona City; I had only heard stories of it from Father's guests. Making sure my head was completely covered, I led Iris into the bustling streets of the city. The setting sun sliced long shadows over the shopping people. I was standing in the center of a crowded street, scanning for inns, when someone grabbed my arm: a man dressed in green robes with the king's emblem embroidered on his chest. I hadn't been in Torona City for twenty minutes and already I had run into a knight!

"What's a pretty thing like you doing wondering the streets?" he asked, still with a firm grip on my arm.

"I was about to find a place to sleep, sir," I replied, trying to release my arm.

"Are you here with anyone?" he asked, peering at the crowds. His eyes returned to my face and they widened slightly, having seen a few strands of white hair from underneath my hood.

"No. I really should find an inn before dark, sir."

"A gem like you, sleep in a dirty old inn? Oh no, you're staying in the castle. It's safest there." Without waiting for a reply, he tightened his grip on my arm and led me down a road—the castle looming closer with every step.

I had never seen Torona Castle but that didn't mean that I didn't know anything about it. It had a hundred rooms: dining rooms, ballrooms, sitting areas, libraries, and no less than sixty-seven bedrooms, not to mention dungeons and twenty-three towers. Even though I knew all this, I was still taken aback by the sheer size of the castle. I couldn't help feeling that it looked *too* grand.

We entered a courtyard containing ten large fountains with statues of horses and maidens.

"We'll leave your horse here. The stable boy will pick her up."

He smiled and I looked away nervously. How was I going to get out of this? He didn't release his hold as we went through the castle doors. For a moment, I completely forgot about the knight. I stared stupidly at the overflowing grandness of the castle. The walls were covered in large portraits, and expensive furniture and statues cluttered the rooms and hallways. Tapestries and gold vases encrusted with diamonds and sapphires were everywhere. I saw tall, large rooms with impressive chandeliers that shimmered brilliantly. Servants bustled here and there with their arms full of laundry or dust rags. It was so different from Aris, and I couldn't help but prefer Aris's elegant simplicity.

"This way," said the knight, who didn't seem to have noticed my dumbstruck expression. He pulled me to a staircase, shooting furtive glances as we went. "We're not supposed to bring people in without reporting to the captain," he said quietly. "But he's away…just be our little secret, eh?" He winked and my unease tripled. Oh, I was in big trouble, all right.

We walked up one set of carpeted stairs and then down a hall with portraits of expensively-dressed members of the Royal Family. He tugged me in front of a door.

"You can stay in this room," he said, holding it open.

As I stepped in, I thought that it was a very simple room for such an imposing castle.

"I'll send someone along to fix you up," and with another wink, he closed the door.

I stood in the center of the room, nervously twisting my hands. Now what? I turned the doorknob—locked. I had to get out of here before Sir William and his knights got back. I ran to the window and flung it open. I grimaced. It was a good thirty-foot drop to the cobbled courtyard below. There was no way I could climb down. I yanked the window shut with a *snap.*

I glowered at the darkening sky. I was stuck once again. I wasn't any farther on my mission and Sir William could clatter into the city at any moment. I had to find a way to leave the city as quickly as possible.

Just then, the door swung open. I whirled around, expecting to see the knight who'd brought me here. Heat rose unpleasantly in my cheeks. There, looking as handsome as ever, stood Prince Philip. He had a strange smile on his face as he asked, "How do you do?"

"As well as could be said, Your Highness. Y-you?" I stuttered.

"I bumped into Sir Alfred," Philip said, closing the door. "He was positively gibbering about you. I had to see for myself if he was telling the truth."

My mouth had gone very dry. I followed Philip's eyes as they focused on the hair visible under my hood.

"Lady, you are the most stunning woman I have ever had the pleasure of laying eyes upon."

"How kind," I said with a nervous laugh. Philip took a step closer and I, in turn, a step back. My back bumped into the window.

Philip reached for my hand—

"Philip, oh, was I interrupting?"

Philip spun around and I gasped as another familiar face was brought abruptly back into my life. Lydia was standing imposingly in the doorway.

"Ah, Lydia, glad you found me," said Philip quickly. "I was greeting a new guest."

But Lydia wasn't listening. Her icy gaze had moved from Philip to me. I watched her eyes drift scathingly from my face to my toes and back again to settle on my hooded face.

"I thought you were going to escort me to dinner, Philip," Lydia said, turning her head and batting her eyes at him.

"That's exactly why I was coming down this hall," Philip said, walking toward her. "Shall we go?"

Lydia smiled at him after giving me a glistening glare. She left the room and Philip followed her without a backwards glance.

I suddenly noticed how cold the palms of my hands were and lifted them from the window. I sat down in a chair and rubbed them together. I was half glad that Lydia had interrupted when she did and half annoyed.

"He didn't know it was me," I mumbled to my hands.

All of the sudden, a great commotion erupted outside. I looked out the window and saw a band of knights clatter down the cobblestone bridge and skid to a halt. The leader of the group jumped from his steed and rushed into the castle, but not before I had recognized the sharp outline of his nose and his familiar pompous gait—Sir William had returned.

My heart pounding, I opened the door that Philip had not locked and ran into the hallway. I quickly looked right and left and crept silently down the deserted hall to the stairwell. There, I hid behind a statue and saw Sir William appear in the great hall below, panting heavily.

"I must see His Highness!" he said in a wild fury to a butler.

"He is getting ready to dine, Sir William," the butler answered.

"It is urgent news," Sir William said loudly, his voice echoing around the great hall. "I must—"

"Shanklin," a voice boomed suddenly across the hall. "What's all this noise?"

I crouched frozen as I watched King Rowan march across the marble floor toward Sir William and the butler. Sir William jumped forward and performed a ridiculously low bow.

"Your Highness! I have news that will help the hunt!" He seemed beside himself with pride.

"Really?" asked King Rowan. He turned to the butler and said, "Leave us."

When the butler had disappeared from the great hall, King Rowan turned back to Sir William and said, "Well?"

He didn't seem pleased. A little flutter of hope quivered in my chest. Maybe the hunt wasn't going well?

"I know of someone who can find the unicorns!"

My stomach dropped a few notches.

"A girl, My Lord! A girl is all we need. One that has ethereal beauty."

I stood as still as the statue I was hiding behind.

"A girl?" King Rowan spat incredulously. "What is this rubbish, Shanklin?"

"I tell you, My Lord, its true! I just found out from the witch—"

"*Be quiet fool!*" King Rowan barked. He looked around to make sure no one was there, but the great hall was quite empty. "Come to my chambers and we will discuss what you have learned."

I watched them leave my vision with mounting dread. Sir William would tell him about the 'white-haired girl' and they would run into Sir Alfred or Philip and learn that there was indeed a white-haired girl in the castle at that very moment!

I ran back to the room and grabbed the Replenisher. Then, just as quickly, I ran back to the statue, my hand gripping my hood to keep it from flying off. Slowly and quietly I tiptoed down the stairs, and when I knew the coast was clear, I sprinted for the door.

I found the stables quickly and ran past many stable-hands. Before they could even react, I had mounted Iris and pushed her into a full gallop over the bridge. We rushed into the city as people cursed and jumped out of the way, shaking their fists at my retreating back. I looked over my shoulder to see if the knights were following me yet, and when I turned to face back around, I let out a yell. A boy on his horse had suddenly emerged from around a corner and Iris reared in panic. I fell heavily on the road, my elbow banging the cobblestone road. My hood fell off and I looked up at the boy still on his horse, ready to curse him for making me fall when—

"Leah?"

I sat up and looked at the boy's face as he leaned over his horse, looking down at me. He had flaming red hair.

"Ian?"

"Why, who would have guessed it?" Ian said loudly, a smile spreading across his face. "We just keep bumpin' into each other! You okay? You hit the ground hard."

"I'm fine," I said crossly, rubbing my stinging elbow.

Ian smiled wider, but then he looked up over his horse's head and the smile disappeared slightly. I turned and heard the pounding hooves of a large group of horses.

I leapt up, ignoring Ian's puzzled look, grabbed Iris by the bridle and hid behind the corner of the building where Ian had appeared. I peered cautiously around the corner and saw that Ian had dismounted and was staring up into the faces of five very angry knights.

"Boy," one of them barked, "did you see a girl pass by here not too long ago?"

"A girl, sirs?" Ian asked with a bewildered face. "I've seen quite a nice amount of girls pass by, sirs. They didn't have much interest in me though … "

"You worthless dog," another spat, and this one I recognized as Sir Alfred, the one who had brought me to the castle, "have you seen one with white hair, you fool?"

"Ahh, now that narrows it down a bit, sirs," Ian said, a look of dawning comprehension spreading across his face. He pointed down the opposite road and said, "Yes, sirs, she went bustle'n down there. Chickens flyin', people screamin' … she scared poor Merlin here," he added with a slightly injured tone, indicating his horse.

But the knights weren't listening anymore. They were already halfway down the road before he had finished. Looking slightly bemused, he tugged at his horses' reins and walked over to where I was hiding.

"Now then, are you going to explain why some knights were chasin' you?" he asked calmly.

"Not here," I said tersely.

"Well, you can where I'm stayin'. It's just down there."

Ten minutes later Ian opened the door to his room, on the second floor of a decrepit looking inn, and I sank onto a squeaky bed with a slight shiver.

"*So*," Ian persisted. "Why were some bloody knights chasin' you?"

I stared at my feet in response.

"Oh no," said Ian, as he shut the door with a snap. "We're not playin' that game again." He walked over to a chair, dragged it in front of me and turned it around backwards. He leaned on it for a minute and said abruptly, "I'll make tea."

I sat numbly on the bed and watched him boil water. My mind was horribly blank.

"There," he pushed a mug of tea into my hands and sat down, wrapping his arms around the back of the chair and staring at me expectantly. "*So?*"

"It's a long story."

"I got time."

I glared at him. I could lie, but for some reason, I couldn't bring myself to do it. I had been running for so long, and suddenly, I couldn't take another step. Before I had even tried to consider what might happen if I told him the truth, words spilled from my mouth.

He sat in silence, nodding occasionally as I told him everything. Flashes of the ball, Lavena, Father, King Rowan's plan, the sickness, the recovery, the elves, the monsters with red eyes, and Mora all sped through my brain and out of my mouth. His eyes darkened at the mention of Mora and his mouth tightened, but he didn't stop my narrative.

"And I just saw Sir William Shanklin tell King Rowan what he learned from Mora and now he's looking for me. He'll use me to find them, I'm sure of it—that is if Mora doesn't get to me first. But I don't know where the unicorns are and I'm tired of running!"

Ian rose from his chair and walked to a grimy window with his back to me.

"We'll just have to find them then, won't we," he said finally.

"What?"

He turned to me, his face set.

"The unicorns. We've got to find them. You're the only one who can talk to them, so you're the only one who can warn them. We'll have to leave now though. I'm sure King Rowan will have the whole city searched by mornin'."

"Yes, but what's with all this *we* business?"

"What? Didn't you know? I'm coming with you." Ian grabbed a sack, walked to the door, opened it and headed down the hall as I followed him.

"No you're not."

"Yes I am."

I glared at him.

"My dear Leah, I don't believe you've had the pleasure of meeting my stubborn side," he said with a smile as he started down the stairs.

"But—but what about your future and all that?" I asked desperately as I hurried to catch up with him.

"My mother gave me one piece of advice as I left our humble home," Ian said conversationally, "She said, *'Don't you follow anything mysterious!'* And you, Leah, are the most mysterious thing I've ever met."

"But your mother told you not to!"

We were outside once again and mounting our horses.

"Yes, and you might also need to know that I always do the exact opposite of what my mother wants," Ian said, and with that he started off at a gallop, with Iris and I following in his wake.

## Chapter 23
# Light in the Dark

The sun was full in the sky and Torona Castle's many towers were no longer visible. We had traveled all night and all morning without stopping.

"So they didn't tell you anything?" asked Ian suddenly.

"Who? The elves?" I asked.

"They didn't tell you *at all* where they were head'n'," Ian asked, one eye cocked.

"That's right," I replied rather defensively.

"But *why* would they do that? From what you told me it sounded like they were on your side, so why all the secrecy?"

"I got the feeling from Angora that she felt someone had turned traitor. I wasn't even sure if all the elves knew where the unicorns are."

Ian nodded darkly. "That makes sense."

"Or maybe," I said frowning, "she didn't want certain *other* people to know—people who might get hold of me, like Mora or King Rowan."

We exchanged dark, significant looks and I tugged my hood lower over my eyes as we passed a wagon. The scenery rapidly changed as we continued. The flat meadows mounded into rolling uneven wet ground and the trees became sparse and few. As night began to descend, I asked Ian, "Where are we going, by the way?"

"I was thinking about head'n to Bell Sound—it's where I live. We can rest there, get supplies, figure out our next move. In fact," he pulled on his reigns, "we'd better stop here. There won't be much firewood ahead."

"Why's that?" I asked curiously.

"Because ahead's the Ash Moors."

"Why are we going through the Moors?" I asked, taken aback. "There's got to be another way to Bell Sound." I hadn't yet forgotten Sir William's description of the Moors and I was not in any mood to see if he had been exaggerating or not.

"Sure, there's another way," Ian said in an off-hand sort of voice, "it'd just take us two weeks. Goin' through the Moors will be faster."

I bit my lip uncertainly.

"Come on, the sooner we get to Bell Sound the better," Ian pressed.

"You *do* know your way through the Moors?" I asked as we started to make camp. "We won't be going through the Braxton Bog, will we?"

"'Course we won't! What d'you take me for?" Ian replied indignantly.

"All right, all right!" I said, picking up sticks for the fire.

Twenty minutes later we sat around a small fire and I pulled out the Replenisher. I had forgotten that Ian had never seen it before. When I had pulled out two flasks of wine, four nice-sized dinner rolls, a large hunk of blue cheese, a skillet, a piece of beef, two glasses, knives, forks, and two large bags of grain for the horses, I looked up and saw that his eyes were as large as saucers.

"H-how did you—" he whispered as he pointed a shaking finger at the Replenisher.

I unwrapped the beef, put it in the skillet, and set the skillet over the fire.

"Lavena let me borrow it," I said, handing him a flask of wine. "It's quite handy."

Over dinner I explained the Replenisher to Ian, who couldn't get enough of it.

"So whenever I open it, it'll always have food in it?" he asked in awe. The Replenisher was in his lap and he was holding it like his new-born child. "Simply amazin', and yet it's as light as a feather."

"The food only appears when you open it," I said, hiding my smile behind my glass.

"And it's somethin' new each time?" he asked gleefully, opening and closing it over and over.

"Yes, but you can think of something in particular that you want and it'll appear."

He gazed down at the weather-worn sack like it was the most valuable treasure in the world.

"I've gotta tell mom about this," he whispered.

❦

The next morning, a glowing yellow orb rose through a hazy fog. Ian was already packing up his horse, Merlin.

"We should get movin' after breakfast. The king's men have probably realized you aren't in the city by now."

We ate once again from the Replenisher (Ian couldn't help but make a few more adoring comments) and we were off.

We traveled all morning, as the land around us grew more and more different. At midday, we stopped and stared at the Ash Moors stretching before us. Fog hung in thick layers over the marshy land, enveloping it in shadowy darkness.

"So this is . . . "

"The Ash Moors," Ian finished grimly. "We should best dismount. Easier to see where we're steppin' . . . take it slow."

"So we won't run into the vors," I said nervously, dismounting, "since we won't be going through the Braxton Bog."

Ian didn't look at me as he replied rather quickly, "Nope, sure won't. Well, let's be off then!"

I followed him with my eyes narrowed in suspicion.

"You're *sure* you know where you're going?"

Ian grumbled incomprehensively, gripped Merlin's reigns, and walked into the fog.

I closed my eyes and took a deep breath.

"This really isn't worth it," I muttered to Iris. She snorted in agreement.

Even though we were on a road, our feet squelched in the wet, thorny grass. I could barely see anything. It was as if someone had placed a bowl upside down on top of us, trapping the dense fog in. Soon, I forgot it was only mid afternoon. I saw only one or two trees in the entire day's trek and they were quite disturbing. They were bent over as if in pain from the blustering winds that whistled through sporadically, and their roots grew out of the ground as if trying to climb their way out of the disgusting muck.

"It's lucky you have that nifty sack," said Ian happily over his shoulder. "Huntin' in the dark isn't fun."

"I'm so glad I've helped make this trip less unpleasant," I said dryly, as I pulled my foot out of a particularly muddy puddle. "We won't sink in anything, will we?"

"No, the people who built these roads were very careful to keep away from the big pools."

Some time later, Ian stopped and I almost ran into him.

"Shall we settle down for the night?" he asked pleasantly, as if we were taking a stroll through a sunny meadow.

We sat down on the driest patch of grass we could find and ate a cold dinner. We didn't even bother trying to make a fire; the few trees were far too wet to catch flame. The only thing that allowed me to go to sleep was Ian informing me that we should make it out of this muck in the morning.

We woke early, spurred on by the vision of leaving the Moors. But we kept walking . . . and walking . . .

I stopped and stared around. Something wasn't right. The fog should be lifting, but it was growing denser and the ground was certainly wetter. The haze was so dense that for a moment I thought I could scoop some up in my hand. Silence pressed heavily against my eardrums. A sudden burst of cold wind suddenly whistled through the fog, nearly knocking me over.

"Ian, Ian! This doesn't look right," I called to him.

He had stopped a short distance ahead of me and was also staring around at the fog, hands on hips.

My foot suddenly sank deep in the mud and I grabbed onto Iris to keep from falling. Ian was making his way to me with difficulty—his feet kept sinking into the muck.

"I don't like to admit this," he said grimly, "but I think we're lost."

I felt myself sink even lower.

"*Lost?* I thought you said you knew where you were going?" I yelled furiously.

"Well, it all starts lookin' the same after a while," he snapped.

I glowered at him. Lost. We were *lost* in the Ash Moors! This was perfect, oh, yes, this was—my stomach turned over.

"We're not—Ian, are we in the Braxton Bog?"

Ian looked around uncomfortably before mumbling, "I think so."

"WHAT?"

Ian waved his hands at me wildly, saying, "Shhhh!"

"You said you knew where we were going!" I yelled, ignoring him. "You said we'd stay clear of the Bog!"

"Well, it's been awhile since I was last in the Moors," Ian fired back, just as loudly. "Perfectly honest mistake! Don't see why you're gettin' all worked up!"

"Don't know why I'm—" I repeated hoarsely, "*Worked up?* Ian, the *vors* live here and you're wondering why I'm *worked up?*"

He opened his mouth to reply, but a distant howl that made my heart stop beating reached our ears through the fog. Ian and I both whipped around, our argument forgotten, and Iris's and Merlin's ears twitched toward the sound, their eyes wide. The howl reached a high pitch before slowly growing faint. I breathed quickly, gripping the air beside me for Iris.

"Ian—"

"SHHH!" He extended his neck, his eyes wide as he stared into the surrounding fog. I couldn't see anything through it.

Another howl erupted from a different direction than the first and was quickly accompanied by three others. The hair on my neck stood up as the gut-wrenching howls grew in number.

"Ian," I whispered, tugging on his sleeve, "*Ian.*"

"Right," he breathed, taking a step back. "We need to find the road."

Then, abruptly, the howling stopped. We stood frozen in the mud, straining our eyes and ears.

"Run," Ian whispered. "RUN!"

We turned and bolted, sloshing and tripping through the mud. I looked over my shoulder and would have screamed, but there didn't seem to be any air in my lungs. In the fog, standing on the top of a fallen twisted tree, was a vor, and it was ten times worse than Sir William's description. Its fur was a matted dark mass, and its jaws were unnaturally long and large. And it was huge; it would have towered over the average dog. As we ran, Ian and I jumped onto Iris and Merlin and plowed through the fog. I bent over Iris, begging her to go faster.

A vor leaped into the air and hit Iris. I fell off and hit the mud hard. A sharp yell cut through the mist and I saw Ian stabbing at the vors with his dagger. Merlin had tripped on a stump and was whickering loudly at a crouching vor. I heard a low rumbling growl a few feet away and turned to see a frothing vor bearing down on me.

I had no weapon; fire was the only thing that frightened them. I rolled on my back and crawled backward. The vor gave a final growl, bared its large teeth and pounced! Instinctively I threw up my right hand to cover my face from the blow and shut my eyes—but the vor didn't attack; in fact, it let out a frightened yelp. I opened my eyes and squinted painfully. A blinding, white light was glowing from my finger, the one with the little, silver mark. In seconds my eyes adjusted to the light and I saw the vors barreling away from the light, their tails tucked, each one screeching and howling into the mist. When all the vors had gone from sight, the light slowly faded and the Bog became dark and silent once more.

# Chapter 24
# Bell Sound

"But how—what—what happened?" Ian stuttered, staring at me in alarm. We had found the road and were walking down it as quickly as possible.

"I don't know," I replied, rubbing the finger with the mark, "that's never happened before."

"You aren't magical, are you?" Ian asked shrewdly.

"Lavena always said I wasn't."

"Well, she didn't see you do that," Ian said, pointing at my finger. "That wasn't normal."

By the time we had left the Ash Moors, Ian had stopped trying to figure out why my finger had suddenly 'activated' and was now focused on the direction of his hometown, Bell Sound.

I closed my eyes and breathed in the fresh, cool air as I listened to the chirping birds. Iris was even gladder than I was to be out of the Moors. She pranced a few steps and swung her head up and down in delight. When the misty Moors were completely out of sight, we came upon a fork in the road. In the middle was a sign with two arrows. One said 'Yarmouth' (to our left) and the other, 'Bell Sound' (to our right.) Both roads were deserted.

"We should be there in a few minutes," Ian said happily.

At first we were the only beings on the road except for a bird here and there. But I started spotting more and more sheep grazing on pastures the farther we went. When the muscles in my back and legs were beginning to ache in pain from riding, I saw Bell Sound.

The roads in the village were cobblestone and people bustled from shop to shop. We entered the town and a few people turned their heads in our direction. I nervously tugged at my hood as their eyes wandered over me.

"Ian! Why, I didn't know you were back in town," yelled a short, buoyant woman, grinning widely. Her hair was frizzy and her shopping bags swung wildly as she waved at Ian.

"Just stopp'n by, just stopp'n by," Ian called back.

Many people knew Ian. Quite a few waved at us as we passed and called out cheery words of welcome. A little farther into the town, Ian pulled on Merlin's reins and dismounted before a small store. There was an old, wooden, sign hanging over the door with bold, yellow letters: Daffodil Bread.

"Why are we stopping here?"

"This is m'Dad's shop."

A small bell attached to the door tinkled merrily as we entered the shop, and I halted in the doorway, momentarily stunned. We were in a bakery filled with the most delicious looking sweets and breads I had ever seen—round wheat breads; long, skinny, white breads; breads that were covered with seeds; huge loaves of brown breads the size of wagon wheels. They were all placed on shelves behind a long counter.

In front of the counter were delicious pastries. Some had delicate designs on top while others were simply oozing in sweet, sticky sauces and creams. On the walls were jellies and jams. They were all in the strangest containers. Some were tall and skinny while others were round and squat. Some looked like the maker had gotten carried away, resulting in a bottle that looked twisted in knots. The walls were the same color yellow as the letters on the sign outside and the old wood of the counter and shelves added a touch of quaintness.

"Is there something I can help you with?" asked a balding, plump man who had emerged from under the counter, though his attention seemed to be elsewhere. He scanned the floor around him as if he had dropped something. His copper hair was fading in color, but his round face was smooth.

"I'll take one of everythin'," said Ian, slapping his hand on the counter.

"Now how am I supposed to pack—" The man stopped as he finally looked up at us. "Ian m'boy! Back so soon?"

"Well, you see, I ran into somebody." Ian pulled me forward.

Ian's father looked at me, but must not have seen any white hair under the hood, for he didn't react strangely. His smile broadened mischievously as he looked back at Ian.

"Got yourself a girl! And a pretty one at that."

Ian turned the exact color of his hair.

"What! No, you've got the wrong idea, Dad. It's nothin' like that. I'm just helpin' her!"

"Sure," he said with a wink.

Ian mouthed like a fish out of water.

"You have a lovely shop, sir," I said, trying not to laugh at Ian.

"Thank you, miss. I take much pride in what I bake," Ian's father said, slapping his round belly jovially.

"Glad to hear it. I know a chef that would be envious of what you have here," I said, thinking of Frank, but I stopped quickly. It was painful to think of home.

Ian's father chuckled appreciatively. He smiled at me broadly and said, "So where did m'boy meet you?"

"At the Quail Inn," Ian said quickly. "In Vitnor."

"Ah, very nice place, Vitnor, I should go there more of'n. Uh, do you live in Vitnor?"

"No, I—"

"Really, Dad, I'm sure Leah here would *love* to answer your questions," Ian interrupted smoothly, "but we've had a rough time of it and were hop'n we could stop at the house for a bit."

"Why didn't ya say so," Ian's father exclaimed. "Good Lord, I hav'n even introduced m'self." He thrust out his hand and said, "Name's Tarren, Tarren Grinshaw."

"Leah Vindral," I replied as he shook my hand energetically.

"I was just about to head back there anyway. We can go together," Tarren said to Ian. "I'll be right behind ya. Gotta take care of a few more things. I'll just leave Dana in charge. Dana! Dana!"

He disappeared through a door behind the counter and a few moments later he had reappeared, pulling on his cloak, "And don't let that old Tipton take anythin' else without first paying for the half dozen loaves he owes me!" He closed the door behind the counter and said jovially, "Let's be off!"

We left the shop and Ian and I mounted our horses while Tarren disappeared around the back of the building. He returned on a cream-colored horse that moved slowly with a slight limp.

Bell Sound seemed like a peaceful place to live. The houses were small and made of stone, and the children ran about in the yards while their parents talked over fences. A strand of white hair fell forward and drifted lazily before my eyes. I hastily tucked it behind my ear, but nobody seemed to have noticed. I wondered ruefully how long I would have to keep my head covered.

The Grinshaws lived at the other end of the village. Their house was a three-story stone building surrounded by a sea of pale, green grass. I pulled my cloak tighter as a sharp wind blew past. A barn was erected a little ways from the house with a fenced-off area for the animals. When we were almost at the house the door banged open as three children rushed toward us, yelling at the top of their lungs.

"Daddy's home!"

They all grabbed their father and hugged him tightly, completely ignoring Iris and I. They then caught sight of Ian and grabbed hold of him.

"Mommy said you wouldn't be back so soon," a little boy said to Ian.

"Ha," Ian laughed. "Won't Mommy be surprised."

"How's your Mother?" asked Tarren, as he lifted the smallest of the children into his arms and continued to walk up to the house.

"Fine," chirped the girl in his arms.

I walked behind them in silence; I didn't want to interrupt but I didn't know where to put Iris. Just then Tarren turned around and said, "Now which one of you wants to show our guest, Leah Vindral, where the stable is?"

As if they had been offered one of the greatest pleasures in life, the children jumped up and down, pleading for their father to pick them.

"Let's see, Timmy, how about you show her."

Ian put the boy down. He smiled a toothy grin, and said, "Over here," and ran as fast as his legs would carry him, making the chickens flap furiously out of his path.

"You'd better hurry up," said Tarren with a smile.

I led Iris after Timmy and soon spotted him standing before a wooden stable. The smell of straw was heavy in the air as I put her in one of four stalls.

"Who are you?" Timmy asked bluntly.

I closed the stall door and faced him slowly.

"Leah Vindral." I bent down, hands on my knees, and asked, "How old are you?"

"Seven," he said puffing out his chest.

"Your mother and father must be proud."

"They are."

I couldn't help but smile at the pure smugness that bubbled from the little boy.

"Do you think you could show me to the house?" I asked, straightening up.

Without hesitation he grabbed my hand and pulled me out of the stable to the house. The sun was close to setting and I could see the shadow of the moon in the sky. The windows of the house glowed warmly. Timmy opened the door and walked in. Tarren and Ian, surrounded by the other children, were sitting at a wooden table in the kitchen.

"Ah, Leah there you are. I thought Timmy had given you a tour of the grounds," Tarren said, standing up and walking up to me.

"If he had, I'm sure it would have been wonderful," I replied. Timmy stood peaking up at me from behind a woman, who I could only guess was his mother, smiling bashfully at such a compliment.

"So this is the girl you were telling me about?" asked the woman. She shot a glance at Ian whose ears were a bit red. He picked up a potato and eyed it closely.

"Yes indeed!" Tarren grabbed my wrist and pulled me to the center of the room, near the table. "Everyone, this is—"

The door opened and another young girl entered.

"Meg where have you been?" asked her mother, advancing toward her, holding the spoon in her hand like a sword.

"Don't worry, Mother" said the girl, slightly exasperated. She looked around thirteen or fourteen, with wild hair and blue eyes.

"You better not have been at that lake again!"

"I can swim," Meg said indignantly.

"*Hem hem.*"

They all turned to stare at Tarren who still had hold of my wrist.

"Oh, my," Ian's mother said, color tinting her cheeks, "how rude you must think us, my dear. I am Amelia Grinshaw." She extended her hand to me and I shook it politely.

"Like I was sayin'," said Tarren, clearing his throat again, "I had a very interesting day and around late afternoon Ian and this young girl appeared at my door."

"You are very welcome to stay my dear, but I'm sorry to say that we don't have an extra room. You'll have to share with one of the girls," said Amelia kindly.

"I really don't mind," I said, smiling. "It'll be nice to sleep inside for a change."

Ian was the only one who laughed. Amelia stared at me worriedly but she quickly recovered.

"Well, it—it's wonderful to meet you, Leah. You already know Tarren and Ian. The littlest one is Carey… the one with the brown hair is Linda. The one that just walked in is Meg, and from what I've heard you've been introduced to Timmy already," she said, putting her hand on Timmy's head. "Everyone, dinner's ready."

I sat between Meg and Timmy. As I scratched my ear, my hand brushed my hood. It must have looked very foolish to the others so I uncovered my head.

Amelia stared at me with wide eyes, her back stiff in her chair. Ian sat hunched over his plate with his eyes darting from person to person. The young children gaped and little Carey pointed. The only one that didn't act shocked or bothered was Tarren, who hadn't noticed anything since he was loading his plate with carrots.

Heat flooded my checks and I looked awkwardly at my hands as they twisted in my lap.

"Why isn't anyone eating?" asked Tarren who had finally noticed the silence at the table. He looked up, caught sight of me and looked momentarily stunned, but then his whiskery face broke into a wide smile and he turned to Ian. "So this is what you meant!" He laughed at my confused expression. "When you were in the barn, Ian told us there was somethin' different about you," he explained with a kind smile. "Pass the roast, Meg, would ya?"

With that, we ate. The children continued to shoot curious glances at me and finally, I allowed Timmy to touch my hair. His complete awe was enough to keep me laughing for days.

When dinner had finally come to an end and the last dish was washed, Amelia turned to me and said, "You can share Meg's room. I can bring down an extra mattress from the attic. Come on now, all of you off to bed."

Out of the corner of my eye, I saw Tarren put a hand on Ian's arm to make him stay. I pretended I hadn't noticed and followed Meg and the others up a flight of stairs.

Meg took a right at the top of the stairs and opened a door to a small room with a bed and dresser crammed inside.

"We can put the mattress over there," Meg said with a wave to the corner. She averted her eyes and sat down on her bed.

I stared around the room in silence and Meg focused on her shoes. Then I heard the sounds of heavy footsteps and turned to see Amelia walk into the room, dragging an old, dusty mattress and a handful of sheets.

"It's the best we can do," Ameila said. She dropped the mattress on the floor in the corner. "Meg, give Leah one of your pillows, won't you."

"Sure," Meg said.

"Well, sleep well girls," Amelia said with a small wave, as she closed the door.

I could hear her feet on the stairs. She was going back down to the kitchen where Ian and Tarren were. With sleep itching at my eyes, I bent over to fix up my bed. It hadn't been long when Meg finally spoke.

"Who are you?"

I straightened up and looked at Meg. She sat on her bed with her hands gripping the mattress as if bracing herself for some kind of shock.

"Leah Vindral," I replied.

"No, I mean where did you come from?"

I stared at her, my mind working furiously. I had told Ian everything; should I tell Meg, even if she was Ian's sister?

"I used to live in a manor a good ways from here," I replied, turning back to my bed.

"In what village?" asked Meg quickly.

"It wasn't in a village exactly, but close to the Langdale Mountains."

"How did you … you know … "

I looked at her and knew that this was what she really wanted to know: how in the world did I get to look like that? Meg seemed to know that this was something she shouldn't ask and leaned back looking unconcerned, as if she really didn't care about how I looked that way.

I got into bed and pulled the covers up to my chin.

"Sleep well, Meg," I said, pleasantly.

She grunted and blew out the candles. I heard the creak of her bed as she settled down but I didn't hear the tell-tale sounds of sleep from her for an hour. Just as I was dozing off, I heard a group of muffled foot steps making their way up the stairs and I knew that Ian, Amelia, and Tarren were finally done talking. The question that was gnawing inside of me as I closed my eyes was: how much did Ian tell them? I trusted him, but I didn't know about his family. I liked Tarren, and Amelia seemed polite enough, allowing me room and board. But I was on the run from knights, and Mora was still out there plotting who knew what. It was as if an ice cube had slipped into my stomach as her cold face drifted before my eyes. Clutching the covers tighter around me, I tried to suppress a shudder.

# Chapter 25
# The Tale

The next morning, I awoke to an empty room. A brilliant stream of sunlight beamed over Meg's unoccupied bed. I sat up, stretched, and yawned.

"LEAH!"

I lowered my arms and stared at the door.

"Leah, if you want breakfast you better come now!" Ian yelled up the stairs.

With a sigh, I stood up and went slowly downstairs, bracing myself for more stares and questions, but Ian was the only one in the kitchen.

He was stirring a large pot that bubbled thickly. Ian put a ladleful in a bowl and handed it to me with a hunk of bread. "After you eat we can take a walk. Timmy missed you this mornin'. He kept askin' me when you were gonna wake up."

"Sorry to keep him waiting for so long," I said with a smile. "Where are the others?"

"Mom and Dad and Carey are off in town and the others are somewhere 'round the place," Ian said.

When I finished, Ian and I went outside, walked through a flock of chickens, all clucking merrily, and headed straight for the stables. Iris was very happy to see me. She rubbed her nose against my cheek and neighed softly.

"She was whinnyin' like a storm this mornin'," Ian commented.

I brushed her nose and whispered more to myself than anyone else, "I don't know what to do."

Ian cocked an eyebrow and opened Merlin's stall door just opposite Iris's.

"Go on and take her out," he said over his shoulder. "We'll take them down to the lake."

When Merlin and Iris were ready, Ian led the way across the yard and down a hill. By the time we arrived at the lake, the only part of the house we could see was the tip of the roof. The lake was large and sparkled brilliantly under the sun's rays. A group of swans cut their way smoothly across its surface. Ian and I sat down under some trees and watched the swans as Iris and Merlin grazed a short distance away. I could just hear Timmy and Linda playing in the distance.

"So what's the problem?" Ian asked calmly.

"So many strange things have happened, and none of them make any sense." I twirled my marked finger around a blade of grass. "I know I need to find the unicorns, but I don't know where to start."

Ian stared across the lake in silence, his forehead furrowed. He closed his eyes and said slowly, "This all started when you got sick, right?"

"That's right."

"So this illness must have been the cause of everythin'."

"But my father said that the antidote altered me."

Ian sighed deeply and grimaced. "But it still started with the illness." He opened his eyes and turned to me. "D'you know the name of it?"

At first I didn't think I did, but then I remembered what Angora had said. "The sleeping sickness."

"Never heard of it."

"Do you think Amelia or Tarren might have come across it?"

Ian shrugged.

"By the way," I said with narrowed eyes, "what did you tell them last night?"

"Everythin'."

"*Everything?*"

"Yes, Leah, everythin'," Ian replied forcefully. "Don't look at me like that! I trust 'em—I know 'em. They'd never turn ya in."

"And they believed you?" I asked frowning.

"Course, I'm they're son, ain't I?"

"Well, what'd they think?" I asked, trying to retain some dignity.

"Not much more than us, I'm afraid." Ian picked up a rock and threw it into the lake. "When Mom was little she heard stories of unicorns but that was what they were—stories."

Ian continued to stare in frustration at the swans and an idea suddenly came to me.

"But King Rowan believes they're real," I whispered.

"What?" Ian grunted.

"Who convinced King Rowan that unicorns exist in a country full of people who think otherwise? In fact, the only ones I've come across who do believe they're real are magical."

"So you're tellin' me that some magical person knocked on King Rowan's door, convinced him that they're real and to hunt 'em?" Ian said with a quizzical eye. "But why? Why King Rowan of all people?"

"I don't know..."

We sat in silence again. My mind was quite blank as I stared at the swans.

"You know," Ian said, "I hadn't even heard of King Rowan huntin' the unicorns until you told me."

My eyes widened.

"You mean, he hasn't told the people?"

"Nope."

"So he must be trying to keep the hunt quiet so people won't start calling him crazy."

"He already seems kind of insane to me, personally."

Ian and I spent a good part of the day by the lake and when we finally headed back up the hill it was past noon. After lunch, we enjoyed ourselves watching Timmy and Linda chase the chickens. Meg stood a good distance from me and kept shooting odd glances in my direction, but I was surprised by how little I cared.

A short time later, when Timmy and Linda had finally gotten tired of chasing the chickens, Amelia, carrying a large bag in one hand and gripping Carey tightly with the other, appeared marching up the road. At the sight of her, Timmy and Linda rushed at her with gleeful cries, "What is it? Tell me! Tell me! Is it for me? Is it!?"

"Hush, you two!" Amelia commanded, but she smiled warmly at them. "Hurry up to the house so we can start dinner."

They flew past Ian and me, up the steps and into the house. Meg was the only one who had stayed leaning against the house with her arms crossed.

"Come on," Amelia said with a slight pant as she climbed the steps to the door, "I'm planning a nice large dinner. I'm gonna need as many hands as possible."

Meg followed her mother stiffly into the house.

"I don't think Meg likes me," I muttered to Ian under my breath.

"Nah. She hasn't gotten used to you yet, that's all. She's fourteen anyway; everybody's stupid at that age."

"Leah, I got you a dress," Amelia said to me as I entered the kitchen, pointing at the brown bag sitting on a chair.

"You didn't have to," I said taken aback.

"The dress you're wearing is torn and muddy," Amelia said with a sweeping gaze. "You need something better to wear. Now I need you over here."

She gave me a knife and a pile of potatoes.

"Cut these up for me, dear."

I nodded and she smiled sweetly and walked away. As I started cutting the first potato, I wondered why she was treating me so warmly. By coming here, I was endangering her family. Wherever I went, Mora and knights were sure to follow. I looked over at Ian who was getting instructions from his mother and rolling up his sleeves. Now, more than ever, I wanted to know what Ian had said about me.

It surprised me how much I enjoyed cooking. I had never done it before, unless you counted making potions as cooking. But it wasn't just the act of cutting potatoes that was peaceful, it was being with Ian's family. They treated me like one of their own, as if I was a distant cousin who had dropped by. Even Meg dropped her cold demeanor to help me slice onions. We were having a wonderful time, laughing and joking, when Tarren came home looking exhausted and wind blown.

"Hell of a day," he huffed as he took off his floppy hat and threw it on a chair. "First, old Tipton came by demanding three loaves of *sunflower* seed bread. I told him I didn't have anymore sunflower seed bread; why not instead a nice *poppy* seed loaf? No sir! *Sunflower* seed was what ol' Tipton wanted and he spent thirty minutes demanding to have them while I tried to convince him I didn't have any! And of course he still has'n paid me for the loaves from last week!" he grumbled.

"Don't let Tipton annoy you," Amelia said.

"But that's not all!" Tarren announced to the room. He slapped his hand down on the table. "People comin' in all day askin' for things I didn't have and Dana refusing to talk to me, much less help the customers. *And* I nearly got blown off the road comin' here! Hell of a storm's comin'."

"Here, you can vent your anger on these carrots, dear. Chopped, not sliced."

Tarren was right; there was a hell of a storm that night. As we set the table I could hear a faint whistle which grew into a steady howl that I feared would pick up the house and sling it across the yard. Rain pelted down on the house and lashed at the windows violently, but inside was warm and cheerful. Even Tarren couldn't stay in a bad mood as he stared at the steaming pots and pans on the table.

When dinner was over and Timmy and Carey were rubbing their eyes and yawning widely, Meg, Linda, and I rose from the table for bed, but Amelia stopped me.

"Leah, could you stay a little longer?" she asked pleasantly. "I'd like a word with you."

I nodded and sat back down, but with a slightly sinking feeling. Amelia shuffled the others up the stairs but not before I caught Meg shooting a suspicious look over her shoulder, obviously wondering how she could listen in on the conversation without her mother knowing.

"Come on, the rest of you up to bed," she shooed.

Their footsteps sounded loudly on the stairs and then, moments later, above our heads. Ian looked at me, opened his mouth to speak, but closed it and stared at his hands. My eyes wandered to Tarren, who was leaning back in his chair, staring at the ceiling, a far-away look on his face. We continued to sit in silence, listening to the wind howl and rain slash against the windows, until Amelia's feet sounded on the stairs and moments later, she entered the kitchen. She brushed her hair out of her face and sat down.

"There's no point in beating around the bush," Amelia said with a kind smile, "Ian's told us your difficulties"—Ian shot a quick glance at me and returned to studying his hands—"and Tarren and I want to help."

"I don't know how you can," I replied, slightly shocked at her pronouncement. Like Amelia said, there was no point in dodging the facts. "Unless you know how to find unicorns."

"What makes you so positive that they're real and not just fairy tales?" Tarren asked.

I hesitated.

"Because too many people are after them for them *not* to be real," I said. "If the unicorns weren't real, then Angora wouldn't be so scared of Mora returning to power, and Mora wouldn't be interested in helping King Rowan with his hunt."

Amelia closed her eyes tightly at the mention of Mora and Tarren's kind face darkened as if a cloud had passed overhead.

"I'm sorry," I said quickly, "You know of Mora?"

"How can we not know of Mora?" Amelia said bitterly. "I don't like thinking about those years if I can help it."

Tarren reached over and gripped Amelia's shoulder tightly.

"So these unicorns, they can bring Mora back?" Tarren asked.

"That's what Angora said, but I don't know the details."

"So everything rides on them," Tarren said, frowning.

I nodded and Amelia looked at her husband, concern etched over her face. He cleared his throat.

"Why don't you start at the beginning?"

"But I thought Ian told you everything." I shot a curious glance across the table and Ian shrugged in return.

"It's always best to hear the story from the horse's mouth," Tarren stated.

I took a deep breath and replied gloomily, "It's lengthy."

"We have all night," Amelia said with an encouraging smile.

I glanced at Ian who nodded slightly and, with a swallow, I started my tale.

Some parts were much harder to voice than I had expected. I hadn't yet realized how homesick I was until I had to speak of Father and Lavena in as much detail as Tarren and Amelia insisted. What I had told Ian had mostly been a summary of past events. My voice cracked unpleasantly whenever Father or Lavena entered the monologue. When I reached the sleeping sickness, Tarren and Amelia had such strange expressions that I asked with a hopeful edge, "Have you ever heard of it?"

"No," Tarren remarked, and Amelia shook her head in agreement. "Please, continue."

I started again, this time telling of my departure from Willow Manor and my encounter with the elves.

"Wait," Amelia interrupted. "You've been traveling all winter?"

"Yes." I found this an odd question.

"Didn't you get sick?"

"No."

"But that's impossible."

I shrugged my shoulders.

"I have wondered that before now," I admitted. "But I didn't bother worrying too much about it."

Tarren nodded his head for me to continue, but Amelia stopped me yet again when I mentioned the mark on my finger. I held my right hand out to her and she studied it closely. Tarren leaned toward it as well and said, "I've never seen anything like that before. It lit up, you say?"

I nodded, "I don't know how it happened, but it did."

"And the light scared the vors away?" said Amelia skeptically.

"Yes."

"Vors are only afraid of fire."

I shrugged.

"If that hadn't happened," Ian said quietly, "you wouldn't have had the pleasure of meetin' Leah or seein' me ever again."

"I'm sorry if I sound doubtful." Amelia released her hold. "It's just that anything that has to do with vors makes chills run down my spine. There have been too many close encounters with them over the years for my liking." She shuddered involuntarily.

I continued and finished without interruption.

"It's strange that I haven't heard of King Rowan's plan," Tarren said with a frown, rubbing his scruffy chin.

"Leah and I were discussin' that earlier today," said Ian. "We were wonderin' who might have convinced King Rowan of their existence."

"Someone would have had to," Tarren replied, nodding. "King Rowan always believed solely in concrete facts. He wouldn't believe there were giants 'less he saw one walk past him. And when he did, they almost became extinct. Maybe the unicorns are smarter than we think, staying in the dark," he added with a dry smile. "That's what's bothering me—why the sudden change?"

"Maybe he saw one," Ian suggested.

"I don't think so," I said with a frown. "I think he would have told my father if he had. He really wanted him to join the hunt."

"So someone must have gone to him," Amelia concluded. "So the question remains: why and how did he convince the King?"

"Could it have been Mora?" Ian asked. "She has the most to gain."

I frowned as Amelia and Tarren looked from Ian to me.

"I don't think so," I said slowly.

"Why not?" Ian persisted. "She may not have done it herself. She could have sent some messenger."

"Yes, she could have done that," I said frowning.

"You don't sound convinced," Tarren observed.

"Angora didn't think Mora knew about the hunt."

"Angora could have been wrong," Ian argued.

We looked at each other in silence. Finally Tarren cleared his throat and said, "I think you should stay here for a while, Leah."

"But the knights will be searching every village close to the city. They're bound to come here," I replied, but I was still grateful for his care. I didn't want to leave their home; I had been reunited with a sense of family. But at the same time, I couldn't bear the thought of them being in danger because of me.

"It's better to have a plan than to go wondering around," Amelia countered. "You'll be safer here."

I opened my mouth to argue, but with one look at Tarren and Amelia's determined faces I closed my mouth and nodded, smiling.

A few minutes later, we left the kitchen and went to bed. Meg was sound asleep, even with the continuous pounding outside from the storm. I closed the door softly and was slowly crossing to my mattress in the corner when I saw it. Right outside the window, sitting on a swaying branch, was a raven. Its black eyes stared into mine for half a second before it suddenly opened its wet wings and disappeared into the stormy night.

# Chapter 26
# The Raven's Eye

"Leah. Leah wake up!"

"Wha—"

"I want to know what happened last night!" said Meg, pushing my shoulder.

I rolled onto my back and squinted at her.

"I want to know what happened last night," she repeated.

"You mean you didn't sneak down and listen in?" I rubbed my eyes as I sat up.

"Mom would have skinned me!" Meg gasped, horrified by the very idea. She leaned back on her heels as I yawned. She waited a few seconds before blurting out impatiently, "*Well?*"

"Well what?" I must say, I was enjoying tormenting her.

She glared at me and jumped when a knock sounded against the door. It opened and Amelia's face appeared.

"Hurry up, you two and come down for breakfast."

Meg and I dressed quickly. The outfit Amelia had gotten for me fit surprisingly well, given that she didn't know my measurements. It was a plain brown and green dress that reached my ankles and was much easier to move around in than the long gowns I had been wearing before.

I stood by the door, waiting for Meg to finish getting dressed. My eyes roamed the room lazily before resting on the tree outside of the window. The storm had blown through, leaving the scenery looking washed, much like a watercolor painting. I focused on a small brown bird that had just landed on a branch, twittering loudly. In a flash, I was completely alert. A raven had been perched there last night. But it was just a bird, wasn't it? A simple bird that got lost in the storm. Then why was I suddenly cold?

"What's the matter?"

I jumped slightly. Meg stared at me, a puzzled frown creasing her forehead.

"Nothing," I replied quickly. "Ready to go down? I'm starving."

Meg continued to frown curiously as we went downstairs.

Everyone was in the kitchen eating when Meg and I entered. Tarren looked at me over his plate and smiled as I sat down, and Amelia passed me a dish of eggs.

"Sleep well?" Amelia asked.

"Yes, thank you," I answered.

Tarren swallowed a large mouthful of eggs.

"Leah, I'd like you to stay at the house," he said. "It'd be best for you not to make contact with the villagers."

He rose from the table, grabbed a biscuit and said, "I'm off to work."

"And keep your ears open," Amelia yelled after him as he put on his coat and hat. She looked at me and explained, "It'll best to know if the knights are near the village."

I nodded and finished eating. I didn't want to tell Ian about what had happened last night in front of Amelia. It would have likely put her even more on edge and I wasn't even sure why *I* was on edge. I caught Ian's eye and signaled toward the door. He got my drift and—slightly crestfallen—returned the serving spoon back to the eggs and followed me outside.

"What is it?" he asked the moment we were out of ear shot.

"Something weird happened before I went to bed… " and I told him about the raven outside Meg's window.

"But it was just a bird," Ian said dismissively.

"Or was it?"

"What d'you mean?"

I took a deep breath. "Mora has a raven. I saw it. It looked like a pet."

"So? People have pets. And anyway, we have ravens 'round here."

"You didn't see it," I replied shortly. "It didn't look normal."

"What wasn't normal about it?"

"It—oh, I don't know! I just got a strange vibe from it."

Ian cocked an eyebrow and stared at me in amusement.

"Look, don't you think it's an odd coincidence that I met Mora who happens to have a pet *raven* and then, some weeks later a *raven* is outside the bedroom *I'm* staying in?"

"So what, you think a raven's spying on you?" he asked with a hint of disbelief in his voice.

"Maybe she can talk to it," I said, my temper rising. "I wouldn't put it past her. Lavena can talk to her owls."

"Leah, I think you're gettin' too jumpy," Ian replied. "It was just a bird. The odds of it bein' Mora's—"

"If you don't want to believe me, then fine," I snapped angrily.

"What is it you want me to believe?" said Ian, laughing. "There was a raven outside the window, so what?"

"Look, forget it. It doesn't have anything to do with you."

I turned away from him and marched back up to the house.

"Hey!" Ian yelled at me angrily. I could hear him running to catch up with me.

"You don't have to get all worked up about it!" Ian huffed as he caught up with me.

"It doesn't concern you, Ian."

I sped up and chickens flew out of our way. I marched up the stairs, ignoring Ian as I went. I entered Meg's bedroom and shut the door in his face.

"Hey!" He shouted, insulted.

"I need some time alone," I said through the door. "I'm sorry."

"No, no, don't apologize," he said dramatically. "I don't want to hear it." His feet banged against the stairs as he stomped to the floor below.

I turned slowly on the spot and stared around the room. No matter what Ian said, I *knew* that raven wasn't a normal raven. There was something different in its eyes... something intelligent... something *human.* I had long suspected that someone had been following me.

I had wanted so hard to believe that Angora was right—that Mora didn't know about me, but the truth was she did. She had given Sir William my description. *How* had she known? *How* had she discovered my existence while Angora had been so sure I was hidden? An icy feeling of dawning slowly crept into my stomach.

A mental image from long ago flashed before my eyes. I had been sitting in my bed, reading Philip's letters after my illness. I had turned to the window and saw a bird fly past. It had been very close. It must have been perched in the tree right outside the glass. It had black feathers.

My heart was racing. Could it have been a raven? If it had... if it had been Mora's—my stomach turned queasily—then she had known about me a long time ago. She had known about me the day after my recovery. I felt like I had been slapped in the face. I had seen so many ravens when I left Willow Manor, but I hadn't suspected them. I was in Raven Wood, after all. Could they all have been Mora's? Or was I just overacting?

I paced the room fretfully. If I was to believe that the raven I had seen last night was Mora's and if I was to believe that the bird outside my room at Willow Manor was Mora's, then why hadn't she done anything? If she had known about me from the start, then why hadn't she swooped down and grabbed me? She could have easily snatched me when I was at her cottage, so why hadn't she?

I stopped pacing and wrung my hands nervously. Maybe… maybe she was biding her time. She wanted her powers back—that was her goal, after all. She knew that I was connected to the unicorns. It would have been the smart move to stay in the background, waiting patiently for something to happen, send her raven to keep watch over me…

I looked down at the shiny mark on my finger. Rubbing it softly, I sank down onto Meg's bed and gazed at my knees, wishing more than ever that I was back home.

The sun's rays shot through the one, small window, casting a yellowish glow on the walls that slowly dimmed until I sat in darkness. There was activity down below my feet. Amelia's commanding voice drifted up through the floorboards along with the rattling of pots and pans. I knew I couldn't hide forever. With a deep sigh I stood and left the room.

Ian looked at me when I entered, but quickly turned his attention back to a heap of garlic, his back unnaturally stiff.

"Can I do anything?" I asked Amelia.

She spun on her heel, her hair falling wildly from her bun.

"No, no. I think we have everything under control, dear. Why don't you have a seat."

I glanced at Ian as I took a seat, but he didn't return my gaze. I bit the side of my mouth and stared at the wall.

Suddenly the door banged open and Tarren rushed in, wide-eyed and terrified.

"Tarren, what's the matter?" Amelia asked, looking alarmed.

"No time to talk Amelia!" Tarren's voice was strained and hoarse. He shut the door hastily. "They're here!"

"Who?"

"The knights!"

Ian dropped the garlic and I stood up so quickly that I knocked my chair over.

"Here? Now?" I whispered.

I couldn't believe it… they couldn't possibly have gotten here so quickly. They must have chosen to search Bell Sound first.

"I saw them coming this way," Tarren panted. "I only had a short head start. There's no time for Leah to leave."

We stood in silence, our minds suddenly blank.

"GO!"

Amelia pushed me up the stairs, Meg and the other children running behind us. We ran past Meg's bedroom and down the hall.

"In here."

Amelia opened a closet door that was filled with blankets and sheets. I stepped inside and crouched down as she and Meg threw sheets over my head. Just as Amelia shut the door I heard a pounding at the door below us.

Sweat beaded on my forehead immediately. I could barely breathe in the hot, stuffy, closet—but I could hear. My heart thumped horribly when Sir William's bellowing, yet muffled, voice come up through the floor boards.

"By order of His Majesty, I have permission to search your home."

I didn't hear a reply but Sir William must have gotten his way. Soon, the pounding of armored feet echoed through the house. I sat as still as a rock, not daring to breath. What if they searched the closet? What would I do?

The door suddenly opened and someone was tearing the sheets off me. I prepared myself to bite, claw, kick, anything to get away—but instead of a knight's, Ian's face appeared over me as the last sheet was removed.

"Ian!" I could have kissed him, I was so relieved.

He opened his mouth, but—

"Boy! What are you doing there!"

Ian slammed the door and I was plunged once again into darkness.

"Helpin' with the search, sir," Ian replied to Sir William. "If there's a criminal about I want to make sure my family's not harmed."

Sir William's footsteps grew louder until they stopped abruptly. My heart hammered as his shadow cut off some of the light at the bottom of the closet door.

"What's your name, boy?"

"Ian. Ian Grinshaw."

"I hope I meet you again. You'd make a good squire."

"Thank you, m'lord."

The doorknob turned slightly.

"There's no one in there, m'lord," Ian rushed. "I just searched it."

"I'd like to see for myself."

The door cracked open an inch and then—*CRASH!*

"What was that?" Sir William barked.

"I don't know."

The frantic movement downstairs grew louder and Sir William's footsteps banged down the hall toward the commotion. The door swung open again and Ian pulled me out. We ran down the hall and up a flight of stairs that led to the attic. He let go of my hand and started pushing against a large, dusty, window.

"What are you doing?" I heard another faint crash.

"This is the only way out." Ian gave another shove and the window creaked open.

*"Are you insane?"*

He nodded.

"With all that noise all the knights should be inside by now. We'll climb onto the roof and head for the stables." He acted like it was as simple as a stroll through a park.

I blinked at him, too stunned to reply.

"*Come on,*" he said fiercely. "Do you want to get caught now or later?"

I gaped at Ian as he forced himself through the small window. I moaned and quickly squeezed through the small window after him. As I stepped onto the roof, I heard another loud BANG downstairs. Walking on roofs, what would Miss Perish say if she saw me now?

"This way and stay low," he hissed.

Gritting my teeth I gripped my way over the roof. *Don't look down, whatever you do, don't look down.* We were at the back of the house and Ian pointed down at a trellis that was up against the wall. I nodded and he started climbing down it like it was a ladder. I followed him and we crouched low on the ground.

"We need to get to the stables," Ian whispered. "Let's make a run for it."

Staying low, we scurried to the barn.

"Go on in," Ian whispered, looking back at the house.

Iris was startled to see me so late.

"We're leaving," I whispered to her as I quickly put on her saddle and bridle.

The floor gave a creak and I spun around. It was only Ian. He walked over to Merlin's stall and started getting him ready as I returned to Iris.

"They didn't see us, but we don't have a lot of time," he said tensely.

When Iris and Merlin were saddled, we silently and cautiously headed for the woods. I kept looking over my shoulder, expecting to see Sir William and the other knights rushing from the house and toward us.

Like ghosts we flew through the woods, farther and farther from the danger of the knights. But I knew the truth. I would never be safe again until I found the unicorns. What had I gotten myself into? If I hadn't left Willow Manor none of this would have ever happened. I'd be safe in my bed with not a care in the world.

We traveled all night. I didn't ask where we were going; I was hoping Ian had a plan because I certainly didn't have one. By morning the trees had thinned and large patches of muddy soil ran between them. My eyes itched with sleep and my stomach growled loudly. Then I remembered. With a gasp I grabbed at my sides.

"I didn't bring it!" I exclaimed.

"Bring what?" Ian turned in his saddle.

"The Replenisher."

"We'll have to get food the old-fashioned way, won't we?" said Ian grimly. "There's an inn farther up ahead. We should be there by evenin'. We'll stay there until we decide what to do."

I nodded my head in agreement, disgusted with myself.

Soon we found the little inn, in the middle of a field, with a round, rosy-cheeked innkeeper.

"Ian, my lad, how y'doing? Amelia and Tarren well, I hope?" chattered the innkeeper loudly. "How y'sisters and brother—still running round like mad I presume? But I mustn't babble on. What has brought you, my lad, what's brought you?"

"We need a place to stay for the night, Seb," Ian said as he warmed his hands by the fire in the hearth.

"You and . . . ?"

I had just walked through the door. He stared at me as if transfixed. I pushed my white hair out of my eyes and stared at the innkeeper. Forgetting the

Replenisher had not been our only mistake. We had been forced to leave without cloaks.

"Yes," Ian said firmly, breaking through the heavy silence.

I felt a spurt of respect for Ian.

"This way," said the innkeeper tersely, as if he was doing this against his better judgment.

We followed him up a set of stairs and down a narrow hall with doors placed evenly down both sides. He shuffled past three doors and stopped in front of one on the right.

"Your room," he said to me pointing at the door, "And yours." He glanced at Ian and pointed at the door to the left, just opposite mine. He gave us our keys, mine rather roughly, and left.

I unlocked the door and entered, closely followed by Ian. It was small and simple, though a little dusty, with a bed and a single circular window. Ian shut the door, crossed his arms, and leaned against it.

"So, where to now?" he asked.

I bit my lip, my gaze focused on the window. The sky was steadily darkening.

"I don't know. We haven't learned anything to lead us to the unicorns."

He moved into the room and sat down on the bed, looking at his feet. I walked past Ian and swung the window open. Spring was well on its way. A cool breeze gently played on my face. Where could the unicorns be? No one seemed to have any idea, except the elves and they weren't exactly around to ask. If only I had more information about them.

"I've got it!" I yelled, excitedly, making Ian spring up from the bed in surprise. I spun around from the window. Why hadn't I thought of it before?

"You've got what?" Ian asked, looking at me with concern, as if—in his opinion—I had finally lost it.

"Right before I left Willow Manor I looked up unicorns in the library."

"So?"

"*So,*" I said, hardly able to contain my glee. "I found a drawing of one and it had *mountains* in the background! Don't you see? *Mountains!* The unicorns must live in a mountain range!"

Ian smiled triumphantly, but then he frowned and said shrewdly, "Are you sure? What if the book was wrong?"

"Well, it's all we've got," I said, still amazed that I hadn't thought of it earlier. "What are the different ranges—Langdale . . . ?"

"Autorian and Brendor," Ian finished.

"Which do you think we're closer to?"

"Pretty sure the Brendor."

"Then we go to the Brendor first," I said happily, clapping my hands together.

"We should probably leave early," Ian said, his expression suddenly hardening. "That Sir William won't stop before he's found you."

"If he asks anyone in the village for a girl with white hair, he'll be told about you too," I pointed out. "You're not safe either. Plenty of people saw us together."

Ian rubbed his chin, frowning slightly.

"You hungry?" he asked suddenly.

"*Starving.*"

Wishing that I had a cloak so that I could cover my head, I followed Ian downstairs. He was familiar with the inn and headed straight to the kitchen, where a woman served us lamb and potato stew with bread. We ate quickly, trying to stay hidden in a darkened corner. Thankfully there was only one other pair of people eating.

Ian and I said good night and I locked my door. My head throbbed with exhaustion. I dragged my feet to the small bed and, without getting undressed, collapsed on the sheets and immediately fell asleep.

I dreamed I was home. I stood in the middle of the ballroom as the orchestra played a waltz and masked people danced around me. Father stood to one side, laughing and smiling at the revolving figures. But then the room changed. Instead of the colorful, warm ballroom, I stood in a dark bedroom where a girl slept. A chilly wind blew through a circular window. Quietly I inched closer to the sleeping girl… I saw her white hair… her pale skin…

I jerked awake, gasping for breath as if I had just run a race. Pale moonlight partially illuminated my dark room. My blood turned glacial—perched on one of the bedposts was a large raven. It ruffled its wings, its black eyes reflecting the moonlight. Suddenly, it cawed loudly, making me jump, and without warning opened its wings and flew through the open window. I flung off my sheets and rushed to the window, snapping it shut and bolting the latch.

# Chapter 27
# The Brendor Mountains

I'm not sure how I made it through the night. I sat on the bed, my back hunched up against the headboard, my arms wrapped around my bent knees. Now and then, I would drift off to an uneasy sleep before jerking awake again and quickly scanning the room for any intruders. When my room was lit by the soft early rays of daybreak, I heard movement downstairs. I sat frozen on the bed, listening carefully. The innkeeper must be awake and, from the sound of the rattling of pots, the cook as well. I slid off the bed, crossed the room, opened the door and pounded on Ian's. After a moment's silence, I heard shuffled footsteps on the other side and the door cracked open. A very tousled, bleary-eyed Ian blinked at me sleepily.

"Wha's matter?" Ian asked groggily.

"I think Seb and the cook are up." I couldn't help looking up and down the deserted hallway.

Ian inclined his head to listen.

"Sounds like it." He yawned loudly. "It can't even be daybreak. Why do you want to leave so early? Leah, what's the matter? You look terrible!"

"I just want to get out of here," I replied.

He nodded. "Just let me get dressed."

He closed the door, leaving me to wait in the corridor, and a moment later he reemerged from the bedroom.

"The cook will be very surprised to see us so early," said Ian.

And so she was.

"We have a long way ahead of us," Ian explained to her.

She gave us our eggs and boiled ham, and, as we sat down, I saw Seb walk past the kitchen's open door.

"How long have you known Seb?" I asked Ian, who was shoveling food into his mouth.

"Most of m'life," Ian said after a large swallow. "Why?"

"I think he's suspicious of us," I muttered.

Ian let out a short laugh that sounded more like a bark.

"Seb tries to get into everybody's business. Don't worry 'bout him. Now you tell me," he said, suddenly serious, "what happened to you? Y'look like you didn't sleep a wink."

After I had made sure we were alone, I told Ian in an undertone what had happened.

"There was a raven in your room?" Ian asked stunned.

"Yes. You can't call that normal."

"No, I suppose not." He frowned at his fork. "Gettin' a bit more dar'n, isn't it?"

"So, now you believe me?" I asked waspishly.

He smiled weakly and looked down at his ham.

"Do you think it was Mora's?" he asked.

"I think so. I think she's having it follow me." And I told him how I suspected the raven had been following me ever since I recovered from the sleeping sickness. He didn't argue with me.

"So, do you think I'm right?" I pressed.

He didn't reply immediately. "Yeah, I think the raven's following you."

We sat in silence before he suddenly said without looking at me, "You could have come to me, you know."

"I didn't want to bother you," I replied, slightly taken aback, but pleased all the same. "Anyway, the raven flew off ... I just would have felt ... silly ... " I was suddenly aware that my cheeks were turning red and, horrified, I quickly looked down, busying myself with buttering a biscuit.

Ten minutes later we had paid for our rooms and had saddled Merlin and Iris.

"Where you off to in such a hurry, Ian?" called Seb from the doorway.

"Nowhere you'd be familiar with, Seb," replied Ian jovially over his shoulder.

I mounted Iris and started her down the path away from the inn.

"Shame to see ya go so quickly," Seb said conversationally. "Well, just want to make sure ya don't get into trouble, son. You know where I am if ya need help."

My back stiffened. Ian mumbled his thanks and soon Merlin was trotting up beside Iris.

"You could have at least said goodbye," Ian scolded.

"Seb doesn't like you being around me," I said, ignoring Ian's remark. "He thinks I'll probably curse you."

"Don't be ridiculous!"

"Don't tell me you didn't see all those scathing looks he gave me."

"Scathin's a bit harsh. He just doesn't know you."

"How long till we're there?" I asked in exasperation.

"The Brendor Mountains? They're a good week's journey."

I felt myself sink in the saddle. *A week*—maybe more if we got delayed, and no Replenisher. It would be horribly risky to go into towns for food. Sir William was probably asking everyone about a white-haired girl.

"Have you ever been to the Brendor Mountains?" I asked.

"No, but I know how to get there!" he rushed at the look on my face. I hadn't forgotten the Braxton Bog fiasco. "No, honestly—m'dad's been there and he's told me the way ... he wanted to take me along, but Mom wouldn't let me go."

"Why?"

"Dragons."

I pulled on Iris's reigns and she reared slightly.

"What?" Ian asked, looking over his shoulder at me.

"There are *dragons* in the Brendor Mountains?"

"Course, didn't y'know?"

"Dragon habitats aren't exactly a lesson topic for a governess's pupil."

"Don't worry," said Ian, waving his hand lazily, as if dragons were hardly worth worrying over. "Dragons usually stay deep in the mountains. We probably won't even see one's tail."

As we galloped over the rippling fields, with daffodils dotted here and there, I hoped he was right.

We stopped for dinner in an open field. Ian caught a large hare for us while I gathered firewood. We were both stretched out on the ground, stomachs full, sleepily staring up at the stars.

"What are you going to do once we've found the unicorns, Ian?" I asked suddenly.

"I don't know," he said peacefully. "I guess I'll go back to what I was doin' before I met you. You'll be headin' back home, right?"

I swallowed. There was suddenly something large and painful in my chest.

"Ian, have you ever judged someone too harshly?"

"Plenty o' times."

"Did you give them a second chance?"

"Have to when they're family," he said with a gloomy sigh. "Why?"

"No reason," I sighed.

The long trek to the Brendor Mountains was not an easy one. For three days rain swept over us, and the sky stayed a steady, gloomy gray. A few times, Ian had to ask passing travelers or farmers for directions, to make sure we were heading the right way. During these encounters, I would stand beside Iris, using her to hide me from curious eyes. We didn't enter villages, if we could avoid it. Usually, Ian would catch something to eat, but sometimes the rabbit would get away, and he was forced to enter a village and buy food while I waited on the outskirts. I was relieved, but my happiness was tinged with apprehension when the tall peaks of the Brendor Mountains finally jutted against the horizon.

"They certainly are tall," I said, hoping to sound indifferent.

"The Brendor Mountains are the tallest in all Torona. Surely your governess taught you that."

"Maybe," I said, shrugging. "I never paid much attention in her lessons."

I could feel a huge lump in my throat grow larger with every step that brought the mountain range closer. They were massive—a giant could have made each mountain its home—and ended in sharp, jagged peaks.

"Ian," I said, looking up at the mountains doubtfully, "I don't think unicorns live there."

"There are valleys and nooks in the mountains," Ian answered. "M'dad told me all 'bout them. That's where most of the villages are. I'm sure there are valleys hidden away that are a bit more difficult to get to. That's where we should look."

By nightfall we were half a day's journey from the first mountain. I rolled on my side and stared at a pebble, listening to the night sounds. Soon, Ian's snores accompanied them. Somehow, I drifted off to sleep…

The next morning, Ian woke me bright and early. On the way to the mountains, I spotted a few strangely sticky plants with pink flowers that I immediately recognized as Feverfew. Lavena had told me that Feverfew, when used in the correct potion, deflected dragon fire. She had never told me how to make it, but I dismounted anyway and plucked a few leaves and flowers from the plant. Maybe, just by itself, it could keep a dragon away? Maybe they didn't like the smell of Feverfew. It did have a very pungent smell, like that of an overripe melon.

Ian had stopped Merlin and was staring at me curiously.

"What are you doing?"

"Picking Feverfew," I answered. "It's used in potions to deflect dragon fire."

"That's great and all, but I don't think we have time to make a potion."

"I couldn't even if I wanted to," I said, pocketing the sticky leaves. "I don't know how."

"Then why waste your time picking the plant?"

I glared at him.

"Because it may keep them away. You can have some too, if you want."

"No thanks," Ian said grinning. "I'll take my chances."

I mounted Iris and we continued to the mountains, but I stopped and picked more Feverfew whenever I spotted any. Soon, my pockets were bulging and Ian only shook his head in exasperation as he watched me stuff my pockets. I think he thought I was utterly mad, and even though a part of my brain agreed with him that it was probably pointless, it made me feel like I was doing *something* other than fretting about what lay before us. By midday we were staring up at the first mountain's sloping hillside.

"There are paths, but it's gonna be tricky," Ian said, as he led Merlin up the hill.

"What have I gotten us into?" I mumbled to Iris. She shook her head and slowly we followed Ian and Merlin.

The climb was slow and demanding. At times the path was so rocky and narrow I had to put my hands down to steady myself. Iris's hooves slid under her occasionally. Up ahead, Ian and Merlin were having the same difficulty. The higher we went the rockier everything became. There were no trees, but every yard or so there were scrawny, thorny-looking plants that barely came up to my waist. The ground was dry and dusty. As I wiped my sweaty brow, I wondered how anything could live here.

"Ian," I yelled after hours of climbing, "I really don't think the unicorns could be here." Ian poked his head back around a corner he had just passed.

"The valleys are a lot different than this. At least, m'dad said so. I think that's where all the animals live … 'cept the dragons."

"Of course, you *had* to remind me about the dragons," I said sarcastically.

"What?"

"Nothing."

Some time after that, when my hair was glued to my sweaty face, I stopped and turned around, looking back in the direction we had come from. My stomach flopped sickly. I had no idea we had climbed so high. The wide expanse of fields and trees stretched far down below me for miles, looking more like a patchwork quilt than anything else. My hand shook slightly as I brushed my sweaty hair out of my eyes and turned back around.

The ground was so uneven I had to watch my feet to keep from slipping. A butterfly fluttered just above my knee. Smiling, I followed its progress upward and toward the face of the mountain. On the stone were three long, jagged scratches, each one at least three feet long. A scorch mark the size of cow blackened the wall next to the marks.

Iris and I ran as fast as we could and soon bumped into Ian.

"Hey, watch where you're goin', Leah!"

"A—a dragon—a dragon was over there!" I gasped.

"Did you see it?" Ian asked, his eyes widening.

"No—but it was there."

Ian cocked an eyebrow.

"It was!" I yelled in fury. "There was a scorch mark and—"

"There must be thousands of scorch marks here. Don't be so jumpy."

"*Don't be so*—fine!"

I flipped the hair out of my face angrily as Ian continued and disappeared behind a bend. Just as I took a step to follow him, Iris pulled her head back sharply.

Something was very wrong. Her eyes were wide, nostrils flared, ears pricked back.

"What is it?"

Her head pointed at the sky and she reared wildly. Looking up, I stood momentarily stunned. Hundreds of feet above me hovered a dragon.

It flapped its wings once and *dived.* I was frozen—my mouth opened in a silent scream. Its jaws opened wide revealing rows of razor sharp teeth, its cat-like eyes contracted, and in a *swoosh,* I was grasped tightly in its claws. My stomach lurched sickly as Iris shrunk to the size of a dog.

The dragon soared over the mountain side and dived sharply, making my insides flip. I was sure we were going to crash into the side of the mountain, but a cave's opening appeared. The dragon landed with a tremendous thud, but it kept the claw holding me held high so that my feet barely brushed the ground. It was as if my voice had been left behind with Iris; I couldn't make a sound.

The dragon's cave was cool and wide, filled with mounds of bones and skulls, and smelled distinctly of charcoal. Every few feet there were scorch marks and jagged cuts in the walls.

The dragon snorted and tossed me into a pile of old bones. It towered over me, as I quivered like a hyperventilating mouse. A deep growl rumbled in its broad chest as it opened its mouth—

"*Damn it!*"

The dragon snapped its head toward the far end of the cave. I tore my eyes from the dragon and saw a small figure shuffling toward us.

"Zarendor, you bad dragon!"

The figure walked into the light, and I saw a very short, old, wizened man, shaking a gnarled staff in the dragon's face.

"If I've told you once, I've told you a thousand times—*don't bring humans to the cave!*"

The dragon hung its large, green head in disgust and jerked its tail much like a disgruntled cat. I flung my arms over my head to deflect the bones bouncing off the walls.

"I'm sorry, miss, bu—*leapin' lizards!*"

The man had turned to me and jumped back as if he'd stepped on a snake. With a clatter his staff dropped to the floor, and he hurriedly picked it back up. His face full of frustration, he rounded on his dragon.

"Your eyesight's getting worse everyday! Do you realize who you just caught?"

Zarendor leaned closer to me while I pressed myself flat against the wall. He sniffed and snorted loudly.

"Zarendor get!" the man said, exasperated.

The dragon stomped past the man and curled up like a cat in a corner, smoke unfurling moodily from its nostrils.

"I'm terribly sorry, miss," the old man said again as he wrung his gnarled hands together. "But he does have horrible eyesight."

"Oh?" I said, still plastered against the wall.

"I am Talen the Magician."

"A magician?"

"A *retired* magician. So don't even try to ask me to save some doomed kingdom because I just won't do it," he said, suddenly defensive. "That's why I yelled at Zarendor. I've had so many damsels in distress and knights knocking at my door that I just couldn't take it any more. I won't have it, I tell you! I won't!" He banged his staff angrily on the floor.

"Then I guess I'll be on my way," I said weakly. I started to rise, but Talen held out a wrinkled hand.

"What?" he asked startled. "Go? You can't go! Not yet!"

"Why not?" I asked taken aback. He hated visitors and now he suddenly wanted me to stay?

Talen stuttered and muttered as he twisted his staff jerkily, obviously agitated.

"Leave! The *nerve*. Barge into my cave and expect to walk out like nothing."

"I didn't *barge* in," I said, annoyed. "Your dragon brought me here!"

Zarendor snorted from the corner.

"The least you could do is show some manners," Talen snapped.

"Fine," I said and without further ado, I sat back down.

"You're staying, are you?"

"Don't you want me to?" I shot back.

Talen glared at me and finally murmured, "Truth be told, another human being is a pleasant change. Zarendor's a good companion and all, but it's nice to hear someone talk other than myself."

I smiled slightly at the old magician. For the first time, Talen stared fixedly at me, his eyes lingering on my face and hair before quickly inspecting his wooden staff.

"Zarendor *had* to catch … well, just my luck, I s'pose," he muttered under his breath.

"Sorry?" I said.

"You have the connection," he said in an audible whisper. "I haven't seen anyone with the connection in all these years."

A chill ran up my arms, even though it was quite warm in the cave.

"You know about the sleeping sickness?" I asked. "You know why I look the way I do?"

"Of course," Talen chuckled. He gazed down at me kindly. "You're very lucky."

"*Lucky?* How in the world am I lucky? Mora and the knights are after me. I can't go anywhere without people staring. I—"

Talen was chuckling and I stared at him, lost for words.

"How?" I asked. "How am I lucky?"

Talen took a few short steps toward me and his eyes seemed to glow.

"You've never met one, have you? No, you couldn't have." He slowly knelt down so that we were face to face. "But when you do, you will understand."

"Have you?" I whispered.

"Ah, yes." He closed his eyes blissfully. "Yes, I have. It was many, many years ago, but I still remember it clearly." He opened his eyes and said suddenly sharply, "But why are you here?"

"I'm trying to find them."

The magician's eyes widened, his eyebrows completely disappearing in his white hair.

"But they're not here," he said.

"You're sure?" My heart plummeted like a rock.

He nodded his head. "Quite sure."

I glared at the ground. All that trouble and for what?

"But I'm pretty sure they live in the Langdale Mountains, if that helps at all."

"Langdale?" I stared up at him.

"That's where they were rumored last," he shrugged.

I jumped up so fast that the magician stumbled backwards and dropped his staff again.

"Thank you very much!" I ran out of the cave and down the path.

The magician poked his head out of the cave and yelled, "You're welcome!"

***

I couldn't believe it. All this time searching Torona and they had been right next door to Willow Manor all along. All I had to do was find Ian and head for home. I actually got a small excited flip in my stomach at the thought of seeing Father and Lavena again. I had been away from them for so long—with a smile I thought to myself, *grudges aren't meant to last forever.* I was ready to go home.

I stopped running and walked quickly down a narrow path. How was I going to find Ian? It was very quiet. Talen's cave was far out of sight. Maybe I should go back and ask for his dragon to help me find Ian? Just as I was considering this idea, I heard frantic movements from behind a corner, and a few seconds later, Ian came blasting into view, Iris and Merlin shortly behind. He caught sight of me, gave a strangled cry and rushed to me.

"Ian," I yelled happily, "Thank goodness! I— "

"No time!" he panted, grabbing my wrist and pulling me into a jog.

"Ian, Ian stop!"

"You're right," he said coming to a halt so suddenly that I ran into his back. "Quick! Behind these boulders!"

He dove behind a large group of rocks and pulled me down to crouch beside him. "It'll see us for sure if we just run for it," he continued with a wild glint in his eyes, "we'll have to go slow—it won't be expectin' that—and duck behind—"

"Ian, will you stop?!" I yelled, trying not to laugh.

"You're right!" He stared at me shocked. "We're wastin' time—that dragon could already be after us! Did it hurt you? You look like you can run. Quick!"

He leapt up from behind the large, scorched boulder with his eager gaze focused on a thorny bush and was about to sprint like a prisoner to safety when I grabbed his arm.

"Ian, he let me go."

"There's no time, Leah. We have to—he what?" For the first time since my return from the dragon, the manic glint in his eye disappeared; his ruffled hair even seemed to wilt in disappointment, but then he shook his head, frowning. "It's put a spell on you, it has."

"Don't be ridiculous!" I laughed. But Ian still looked stubbornly unbelieving, so I grabbed his arm and nearly dragged *him* away. "I'll explain it on the way, now can we simply walk?"

I explained everything that had happened in the cave to Ian on our descent of the mountain.

"He said the unicorns are in the Langdale Mountains? Are you sure you should believe him—a magician?"

"Why not? If he wanted me hurt he could have easily let his dragon eat me and no one would have known. Anyway, the mountains in the drawing didn't look anything like the Brendor Mountains."

That night we reached the base of the mountain. Before I settled down to sleep I watched the sunset turn into a brilliant twilight, feeling more peaceful than I had in a long time.

## Chapter 28
# Imprisoned

The towering peaks of the Brendor Mountains sank into the horizon and slowly out of sight as we journeyed for a week with our backs to them. Our plan was simple: skirt the perimeter of the Ash Moors and head southeast. What direction southeast was exactly, I had no idea, but we stopped at each village we passed. I would stay on the outskirts of the town, making a fire, while Ian asked for directions and got food. Safe and perfect ... at least it seemed that way in our heads. But I should have known after all my traveling that it wouldn't be so easy.

Some villages, it seemed, had heard of me—or at least had been told what I looked like. Ian had to be very careful in these towns because his description had also been reported by the knights. It seemed that someone in Bell Sound had told Sir William that the boy, Ian Grinshaw, had come to his hometown with a strange girl. I worried that it was dangerous for him to be seen by people, but Ian always argued that he was careful to stay in the shadows.

One day, one week after we had left the Brendor Mountains, we were walking slowly down a dirt road. It was late afternoon and there were only a few more hours till sunset. We were headed to Vitnor, the town—oddly enough—where Ian and I had first met. A sign a good ways behind us had said it was only a half mile away. Iris and Merlin walked at a slow, steady pace and the road was deserted. I was glancing into the woods when I spotted it. I pulled on Iris's reins and stared at a small bunch of plants at the base of a tree. They were very distinctive with their blue, jagged leaves.

"Leah? What are you look'n at?"

"Nothing," I said, pushing Iris to a walk. Ian had been teasing me about my Feverfew ever since we had left the Brendor Mountains. I wasn't in the mood to give him another plant to use against me.

On the outskirts of Vitnor, we stopped and made camp in the shelter of some trees. I started a fire, and Ian headed toward the town on foot. Iris and Merlin poked around the scraggly grass while I sat by the crackling fire, waiting for Ian. The sun was setting, bathing the sky in brilliant colors of orange, red and pink. It was beautiful and I was pleasantly entertained. Then, when only a sliver of the sun was still visible, I started to get worried. Ian had been gone an awfully long time. Had he been recognized? Had he been caught?

There was a sudden shuffling of leaves to my right and I jumped up. After a tense moment, Ian stumbled through a clump of bushes.

"Ian! I've been worried. What-what happened?"

Ian had just stepped close to the fire. His entire sleeve was red with blood.

"It's nothing. Nothing," Ian grumbled as he jerked his bloody arm out of my reach. His face was horribly pale and he swayed slightly. He gripped his arm tightly and I saw a long rip in the stained sleeve.

"That doesn't look like nothing. Ian, sit down." I helped lower him to the ground. "*Sit.* I'm going to find some Farlex; I thought I saw some on the way here."

"Farlex? What the hell is that?" he said through gritted teeth.

"Just stay here. Will you stay?"

"Yes, mother," Ian grumbled, gripping his arm.

I had already taken five strides from him toward the dirt road we had come from. The sky was a soft blue that was darkening quickly. I needed to find it soon. I walked off the road into the canopy of trees, searching the ground for the small, dark green plant. It had been somewhere near here … or maybe farther on?

"Aha!" I yelled joyfully.

There next to the base of a tree was a clump of Farlex. I hadn't been able to inspect Ian's arm, but from the looks of the rip in his shirt and the large amount of blood, it was deep. I picked a handful of the jagged blue leaves and rushed back to Ian.

"What's that?" Ian asked suspiciously as I knelt beside him.

"Farlex. It'll heal your cut."

"A bunch of leaves?" Ian snorted skeptically. "I don't—hey! What d'you think you're doin'?"

I had just reached for his bloody arm which he had jerked away from me.

"Ian, I know what I'm doing," I said patiently. "Now will you let me help you?"

He eyed me uncertainly before he allowed me to see to his arm.

"Don't see how some leaves are gonna do anything," he muttered darkly.

I bit back a retort as I placed the leaves on his gash. It was deep and long, slashed across his forearm.

"How did this happen?" I asked.

"Well, I went into an inn, got directions to the Langdale Mountains and, by the way, we're dead on course. So I say, 'Thank ya' and head out. I'm walking down an alley and all of a sudden, I get jumped. Do you remember those buffoons that were at the Quail Inn, the ones I kept from gettin' into your room?"

I nodded.

"They recognized me," Ian said grimly. "I barely got away."

"Do you think you lost them?"

"Yeah, I think so. Ouch!"

"Sorry." I ripped off a piece of my dress and wrapped it around his forearm. "There. It should be good as new in the morning."

Ian stared at it critically before saying, "Thanks."

There was a silence between us and I fiddled with a broken twig next to my foot, feeling heat rise in my cheeks.

"Did you manage to get food?" I asked, still looking at the twig.

"Just a little, sorry to say. I got it before I went to the inn, but some fell out of the bag during the fight."

I opened the bag that he passed me with his good arm and extracted two small flagons of mulled wine, two loaves of bread, and a hunk of cheese.

"So," Ian was now examining his bandage, "What are these leaves going to do, exactly?"

"Heal your wound," I said, passing him some bread. "Lavena told me about Farlex. Don't worry, it'll work."

"I'm not *worried*," said Ian.

I smiled behind my flagon.

In the morning, we saddled up Merlin and Iris, and Ian—with much trepidation—unwrapped his bandage. It took all the strength I had to keep a straight face as he stared flabbergasted at his perfectly normal, unscathed arm. He didn't tease me anymore about the Feverfew.

We were far from Vitnor, riding down a long, dusty, dirt road. The weather was lovely now that spring had finally taken the place of winter. A slight breeze was blowing gently, birds sang happily, a few puffy clouds dotted a brilliant blue sky, and suddenly Iris stopped so abruptly that I nearly flew over her head.

"Iris," I snapped crossly. "What was that for?"

Iris snorted and Merlin reared a few feet in agitation. I strained my ears as I stared up the road. A clip-clopping sound was coming toward us.

"I think we need to get off the road," Ian said tersely.

But before we had even made a move, a group of men in green robes on horseback erupted from around a bend in the road. Seconds later, two more knights appeared through the brush on either side of the road. In a flash, we were surrounded.

From the group of glaring knights before us stepped a large molasses-colored stallion. It swished its tail and snorted at us imposingly.

"We meet again," Sir William said smugly from atop his large horse.

I expected him to look at Ian. After all, Sir William had just met him. But he didn't. He sneered down at me.

"His Majesty requests to see you … Leah Vindral."

I felt like I had been plunged in icy water. *How?* How did he know it was me?

"I'm afraid I don't understand you, sir," I said, hoping my face looked innocently curious.

"Don't bother trying to fool me girl!" Sir William barked. "You're coming with us, and if you even try to escape I will deal with you personally," he added in a cold whisper, his eyes darting between Ian and me.

There wasn't much Ian and I could do. We were surrounded. The knights formed a line with a knight on either side of Ian and me. Sir William trotted to the front of the line as if he ruled Torona.

"Forward," he commanded.

❧

I didn't know how far we were from Torona City until I overheard one disgruntled knight say to another,

"We'll be in Torona City in two days, won't we?" I saw him shoot a nervous glance toward me. Ian and I didn't dare speak to each other as we traveled down the road. We had to find some way to escape, but how? If I made the slightest move the knights would have me, and what did I have to fight them with? And I hadn't even begun to answer the question of how Sir William knew who I was.

Shortly after the knights had found us, it started to rain—a light steady rain—and the dreary weather continued until we came upon a small meadow. Sir William stopped and swerved his horse to look back at us.

"We'll stop here for the night," he boomed. "All knights set up camp except for you three"— he nodded his head at three burly knights —"keep watch on the prisoners."

*Prisoners?* I understood that Sir William enjoyed the role of commander but this was going overboard. The knights immediately jumped into action. The three knights Sir William had indicated marched over to us.

"Dismount," one said harshly.

My foot slipped slightly so that I fell closer to the knight than I had intended. He jumped backward as if he had been stung. I smirked inwardly. Not so tough after all, eh?

"Over there, against that tree," the knight spat.

The knights kept Iris and Merlin away from us, tethered to another tree. The three stood a good distance away, but their eyes never left us.

"Come up with a plan yet?" Ian whispered.

"I was hoping you had," I mumbled back.

"There's no way we would be able to sneak out of here. Sir William would rather give away his own children than lose us," Ian said darkly.

I nodded in agreement as I watched the scurrying knights. They moved quickly, setting up large tents. It seemed that ours would be last. I shivered and wished I had a cloak. The sun was setting rapidly and the temperature was going with it. We received our small portion of bread and cheese, accompanied by a miniature flask of water, our backs against a tree.

"She's an odd one she is. I tell you we never should have grabbed her."

My hand froze midway to my mouth as I heard a nervous voice a little way off. With a slight tilt of my head I could see five knights standing in a close circle. Ian and I exchanged looks and he tilted his head to hear better.

"You know His Majesty's orders!" said a young knight, who, from the looks of it, was flabbergasted at the idea that anyone wouldn't want to obey the slightest command from King Rowan.

"They're stupid orders, if you ask me!" said a short balding knight with a long pointed nose. "He always gives us a reason to go looking for someone. If it's a princess, she's been pinched by a bloody dragon. If it happens to be a damsel in distress most likely she's locked in some tower. Well, where are those reasons now, eh? Eh?" He looked around the group and a knight with jet black hair shouted "Here-here!"

"And look where we are, mates," said the short knight with enthusiasm. "Standing in mud, that's where. All because of the stupidest order that I think I've ever heard." He lowered his voice and straightened to his full height, poked out his chest and pointed down at an imaginary person. "Go find the girl with white hair and bring her to me for questioning, even if it means you'll freeze to death in the process."

The group of men laughed at his impersonation of the king, but the young knight frowned in distaste.

"I think you're right," said the man with black hair who had shouted his agreement with the short knight. I saw him shift his eyes to the tree I was sitting under. "I just have a bad feeling about that girl."

"Sean, you're too superstitious," said another, patting the knight on the back.

"I don't know John, I've seen enchantresses and she's a spitt'n image."

"Then why didn't she turn into a bird and fly away when we advanced on her?"

"Don't ask me how enchantresses think!" said Sean, a look of pure terror etched on his face. "They're frightenin' creatures!"

"Then why were you eyeing her while Sir William was interrogating her? Ehh?" said the short knight slyly.

Sean turned the color of a tomato on a hot summer's day.

"Don't feel bad Sean," said the knight named John, between gales of laughter. "Nobody could take their eyes off her, poor girl."

The short, balding knight stopped laughing long enough to notice a newly rustling fire: "Oh, perfect! Look, the idiots have finally started a fire. If you need me, I'll be over there trying to thaw out," he said, and without further ado, he hastily left the group with the rest of the men following him, still chuckling.

I ate another piece of bread.

"Enchantress, puh," Ian said with disgust. "You don't look anythin' like an enchantress. They're much taller and don't have white hair for starters."

"But I look like I've been touched by magic," I replied. "That's enough for superstitious folk."

Just then our tent was finally raised and we crawled inside.

The next two days went by quickly. The knights never bothered me, and, to my relief, Sir William never even looked at me. On the morning of the second day, Torona Castle's familiar towers loomed above us. The temperature seemed to drop around us as I gazed up at the impressive structure. A knight pushed me roughly to get me moving.

Sir William had us dismount in the courtyard and led us into the castle, along with several of his knights. My neck tingled as the knights surrounded Ian and me. That uneasy feeling increased dramatically as Sir William led us down an empty, torch-lit passageway. I didn't recognize anything around me, and I noticed that we were on a steady decline. The walls lost their handsome shine and became rough, dirty stone. The temperature decreased horribly and I heard the distant rattling of chains.

Ian had already guessed where we were heading. His eyes were dark, his mouth a thin line, and his face as white as a sheet of parchment. I looked at the back of Sir William's head in disbelief. No, no matter how pompous and arrogant he was, he would never send Ian and me to the dungeons. Ian had done nothing and if he really *did* know it was me, the daughter of his friend ... surely he wouldn't.

We passed several cells, each one dark and disgusting, filled with moldy, decaying hay and pitiful rags, which I soon realized were actually prisoners. Some cells were vacant but the ones that weren't horrified me most. Most of the prisoners rushed to the barred doors and groped the air for us with skeleton hands. Others sat hunched over in corners, their eyes glittering hollowly through the gloom.

The knights pushed us roughly onward, completely ignoring the screeching occupants. The pitiful cries and screams from the prisoners slowly faded to dull echoes as we marched down a nearly deserted hall. The knights unlocked two cells side by side and shoved us in. I felt like my heart had stopped for some seconds and jerked back into motion as the iron doors slammed shut. The knights left us, Sir William smirking triumphantly as he walked past my cell.

## Chapter 29
# Owl Sighting

"Leah! Snap out of it!"

"I can't believe it," I repeated hysterically for the fifth time. "*I can't believe it!*"

"You'd better start," Ian said sharply. "We've got to get focused."

My head swung around to stare at him through the bars.

"Focused? *Focused?* We're trapped in King Rowan's *dungeon*!" I said feverishly.

"And it's obvious why," Ian said bitterly. "Just imagine how high Sir William will go now that he's *personally* delivered you to the king. He may very likely become the king's right hand man."

Of course, the only thing that mattered to Sir William was power, and he wouldn't let anything stand in his way, not even the so-called friendship of my father.

"That's why you need to stay calm, Leah," Ian continued, a sound of urgency now in his voice. "You'll be interrogated. Sir William … he might try anythin'. Don't tell him anythin'."

Then it dawned on me—I might be tortured. But no, surely he wouldn't *torture* me. If Father found out—but what could Father do? He wasn't more powerful than Sir William, not powerful enough to override him. Suddenly, I felt disturbingly calm as I looked through the bars at Ian. Ian thought I couldn't handle it. He thought I'd spill everything.

"We have to get out of here," I whispered.

"But how—" Ian was cut off by sudden footsteps that echoed down the stone passageway.

A few seconds later, two knights appeared before my prison door. Without a word they unlocked the door and led me down the hall, out of the dungeon, leaving Ian behind.

The knights led me into the main castle—my eyes blinked painfully at the bright light—and stopped before a pair of extravagant doors. One knight knocked and opened the door, and the other pushed me roughly inside.

It was an expensively-made room, more so than the others I had walked by. The floor was a shimmering, rich maple; the ceilings were at least twenty-five feet high. Large statues lined the room, jewels and diamonds sparkled wickedly behind glass, comfortable chairs beckoned invitingly, and a huge chandelier hung impressively on the golden ceiling. And there, sitting on a raised pedestal, was King Rowan.

"The prisoner is here, Your Majesty," one of the knights said crisply.

"Thank you, Sir Grith." King Rowan twitched his heavily jeweled fingers.

Sir Grith bowed low, turned on his heel, and marched out, shutting the door behind him.

"Please, my dear, take a seat," said King Rowan, his voice echoing impressively off the oak walls.

The hairs on the back of my neck rose sharply. I doubted that King Rowan was usually polite to prisoners. Pushing my worries aside slightly, I sat in the chair opposite his; it nearly engulfed me. His eyes darted over me before continuing.

"I ask your forgiveness for halting your travels to bring you here to my castle … but I have an extremely important problem to which you may hold the solution."

I glared at him, my uneasiness growing rapidly, as he turned to take a goblet from the table next to him.

"You must not have any idea why I have ordered my men to bring you here." The king's voice was too soft, too fatherly. He was trying to make me trust him … convince me that it was purely accidental that Sir William ran into me. "There is nothing to fear, my dear. I just need to ask you some questions that—"

"Your Majesty, there's no reason to continue this charade."

King Rowan looked up from his goblet with wide eyes. I'm sure he had never been interrupted in the middle of a speech before.

"Don't treat me as if I don't know what's going on. I know for a fact that your knights have been looking for me for some weeks on your orders." I paused, aware of how dangerous I was making my situation. "There is also no reason to pretend that you don't know who I am. If Sir William does then I am sure you do."

I had no idea how King Rowan would react to my assault, but what he did certainly unnerved me. He smirked widely and burst into laughter. His booming voice echoed throughout the large room, sounding twice as loud, and he shook with mirth. He placed his goblet down, still chuckling, and said, "You're smarter than I remember. I should have paid you more attention." He pondered me for a moment before saying, "Since it's clear that I know who you are, there is no point in hiding your secrets any longer."

"My secrets?" I asked blankly.

"Unicorns!" King Rowan hissed. His hands gripped the chair's arms as he leaned forward. "*Where are the unicorns?*"

My throat tightened uncomfortably.

"I've been searching far too long to have you suddenly play dumb. I know that you are the one who can find them and communicate with them."

"I don't know what you're talking about. Surely Your Majesty knows that unicorns don't exist?" I said.

King Rowan stayed silent for a moment, his face expressionless.

"We'll see if the dungeons jar your memory," he said quietly. "I wonder how long a manor girl can cope surrounded by rats. Sir Grith!"

The doors opened behind me.

"Take her back to the dungeons," King Rowan said harshly.

Five minutes later, I was locked once more in my cell.

"What happened?" Ian asked the moment the knights' footsteps stopped reverberating down the corridor.

I told Ian everything that had been said.

"He's positive that I know where they're located," I said resting my back against the stone wall.

"We'll have to stall him," Ian began. "He can't—"

"What if he tortures you?" I interrupted.

Ian stared at me.

"I don't think King Rowan has any intention of harming me," I said quietly. Ian opened his mouth to argue but I cut him off. "I'm too important. He has no idea where they're located. For all he knows they may be halfway across Torona and he'd need me in tiptop shape for a long journey. No. I'm more worried about him hurting you, Ian."

Ian smiled slightly, trying to look unconcerned, but I knew better. He cocked an eyebrow and said, "Then we'd better find a way out o' here fast."

I slept fretfully, even though it was nice not to sleep outside. There was hay in a corner where we were to curl up and rest for the night, but I opted for the stone floor. It may have been harder and colder, but at least it didn't smell of mold and must. What kept me awake, for the most part, was the horrible scratching of many tiny feet on the stone floor. I once opened my eyes and saw a long, ugly, hairless tail zoom through a small pool of moonlight shining from a barred hole in my prison wall. It was no surprise that I wasn't refreshed in the morning.

Around early dawn I gave up on the possibility of any more sleep, and sat with my back against the stone wall, gazing unfocusedly at a small pile of rocks in the far corner. The sun's weak beams shown dimly through my small window; I distracted myself by watching dust swirl in the light. Slowly, it became light enough to make out the lump that was Ian.

Suddenly I heard the rustle of wings and a soft hoot. My head jerked up to look at the window. On the other side of the bars stood a weather-beaten barn owl. There was something slightly familiar about it, but before I had gotten a better look, it had flapped its wings and was gone.

I spent the next couple hours racking my brain, trying desperately to think of some way out of the castle. When Ian woke we put our heads together but we didn't get anywhere. Our only hope was that King Rowan thought us useless and let us go, but somehow I didn't think that was likely.

After the guards had brought us our breakfast (a pitiful bowl of slop and an old, stale piece of bread) we decided that no matter what happened, we would not tell King Rowan the location of the unicorns. I had just swallowed my last mouthful and pushed the bowl aside when my prison cell was visited once again.

This time there was only one knight—Sir Grith. I braced myself for another interrogation and left my cell once more. He led me again to King Rowan's sitting chamber. Sir Grith knocked and opened the door. I stepped inside and the door shut immediately. I had expected to see King Rowan, but he wasn't in the large room. Instead—my heart rate doubled—there was Prince Philip standing near a table, his arms crossed, with a bemused expression on his face as his eyes drifted over me.

"We meet again, miss," Philip said pleasantly.

I had forgotten about Philip. If I couldn't trust King Rowan, did that mean I couldn't trust Philip? If I told him ... if I explained to him what was at stake? Would he help me? An image of Ian's shocked and angry face floated into my mind as the idea of intrusting Philip entered my brain. Ian thought I would tell them everything. Ian thought that no one in the castle could be trusted. *But Ian doesn't know Philip.*

"Miss, do you know who I am?"

"Of course, who doesn't," I said with a nervous laugh that died almost instantly.

Philip nodded, a steely smile on his face. His eyes swept over my face.

"And do you know why you have been sent to my father?"

I could lie to him and play a simple airhead but I didn't want to ... I wanted Philip to guess who I was. Maybe he already knew. Sir William and King Rowan did.

"I do. But I'm afraid I can't help him," I replied politely.

"You can't?" Philip raised an eyebrow. "Well ... I suppose most people can't," he said in an undertone. He looked up at me and continued, suddenly casual, almost as if he were bored, "I recently received a most distressing letter." He lifted a piece of paper off the table and stared at it lazily. "In it was the most *fascinating* information." His eyes left the paper and focused on me. "Do you know what it said?"

There was something wrong about his demeanor. There was something in his gaze … I fought the impulse to back away from him.

"No, Your Highness, I don't."

"It was from a man that I paid a visit to last December." Philip's eyes returned to the parchment. "It seems that in February his only daughter ran away." Philip's eyes shot back to me, but I kept my face expressionless. His smile widened. "I don't mind telling you that he was quite beside himself. Supposedly he's been scouring the countryside, trying to find his daughter, but to no avail—that's why he wrote to me. He seemed to think that his daughter and I were close." Philip suddenly chuckled.

I frowned, suddenly angry as well as uneasy.

"What's so amusing?" I asked, trying and failing to keep the irritation at Philip's attitude at bay.

Philip's eyes glittered like the many jewels locked away in the glass cabinets lining the walls.

"I was told to befriend the daughter … told to get close to her. My father seemed to think that Sir James would be more likely to do whatever my father wanted if I courted his daughter. And look at how wonderfully our efforts paid off." Philip slightly shook the parchment in his hand. "He told me everything, Leah," Philip said quietly.

I felt like I had been slapped.

"It was all an act?"

“I never had any interest in you,” Philip sneered. “It was fun leading you along. Watching you blush whenever I looked at you. Though, I must say, the change you have undergone is quite ... pleasing.”

I was shaking. I had balled my hands into fists. I watched him continue to smile, amazed that he didn’t feel the angry waves radiating from me. He took a step toward me, placing Father’s letter back on the table.

“Now Leah, Father informed me that you were being annoyingly difficult. But I think you’ll tell me everything,” he said smugly, crossing his arms.

“Really?” I spat. “And why would I do that?”

“Because I’m sure you want to see your father again ... or at least save him from dying of grief ... what you have to do is very simple. *Just tell me where the unicorns are.*”

# Chapter 30
# Dark Ambition

I laughed humorlessly, "Really, Philip, I'm a bit tired of this game—"

"That's *Prince* Philip," he interrupted harshly, "and this isn't a game." He glared at me before recovering himself and then said in a calmer tone, "I, for one, also believed they were fairy tales, that is, until we were given the horn. Some old woman brought it to us... she was convinced it was from a unicorn. So convinced, my father believed her."

"You found a unicorn's horn?" Even in my anger, I couldn't help but be curious.

"Just a piece. The bottom half had been broken off. Nothing to get excited about."

"But how do you know it's a *unicorn's* horn?" I pressed.

"You're not the one asking questions," he snapped.

"Where is it?" I asked, ignoring him. I glanced around the room, expecting to see it sitting on a stand in clear view. Surely, the king would display it.

"It was stolen. But enough of this talk," Philip retorted. "I just want one small piece of information from you, Leah dear—"

"I'm not telling you anything," I said vehemently. "I don't know where they are."

"Then you'll never see your father again," Philip continued pleasantly, as he studied his finger nails.

"You can't keep me from my father, Philip—"

"*Prince* Philip," he repeated heatedly. "If you really enjoy playing this little game, then I can send you back to the dungeons right now and go through this again tomorrow. Or maybe I should torture the fellow who's with you."

"Don't you touch Ian!"

"Ooh, hit a cord, have I?" he smirked.

"Why are you doing this?" I blurted out. "We know each other!"

For a second Philip's face was as blank as parchment. He took a step toward me.

"You would make a beautiful queen," he whispered.

I stared at him repulsed. He smirked yet again at my expression. Suddenly, the door opened and Sir Grith stepped into the room. Philip spun around.

"What do you want, Grith?"

Sir Grith looked uncomfortable. A piece of paper was clutched tightly in his hand and his eyes kept shooting at me.

"Speak up, man!" Philip snapped irritably.

"The messenger has just sent this."

He held up the paper and Philip snatched it from him. He read it quickly, a cold smile growing larger and larger. He looked at me and said, "This simplifies things, but I still have a use for you. Take her away," he barked at Sir Grith.

Without looking back, my skin crawling as if ants were creeping along my arms, I left the chamber and followed Sir Grith to the dungeons.

Back in the dungeon, Ian paced with the darkest frown I had yet seen on his face while I sat in a corner staring into space, only hearing snatches of his mumbling.

My conversation with Philip had greatly shaken me. The very thought of him made me sick to my stomach, but something else was nagging me. What had been written on that paper Sir Grith had given him? Surely he didn't feel like he had to hide anything else from me. In his mind, I was at his mercy. Philip and King Rowan were going to force me to show them the unicorns. How could I stop them from doing that and *not* get Ian and myself killed? Sure, I could lie to them. Tell them they were in the Brendor Mountains and hope a dragon gobbled them up, but I knew that was hoping for too much. They would most likely take me along, just to be sure.

"... No other way," Ian murmured. "You'll have to give them false information and hope we can get away when they're not lookin' ... if only we had a decoy. Some distraction ... "

"Ian," I whispered suddenly.

He stopped his pacing and looked at me.

"I'm really worried ... and I'm so sorry I got you into this."

He leaned against the bars separating us, a small smile playing on his lips.

"I'm not sorry at all."

I smiled and looked away, wiping my eyes.

Our lunch had arrived, but it sat untouched. We waited in silence for the return of the knights. King Rowan and Philip were bound to be losing patience with me. Many times I glanced at Ian, wanting to say something, but the words never seemed right. I had made up my mind, though. The unicorns' safety wasn't nearly as important to me as Ian's. If they tried to hurt him, I would agree to lead them to the unicorns. Maybe I could buy some time on the journey and hope to find a way to escape.

*The messenger has just sent this* ... What had Sir Grith meant? Philip had looked so triumphant. He had learned something ... something that made his situation simpler. I gasped, horror struck.

"Leah?" Ian stared at me in concern through the bars.

"He knows!"

"What are you talk'n about?"

"That letter Philip read. Sir Grith had gotten it from 'the messenger.' The raven! Mora's raven is the messenger."

Ian looked surprised.

"We don't know that for sure," he said. "King Rowan isn't working with Mora."

I shook my head violently.

"Last time I was here, I overheard King Rowan and Sir William talking about Mora's information and it was obvious that King Rowan didn't want to be overhead." Ian opened his mouth to argue, but I cut him off. "Listen to me, Mora wants the unicorns, she's been sending her raven to follow me, she knows the king is after them. Isn't it possible that King Rowan wants them so badly that he's willing to work with Mora if she could give him more information? Her raven could have heard us talking about where the unicorns live."

Ian stared at me.

"I just . . . I just have a feeling that he knows something," I said, biting my lip.

*Clang!*

My head jerked in surprise at the loud echoing noise. Ian leaned against his bars, trying to see down the dark corridor.

"AHHH!"

Ian had jumped back as if electrocuted. There, wedged in a small crack in the stone floor outside of the bars, exactly where Ian's hand had been, was an arrow. I sat staring at it in dumb disbelief.

"It's a pleasure to see you again, Leah," said a face that loomed toward us in the darkness.

"Kindlen!" I yelled in joy. He was alive!

"Sorry about that," said another elf, staring at Ian. "It ricocheted off a knight."

"No problem," Ian gasped.

There were more elves gathering around our bars now.

"Where's Lavena?" Kindlen asked the crowd.

*Lavena?* I stared numbly, not daring to believe it, as a short, old woman pushed through the crowd of tall elves. My heart pounded furiously, my stomach flipped, and my face broke into a wide, watery smile.

"I'll get you out of here, Leah," Lavena said hurriedly.

I wanted to say something—anything, but words wouldn't come. From inside her cloak, Lavena pulled out something that was wrapped up in leaves and tied with string. She crammed it into the lock on my prison door, snapped her fingers (a small flame erupted), lit the contents in the lock, and stepped back. The lock sizzled, smoked and suddenly blew apart. An elf pulled the door open and Lavena grabbed me in a tight hug.

"Ian. Let Ian out too," I said when Lavena had released me.

Lavena looked taken aback for a moment, but she quickly placed another lump of the explosive in Ian's lock and seconds later, Ian stood next to us.

"Thanks," he said, shaking Lavena's hand jovially. "Y'must be Lavena. Pleasure to meet you!"

"Likewise," Lavena said with a smile, staring at him curiously.

"We must move. Now," Kindlen said sharply.

With that Lavena grabbed my arm and pulled me down the corridor. Unconscious knights lay sprawled upon the floor.

"How are we getting out?" I panted, as I jumped over a knight.

"Never you mind," said an elf beside me. I recognized her. She was Orena.

The elves made a sudden left turn and we ran further on. Our path was still littered with the fallen knights. I was just beginning to hear faint, startled yells echoing distantly down the corridors.

"We must hurry!" Lavena gasped.

We ran down another particularly dark corridor and stopped abruptly halfway down it. Kindlen and an elf pushed and heaved against a piece of wall. They grunted as the yells of the knights grew louder. They must have come across their fallen comrades. Then, miraculously, a small portion of the wall slid away, exposing a long, dark tunnel.

"Go! Go! Go!"

Lavena pushed me and Ian through behind Kindlen. The rest of the elves filed in and slid the wall back into place. I released a tense breath. *We were safe.*

# Chapter 31
# The Horn

"This was put in for the servants to escape through if there was ever an attack," whispered Lavena. As she walked steadily forward she clapped her hands together and a ball of brilliant flames blazed in her outstretched hand, illuminating the dirt tunnel. She was so short that her gray head hardly brushed the ceiling. The rest of us weren't as well off, especially the elves. They grumbled darkly under their breath as we walked doubled over, like trolls. "It leads out of the castle. Lemor and Rendor are waiting for us with the horses," Lavena continued.

*Lemor. Rendor.* They had both been in the ambush. But I didn't recognize most of the elves around me, only a few. I felt a horrible dead weight in my stomach. I knew that all the elves couldn't have survived that brutal assault in the woods, but I had always hoped they had.

"But the knights must know about this tunnel?" I asked.

"This isn't the only tunnel," Lavena answered in an undertone. "And by the time they realize you've gone, we'll be far away from the castle."

We continued onward in silence. I could only imagine what was happening inside the castle. The knights must have informed King Rowan and Prince Philip of our escape. I would have hated to be the one to tell them the bad news.

My back had begun to ache from being bent over for so long—surely we were almost there…

"We're at the end," came Kindlen's voice ahead of us.

We had come to a set of dusty stairs. We walked up them for a short time and then Kindlen stopped and I heard him pushing at what must have been a trap door. Ian squeezed up next to him and placed his hands on the stubborn exit and pushed. With their combined efforts it released and the cold air flew in to chill our bones instantly. Ian grabbed my hand to help me out and Lemor and Rendor ran to us with a slew of horses, Merlin and—

"Iris!" I yelled joyfully as Iris pushed her head into my hands and neighed happily.

"Let's move," Lavena said tensely. She clapped her hands together and the flames were extinguished. "They'll be swarming the grounds any minute."

I looked around as everyone mounted. I couldn't see the castle at all, nor any part of the city. We must have climbed out into one of the far patches of woods that dotted its border.

"Leah! Quickly!" hissed Lavena.

I shook strands of hair out of my face, leapt onto Iris's back, and followed the others farther into the woods.

We rode for the rest of the day. Lavena insisted that Ian and I hood ourselves. Two elves gave us theirs.

"And neither of you even dare to take them off," she said seriously. "Not until I tell you to."

"Lavena, where are we going?" I asked

"I'll explain everything later," she replied.

By nightfall we had reached a cozy inn on the outskirts of a small town. The innkeeper looked slightly surprised to see a small army walk through his door. There were thirty of us total. Ian and I stood in the middle of the crowd with our heads bent as Lavena booked our rooms. With a bemused expression, the innkeeper handed out our keys.

"Tis good only one room was booked already. You lot 'ave taken over the place."

Lavena smiled back pleasantly. "Could you tell me what room that is? I'm meeting those people."

The innkeeper raised his eyebrows even farther but told her it was room twenty.

With a quick nod toward Ian and me, she led the way up the stairs. Moments later we stood outside room twenty as the elves continued down the hall to their rooms, except for Kindlen who stayed standing behind me. Lavena knocked sharply and immediately the door swung open. A dark-haired man stood in the opening. His eyes shot from Lavena to me and back again.

"You made it," he said rather breathlessly. "Were you followed?"

"I don't think so," Lavena said. She pushed Ian and me through the door and Kindlen closed it behind us. There were eleven people sitting, pacing, and standing in the room. Each one stared at me before shifting their gazes. Some glanced curiously at Ian.

Ian bent his head and whispered in my ear, "What's this about?"

Lavena turned to Ian and me and said, "You can take your hoods off now."

"Wait! We can't let him in here! We don't know who he is."

I recognized the voice almost immediately. A tall woman had risen and crossed the room in three strides. She towered impressively over us.

"Leah asked for him to be saved, Myra," Lavena said calmly.

Myra snorted loudly.

"Yes, but can he be trusted?"

"Lavena, *Ian* and I really need to talk to you," I interjected with a cold glare at Myra.

"Whatever you need to say can and should be said before us all, Leah," Lavena said. "We are the Council, except for Kindlen. He is here on behalf of Angora. You are already acquainted with Myra. This is Sylvia—" a small wispy woman smiled back at me.

"I'm not saying anything if Ian isn't with me," I interrupted stubbornly, crossing my arms.

Ian and I had been through too much to suddenly be separated, just because some Council I'd never heard of said so.

"That's fine," Lavena said with a nod. "What do you need to tell me?"

I glanced at Ian who nodded. I took a deep breath. "I have a feeling that King Rowan may know where the unicorns are."

Several of the people around us gasped; others just stared with grim realization.

"*How?*"

"How indeed, Sylvia," said Myra coldly. "Did you break down in those dungeons, girl?"

"She didn't tell him a bloody thing!" Ian exploded.

The Council stared at Ian as if daring him to speak again, but Ian simply glared back at the lot of them.

"Why do you think this Leah?" Lavena asked, frowning slightly.

"Philip read a letter that was from 'the messenger.' I don't know what was in it, but whatever it was, he didn't seem to need me as much. I think Mora used her raven to deliver the message."

Frantic whispers erupted from everyone.

"She can't use her raven," said a strong-jawed man.

"I'm sure she can speak to it," I countered.

"Impossible. That power was taken from her. *All* her powers were."

"Listen to me," I said, trying to keep the frustration out of my voice. "Mora has known about me all along. I saw her raven at her cottage—"

"When were you at her cottage?" asked Lavena, shocked.

I ignored her.

"The same raven has been following me. I'm sure some of you have seen it. It doesn't look or behave the way a raven should. It's—it's almost human-like."

They stared at me in stunned silence. Then the small woman named Sylvia said quietly, "Angora always argued that Mora might retain some powers."

"Then we will assume she has," Lavena said grimly.

"An old magician told me where the unicorns were rumored last," I told the Council. "The raven must have overheard Ian and me talking about it."

"So King Rowan's heading for the Langdale Mountains," Myra said darkly. "We'll have to get there before he does."

"Wait. How do you know that they're in the Langdale Mountains?" I asked.

"We've always known where they are," Lavena said with a dismissive wave of her hand.

"You've known?"

"The unicorns are guarded, though," the strong-jawed man said, ignoring me.

"That guard, as good as it is, won't stand a chance against an army, Ven," Sylvia said grimly.

"King Rowan will search every inch of the mountains until he finds them," Kindlen agreed. "We have to find the unicorns first and somehow protect them."

"And how do we do that?" asked Ven.

"By letting Leah take over."

It surprised me that Myra had spoken. She shot a questioning look at Lavena who silently agreed.

"But what am I supposed to do?" I said nervously, as all eyes turned to me.

You're the only one who can communicate with the unicorns," said Lavena. "You'll have to warn them... have them hide somewhere until the danger has passed."

"But I don't know *how* to communicate with them."

"You'll know when the time comes," Lavena said confidently. "We'll handle the knights; you take care of the unicorns."

An hour later I sat in my room, bits and pieces of the meeting drifting through my head. I had to tell them to hide. But what would hiding accomplish? The elves and Council wouldn't be able to kill or scare off all the knights. And even if they tried, we'd be facing a possible war. All for what? For the safety of these unicorns? These creatures that no one had even seen before? It was mad. Why couldn't we let King Rowan have a few and just protect them from Mora? What harm would it do?

*We don't know where the unicorns are in the mountains, but you'll be able to find them.* Lavena had spoken with such belief. But belief was the last thing I felt at the moment. Stress, anxiety, anger—but not belief. Not only did I somehow have to protect the unicorns, but I also had to find their secret guarded hiding place? I snorted loudly. I was beginning to wish I was back in the dungeons.

I sat cross-legged on the bed staring moodily at the door. Lavena was rooming with me along with a strange-looking woman named Poppy with wild hair and slightly green skin. I had a hunch she was a wood nymph, but I wasn't sure. Lavena had insisted that

Ian and I go to our rooms while they continued the meeting. How in the world was I supposed to do anything if I was left in the dark? I yelled in frustration and threw a pillow at the door just as it opened.

"Oh!" Lavena said as the pillow hit her in the stomach. "The meeting's over."

"Decide anything new?" I asked vehemently, as Lavena bent over to pick up the pillow. Poppy poked her head through the door and my cheeks turned slightly red with embarrassment.

Lavena grabbed the pillow, smiled, and turned to Poppy.

"Would you mind letting us have some time alone, Poppy?"

"Oh. No, of course not! I promised Quin and Warren I'd help them sharpen our swords before we leave tomorrow anyway."

"Could you find Leah and Ian something, too?" Lavena asked. "They're going to need it."

"Sure will," Poppy said briskly, and, with a wink at me, she turned and walked down the hall.

Lavena shut the door.

"I'm sure you're upset that you still haven't been told everything," Lavena said, placing the pillow on one of the beds. "And you have every right to be. I should have told you everything from the very beginning. It certainly would have saved you a lot of trouble and your father and me a wagonload of worry," Lavena added dryly.

"Well?" I pressed as she sat in a chair, facing me.

"It all started, I guess, with Mora." A darkness

seemed to settle behind Lavena's eyes. "You've heard about Mora from Angora, haven't you? She was the most dangerous witch in Torona. Still is, in fact."

"Yeah, I know all about Mora," I said impatiently.

Lavena raised her eyebrows before continuing.

"She killed hundreds and tortured countless more until they agreed to join her. As she grew stronger and more dangerous, I realized we had to do something to stop her."

My chest constricted as I remembered the Wall of Names.

"That was when I began the Council," Lavena continued. "We were a group who was willing to stand and fight against Mora and her minions. After some time, we finally caught her. In fact, it was shortly after your second birthday." Lavena sighed heavily. "I rushed to where they were holding Mora and we decided to strip her powers. Shortly after our decision, I received news from Sir James of Lady Castilla's possibly fatal condition. In the letter he told me that no doctor could save her and that I needed to come immediately. But the entire Council was needed for the Binding Charm. I moved the charm along as quickly as I could. We couldn't hope that Mora would remain captive for very long." Lavena's voice cracked slightly. "The moment Mora was taken care of, I rushed back to Willow Manor … but I was too late."

"That's why Father was so angry?" I said quietly. "That's why he never told me about you?"

"Sir James was sure I could have saved her. He did what any grieving husband is likely to do. I don't blame him. When I healed you, the ice melted some," Lavena said with a half smile. "After we bound Mora's powers we banished her to a solitary life—"

"Why didn't you just kill her?" I interrupted.

Lavena stared at me, her eyes searching my face.

"Some of us wanted to. There was much arguing over her fate. I, for one, do not enjoy the idea of killing, for any reason. Murder and revenge does not make the pain or loss go away. It only adds more bloodshed. And I was tired of bloodshed."

I couldn't look Lavena in the eye. There was a small pause before she said, "With her powers bound, she would never be able to use any magic, and we *thought* that she wouldn't be able to communicate with the ravens anymore," Lavena laughed bitterly. "I guess we underestimated her."

"Angora told me that she thought Mora could have fortified herself against losing her powers."

"Yes, she could have, but we didn't want to believe it. Either way, Mora can still make potions. That's why the Council has taken turns checking on her because there is *one* potion that can reverse the charm and give her back her powers. We were sure that she would never be able to complete the potion because of one ingredient—*three complete unicorn horns.*"

"But why can't we just let King Rowan have one?" I blurted.

"Leah think. Is King Rowan likely to be happy with *one*? He wants them all. And anyway, who are we to decide *which* one?"

"You talk about them as if they're human," I snorted.

Lavena's eyes twinkled.

"They're more than what you think they are," she said quietly.

"The unicorns are guarded and well-hidden," Lavena continued as if I hadn't interrupted. "Mora wouldn't possibly be able to find them." Lavena suddenly looked tired. "Then I discovered how horribly wrong we were. Mora had been slowly gathering the ingredients to the potion that would return her powers. She knew she was being watched, so she had to do it slowly. None of us knew how far she had gotten until my owl told me something very strange. He told me that Mora had disguised herself as an old beggar and gone to Torona Castle, where she then gave King Rowan a unicorn's horn."

"What?"

"Yes, I thought it odd," Lavena said, frowning. "Why would Mora give the key ingredient to King Rowan? And that's when I became frightened. Mora had somehow found a horn, but had discovered that an *incomplete* horn was useless to her. So instead of giving up on the possibility of finding a complete horn, she set her sights on the king."

"But why go to King Rowan?"

"So that she could manipulate him. So that she could play on his greed and desire for grandeur. Can't you picture it, Leah? Mora can spin her words very well. She would have found it easy to convince him of the horn's authenticity—and its power. A unicorn's horn lasts forever, Leah. King Rowan would have been mesmerized by the possibility of controlling creatures with so much stunning beauty and power."

"So she left the broken horn with King Rowan just to get him to hunt them?" I asked.

Lavena nodded.

"She was behind it all. Mora was sure that we would notice the knights searching for the unicorns."

"What? She *wanted* the Council to know?" I asked, shocked.

"I believe so, yes. I think she wanted everyone to be so terrified of her finding the unicorns, that *they* would find them for her."

"Then we're playing into her hands!"

"I know, but we have no choice. The knights won't stop their search; therefore, we can't stop ours."

I glared at my ankles. What a mess. If King Rowan hadn't become involved then this wouldn't be happening. Then I remembered something.

"Philip said the horn they had been given was stolen."

"Yes," Lavena sighed, her eyes closed. "I did. I stole it."

"*You?*"

"I had to." She opened her eyes and they were bright with tears. "The night my owl told me Mora had given King Rowan the horn was the same night I discovered you were ill. Hearing the trees—"

"I'm sorry, *trees?*"

"Yes, the trees speak. Only unicorns hear them. Why, I don't know—I've never been able to ask one. The sleeping sickness resided in you long before it fully took hold. It could have been in your system for years—maybe shortly after birth. It's not just the cure that altered you—the illness itself does a good deal. No one knows why, but the disease gives you certain similarities to unicorns—their senses, their feelings. The time that you overreacted when the stag was killed, that wasn't just you. Your emotions of disgust and anger were enhanced by how a unicorn would feel. I am right to assume, am I not, that you have had other instances when your feelings were not entirely your own?"

I swallowed.

"The time—the time when I overheard King Rowan asking Father to help him hunt the unicorns. I almost fainted."

Lavena nodded. "Hearing the trees is one of the signs of the illness, but when you told me, I forced myself to believe you'd just imagined it—only hearing them once—but when you told me you'd heard them *twice* . . . well, I knew I had no choice."

I stared at Lavena and I finally understood.

"The horn."

"The horn," said Lavena, nodding. "Unicorns are very powerful, magical beings. Their powers and abilities are not meant to be shared with a mere human. Without the horn, you would have died. It's such a rare and strange illness that even I don't understand it fully. But horns have incredible healing properties, and somehow the combination of the horn and the sleeping sickness allowed for your deep connection to the unicorns."

Lavena looked at me, and a few tears slid down her cheeks. "The horn was easy to steal. I really should be thanking Mora for giving that horn to King Rowan."

My stomach turned. I was alive because of Mora.

"So you didn't need a complete horn to save me?"

"No," Lavena said as she shook her head, "just a piece, no matter how small."

"Did Mora ever find out that you stole it from King Rowan?"

Lavena ran a hand through her wild hair distractedly. "I didn't think so, but now ... you believe that Mora has known about you all along?"

"Yes, I do." I sat up straighter. "When I woke up from the illness, I saw a raven fly by my window. When I ran away, I felt that I was being watched. Then, when I was at Ian's home, a raven was perched in a tree, looking at me through a window. And at an inn, I woke up and a raven was in my room."

"She has hidden the fact that she can still speak to the ravens very well. All these years of watching her and we never suspected."

"She can speak to multiple ravens?"

"Yes, but she has an affection for one in particular."

"The one that I saw in her cottage?"

"Yes."

Lavena sank into a brooding silence. I looked around the room, trying to think of something to interrupt the sudden silence.

"What were the creatures that ambushed the elves and me?"

"Crags. Mora used them when she was in power. They do her bidding because she can give them fresh meat. It doesn't hurt that they are a bloodthirsty race either," Lavena said with a dry smile. "They enjoy fighting."

My heart was beating a bit faster than normal as I remembered the glowing eyes, the gaping mouths full of broken teeth ...

"So Mora must have had her raven watching King Rowan to see what he would do with the information she had given him. And, when the raven saw me steal it, Mora must have sent her raven to follow me, to see what I would do with the horn," Lavena continued. "I can only imagine how she reacted when it informed her of you."

"She's known about the sleeping sickness all along, hasn't she?" I asked.

"Yes, she knew that the illness strikes every hundred years, and that the date was approaching. She knew that you could find the unicorns. All she had to do was hope that I told you about the horn; surely your curiosity would get the better of you and you'd try to find them." Lavena looked at me sadly. "That's why neither I nor your father could tell you. We were afraid telling you would make you all the more vulnerable to Mora's plans."

"Father knew about Mora?" I asked. "He never said anything about her to me."

"Oh, yes, he knew about Mora. I've never seen him as frightened as when I told him she might be after you. The Council, however," Lavena's tone hardened, "knew what I'd done with the horn and about King Rowan's plans, but I refused to have you involved. Much like Sir James, my attempts at protection didn't work very well." She smiled wryly. "I've been looking everywhere for you. When I ran into Kindlen I cried from relief. He'd seen you ride away from the battle with the crags—you were alive, lost but alive."

"I didn't know where to go. Angora never told me where the unicorns live. I made myself keep moving just to stay sane."

"Angora feared Mora was getting information," Lavena explained. "Angora was the first member of the Council to know that a small piece of a unicorn's horn had been discovered. She relayed the information to me personally. Angora was very careful—not even her inner Council knew—but somehow Mora still found out."

"The raven!" I exclaimed.

"Yes, I think so. After the leak, Angora was even more cautious; she only told Kindlen their location."

"You're sure that King Rowan knows where the unicorns are?"

"I fear that it is too foolish now to think otherwise," Lavena replied gravely.

I suddenly felt sick.

"How many unicorns are there?"

Lavena looked thoughtful for a moment.

"I'm not really sure. Like I said, I have never seen a real one before."

"Talen—the magician who told me where to look—has."

"A lucky few have," Lavena replied with a small smile.

I frowned at the floor. There must be more than three unicorns.

"If Mora gets three horns, will you be able to bind her powers again?" I asked, but I thought I knew what the answer would be.

Lavena shook her head.

"No, the unicorns' magic works in powerful ways. She will have her powers forever. Don't blame yourself, Leah," Lavena said as if she'd read my mind. "Mora was bound to find the unicorns' location eventually. There's no point in us denying that fact any longer. We should—*I* should—have told you about it long before now. Never think that this is your fault. You are stronger than you think. The fact that you've been searching the countryside for months should prove that."

"Ian helped," I said.

"Yes, tell me about this Ian fellow," Lavena said archly with a crooked smile.

"We're *friends*, Lavena."

"That's what they all say, dear."

## Chapter 32
# The Gathering

We slept for only four hours. When Lavena woke me it was hardly dawn. We ate quickly and I tried to ignore the tension in the air.

"Here's some weaponry for you," Poppy said as we saddled up. She handed Ian a long, wicked sword that he quickly tied around his waist. "And this one's for you." Poppy held out a sword that was thinner but still as dangerous.

"Keep your eyes open," Kindlen said to our large group. He had mounted, and everyone, including the Council, did as well. "The crags attacked once before—we don't want that to happen again."

A chill ran up and down my spine.

"If we are attacked," Lavena said to Ian and me, "I want you and Ian to run. Continue the search. Find the unicorns. You *must* find them, Leah."

I nodded my head, not trusting my constricted throat. My stomach hadn't stopped twisting nauseously since I woke up.

"Leah, Ian. Hoods on," Myra commanded as she pushed her horse past us. We did so and quickly joined our small army.

❦

The strong-jawed man who had argued with me the night before was named Ven. He informed Ian and me that it was a good five day's journey to the Langdale Mountains.

"But we should be a little ahead of the knights," he said swiftly. "They're starting farther behind us. And I don't think King Rowan would have sent his knights after you last night. He would have waited until dawn."

"I'm sure they won't make many stops, though," Ian said, nudging Merlin into a trot alongside Ven.

"And neither will we," Ven replied. "Only to sleep and eat."

That was almost exactly what we did. I pushed Iris to her breaking point as we plowed through the countryside. The closer we got to the Langdale Mountains, the faster time seemed to speed by. Before I knew it, the rolling silhouette of the vast mountains—a silhouette I had taken for granted for so long—loomed on the horizon.

I had never been to the Langdale Mountains, even though they were only a good day's journey from Willow Manor. They had only been a distant landscape from the Manor, nothing more. I feared they would be like the Brendor Mountains—jagged and harsh—but actually, they were quite beautiful and gentle. We traveled at a steady upward angle, but there were breaks when the ground would level off before sloping upward again.

The sun was beginning its slow descent. Shadows lay long and thin upon the uneven ground. As we weaved through the trees I couldn't help but be amazed at how close I had always been to the unicorns. None of us spoke. I looked at the elves and each wore the same tense frown. We were close. Ian looked more excited than I had seen him in some time, and Lavena's face was contorted with concentration. I felt more nervous than anything else. I had to find the unicorns before the knights or Mora, and I didn't have a clue how. Then there were the ravens. What if we were too late? What if Sir William and the knights were already here? I frowned and thought grimly, *then we'll fight them.* We couldn't let Mora have the horns.

We continued at a hurried pace, never stopping. But then we came to a large section of forest that was strangely mute. A breeze blew past us, increasing my sense of unease tenfold. The hairs on the back of my neck rose sharply: we were being watched. My eyes strained to glimpse what I feared was hiding just out of my visual range. Ian was slightly ahead of me. He stopped suddenly and Iris reared slightly to keep from bumping into Merlin.

"Ian—what?"

But Ian shook his head, as the others turned to us with severe glares, and pointed a slightly shaking hand up at the trees. What seemed like a thousand ravens were perched in the high limbs around us, each one staring down at us, ruffling its wings. The temperature seemed to drop horribly as Iris took a step back; my eyes stayed glued to the foreboding birds.

"Mora," Myra hissed vehemently.

"My God," Sylvia whispered. "She controls them all."

"Leah," Lavena said tensely, keeping her eyes fixed on the ravens, "No matter what happens I want you to get out of here and find the unicorns. Warn them, tell them what's happening. Don't forget about the guardian. Don't worry about us, just find the unicorns."

I nodded, swallowing with difficulty. The elves were quickly cocking arrows to their bows as everyone else dismounted and drew their swords. The long piece of metal felt clumsy and heavy in my clammy hands. I had never fought before. I didn't stand a chance.

*SCREEEEE!*

I jumped, my heart hammering, as the blood-curdling scream echoed through the trees. I had barely recovered when I saw them pounding through the sun's slanting red rays, their orange eyes glowing brightly. And they weren't alone. Thundering behind them on their armored steeds were King Rowan's knights.

"She's sent the crags!" Kindlen cried as he released his arrow. "FIRE!"

A hailstorm of arrows speeded through the still air toward the advancing crags, but there were either too many of them, or the arrows merely stung their thick hides, because they hardly stumbled at the onslaught. The air filled with the monsters' screams and the knights' battle cries. Was King Rowan mad? How could he possibly agree to use the assistance of these monsters?

I stood as if in a dream—my mind blankly numb as I watched the forces collide. I saw Ian whacking at a knight and crag viciously, a bloody streak on his forehead. Lavena was mumbling under her breath steadily, sending a never-ceasing explosion of red sparks at the crags, forcing them away from her, but now the ravens had joined the fray. They swooped from the trees cawing wildly and clawed at our fighters' eyes.

"Leah! What are you doin'!" Ian yelled furiously as he ducked a crag's sweeping arm. "GET OUT OF HERE!"

I stumbled backward. It was as if I had been filled with lead. My sword hung uselessly at my side. Then I felt a small, insignificant tingle (I was amazed I even noticed it) from my finger. I looked down and saw a small glow shining from my hand.

"LEAH!"

My head jerked up to see a crag bounding toward me. I could count its broken teeth as it raised its large club in its unnaturally large hand ... without a second thought I dropped the sword and flung my right hand out before me, facing the creature. A white, blinding light erupted from my finger, bathing everything in its glow. My eyes burned painfully before adjusting to the blinding light. The crags were running full out away from the light, screaming in pain and fear, covering their large eyes. They couldn't stand it...just like the vors.

Moments before we had been surrounded by the crags, but after just a few seconds they had all disappeared; even most of the ravens had taken flight from the burning light. When the light faded, I realized the battle had halted; the knights, elves, Lavena, and Ian all stared speechlessly at me, slowly lowering their hands from their eyes.

"You didn't tell me ... " Lavena began, her face full of astonishment.

Unnerved by all the eyes upon me, I opened my mouth to reply... but a soft hum reached my ears. A hum so peaceful, so calm, that I couldn't help but be filled with those emotions, even though I was scared and exhausted. I slowly looked over my shoulder and stared unbelievingly as a pure white creature with a white horn galloped soundlessly toward us. It slowed and stopped a few feet away, tossing its slender head and swishing its lion-like tail, eyeing our party curiously. All of us, the knights included, gaped at the unicorn. Then the hum came again, this time stronger. I had the strangest feeling that it was coming from the trees...

"Look," Ian whispered.

I tore my eyes from the unicorn and received a jolt. The forest shined with unicorns. They were everywhere. There must have been a hundred, each one as stunning as the next. A light glow pulsed from them as they tossed their delicate heads. They were the most beautiful creatures I had ever seen. They were nothing like the drawing in the library book. They were ethereal. They stood silently with their pearly, white front hooves placed closely together, as if waiting patiently for something to happen.

"What are you waiting for?" came a harsh voice through the shocked silence. I spun around and saw Mora step out from behind a tree. Dark excitement pulsed through her frame as she eyed the unicorns greedily. She looked at me sideways, a wide smile spreading across her sickly, pale face.

"I thank you for calling them to me." She pointed a long steady finger toward a unicorn. "TAKE THEM!"

## Chapter 33
# The Guardian

Everything happened so quickly. I could hardly react. Like a stampede, the knights charged toward the unicorns, while the elves ran to intercept them. Mora hadn't moved from her spot but continued to shout out orders and howl with glee as the knights stabbed at the elves. The unicorns pawed the ground nervously, but stayed where they were, shooting uncertain glances at me.

Why? Why weren't they running? Didn't they see the knights swinging their swords through the air, gaining a few feet every second? They knew something was wrong by the way they flared their nostrils and stamped the ground, but… but they had come to me… I had called them to me. The mark on my finger must have brought them.

It didn't take me any more time to decide what to do. I looked at the battle, searching for a few seconds before spotting Ian and Lavena. They were both well distracted. Iris had been pushed to the opposite side of the fight, rearing and snorting angrily. Even Mora seemed to have forgotten me … I was no threat—just a stupid girl wringing her hands on the sidelines of a slaughter. I gritted my teeth and ran through a crowd of battling knights and elves straight to the line of unicorns, ducking arrows and swinging metal.

I'm a small person, smaller than average, so I was hardly noticed as I streaked and dodged through the battle. When I reached the span of trees that held the unicorns, my mouth went horribly dry. Would it let me?

The unicorn tilted its slender head slightly and stared at me with large, blue eyes. I received a shock as I realized they were the same piercing blue as my eyes. I swallowed and said clearly.

"We must leave. May I ride you?"

The unicorn simply stared at me. I felt stupid for even asking an animal for permission but before I could do anything else an explosion of triumph shattered the forest. My head jerked around and I saw three knights wrestle a unicorn down to the ground. As I watched they tied its legs together.

Panicky, I turned back to the unicorn, but it wasn't looking at me anymore. All the unicorns stood like statues as they stared at their fellow creature, their necks arched back, clearly aghast. Then a shiver ran through them. Hot anger emanated from their svelte forms.

"Please, we must go," I said, forgetting to hide the panic in my voice. Mora had gotten her first horn; she could *not* get anymore.

The unicorn before me looked down and *nodded.* It wasn't like a nod from Iris—it was somehow a *human* nod.

"Move quickly," it said.

My jaw dropped. *It could talk?* It hadn't moved its mouth but I had heard the words clearly—just like the trees.

"*Quickly,*" it said again.

As if its word was a whip, I ran to the unicorn's side. As I leapt on to it I thanked Father for teaching me to mount bareback.

"Hold on tightly."

I looked before me. It felt rude somehow to grab those floating white strands of mane. Then, the unicorn took off so suddenly and quickly that I almost fell off backwards. I flung my arms around the unicorn's neck as it ran through the forest away from the battle.

I looked around and saw a sight that I will never forget. Unicorns galloped all around us, their coats shimmering in the setting sun. It was the most beautiful sight I had ever seen. The entire forest glittered and shined with a silvery glow. I heaved a sigh of relief: they were following us away from the battle.

The ride was like nothing I had ever experienced. The unicorn moved so gently that I could have sworn we were hovering inches above the ground. We traveled so quickly that my eyes watered from the sharp wind. Iris could never surpass its speed, no horse could. The trees were black blurs as we rushed by. I was sure we hadn't been traveling for very long, but we must have gone a good distance, because when we stopped before a large cave half-concealed by overgrown foliage, all noise of the raging battle was gone.

I dismounted quickly and grabbed onto the side of a tree to steady my wobbling knees.

The unicorn faced me once more, as if it was sizing me up. All around us the others slowed and entered the cave, each giving me a long, calculating stare as it went past, but two gathered around the tree I was leaning against.

"Are we allowing her to enter?" a unicorn to my right asked. How I knew which had spoken, when they didn't move their mouths, I have no idea.

The one that I had ridden nodded its head.

"I think we should," it said and suddenly, I knew it was female. The one to the right was a male and the one to the far left, another female. "She called to us."

"What about Aereus?" the other female cut in. "We never should have left him."

"We do not fight," the male stated.

"That doesn't mean he should be left to be murdered!"

"Aereus may not be harmed ... yet," I said quickly, wanting them to stop bickering. Too much time had passed.

The three unicorns turned their eyes on me.

"We are safest inside," the first female said shortly.

The unicorns turned from me and began walking to the mouth of the cave, and then I remembered.

"But what about the guardian?" I said, hesitant to enter the cave.

"She will not harm you if you are with us," the male said smoothly, looking back to me.

Still wary, I nodded and hurried behind them. My eyes scanned the front of the cave for where the guardian might be lurking but I spotted nothing unusual, even inside the cave. The unicorns didn't speak as we marched down the narrow tunnel. It was odd. Why would unicorns—creatures obviously meant to run in open spaces—choose to live in a cave? We had just turned a corner that blocked the cave's entrance from sight when I stopped in my tracks and whirled back around.

"They must have gone through there," a crisp voice rang through the cave.

"Your Highness, maybe I should go in after her," said a silky voice that I recognized immediately as Sir William's.

"That's exactly what I had in mind, Shanklin," Philip replied smoothly. "Your reward for bringing me the girl and the unicorns will be beyond your imagination."

The unicorns had stopped and turned their heads back toward the cave's opening as well. They were unnaturally stiff…wary almost, as if they were waiting for something to happen. My curiosity completely ran away with me, and I inched forward, hiding behind a large jut in the rock wall. I could easily make out Philip and Sir William's forms on their sweaty horses. They must have followed me through all the chaos.

"I would be honored to go in after them, Your Highness," Sir William said, barely concealing the greed in his voice.

"Yes, Shanklin. And do hurry; I hate to wait," Philip replied lazily.

"I will travel like the wind itself, time will not pass in my absence, my—"

"That will do," Philip said curtly.

With a flourish, Sir William dismounted and marched up to the mouth of the cave as panic rooted me to the spot. If I moved, he would see me, but if he went down the tunnel he would find the unicorns! I had to act! But before I could think of anything, a giant creature bounded down from the top of the cave to land before the cave's opening, blocking Sir William's path. Sir William jumped back and drew his sword.

"Get back, beast!" he cried, waving his sword flashily through the air, but the creature merely swished its lion-like tail and sat down on its haunches.

"I said get back, you foul-some sphinx, before I gut you!"

I gasped audibly and Philip stared into the cave frowning, as I pressed myself into the stone wall.

"Threats will not move me," the sphinx answered calmly, as if she had not noticed anything. Her voice was hoarse and gritty. Philip leaned as far back on his steed as possible without tumbling over backwards.

"I will let you pass if you answer my riddle correctly," the sphinx stated. She stood up and began to pace back and forth before the cave's entrance. As she turned I saw her face, the face of a woman with amber eyes but disturbingly sharp, large teeth. The hairs on the back of my neck stood up unpleasantly as I watched Sir William stand like a statue. Philip's and Sir William's horses neighed nervously and tossed their heads, their bulging eyes glued to the sphinx.

"I don't have time for your games, beast," Philip spat.

The sphinx merely stared at Philip.

"Dispose of it, Shanklin!" Philip ordered.

For a moment, I thought I saw Sir William's bold expression falter. Then suddenly, he yelled, swinging his sword through the air at the sphinx. She dodged it and spread her wings wide, flapping them powerfully, forcing dust and dirt up into the air. Sir William covered his face with one arm and jabbed at the sphinx. She lifted one giant paw, the gleaming claws extended, and swiped at Sir William. Her claws made impact and Sir William was thrown into a tree with a sickening crash, his sword flung uselessly ten feet away.

Sir William's horse screamed and ran into the forest. Philip stared at Sir William's silent, broken form and then focused on the approaching sphinx. She moved like liquid, her eyes steadily fixed upon Philip. He spurred his horse and they flew into the wood with the sphinx bounding after them.

I stared at Sir William's body. I couldn't let him bleed to death.

"No!"

I spun around. The unicorn I was most acquainted with stood beside me.

"I can't let him die!" I said.

"He is already lost. There is nothing you can do. See." The unicorn tilted her head and when I turned back I saw the sphinx emerge from the wood and saunter over to Sir William. She kept her golden eyes upon us, for now we were in plain sight.

As she bent her head down to Sir William's exposed neck the unicorn jerked her head, "Come, I do not wish to see any more."

I turned away from the terrible scene and followed the unicorn. We walked far into the tunnel, but the distance did not muffle the sickening sound of tearing flesh.

# Chapter 34
# The Ancient Spell

The unicorn and I were alone in the cave's tunnel. The other two must have continued on down its length. We walked in silence, neither looking at the other. My mind was blank and an odd ringing in my ears made it hard to think clearly. Sir William was pompous, arrogant, dangerous even, but he didn't deserve that. *But the unicorns would have been captured,* a quiet voice broke through the fuzz in my brain. *The sphinx saved them, and in turn you.* I glowered at the dusty rock floor.

"Where are we going?" I asked brusquely.

"To the valley," the unicorn replied. "It is where we live."

"A cave that leads to a valley?"

"You will see."

We turned a bend and I stumbled on a rock, my eyes glued to the scene before me. The tunnel opened onto a small valley. Large trees occupied more than half of the land, and a carpet of grass covered the ground. I looked up and saw that the valley walls jutted high and curved inward, allowing a very small view of the sky.

Upon our emergence from the cave, the unicorns rushed toward us.

"Do you know what is happening, Oreste?"

"Where's Aereus? Where is he?"

"Oreste ... who is that?"

"Please, please," Oreste said over the commotion. "I know as little as you do ... but Aereus has been captured."

"What will happen to him?"

"I don't know," Oreste said quietly.

A chill ran through my spine. I jerked in response and noticed that the unicorns had suddenly gone deathly quiet. Their eyes were wide, their ears pricked up as if listening to something very faint. The trees slowly waved in the air, their new leaves rustling loudly as a brief burst of wind swished through the valley. As I stood there an overwhelming sadness consumed my being, and even though I heard no words, I understood the message.

"Aereus is dead, isn't he?" My voice sounded oddly distant and hollow in the silent valley.

"Yes." Oreste bowed her head.

The sea of faces around me showed a mixture of despair, denial, and emptiness.

"We must act," said a hard voice from the crowd.

"We have been over this before, Sylvan," said Oreste.

"Over what, may I ask?" I said cautiously.

"Who are you?" the one named Sylvan snapped. "Why did you call us?"

"Yes," Oreste replied, though she frowned at him. She turned her slender head toward me. "Who are you?"

My palms prickled with sweat as they all turned to me. It seemed odd to finally give them the message. After all the time searching, I had come to believe that I would never see them, that it would all be for naught.

"My name is Leah Vindral. I have come here to warn you. You are being hunted."

A unicorn to my left swished her long tail back and forth in distaste. Her eyes hardened—eyes that were like the bottom of an ocean—like my eyes.

"We are protected by the sphinx. Those men we saw, they cannot find us."

"One got away," said Oreste quietly.

"That is why you must leave," I said over the unicorns' voices, trying to ignore the sickening fact that *I* had brought the knights to the unicorns. "Philip knows your location. He knows what guards you and he could be back at any moment with more knights than your sphinx can handle!"

The unicorns were silent for a moment and then Sylvan retorted, "Why should we run? We should stand our ground and fight!"

"We are not warriors, Sylvan," Oreste replied.

"Then maybe we should change!"

Arguing broke out fiercely.

"You can't!" I yelled through the angry voices. "King Rowan is not the main threat. The witch Mora—"

"Mora!" Oreste spoke quickly. "You never mentioned Mora."

"She's after you," I said, speaking louder, for a great amount of talk had erupted at the mention of Mora."

"Quiet, please!" Oreste said to the others before turning back to me.

"You know of her?" I asked Oreste.

"We do. You heard or more precisely *felt* the news of Aereus's death." Oreste's voice had become hard. "The trees speak to us. When Mora was at full strength, the news of her destructive path was a daily topic amongst us."

"She's after you." I repeated. "She's working with King Rowan to steal your horns. If she captures three she will be able to make a potion that will allow her to regain her powers."

"And she has Aereus's," said Sylvan forlornly.

"Philip will be back. He will get through the cave, mark my words," I said seriously. "Even if you fought the knights, it is too much to hope that two more of you would not be captured or killed."

"But where do we go?" asked a male unicorn. "We stand out. It isn't easy for us to hide, as I'm sure you have already discovered, Leah Vindral."

I managed a small smile.

"Not if we change," Oreste said softly.

"Give up?" Sylvan gasped.

"We couldn't!"

"It has never been tested!"

The voices pounded in my head and I resisted covering my ears.

"What hasn't?" I yelled over the noise.

A male unicorn stepped forward.

"I am Luce, Leah Vindral. It is an ancient spell." He frowned slightly at Oreste. "One that will erase our features and powers. In other words, we will not be unicorns anymore."

"Is it safe?"

"If we are strong enough... perhaps."

I took a deep, shaky breath. Too much time had passed. Mora and the knights could burst through the cave's tunnel any minute. But who was I to change their lives completely? This was all my fault. No matter what Lavena said, I was sure the unicorns would have been safe if I'd never left Willow Manor. They would have been safe if I had never gotten sick.

My mouth tightened as I braced myself.

"Then that's what you must do."

Upon my words, Sylvan and the others pawed the ground in anger.

"I thought you wanted us to change?" Oreste asked calmly. Her voice contained no bitterness.

"Not that change!" Sylvan cried. "If our magic isn't strong enough... Oreste, the strain could kill us."

Oreste hung her head. The other unicorns were tensely quiet. After a moment, Oreste spoke in such a small voice, I barely heard her.

"I don't like what has become of our lives. I remember the day when we could run through the forest, racing deer. We grazed on the sloping fields...pranced on the shore. *Now*—" She paused, glaring fiercely.

"We were not meant to be contained," she continued in a stronger voice. "And continuing to hide while we turn a blind eye to a future full of bloodshed and fighting that *we* could have prevented...I don't think I could live with that knowledge. Sylvan, you are right, this spell may kill us. But we are already dying."

Her words struck a chord with the other unicorns, reminding them of a truth they had been denying, it seemed. A change had come over them. They stood boldly, their eyes bright.

"Even if we fought the king," Oreste continued, "it wouldn't end—we would be fact, not legend anymore...and we would be right where we were before—always running and hiding. I don't want to be controlled anymore by hunters or my own fear."

But I was struck by a sudden idea.

"Why can't you scare them away? I somehow scared the crags away. If we are connected, won't you be able to do the same?

"Our power does not frighten humans away," Luce explained. "It is odd that you have the power that resides in our horns. That has never happened before."

I opened my mouth to ask why, but Oreste spoke.

"We must agree," Oreste said evenly. "We cannot waste any more time. The cave may be filled with soldiers and Mora's minions at any moment."

There was stillness as the unicorns thought over their plight, and then, almost in unison, they nodded their heads.

"Agreed." Oreste said firmly. "Leah Vindral, please stand back."

I retreated from the group until I was standing against the wall of the cave.

The unicorns quietly formed a large circle with their horns pointing into the center. There were no words, no incantations. A heat seemed to be issuing from them. Each horn slowly grew painfully bright, and the trees tossed and turned as a high wind blew cruelly through the valley.

Something was wrong—I could tell.

"It isn't working! We don't have enough!" Sylvan yelled suddenly.

They were going to be killed. There had to be something I could do …

*The cure connected you to them...* Before I had even realized what I was doing I was running toward the glowing ring.

"Leah, no! Stay back!"

I flung my right hand, the shining mark on my finger already a brilliant glow, upward, pointing at the center of the circle. A burning sensation stung my finger and crept down my arm, numbing it. I began to shake violently. The pain in my arm was becoming more than I could bear. The whiteness of the center became too bright. I shut my watering eyes just as a huge flash of light erupted from the center of the ring, momentarily voiding the valley of all color and substance. The burning in my finger slowly faded. I opened my eyes to find the whiteness gradually vanishing, until it was gone completely.

## Chapter 35
# A New Future

The unicorns still stood in the exact same places they had been during the spell. I stumbled out of the circle, my eyes wide and mouth open. They looked nothing like unicorns. They were *brown.* They were brown horses. Their tails were not like a lion's anymore, but were replaced with long brown mane. Their eyes were not blue, but a deep hazel and their horns were gone. In its place on their foreheads was a small white star—the only thing that signified what they once were. No one could ever tell ... no one would ever guess that these ordinary-looking horses were once unicorns.

They examined each other and waved their heads and swished their tails with a little excitement. When they were done taking in their new appearance they turned to me with wide staring eyes. When none of them spoke, I decided to be the first to break the silence.

"You're free now. There's no way King Rowan's men will ever realize what you once were, and even if Mora does, there's nothing she can take from you now."

The unicorns looked at each other once more, and a few seemed a little frightened. Sylvan stepped forward swishing his long tail impressively.

"Leah Vindral is right. We are no longer confined to this valley; we can roam wherever we please. This—this will take time getting used to, but it has saved our lives—and many others—and for that I am grateful."

I was at a loss for words. Heat rose up my neck and I looked uncomfortably at the ground. Sylvan bowed his head so he could look into my eyes.

"I thank you, Leah Vindral."

Heat rushed to my cheeks as he turned from me. The others bowed their heads to me as well, each one announcing his or her thanks. I felt lightheaded, almost giddy. Then a breeze brushed by me.

*Hurry.*

It seemed that the unicorns had not heard the trees. That power must have left them.

"You must go now," I said quickly. "The knights are coming and they must not see you leaving this cave."

The unicorns pranced slightly in place and then rushed past me through the cave, with me following quickly behind. The knights had not entered the cave yet, but I could hear them advancing through the forest as I neared the cave's entrance.

The unicorns heard them too, and with a final wave of their tails, they darted into the dark forest, in different directions, and in the blink of an eye they were gone.

"So, it's over is it?"

I jumped at the husky voice.

The sphinx stood on top of the cave's opening, staring down at me and Oreste, who had stayed behind.

"Yes," Oreste replied. "I thank you for protecting us for so long."

The sound of the knight's voices increased dramatically and the sphinx smiled cruelly.

"So be it." With a mighty push of her wings, she rose into the air and flew away.

"Let's go," Oreste said.

We ran into the forest and hid behind a large clump of bushes, watching as the knights rushed the area where we had just been standing, each holding a flaming torch.

"In there! In there!" Philip bellowed. "Into the cave, that's where they're hiding!"

Quick to obey, the knights rushed into the cave. A frown crossed Philip's face at the absence of the sphinx. A few tense moments passed, and the knights exited the cave. They shook their heads and a few murmured under their breath.

"Why haven't you brought them out?" Philip asked impatiently.

"There weren't any, your highness," a knight said.

"What are you talking about? I saw them enter that cave with my own eyes!"

"Maybe they left?" a tall knight shrugged.

"They couldn't have left!" Philip yelled.

"Huh, and what about that so-called sphinx," a knight murmured in a loud whisper.

"Are you questioning me?" Philip screeched.

The knights grumbled loudly.

Oreste nudged her nose against my shoulder. I nodded, and we silently slipped away from the clearing. We had been walking in silence for a while, leaving the knights' mutinous grumblings far behind us, when I stopped suddenly.

"This all happened because of me," I said. "If I hadn't left Willow Manor, I wouldn't have led the ravens anywhere. Mora wouldn't have discovered your location and Aereus would still be alive. You would still be unicorns. This is my fault."

"No it isn't." Oreste shook her head. "We had grown restless. A small valley is nowhere for unicorns to live. Our nature is to roam. To explore. Some of us have left the cave to see what the world is like. I left… and saw you."

"When?" I asked taken aback.

"Before you became ill. Yes, I know of the sleeping sickness," she said in response to my surprise. "It is the only way you could look the way you do, the only way you were able to speak to us. I traveled out of the mountains to the surrounding forest. I hadn't left this place for some time, and the urge was too strong to stifle. I came upon a dying rose bush. It depressed me," Oreste waved her head as if shrugging. "I used my horn to awaken it, and you arrived. I must say, you did give me a start."

"And you me," I replied smiling.

"You have nothing to feel guilty about. You freed us."

Oreste turned her head from me.

"But how will you keep from being caught by others?" I asked, frightened by the sudden mental picture of a farmer saddling and harnessing Oreste. "Even as a horse there are dangers!"

"There will always be dangers," Oreste replied simply. "We understood, probably more so than you, the consequences of our decision and you must remember: we were once unicorns. Our knowledge, our past, will help us adapt to the challenges that lie before us."

We started walking again and Oreste said suddenly, "The sleeping sickness is very hard to deal with. You have handled its difficulties admirably."

"Have you seen others like me?" I asked, hopefully.

"Yes, but only one other survived to tell the tale. That was many, many years ago, so many that most have forgotten it."

I stopped walking and brushed my hair out of my eyes. I stared at the ground, my throat oddly constricted, and Oreste leaned her head closer to mine.

"What bothers you, Leah Vindral?"

I swallowed. It was somehow painful to find my voice.

"When-when I helped you change—for a minute I thought—I thought I would change too." I raised my head and looked her in the eye. "That I would look like I did before the sleeping sickness."

"The effects are permanent," Oreste said kindly. "We are now in the same situation, for we can also never return to what we once were."

"I know." I looked anywhere but at her, my eyes burning. "I just never appreciated how normal I was … I feel so different from everyone else."

"What makes us different makes us strong. We are no longer unicorns—we will never be known by others as unicorns, but you, Leah Vindral, you are the last of us."

I looked back at her. Her eyes, that were once just like mine, shined brightly.

"You carry with you our powers, our legacy and our future. You are the last of us."

I didn't know what to say to that, but with her words a warm glow had appeared in my chest.

"Don't regret," Oreste continued gently. "For you saved us. We did not know we were being hunted."

I frowned.

"But why didn't you? The trees never told you?"

Oreste smiled with her eyes.

"The trees never say *exactly* what they mean. They are much more cryptic. I believe they enjoy being mysterious." Oreste smiled more deeply at my expression. "Think about it. The trees could have easily told you our exact location at any point during your journey, but they didn't. It is my guess that they wanted you to find your way to us on your own—with a small bit of guidance along the way. They sent us messages, as well."

"And what were they?"

"That our true desires would be realized—that we would be free," Oreste explained. "That one day, we would live as we once did, so long ago."

I smiled.

"So you must have been expecting something like me to come along."

"Yes and no," Oreste nodded.

"Where will you go now?"

"I don't know," Oreste said candidly. "I think I will visit our old home, see what has become of it. Maybe I will travel to the shore. I barely remember it." Oreste turned back to me, her eyes glowing. "I will go wherever I please, whenever I please."

"Where did you used to live?" I asked curiously.

"What is now known, I believe, as Aris."

"Really?" I asked, slightly shocked. "That's where I think I got my mark." I indicated my finger.

"Yes, your mark seems to act like our horns did—it called us to you. How did you get it?"

"I'm not exactly sure. I touched a lake in Aris and noticed it shortly afterward."

"Ah," Oreste nodded. "We purified the land that is known as Aris. Traces of our magic must reside in the land and water there."

"So when I touched the lake?"

"Because we are connected, it must have transferred some of our powers to you," Oreste finished.

"Does that mean that if I had never gone to Aris, I wouldn't have been able to call you to me or frighten the crags away?"

"You would still have been able to call us, but you wouldn't have had our power. It is very possible, of course, that you were drawn to Aris for a reason."

I liked that idea. Oreste stared happily into the dark forest.

"It must feel nice not to have to hide anymore," I said.

"The feeling is beyond words, Leah Vindral." Oreste turned her back to me. "I know we will meet again!" With a final swish of her tail, Oreste galloped away, and I soon lost sight of her as her brown coat blended into the darkened forest.

"Leah!"

I turned around and saw Ian running up to me, his sword bloody and his face scratched. Behind him were Lavena, Kindlen, and the others.

"Where've you been?" Ian yelled hoarsely, throwing his sword aside and hugging me tightly. "Thank heaven, you're alive!"

"I've been right here," I said happily, but then I saw the large gash in his shoulder. "Ian, you're hurt! You're covered in blood! You need to sit down! I'll—"

But Ian was laughing. He grabbed my hand and said with a smile, "It's worth bein' hurt just to see you so upset about it."

I stared at him and felt my cheeks redden. I suddenly became aware that a large crowd of people were standing around us. Hastily, I stepped away from Ian, who was still chuckling, and turned to Lavena.

"Did you tell them?" she asked.

"They're safer than ever before," I said.

A cheer rang loudly among the elves and Council members.

Night had fallen. We left the forest and settled in a meadow. Lavena sparked a large bonfire, I found some Farlex for Ian's shoulder, and Iris followed me wherever I went, refusing to let me out of her sight. The elves stewed an impressive asparagus and onion soup while we picked strawberries and cherries. Dancing and singing filled the moonlit meadow.

"What happened to Mora?" I asked Lavena, choosing a plump strawberry from a basket filled with the red fruit.

"When you left, the crags slowly came back, and we continued fighting. But we got the upper hand, didn't we Ian?" Lavena had grown fond of Ian rather quickly.

"Yes'm," Ian said through a mouthful of asparagus. "We ducked and weaved and cut and jabbed until they ran back to their scurvy home yellin' and screamin'." He waved his spoon through the air in a great arc, like a sword.

"What about the knights?" I asked. "I know Philip brought a good many of them to the cave, but what about the rest?"

"Ran for it," Ian said, "once we got the upper hand."

"When Mora's followers had left her for good," said Lavena, "she grabbed the one horn she had gotten hold of and fled."

"Where do you think she went?"

"A cave somewhere?" Ian suggested, then he grinned mischievously as he added, "'Spect your friend the magician has a new neighbor?"

I choked on my soup as I laughed.

"I don't think Talen would stand for it," I replied.

I had become a hero. Everyone insisted that I tell how I had saved the unicorns at least three times. I had never seen Lavena glow more than she did that night.

In the morning the elves said their goodbyes and made their way to Aris. As I watched them go I wondered if they would spot a brown horse by one of their lakes. The Council members shook hands with me and Ian and left for their homes as well, but before Myra left, I spotted Lavena talking to her privately. Myra caught my eye as she passed and smiled. Finally, Ian, Lavena and I were left alone to travel to Willow Manor.

"Ian, will you be going to Bell Sound?" I asked, as we stopped for lunch.

He looked up from his small bread and cheese sandwich, oddly flushed.

"I think I'll send word to them. Mom and Dad will never believe what I did." He smiled as he puffed out his chest. "Help save the world, ah, just a trivial task for a warrior like me."

His ears were still red, but I understood. I didn't want to say goodbye to Ian, either.

As we neared Willow Manor, my heart began to pound as the scenery became more and more familiar.

My breathing grew faster when the sloping lawns came into view, their blades of grass waving in welcome. And there, looming like a castle, stood Willow Manor, powerful and strong. As if Iris could read my mind, she took off across the gravel path leaving Ian and Lavena following behind us. Gravel flying, she skidded to a halt at the oak front doors. I bounded off and rushed up the stone steps, taking two at a time, through the open door, and up the main stairs, yelling as I went.

At the sound of my voice doors opened with such force that they banged off the walls. When I reached the landing I grabbed onto the banister to keep myself from falling. Ann rushed to me from the end of the hall and Frank and Guinevere bounded up a side hall. More servants rushed to me from all sides. They swept me up in their arms and held me, sobbing hysterically.

"Leah! Oh, Leah! You're back!"

I finally pulled myself from them.

"Where's Father?" I asked, my smile unnaturally large.

"He's off looking for you," Ann exclaimed. "He was in such a state when you left."

"Leah!"

I turned on the stairs and saw Father standing in the doorway with Lavena and Ian hovering behind him. Our eyes met and for a moment we just stared at each other before rushing together. We held each other so tightly, I thought we would never let go.

# Chapter 36
# Welcome Surprise

"Father, I'm so sorry!" I choked into his shoulder.

"It's alright," he said through his tears. "I'm just glad you're alive!"

I pulled away from him with difficulty and said, "There's someone I want you to meet."

I led him down the steps to where Ian was standing. Ian looked suddenly shy, standing in front of the large oak doors.

"This is Ian Grinshaw," I said. "Without him, I don't think I would have ever made it back home."

For some reason, I was nervous, as if I was somehow afraid he might not like Ian.

"Pleasure to meet you," said Father rather breathlessly as he shook Ian's hand jovially.

"So I take it you met Myra?" Lavena asked cheerfully.

"Yes, she informed me you were on your way here with Leah. Thank you."

Father turned to me.

"You have much to explain."

"Yes, we have to tell you everything!" I said.

"We wouldn't dream of intruding," said Lavena hastily.

"I can't possibly tell the entire thing by myself!"

"Well, if you insist," Ian said, clapping his hands together. He sniffed the air. "M'nose tells me a hazelnut cake is bakin' somewhere."

Father told Guinevere to bring tea and cakes for us as he led us to the sitting room.

When the refreshments where brought in I began. Ian and Lavena stepped in a few times to explain their own sides of the story. It was fantastic. The room was crowded with people. All the servants sat around the table, their faces lit with excitement, awe, and fear as I spoke. When the teapots were empty and the platters relieved of their heavy loads, I had finished my tale. Father and the servants simply stared at me. Frank's mouth had stayed partially open the entire time and Ann kept clutching her chest.

"I can't believe that you did all this," Father finally said.

"You have a very bold and brave daughter, James," Lavena said. "Much like her mother."

Ann stared at me as if she were meeting me for the first time.

"And you, you helped her," Father said, turning to Ian.

"Well—yes, I suppose," he mumbled uncomfortably.

Father grabbed hold of Ian's hand and wrung it energetically.

"You have my blessing, son!"

"Bless-blessing?" Ian stuttered, taken aback.

Ian glanced at me, his ears red once more, but the rest of the table was laughing so loudly that he soon joined in, wringing Father's hand in turn. A short time later, Father rose from his chair and pulled me gently from the room. We went outside, enjoying the warmth of the bright sun after the cool dining room. Slowly, we meandered around the grounds.

"I want to apologize, Leah."

"You don't have to," I said quickly. "If anyone should apologize it should be me."

He shook his head. "No. By protecting you, I pushed you away from me." His throat tightened. "When I realized you were gone ... I was lost. I didn't know what to do."

"I'm so sorry." My chest constricted.

Father smiled wetly and wrapped an arm around my shoulders.

"I truly am proud of you. You risked so much."

We had reached the rose garden now. The weeping willow swayed lazily in the breeze and the roses were just beginning to open.

"Father, why did you refuse to hunt the unicorns?" I asked suddenly.

He slowly withdrew his arm, a slight frown on his tired, shaggy face.

"Your mother was a special woman," he replied quietly. "She was fascinated by the stories of unicorns.

For some reason, thinking of them always made her shine brilliantly. I would never harm anything, fable or not, that touched her so deeply."

As we walked back to the manor, Father smiled at me slyly.

"What?" I asked.

"I like Ian," he said, still smiling.

I spotted Ian and Lavena standing on the stone steps before Willow Manor. Ian waved at us and I said quietly, without blushing, "I like him too."

Father took an interest in Ian's search for a "future or fortune, whichever comes first" and took him to explore the possibilities around Willow Manor. In the meantime, I accompanied Lavena to her cottage.

"I can't even begin to make you understand how proud I am of you," Lavena said as we made our way slowly across the grass.

I smiled bashfully. Suddenly, Lavena sneezed.

"Are you getting sick?" I asked, concerned.

"Probably." She withdrew a bright purple handkerchief from her pocket. "I wouldn't be surprised—trying to track you down in midwinter. I just need a nice cup of my special tea mix." Lavena glanced at me. "Bee in your bonnet, dear?"

"Why didn't *I* ever get sick?" I asked. "I spent a month sleeping in snow and never got a cough."

Lavena smiled.

"A unicorn's horn has purifying powers. When it healed you, it left traces of that purity in you. As I told you before, a unicorn's horn lasts forever, and so does its magic. You will never be sick again."

We entered Raven Wood and traveled the familiar pebbled path.

"Will the ravens still follow me?" I asked.

"I doubt it. Once Mora has realized that the unicorns changed their appearance for good, she will be furious, but won't dare come out of hiding, with the elves and Council looking for her."

"And what about King Rowan and Philip?"

"From what you told me," Lavena said with a small smile, "Philip looked slightly *unhinged* in front of his knights. I think he and his father will try to make everyone forget their attempts at finding the unicorns, just to keep their subjects from believing them mad."

"Will they come after us?"

"Probably not. I truly believe this has cost King Rowan much of his pride, and he will not want to be near anyone who reminds him of that."

At the sight of Lavena's quaint cottage I remembered something.

"Oh, Lavena! I'm so sorry!"

Lavena paused at her door. "What ever for, dear?"

"The Replenisher! It's—"

But an exhausted owl suddenly swooped down to us, dropping a sack at Lavena's feet.

"Ah!" Lavena said delightedly, picking up the Replenisher and dusting it off.

"But—but I left it at Bell Sound. How?"

Lavena simply winked. "Come inside. I would like to show you something." With the owl perched on her shoulder, I followed her into the cottage.

The owl flew to a pot and I watched Lavena extract a small moneybag from the back of a locked cabinet.

"I think this should be in your possession."

She tipped the bag over and what looked like a strange, pointed, white stone fell into her hand. It was about the length of her palm.

"Is that—"

"The unicorn's horn I used to save you, yes. This was the piece I took from King Rowan, and, in essence, the piece Mora gave to the king. There isn't much left after what I used for the remedy, but—"

"It's beautiful."

Lavena simply glowed.

I left Lavena's cottage, the unicorn's horn safely in my hand, and headed back to Willow Manor to find Ian and Father, but as I turned a corner I saw Miss Perish walking hurriedly toward me. She nearly knocked me over with her large traveling case.

"Watch where you're going, girl!" she snapped.

"I'm sorry, Miss Perish," I said politely. "Are you going somewhere?" I had completely forgotten about her. She hadn't come to meet me when I had arrived. Nor had she been with everyone else when I explained what had happened to me.

She seemed to inflate with fury.

"I have been dismissed. Sir James will sorely regret this day, for it is the end of you ever becoming a lady!"

Without waiting for a reply, she swept up her long cloak and marched down the gravel path for the waiting carriage. I smiled as I made my way into Willow Manor.

I knew the perfect place to keep the horn. The attic was dark and quiet. Slowly, I crossed to the back and opened Mother's chest. I picked up an old handkerchief and carefully wrapped it around the piece of horn. After I placed it inside and closed the lid of the chest, I stood and stared at the portraits that stood beside the chest. With a small smile, I left the attic. I had made up my mind. Mother's portraits weren't going to collect dust in the attic anymore. Tomorrow, I would move them all into the brightly lit halls and rooms below.

It had been so long since I had been in my room. I walked through the door with a little trepidation and viewed the scene. It felt strange to be back here when I had feared I wouldn't ever return. I slowly moved over the familiar rug, taking in all the familiar smells, and stepped in front of my mirror and looked at the reflection. Even though I was still sixteen I looked older somehow. My hair was longer and I was slightly thinner. *That won't last long,* I thought with a smile. Father, Ann, and Frank had already fussed over my pale and thin appearance. Smiling, I turned from the mirror and walked to the window. I opened it and leaned on the windowsill, breathing in the cool air. The unicorns were out there right now, living freely. I wondered how long they had been in the cave. *I'll just have to ask them the next time I see them,* I thought.

There was suddenly a large commotion down below me on the gravel road. Miss Perish had entered her carriage and it was clattering loudly up the path, away from Willow Manor. Large dust clouds rose into the air after it. Ian and Father stood to one side, watching it go. They were talking to each other and Father was grinning. Then Ian turned and looked up at me leaning on my window ledge. I smiled widely. A glowing happiness swelled in my chest: everything was going to be all right, now. Everything.

Made in the USA